SONG

of the

CHIMNEY SWEEP

SONG

of the

CHIMNEY SWEEP

TAMATHA CAIN

MAITLAND, FLORIDA

Orange Blossom Publishing
Maitland, Florida
www.orangeblossombooks.com
info@orangeblossombooks.com

First Edition: August 2022

Library of Congress Control Number: 2022905263

Edited by: Arielle Haughee
Formatted by: Autumn Skye
Cover design: Sanja Mosic

Print ISBN: 978-1-949935-38-7
eBook ISBN: 978-1-949935-39-4

Printed in the U.S.A.

She's a road that leads away from home
And she's the only way back
She's a home fire lit by wild fire
She's the ember on a match

-Dominicus Owens

TABLE OF CONTENTS

BETTY,
17 YEARS OLD

JANUARY 1969

The country road that led into town was dark and close and winding, like the stuck-in-your-head refrain of some misremembered old song. It rolled through the farmlands and the blue-ink marshes, a secret passage, with walls made of palmetto bushes and pine trees, maidenhair ferns and bald cypress trees. Their branches lifted on the tailwinds of cars rolling by, and the forest inhaled, then crooned a sweet harmony along with the song of the night.

From the middle of the cramped back seat, Betty Langdon's eyes fixed on the glare of the radio dial. The deep blur of the forest and the crunchy-slick rhythm of the tires rolling on asphalt brought to mind a childhood memory of a night like this one, when she'd also worn her favorite dress and felt the lure of freedom, riding shotgun in her daddy's shiny little blue car. She wished she could remember what kind of car it was, but she still watched for shiny little blue cars and peered at the drivers, hoping to find him behind the wheel.

Betty's best friend Junie sat to her left, staring at the cigarette between her fingers with a faraway, determined look in her eyes. Junie's brother Fred tapped his fingers on the steering wheel, casually driving with the heel of his hand.

"Who are these fool people, spraying fake snow on their windows?" Fred slowed the car and rolled the window down, then set his elbow out the door. "Who do they think they're fooling? Santa Claus?" Fresh air rushed in, bringing blessed relief from the smell of Fred's Old Spice aftershave. The girls patted their hair back in place.

"You know that's got to be some man's idea. I wouldn't want to wash that mess off every dang year," Junie said. The other girls nodded.

Betty's cousin Loreen sat up front, gazing at the little houses and their strings of multicolored bulbs. "The lights are pretty down here, though. When I get married, I'm gonna have the nicest Christmas lights in the neighborhood, I mean to tell you," she said.

"Lights aren't cheap, Loreen," Junie replied. She tapped her cigarette out the window and the ash flicked away. Loreen raised her chin. She'd have lights like that, and better. No doubt about it.

Betty wished she'd gotten a window seat so Junie could have shared the cigarette with the others without passing it across her lap over and over. Some leg room would have been nice, too. She was the tallest, after all. But she hadn't said anything at the house when Junie dispatched them into assigned seats. Warm air blew crosswise through the car, balmy even for a north Florida winter night, and she checked the foam roller holding her bangs above her forehead. The abiding atmosphere of stored humidity and remnant heat emanated from the depths of the forest on either side of the road, biting back at the feeble chill.

Betty, Junie, and two friends had pressed into Junie's brother's faded blue Chrysler Imperial to ride down to a saloon on the Westside to see a local band called The One Percent. Fred had used his last full army paycheck to buy this car after his tour and discharge, and Junie considered it her private taxicab. Junie could always convince them to go along with things they'd never conceive of on their own. Even if they did have crazy ideas and wishes and plans, none of them would have the nerve to say it out loud. Except for Junie. Junie would say it out loud. She'd say anything out loud.

Last week, she'd told Betty and their friends that she'd die—DIE—if they didn't come with her to West Tavern, which was practically right smack in the middle of Shanty Town, to see this band. She was going to leave that tavern with one of those musicians, too, but they had to swear to keep that from Georgie, and did they understand? She didn't want the bother of finding a new date to prom this late in the game. It had been a whole year since she'd warned him he'd have to wear a rose-pink cumberbund and bowtie so they could match.

Betty didn't want to think that far ahead. An anxious knot had been vibrating in the pit of Betty's stomach since it dawned on her there were only ten days left of Christmas break. How did senior year plod along endlessly while the break had practically flown?

Sadie reached across her friends' laps and wagged her fingers. Junie pulled two more long drags before passing the cigarette between them. Sadie pulled a little and coughed, blowing the smoke up to let it suck out the window but missed, and the smoke blew back into the car. Betty coughed. Sadie passed the cigarette back to Junie.

"Almost there," Junie said. "Fred, just turn right up here, then it's just up a little ways." Her brother pulled his elbow from its resting place in the open window and adjusted his grip on the steering wheel. The road ahead was dark as the sky deepened to a blueish black.

"There'd better be some single men in there," Junie said. She pulled a fleck of tobacco from her lip and flicked it away. It landed in Betty's lap. Betty carefully picked it off and rubbed it between her fingers till it was dry enough to drop on the floorboard. She smoothed out the skirt of her new dress, inspecting for a stain.

"Since when do you need them to be single, Junie?" Sadie said. She reached over Betty to poke Junie in the belly.

Junie pulled the band from her ponytail and shook her head. Her hair swung into a silky curtain, just like a Prell commercial. Her voice went low. "I have not stopped thinking about that guitar player at the Willow Branch Park jam Sunday," she said. Betty gave a puzzled smile while the other girls groaned in agreement.

"The hippie?" Betty said. She'd never known Junie to look twice at a boy with long hair.

"Yes," Junie drawled, sucking on the cigarette and blowing smoke out through a whistle. The tip of her tongue appeared and lingered in the center of her top lip.

"That band had a negro drummer," Fred mumbled. "Y'all see that?" He thrummed a phantom beat on the steering wheel.

None of them answered. They side-eyed each other and wriggled in their seats. Of course they'd seen him, with his bear-tooth necklace and tank top, muscles on display as his arms flew over the drum set. The hippie had hugged his neck and called him something exotic, sounded like 'JayMo.' How could they forget? Betty imagined the other girls remembering it the same way. *What a band.*

Betty looked up and caught Fred's eyes in the rear-view mirror. "I don't have no problem with that," he said. "No, sir. I don't have that hang up no more." He looked back out at the darkness and the narrowing road. Betty watched the back of his head. His buzz cut was growing out, and his wiry gold hair hung long around his ears, almost covering the top of a still-angry battle scar high on the side of his neck.

Fred pulled up to the curb and let the girls out in front of the saloon door. "I'll be back in an hour and a half. You hear me, Junie?" He said his sister's name, but he looked at Betty. Betty replied with a helpless shrug as she pulled the foam roller out of her bangs.

"Aww, come on, Fred. How about two hours, huh?" Junie said. She bent to look through the window. "Give you more time to find you some trouble..."

He looked past her to other girls who were looking expectantly back at him. His plans were taking him to a different club, to a meeting not far from the naval base. "Well, all right. Two hours. But I might come back early, so you girls be good in there." He gave the building a cursory once-over, evidently decided it looked decent enough, and pulled away from the curb. He drove off before they could answer, his tail lights disappearing around the bend.

The girls fussed with their dresses and patted their hair. But Fred needn't worry about Betty, she looked forward to the music. Tracking down romance was not on her agenda. The thought of trying to make conversation with some smoky Westsider made her want to wait for her friends in the car. Small talk didn't come naturally, and flirting was as foreign as New York City.

Junie puckered crimson lips around the damp end of the cigarette and took one last drag before dropping it to the gravel. Betty stepped out and covered the smoldering butt, crushing it under the toe of her shoe. The hot end went out with a weak sizzle as it found the damp between the stones. Lifting her foot, Betty checked the sole for damage. She'd bought the already-scuffed red shoes in secret for fifty cents last week at the church rummage sale, stuffing them to the bottom of her tote bag before her mother saw from across the room, where she loudly presided over the baked-goods table. Betty loved them, and she especially loved how they looked with the dress she'd sewn herself from a bolt of blue calico with tiny red cherries, also from the rummage sale.

Looking up from the pulverized paper and tobacco at her feet, Betty started to follow her friends to the saloon doors.

Then she stopped.

A sound came from somewhere down the sidewalk. The other girls sauntered into the saloon, the cheers of an already rowdy crowd pouring out the doors along with the sound of guitar sound checks. As the doors closed behind them, the sound from down the road rose again. Voices. Voices singing.

The dark asphalt road glowed with puddled yellow light. Betty strolled to the nearest light pole and stopped, listening. Her head bobbed along with the music; the harmony buzzing through her belly. She walked to the next light pole, stopped again, one hand against the humid wood. "My Girl". She loved that song—the harmony so sweet, it brought a craving to her tongue. She swallowed hard.

She looked back toward the saloon, then forward again toward the sound. It was coming from one of the small shotgun houses on the other side of the street. It wasn't a record. People were singing. No instruments, only voices. *A cappella*. Like the hymn mama suggested last week at choir practice, mostly to put that haughty organist Vera in her place. Betty leaned toward the source of the sound, then pulled back, anchored to the post.

*Whoa, whoa, whoa...*they improvised, somehow, in harmony. The voices sang on about all that honey and those envious bees. Tantalizing. Her mind filled in the trumpet hit. She set her jaw tight and tilted her head, then stepped out toward the next light pole. She stopped between posts, pressed her clutch against the front of her skirt, clenched her knees together with a shudder. Her shoulders swayed to the rhythm, a rhythm snapped by fingers on a porch across the street.

There were figures. Five men on the porch, singing and snapping The Temptations song. Her mother didn't even like their name, let alone their music.

But her mother wasn't here.

Betty couldn't turn away.

Her eyes adjusted to the light of a single bulb and the glowing tips of cigarettes fluttering like fireflies. A man stood in each corner of the tiny, weathered porch, each singing their parts, their heads tilted toward each other as they found the harmony. Against the front door frame, a tall, narrow man leaned on his shoulder while he crooned the melody. The bare bulb shone down like a spotlight between them. Betty closed her eyes and imagined herself part of an audience, like on The Ed Sullivan Show. Her shoulders rocked as she swayed.

The melody trickled down and stopped, giving way to a melodic hum.

"Live, from the porch on Edison Avenue!"

Her eyes flew open. They'd seen her. She froze.

"Hey, that's all right now! We love an audience. Don't we, boys?"

The harmonizing stopped and they chimed in agreement.

"Sure we do!"

"Yes, indeed!"

"Any requests?"

The tall one came down the stairs and stood across the street. His eyes glinted golden brown in the yellow moonlight and a wave of black hair swooped up from his smooth brown forehead. He wore a collared shirt with short sleeves tucked into pegged trousers. She looked at the ground, but her eyes found the grass at his feet. His shoes were wingtips, brown and polished to a high shine. She focused on them, studied them, to keep from looking up at him. But she didn't walk away.

"You're not lost, are you, ma'am?" he said. His voice was warm and smoky.

"No," she said. It came out dry and squeaky. She coughed and touched a knuckle to the tip of her nose. "No, I'm not. I'm out here, down there, with my friends. To hear a band, at the West Tavern, yonder." She raised her chin and the golden light highlighted the flush on her smooth, pale cheeks.

"Is that right?" he said. "Because, and pardon me if I'm mistaken, but it looks to me like you're down *here*. Listening to us," he tilted his head toward the porch and smiled, a crooked grin, exposing the brilliant whiteness of his teeth behind his wide, full mouth. She bit her own bottom lip.

"Well, I guess I was."

"And?"

"And? And what?"

"*And* what did you think? Seems you are the audience tonight, a private concert for Her Royal Highness, if you will. So, Princess..." he placed his hand over his heart, gave a courtly half-bow, "what did you think?"

The air hummed between them, across the dim street. Only a few yards, but it seemed miles. She stepped out onto the blacktop and he did the same, meeting her in the middle, where two yellow puddles of light overlapped. Silver moths flung themselves at dusty street lights, helpless against the irresistible pull.

"I absolutely loved it. And thank you for the fine concert," she said. A flash of something, a bit of boldness let loose by the fear of losing time, cast about inside her head. Beads of perspiration formed at her temples. She snapped her purse open to fish out a handkerchief, and the purse fell from her flustered hands, landing with a soft thud at their feet. A handful of change spilled onto the asphalt, rolling around them in slow motion. One bright penny found a smooth spot and spun itself silly as they watched, both crouching down as if watching a tiny circus. The penny spent itself and finally lay down on the asphalt between them.

He helped her collect her things—a comb, the foam hair roller, her one precious Revlon lipstick, Cherries in the Snow. She glanced up at him, embarrassed for him to see her private things, but he handled them naturally, as if they were his own. Then they collected her coins. He picked up the shiny penny last and held it up to her, between his thumb and forefinger.

"You keep that," she said, "as payment for the show."

"Oh, no. I can't accept it, Princess," he said, presenting the penny anew, teasing with another little bow. On the porch, the singers counted off an uptempo beat and launched into a bebop version of "Pennies From Heaven."

"I insist," she said. She couldn't have stopped smiling if she tried.

"Well, all right, if you insist, I'll keep it then." He dropped the penny into his shirt pocket. "But not as payment." He patted the pocket and flattened his hand over his heart with gallant air. "I'll save it, as a keepsake." He slid his hands smoothly into his trouser pockets and stepped backward, toward the house. "To remember you by," he dipped his head, "Princess."

He turned and stepped out of their spotlight. She wished she didn't want to follow him. She wished she could turn and go, leave the moment alone and find her friends. Or glue beneath her shoes.

She stepped after him.

"My name is Betty," she said.

He turned back toward her. She offered a hand, the other hand smoothed across the cinched waist of her shirtdress, glad for the little bit of shape it lent her narrow frame. "Betty Langdon."

"Betty. That's a pretty name. My grandmother's name is Elizabeth." *How could a set of eyes seem to convey so much?* "My name's Dominicus Owens." He took her hand. "But they call me Mini."

His hand enveloped hers, warm and smooth. As she looked up at him, towering over her with a smile she couldn't believe was for her. "It's just Betty," she said. "Not Elizabeth. Just Betty. I wish it were Elizabeth, though."

Her hand was still in his. She looked up at his face, at the charming, amused expression and the velvety sheen of his eyes. An explosion of sound broke the cold, quiet of evening.

Raucous music and shouting split the road as the door of the tavern flew open. Three men in jeans and cowboy hats piled into a pickup truck, laughing and hooting as they tore away. The driver's dirty-blond hair whipped against his bare arm as he waved it outside the window, squealing around the curve in the road and speeding away.

Betty and Dominicus looked at each other and laughed. The others hooted and whistled from the porch. "I should get back to my friends," Betty said.

"Well, all right, Miss Betty," he said. A pang of something irrational spiked in her chest. He released her hand and it felt suddenly cold. "You take care now. Come back any time. We practice up there on Sly's porch all the time."

"You fellas a group? What's it called?"

"We are. That's Hank, Zeke, O.T., and Sly. We're The Downtown Sound."

"Are you now?" Betty said. She tried out looking up from under her lashes, but it came out a spasmodic flutter. She pushed her chin out instead. "Maybe I will come back." She patted the handkerchief behind her ear and said before she could think too much on it: "In fact, I know I will. And when I do, I think I'd rather call you Dominicus. Mini doesn't suit you at all." She went on, filled with a sudden boldness, "But I do think Princess will suit me just fine."

His eyes narrowed, then widened, and his mouth spread into a broad grin. She grinned back. He patted his shirt pocket and stopped walking, letting her continue on her own. A hot breeze strained through the bushes, kicking leaves up to swirl at their feet.

Crickets offered rousing applause from their seats in the bushes as one of the porch singers counted off for another tune, uptempo this time.

"It had to be you..." The beat made the old song fresh. "It had to be you...I wandered around and finally found that somebody who..."

Betty turned and walked backward. "Oh, an encore!" she called, bouncing her shoulders to the music. "But I like Ray Charles' s version best."

"Ray Charles's version, huh?" Dominicus's brows arched and he nodded, highly impressed. Betty thought she might burst. It was as if the sun were rising inside her body.

Dominicus watched after Betty until she vanished behind the tavern doors and they closed behind her. Keeping his eyes on the doors, he walked backward to the porch and, catching the beat with snapping fingers, he found his note and took the lead.

"...It had to be you, wonderful you. It had to be you..."

MELODY

2019

Podcaster Melody Hinterson read the last line of her script, adding an extra dash of ominous drama to her voice as she signed off. Her producer Dorian Santos held up one hand, counting down 3-2-1, and then clicked a button on his keyboard with the other hand. "Okay, you're clear."

Across the table, Melody tucked her chin to her neck and found the tiny microphone clipped to her t-shirt. "Thanks, Dor," she said. She nodded at him and pushed her chair back, snatching a slice of room-temperature pizza from its box and flipping the lid closed.

"So did you have a chance to think about what kind of song you want to use for the theme?" Dorian said. He glanced at the pizza box, then set his fingers on his keyboard. The twelve bars of music they chose would be the leitmotif of the whole second season, so it had to be perfect. "Do you want something tense like this?" He finished typing with a flourish and clicked a button. A low progression of string chords played through the bluetooth speakers in the corners of the room, Melody's dining room where they'd set up their recording studio. "Or maybe something more buzzy—more like this?" An acoustic guitar riff played over a melody with a foreboding tone. Dorian's fingers followed the notes, itching for the strings of his guitar.

"Oh no!" Melody rolled her eyes dramatically. "Those 'where art thou' tunes are done to death in the true crime space, don't you think? Like, we get it, the South is sooo gothic…" She wagged her head in a slow figure-eight.

Dorian smiled, then looked back at his screen.

"Dang it, now that 'Constant Sorrow' song is gonna be stuck in my head all day." Melody stood, took a big bite, chewed it over. Her eyes went wide and her jaw worked faster, pushing the mouthful to one cheek. "Oh, oh, oh!" She swallowed fast. "What are the chances we could get the rights to a Lynyrd Skynyrd tune? How perfect would that be? Jacksonville band for a local story?" Her eyes crinkled the way they did when she went into that faraway thinking mode. Dorian smiled and then looked away, turning back to his keyboard, but Melody couldn't miss the red flush in his cheeks. He typed something into the search bar, and the first strains of the organ intro to "Freebird" filtered into the room. Melody grinned.

"Yeah, like that!" she said. "Perfect!"

"Actually…" Dorian said, clicking the keys again, "*this* could be *really* perfect." The evocative first bars of "Simple Kind Of Man" played — guitar and cymbal, followed by bass.

"Oooh my goodness," Melody's head lolled back, "you're right!"

"I know," Dorian said. He shut his laptop down. "But we don't have the budget for the rights to that song."

Melody's shoulders sank. "How much can you use before you have to pay for rights?"

"I think it's still ten seconds."

"How much would full rights be?"

"More than we have."

"What if my mom's cousin went to school with one of their nieces? Do you think that would help?" Melody took a big bite of pizza.

"Did he date her?" Dorian checked the pizza box, found it empty, and closed it back up.

"Kind of, I think." Melody aimed her slice at him, offering to share.

Dorian shook his head. "I'll just starve." Melody rolled her eyes, but smiled around her mouthful of pizza.

"Did he marry her?" Dorian said.

"Not that I know of."

"Not that you 'know of.'" He drew air quotes. "Probably 'no' then." More air quotes.

"Still, we have a better chance than if he *had* married her, and then divorced her, like he did all his other wives," Melody offered. "So there's that. It wouldn't hurt to ask. Maybe I should ask." She made a note in her calendar. Her mom would probably have his latest phone number. Then she wrapped her wavy ponytail around itself till it formed a bun, pulled the end through the middle and tugged.

She flipped her laptop back open and searched the Lynyrd Skynyrd website. Dorian shook his head and gathered his things. Then he stood behind Melody and looked over her shoulder at the screen as he put on his hoodie.

"'Man of Constant Sorrow' is actually public domain, you know," he said.

Melody covered her ears. If she thought about that song, it would be stuck in her head the rest of the day.

Dorian grinned at the top of her head. "When should we meet back?"

She pulled her gaze from the screen and looked up at him as he tried to zip his hoodie. She'd given him that hoodie for his birthday when they were classmates in college. He looked so cute in it that she was suddenly glad it was fall. "I thought we might set that up after you're done editing the trailer and intro episode."

"Let's see. I need to wrap up the ad updates for last season and then I can focus on just this. Probably could have it ready for you to check out by Friday? I can come by and play it—"

"So you can upload to beta for me to listen—Oh, you mean…" He usually sends this kind of stuff digitally… "Yeah, you could come Friday, for sure! If you want to do that, I mean, if you don't mind. Instead."

"Either way—"

"No, yeah, in-person is even better. That way we can discuss it in real time. Maybe go over the script for episode two." Her voice dropped two octaves as she did an eerily spot-on impression of Peter Thomas, the ominous voice of her favorite show *Forensic Files*. "This week's episode: 'Legend Tripping…'"

Dorian pulled at the brim of his baseball hat. "Great. Check your calendar when you get a chance and let me know what time would work." He hefted his bag and slipped the strap over his head.

"Looks like I can do noon." She pointed to the Friday square in her planner. "I'll order another pizza."

"Did you just jot down 'order another pizza' in your calendar?"

"Yup! See you Friday at noon for an episode review and more pizza." She tapped the empty box. And if we can't find an intro song, maybe you could improvise a few bars on the guitar?"

"Sure, sounds good." He turned and strode to the door with Melody smiling after him. "See you Friday!" he called over his shoulder. He stepped outside, but gave her a small smile before pulling the door closed behind him.

The smile dissolved down Melody's chin. *What is going on?* She thought she knew all his expressions, knew the meaning of every different smile—amused, tired, pensive, surprised. That smile just now looked like he wanted to say something, but had thought better of it.

She wanted to know what it was. But also dreaded it.

Their unspoken understanding since starting this podcast together was that they were business partners, and that meant they could never be a couple. Dopey crushes and silly flirting would ruin everything they were working for here. And yet, the room felt empty the moment he left. She stared after him at the closed door, and then blinked hard when it opened again.

"Package!" Dorian said. "The new mystery puzzle is here!" He went to a small wooden dining table Melody kept in front of the picture window in the living room.

She jumped out of her chair and met him at the table. "I was just wondering when it would get here!" *Sure, that's what you were wondering.*

While Dorian sliced the tape on the plain brown box, Melody snapped a picture of a completed puzzle that covered the table. It was a picture of a snow-covered mountain with tiny skiers dotting the white expanse with an enticing ski lodge in the foreground complete with puffs of cotton-ball smoke drifting from the chimney, its roof heavy with more snow. Lights glowed from within. When they'd laid the last piece, the two of them had stared longingly at the lodge, wishing they could see what was inside, behind those windows. She made sure she got a few good shots then quickly broke it down and gathered all the pieces in a basket they kept under the table. Dorian pulled a note from the box and read aloud while Melody rifled through the pieces in the box.

"'Dear Fellow Mystery Puzzler, Good luck with this one!" he read. "We had no idea what it was until we were halfway through it. Your clue is: *Honey Moon.*'"

Neither of them commented.

Dorian carefully dumped the pieces in the tray, and they both leaned in to spread them out. "So we've got yellows, greens, and blues for edge pieces, purple—what are those? Petals?" He held a piece up with one hand and continued shuffling the pieces with the other.

"Definitely an outdoor scene, drawn, not a photo, maybe a forest?" She looked at the piece Dorian held up, then grasped his hand. "Hold still! Let me see it! Yup, that looks like a little blossom, maybe." They locked eyes, then both glanced down at her hand on his. She cleared her throat and drew her hand away.

He wouldn't want to leave now, not until they'd at least gotten the outer pieces in place. Once they were separated out, they divided the pieces by type: tabs to the left, blanks to the right.

"I'm gonna run and change my clothes," Melody said, clearing her throat. "Be right back."

Melody hurried down the hall to her bedroom and swung the door closed behind her. She stopped in front of her dresser, her hands on the handles of her comfy-clothes drawer, and stared at the door, imagining Dorian on the other side. What would it be like to be someone who would slip into something silky right now, to let her hair down and shake the curls over her shoulders, and slink back out to the living room? To sidle up to Dorian and drop an arm around his shoulder, look down at the puzzle pieces with him, pause there till he noticed her perfume and turned his head—

"Mel!"

She jumped up and grabbed a ratty pair of pajama pants. "Coming!" She wriggled out of her work clothes.

"Come back!" Dorian shouted down the hall. "I don't wanna set it up without you."

"Coming, coming!" She hopped one leg and then the other into the pant legs, stuck her tongue out at herself in the mirror, and headed back out, singing to herself.

"'*Oh, I-I-I am a ma-a-an of constant sorrow*'...Dang it!"

She stopped in the living room doorway. He was bent over the table, pinching his bottom lip, deep in thought.

He placed two pieces down and fit them together. A corner. She organized the pieces by color and pattern. They had the process down. They'd lost track of how many puzzles they'd worked on together since they joined the Mystery Puzzlers Club in their senior year of college. It had been the perfect way to fill down time at the local news station affiliate where they both did their internships. The puzzle club director Theodore Philpot (not his real name, for the sake of his 'personal safety') could tell any member at any time precisely how many they'd completed, along with how many they'd failed, how long they took to complete each puzzle, and how many pieces another member claimed they'd lost, down to the spot where the piece would have fit.

Still, it was fun, even if the director did take his job a little too seriously. Dorian's dead-on impressions of him cracked Melody up, and quoting his emails made up a decent percentage of their inside jokes. Every few months, the club members packed up the pieces to their latest puzzle and mailed them on to the next club member. Then they sent the president a picture of the completed puzzle. Once everyone had a chance at each puzzle, the club director would pack up new puzzles in unmarked boxes and mail them out, starting the next round. High drama broke out once in a while with one team accusing another of losing a piece, inciting the accused to protest that the accuser must be making the false claim with the sole purpose of lowering the accused's point count. Last year, a new rule had been put in place stating that such claims must be made immediately upon receipt of the pieces, and some players went so far as to videotape themselves opening the new box and counting out the pieces. That had been Dorian's desperate suggestion, actually, mostly to shut everyone up so they could get on with working on the puzzles. Theodore Philpot appreciated that idea so much that he'd agreed to sponsor the season one finale of the Tabs and Blanks Podcast.

During breaks in recording, while eating lazy dinners or pretending to study, Melody and Dorian always had a puzzle going. When Dorian got tired of working on his thesis, he went to the puzzle table. When Melody couldn't listen to her own voice in the headphones any more, she went to the puzzle table. When they found themselves floundering with the complicated status of their friendship, they went to the puzzle table.

While the other members took the rules and the scores to another level, Melody and Dorian were blatantly unconcerned. They knew their score was subject to minute tallies and scrupulous recording somewhere—probably in Theodore's mother's basement where he maintained a private puzzle lair—but the fact was neither of them could care less about the score.

At the puzzle table, things were simple. They worked together, heads bent close enough to touch, and everything fell into place. All the pieces eventually found their place, fit just right. It all made sense. At the puzzle table, the outside world disappeared, and rules didn't matter.

It was all about playing the game.

TABS AND BLANKS
PODCAST

Transcript
Season 2: Trailer—"The Chimney Sweep"
Narrated by host Melody Hinterson

Voice of Melody Hinterson: *In the world of jigsaw puzzles, the puzzler's task is to fit the pieces together into a complete image, a total picture that tells a cohesive story. The individual pieces of a puzzle have their own names—'tabs' and 'blanks'— and only when each one is fitted into its original place will the puzzle be solved. Only then does it all make total sense.*

Introducing: Season 2 of the Tabs and Blanks Podcast.

This season: The Chimney Sweep.

From Open Mouth Productions, the story of dry counties, wet Sundays, and the mysterious disappearance of a local woman named Betty Van Disson.

We'll hear the words of Betty's husband Randell Van Disson, from his one and only police interview:

(*soundbite*) "...I have told everything I know, which is nothing. And yet here I sit. My wife is gone. My life is gone. My business. My family. Gone. All gone..."

We'll talk to the lead investigator Billie John Whitaker:

(*soundbite*) "...She didn't just up and disappear, I can tell you that. What I *can* tell you is somebody damned-well knows what happened, and I tell you what, I still believe we coulda put all this to rest if Randell had allowed us to search the property..."

Our investigation takes us down asphalt roads and dirt lanes, over boggy coastal marshland and deep scrub forest, to hear from the people who knew and loved Betty:

(*soundbite*) "...She was a good boss, you know. A nice lady. She would do anything for anybody. She didn't deserve nothing like this. She is truly missed..."

(*soundbite*) "Somebody's gotta know something. We just want to let her rest. Rest in peace. Finally. She deserves that, doesn't she?"

Betty Van Disson and her husband Randell ran a roadside motel on Highway 17 in northeast Florida. Randell also had a small side business as an expert chimney sweep, a business he took over from his father. On September 3, 2001, Betty told her husband Randell she was going to visit her mother, an invalid who lived across the Highway 17 bridge, the picturesque blue bridge that connects north Florida with south Georgia. It crosses over the St. Mary's River, a blackwater that meanders along forming the border between the two states. This was nothing new. Betty visited her mother often, bringing groceries, returning library books and picking up new ones, helping with her bath, and setting her hair in rollers. Betty and her mother appear to have been very close.

And so on that day, when she headed out, her husband Randell Van Disson may not have thought much of it. On the days when Betty was away helping her mother, the motel's front desk and the liquor store were both run by their one employee, a young woman named Heather. It was a Monday, the day after their traditionally busiest day of the week, but frankly, things hadn't been busy at the Maryview Motor Inn and Liquors for quite a while. He expected Betty would be back by evening, as usual.

Here at the border of north Florida and south Georgia, the highway frontage of the Van Disson's property used to be the main north-south interstate thoroughfare. Then Interstate 95 was completed, funneling business from the roadside hotels, Florida souvenir shops, and farm stands that had relied on the excitement and curiosity of tourists and travelers thrilled to have just passed that bright green and orange 'Welcome To Florida' sign.

But there was a reason for some folks to keep using Highway 17 even after the convenient new interstate was completed through Jacksonville: the quiet two-lane road led to the nearest legal liquor sales available to residents of the adjacent dry county in Georgia, just over that bridge.

No body was ever found, nor was any other trace of evidence to explain what happened to Betty.

(*soundbite*) "...Randell refused to cooperate. Let me ask you something: How does that look? Hmm? What does that say? If she was your sister, your cousin, your friend—what would you think?..."

I'm Melody Hinterson. And this is Season 2 of the Tabs and Blanks Podcast:

"The Chimney Sweep."

TABS AND BLANKS
PODCAST

Transcript
Season 2, Episode 1: "Duuu-val!"

Welcome back for Season Two! I'm your host, Melody Hinterson, and thanks for tuning in for Season Two. We're adding something new this season that we're pretty excited about. Each week when we release a new episode, you can also head to the website where you will be able to download a professional, annotated transcript of that episode. This will serve as an additional resource for our hearing- impaired fans, and also we think it's pretty cool that at the end, you'll basically have the whole season in manuscript format! Read additional inter-view transcripts, too, as the season progresses by clicking the 'Transcripts' tab. You can access all that, and also download all episodes of this pod-cast, on our website Open Mouth Media dot com. You'll find any documents mentioned in the broad-cast under the 'Evidence' tab. All the resources are fully integrated so you can switch back and forth between reading and listening, depending on your location or preferences.

The Tabs and Blanks Podcast is a production of Open Mouth Media, Melinda Hinterson, Producer, and Dorian Santos, Sound Engineer.

(*soundbite*) "Duuuuvaaal"

Jacksonville, Florida. Yeah, yeah, I know. It's not really known for much, but that's because it's a city with an identity crisis. I grew up here; it's my town. It has its problems. People hate its name. Progress sometimes gets buried in a quagmire murky as any Florida swamp. But hey, it's home.

This city was also the home of the subject of this season's investigation. Betty Van Disson lived and worked here her whole life—until she disappeared without a trace. Her case remains unsolved and mostly unknown. I've lived here all my life, and I had never heard of it until Betty's cousin Nora left a comment on our listeners' discussion board last season. Someone had posted a comment about the pain of losing someone you care about, and how it's compounded when you just don't know what happened to them. Nora had replied, "My cousin Betty disappeared in 2001, and we never found out what happened to her." Well, we think it's time someone looked for her. The community owes her that much.

Some folks are aware that southern rock was born here in Jacksonville, as The Allman Brothers, Lynyrd Skynyrd, and Molly Hatchet all got their start here, and paved the way for others, too. We claim the great and legendary Ray Charles, even if he did leave town for distant Seattle specifically to get as far away from here as possible. Ouch.

Deep down, we know there must have been a good reason for that.

If there's a local food we can claim, it has to be Mayport Shrimp, since we'd also like credit for our role in modernizing the shrimping industry, thank you very much. Then there's the Maxwell House roasting plant that makes the whole city smell like a giant coffee house whenever work is in full swing. The Camel Rider sandwich is a local delicacy as well, owning to the large and vibrant Arab American community.

Lately, one of the city's biggest claims to fame is the frequent name drops by the lovable Jason in NBC's hit show The Good Place. *His blind devotion to this city, and especially to the local football team the Jaguars, may be what most people think of when they hear the name 'Jacksonville.'*

Comedian Katt Williams chose Jacksonville for the recording of his Netflix special Great America, *and he spends a good twenty minutes telling us about ourselves. To our faces. And we laughed.*

It's hilarious because it's all true. We get it. There's something unique about this place.

As the old saying goes—and it's especially true here—"It must be something in the water."

We appreciate the shout outs, don't get me wrong. But there is so much more to Jacksonville, to this place with the problematic name.

There's the north-flowing river, of course—the St. Johns River. One of the first things folks may tell you when you land up here is that Jacksonville boasts the only river IN THE WORLD that flows north. That, of course, is absolutely not true, there being several others in North America alone. Nonetheless, the little nugget spread like kudzu and became local lore. Like many closely-held beliefs here in the 'River City,' people tend to resist loosening their grip even in the face of new evidence.

'River City' is only one of the city's nicknames. There's also 'The Bold New City of the South'—often truncated to the zippier 'Bold City.' We even have an outstanding local brewery by that name. The town is sometimes called 'The Gateway To Florida,' even as many wish it could be more than a pit stop along the way to somewhere sexier, like Miami, or with more characters (I'm looking at you, Orlando, with all your fancy theme parks and whatnot. Although a deep dive into Jacksonville's history reveals some real characters of another sort!). Some like to refer

to the town as Florida's 'First Coast,' which has always been my personal favorite.

Sometimes we don't know who we should be as a city, and so sometimes the desire to claim an identity means we simply resort to mass exclamations, like at the stadium on Jaguars game day when people of all colors and social status join in glorious, harmonious chants of our county's name. 'Duuuu-vaaal!' we shout as one, unconcerned or unaware of whose name it is we're chanting. In those moments, it doesn't matter. In those moments, we own it, together.

I wonder, though: What does that say about a city? What does it mean about us, the fact that we've seen a need to come up with so many nick-names? A statue of our city's namesake stands in the middle of a roundabout in a major thorough-fare downtown—President Andrew Jackson seated atop a powerfully rearing horse. One is obliged to circle it to reach all points downtown on the north side of the St. Johns River. Every so often, someone defaces it, posting a reminder that Jackson was a slave owner or of his role in the Indian Resettlement Act that led to the Trail of Tears and the deaths of thousands of Native Americans.

So maybe that's a reason for the nicknames. Some folks opine that at least 'Jacksonville' is better than the town's rather unimaginative original name, according to local lore, of 'Cowford.' Other folks strongly beg to differ.

Lately, Jacksonville has been making moves toward claiming its place as the birthplace of southern rock, with bands like the aforementioned Lynyrd Skynyrd and The Allman Brothers having formed here and played in local venues before breaking out into worldwide stardom. The humble childhood home of Skynyrd lead singer Ronnie Van Zant now boasts a shiny new historical marker, as does the 'Green House' in historic Riverside where both he and the Allmans lived at different times. Country music superstar Tim McGraw is claimed as a hometown boy, as is legendary R & B musician Ray Charles, who attended Florida School for the Deaf and Blind just south of here and later lived and played backup piano for a while in the historic and storied LaVilla area.

I hear there are plans in the works for a real music museum—right here in River City! Die hard music fans already make Jacksonville a stop on their way to somewhere more exciting, plugging obscure local haunts like the location of the former West Tavern into their GPS and tooling out to the Westside just to see the place that may have inspired Skynyrd's hit 'Gimme Three Steps.' And although it has gone through many changes over the years, the annual Jacksonville Jazz Festival is still a cool event that draws fans and musicians from around the world.

Betty was part of this town. She was one of us. And she went missing. Authorities are no closer today to finding out what happened to her than they were when she disappeared almost two decades ago. That's not okay. We're going to do something about that.

"The Chimney Sweep" is a production of Open Mouth Productions. Sound engineering by Dorian Santos and lighting by Kina Narvaez. I'm Melody Hinterson. Thank you for joining us today, and please subscribe wherever you listen to podcasts.

TABS AND BLANKS
PODCAST

Transcript
Season 2, Episode 2: Legend Tripping

There are folks out there who just love to search, like me and the rest of the team here at the Tabs and Blanks Podcast. We look for the stories of people who've been lost and forgotten, then we pursue those stories through the layers of mystery. Sometimes that takes us to some... well, let's just call them 'interesting'... and sometimes dangerous places. But we do this with the goal of finding out the truth and bringing justice, or at least some sense of closure, for the stories of the missing and for the heartbroken families they leave behind. When I read Betty's cousin Nora's comment on our discussion board last season, it felt as though it spoke directly to me, right to my heart. And once I looked into her disappearance and the subsequent investigation, and once I learned how little had been done to look for her, I felt a certain responsibility to follow Betty's story as far as it might lead. That is what brings us to the last place Betty was known to have been—the motel, now abandoned and run-down, which she ran with her husband Randell.

However, there are people who trek across towns, across the country, and sometimes around the world, to find the most remote, abandoned places they can for the sole purpose of experiencing the eerie and the strange. Welcome to the world of Legend Tripping.

Legend Trippers seek the places others avoid, hoping to capture the worst of it on their phones and their cameras and take it all home to experience again, or to share on YouTube, or in blogs frequented by the like-minded: **Ooh, look where we went. People used to live here. Like this. Can you imagine?**

They shiver and revel in the creepy and grotesque: **here you see where someone left behind a kitchen full of cereal and canned spaghetti, now eaten-through by rats and rusted by years of exposure to the elements. Why did they leave like this? Who were these people?** It gives them a thrill to think about it, to imagine the sad lives that played out in these former living places, offices, shops. They get a sense that those people are still there, watching as they intrude on the ghosts of past lives.

I get it. I'm an investigative journalist, after all. I know from whence the fascination springs.

But I want to be clear: this is not what we are doing here. We are not 'legend tripping.' We are not here at the former Maryview Motor Inn and Liquors, in the decrepit remains of Betty and Randell Van Disson's life, for thrills. Our goal is to take all the information that's out there about this case and finally gather it all together in one place, and then to present it to the public in a cohesive manner, for the first time, in the hopes that someone out there will remember something that can help fit the pieces together. Maybe someone never came forward before because they didn't even know that what they knew might be a clue.

To get here, going north on I-95 from Jacksonville, you'd never know that Highway 17 used to be the main road into northeast Florida. The freeway barrels over the old roadway with barely a passing glance. Blink and you miss it.

We make our way down a covered path along a row of motel rooms. You get the feeling that the end of this business enterprise wasn't a let's-sit-down-and-discuss-the-situation decision. There's no plan, no rhyme or reason to the up-and-left nature of this place's condition. Furniture leans rotting in the humidity, curtains dangle shredded and moldy, alarm clocks sit ready to wake the rats and raccoons who have made these rooms their homes. It's an uncanny scene.

We try to step into one room, the first one we've found with a floor that hasn't completely given way to the dirt below. There is a sodden mattress, sunken in the middle, sliding off its rails. A dull brass headboard displays its fine collection of intricate spiderwebs, like dreamcatchers. A lone suit jacket droops on a rusty DeLuxe dry-cleaning hanger dangling from the knob of the drunken bathroom door. Some resourceful creature has built a nest in the bathroom sink.

We look into the other rooms, but they are obviously not safe to enter. Ceiling fans dangle from wires. Broken window glass glints dully from the panes and from the ground. One room has a small scraggly tree growing through the gaping hole in the floor.

Across the motel parking lot is the former All-Right Souvenir and Liquor Store. This is the spot where visitors from over the border would end up when they turned right off the highway onto the property and then made another right. Right to the All-Right. Clever. There's a shed near the edge of the clearing, locked up with a heavy chain and padlock, and a thickly forested area beyond. We walk the property line, dense with swordlike palmetto bushes, rope-like vines, pine trees and oaks taking up every inch of space they can claim. There is no way into, or out of, this forest.

Old wiring for the busted out neon signs hangs from the motel lobby windows. The faded blue front door still has a sign in its window, clinging to the glass by yellowing cellophane tape:
"Welcome to Florida! We have what you need to make your trip All-Right!"
We know that Betty's father was from South Carolina, so I wonder if the haint-blue front door was meant to keep the ghosts away. The atmosphere here, a feeling of sudden desertion after a time-stopping tragedy, seems to prove it didn't work. If you believe in ghosts, then you would believe they're around every corner of this desolate property.

Believe it or not, a similar scene lies just up the road from here, at another motel, the scene of the disappearance of another woman—Nellie Olfort. We'll talk more about that woman and her tragic case in a future episode, but for now I'll just say: the similarities are hard to ignore. There are notable differences, of course, the biggest one being that Nellie's case was eventually solved.

And now we want to tell you about this week's sponsor, Branches DNA...

(*soundbite*) Voice of host Melody Hinterson: There was smoke reported in the vicinity of the property, never confirmed, but Randell wouldn't actually let you on the property to search. That doesn't help your case, am I right?

This week we speak with the police investigator on the case all those years ago when Betty Van Disson was finally reported missing.

Today's episode features some of my conversation with former Jacksonville Sheriff's Officer Detective William Whitaker, known as Billy John. He was the detective who took the lead on Betty Van Disson's case. I put it that way, saying he 'took the lead' rather than calling him the 'lead detective,' because that is actually what happened. When an investigation had trouble taking off due to Randell's lack of cooperation and a lack of evidence, Detective Billy John took it upon himself to find out everything he could about the Van Dissons—Randell in particular—the Maryview Motor Inn, and the circumstances surrounding the last time anyone saw Betty.

Melody: Thanks so much for letting us come over today. This is my partner Dorian...

We've just arrived on Billy John's wide front porch. He rises from his rocking chair, shakes our hands. We share introductions all around, including Billy John's wife Barbie. They insist it's okay if we call them by their first names, and after half an hour of fascinating conversation—Detective Billy John is a gifted storyteller—I realize I need to steer the conversation back over to the subject at hand.

Melody: So Detective Billy John—I love that name by the way—I guess it's best to just let you start at the beginning, with the things that stuck out to you the most. Like, what happened that day when you came out to the motel to talk to Randell about Betty's disappearance?

Billy John: Well, now you know already he wouldn't let us search the property at all. He got all up in arms, shouting "Y'all ain't gonna find her out here, why aren't you looking for her, I done told you about that man who kept trying to talk to her."

Melody: There was smoke reported in the vicinity of the property, never confirmed, but Randell wouldn't actually let you on the property to search. That doesn't help your case, am I right?

Billy John nods and sinks his chin into his chest.

Melody: Most people out there listening will probably wonder at that. They'll say, "Well, how could he keep them from looking? Couldn't they have gotten a warrant?"

Billy John: Well now, those people wouldn't understand how the law works. I see your face turning skeptical there, but it's the truth. Especially back then. I asked could we search the property. He said no, no use. I already did that, anyway. He said there's no cause to think she's out there, anyway. Said the chain link fence at the back of the motel lot didn't even have a gate to go through if she'd wanted to. Now, I know better than anyone how that's going to sound to your listeners out there, but at the time, that was that. No judge in that county would have overridden Randell's right to say who could and could not come up on his property.

I decide to let that subject slide for now.

Melody: You mentioned a man? A man who'd come by the motel, tried to talk to Betty?

Billy John: Randell said there was a customer, came down pretty much every weekend to buy his liquor, sometimes more often than that. There were a couple of liquor stores down there, but he always came down to the All-Right at the Maryview. Randell said he always knew that old fellow had a thing for Betty and he thought maybe we should have been looking for him. Said the guy was creepy and that he hadn't seen him in the days since Betty disappeared. Or 'went missing.' I think Randell actually used the term 'gone off,' not 'disappeared.' And to answer your next question, I did. I did go looking for that guy, with the little information Randell had on him, and I interviewed him, just based on the fact that Randell thought he was a creepy dude which, by the way, he was. I gave Randell the benefit of the doubt, said 'okay

Randell, I'll do that. But don't you think we should still check the property? Make sure she isn't out there hurt or sick or something?' He said that no, he'd already searched all out there, all along the brush. At one point he even said he had thought maybe a bear might have gotten her. But there wasn't any sign, you see.

Melody: Do you remember anything else about the guy Randell was suspicious of?

Billy John: Randell had the guy's name, and this was interesting, he had it because the guy always took his receipt from purchase and wrote his phone number on it and slid it back over to Betty. Every time. Until Randell started joining Betty behind the counter any time he was there when the guy came in. He said Betty seemed to think it was no big deal, that the customers gave her their number all the time, offered to 'take her away from all this,' et cetera. If she's like my Barbie, I bet she'd bring it up whenever she and Randell got into a tiff. Like, look I have other options out there.

(*laughter*)

Melody: Mm hmm.

Billy John: But the point is, I guess this guy was pretty persistent, different enough that Randell saved a couple of those receipts in the register. I tracked him down up in Woodbine. He claimed he'd been injured in a farm accident a couple months before and been basically bedridden since before Betty disappeared. His wife vouched for him.

Melody: Oh wow, okay. So Billy John, after spending, I'm assuming, a lot of time and energy and resources investigating what happened to Betty, what do *you* think happened to her?

Billy John: She didn't just up and disappear, I can tell you that. What I *can* tell you is somebody damned-well knows what happened, and I tell you what, I still believe we coulda put all this to rest if Randell had allowed us to search the property."

I have been in contact with the nursing home where Randell Van Disson now lives. I've written to Randell personally and left a message asking if he would let us come by to interview him. According to staff at the facility, he is in declining health and they try not to unduly agitate him. We hope to gain permission to meet with him and ask him in person about his memories of the disappearance of his wife.

In a coming episode, we'll be sharing an interview with members of Betty's family. While they each have their own recollections—of her, of Randell, and of what happened around the time of Betty's disappearance—it was the first time they all sat down together to talk about Betty's disappearance, and in sharing what they remember, they reminded each of other of things they'd each forgotten, things they thought were unimportant, or that they told the police but never heard back on. Years have passed, and Betty's family has been forced to go on with no answers. I can't imagine what it would be like to lose a loved one in this mysterious way and then to feel like there was information that never saw investigation, clues that were cast aside as unimportant. Sometimes, when you lift the rug and sweep the crumbs together, you get a new perspective on how dirty things have become.

MELODY

2019

Melody lifted one side of her headphones. "Should we cut in a clip from the new phone call with Detective Whitaker this week? Or would it be better to leave that for next week's next episode?"

"Maybe that one line, when he said 'she didn't just disappear, I can tell you that...'" Dorian clicked at his keyboard as he spoke.

"I was thinking of the line where he said he told Randell maybe they should check the property? Where he said something like, 'What if she's out there hurt or something...'?" Melody did an excellent 'old Southern guy' impression.

"That's good. And end right after he says, 'but he said no,'" Dorian suggested. "Cue my amazing guitar riff."

"Love it!" Melody clapped a little round of applause. "Great job on the editing this week, Dor. The cutaways are so spot-on, as always. *I* was on the edge of my seat, and I already knew what was happening!"

She took another slice of pizza and slid it onto her paper plate, already splotched with translucent pepperoni grease. She turned the box toward Dorian, exaggerating politeness. He didn't want another slice, but she was offering, so he took one anyway. "Thanks. So do you have any plans for—"

Melody clicked her phone screen with a clean knuckle. "Our subscriber count jumped this week—oh, sorry!" She looked up. "You were saying something?"

"Wh—yeah. I mean no, no big deal. I was just going to ask what you're doing this evening. Big Friday night plans or —?"

"Oh! Um, no. Nope. No big plans," she dusted pizza flour from her hands over her plate. "I'm just so wrecked from this week, you know? I had four free-lance jobs due, picked up a few more that needed some pre-writing research. My eyeballs are spinning." She made the googly-eyes that never failed to make him smile and spun two fingers in circles beside her head. As expected, he did smile, and her eyes glinted, shining mahogany under dark, curly lashes. Her mascara had reached its twenty-four hour wear time, and little black flecks dotted the smile-crinkles around her eyes. "And so, I'm staying in." She checked her phone. "Is it really three o'clock already? Yeah, guess I'll go home and binge Mad Men till I pass out on the couch."

She paused, waited. He looked at the slice drooping from his hand. His mouth opened and he inhaled sharply.

"You could watch an old movie," he said, taking another unwanted bite and grinding his teeth over it dryly. "Some old Bette Davis joint..."

For a brief second, she thought he might offer to join her on the couch. Instead she watched his jaw tighten as he swallowed hard, leaving a moment of question hanging between them.

"You know what I realized?" Melody blurted. "I finally realized I just don't like Bette Davis! I don't know what it is about that chick. Her eyes maybe? I don't know *what* it is, but she gives me the willies."

Dorian gave a vague nod, scratched the back of his head, and stared at his pizza.

They'd figured out early on that they shared a love of Golden Age movies and vintage television shows. One afternoon in the fall semester of junior year, they'd watched Alfred Hitchcock's *Rebecca* on his laptop. It was a brilliant sunny day, and they'd sat at a picnic table at the edge of campus. An impudent gray goose had waddled around at their feet while they ate lunch hunched together to peer at the screen, sharing a set of earbuds. A crepe myrtle nearby kept sprinkling tiny pink blossoms on the keyboard and she'd been surprised at herself for not minding that he watched her lips when she blew them away.

"I have a mind to start speaking like a 1930s gad-about, *Dahhh-ling*," he said as the last scene faded to black. "How's this?" He cleared his throat and tucked one hand in an imaginary breast pocket. "Now see here, Ms. Melody!" He gave a slight, galant bow of the head. "Oh, very well, we *shall* throw a fancy-dress pah-hhty." She laughed until she nearly fell off the bench.

But here it was again—this new, terrible precariousness, dangerous yet somehow fascinating, like a pot on the verge of boiling over.

It used to be so easy, so effortless between them. Teaming up back in college had made so much sense.

Theirs was a collaborative field, and one that was flooded with talent. But their partnership simply flowed, each of them feeding off the other's ideas. It showed in their work, the natural syncopation that drew the admiration—and frustration—of other students. Melody's instinct and insight, Dorian's artistry and technical knowledge, and the magic that happened in the combination made their work stand out, a reflection of the ease and balance between them. Their projects consistently earned high marks, and they'd even worked their capstone internship as a team, covering local stories for the local news affiliate.

So why was it like this lately? Nothing had changed. They both worked so hard to make sure they stayed on the same page, with laser focus on their professional goals. In moments like these, when the growing divide made itself obvious, they each perceived it with the same acuity, but in painfully separate ways.

The podcast was growing in listenership every week, doing well enough that they'd been able to hire a lighting tech, Kina Narvaez, to help bring video to the companion website. Ad revenue was increasing, reviews of last season's show were overwhelmingly positive, and their fans had clamored to download episode one of the new season. As far as the podcast was concerned, things were going just as they'd hoped.

But the two partners were definitely, exasperatingly out of sync.

Once, a fellow student, in high spirits after completing a live news report project, barreled ahead and asked them straight-out why in the world they weren't dating.

"You're obviously perfect for each other. So what's the deal?" she'd asked, still in her 'details at 5:30' reporter voice.

Melody wondered if Dorian ever played and replayed the way the next moment occurred, the way she still did: her first reaction to the question had been to smile. What had that smile meant, if it meant anything at all? Was it a flash of her true feelings, or an attempt to hide her disgust at the very idea? And what about the sing-song inflections as she said: "Just because we're a straight male and a straight female doesn't mean we have to be a couple." Did the teasing tone mean she didn't really believe her own words, but maybe felt compelled to say them? *What a stereotype. Right, Dorian? How presumptuous...* Or had the tone indicated sarcasm? *Yeah, right. Me and Dorian! Pshhh! As if...* What if he had interrupted her right then, let her off the hook with some cute but ambiguous declaration? *I don't know, Melody, whadaya think? Is she right?* Things could be so different now, with just a few choice words in that one moment.

But she'd shaken her head, just slightly. She still didn't know why, and the smile he had captured with his camera countless times had faded when he hadn't said a thing, and then the moment was gone. She'd shrugged the question off as a silly, insignificant bracket of words in the endless stream of words that was the daily life of journalism majors. But two years later, she still played and replayed that moment, pouring fuel on the fire that burned down any ideas of becoming more than friends, more than coworkers.

She was overthinking it, as always. She'd chastised herself then, too, her skin turning hot and uncomfortable, like standing too close to a snapping fire. They were firmly in the friend zone, she'd told herself, then kicked herself for the lame rom-com nerdiness of that played-out inner monologue. Such unoriginal lines, regardless of the truth that inspired them. There was a reason friend-zoned people the world over thought the exact same way. The trope followed the truth.

But man, what a stereotype she was becoming! Like a Taylor Swift song. *The nice girl never gets the guy.*

The thing was, yes she did. In the end she did. If she were patient and long-suffering enough, and if she gazed after him as he ran down a grand staircase or a romantic fire escape, looking gorgeous on his way to another big date in the big city with someone way more fabulous than her. If she were there when he came home, disappointed yet again, and if she gave him hot cocoa with extra marshmallows just like he liked it and let him vent about how he'd never find the right girl. Eventually the music would rise and he would look over at her and finally see. She was there all along.

And then her head and her heart would have to duke it out.

BETTY,
17 YEARS OLD

1969

"Betty? I hear you coming in there. And well on past a decent hour." Her mother's raspy voice pierced the precarious silence and Betty froze. "Where have you been? No, you know what? You go ahead and keep that to yourself. I reckon I might not want to know."

Betty winced at the sound of her mother's voice: Delores Langdon was in one of her 'states.'

"I am in a high state, let me tell you, miss! A high state indeed. Bad enough I have to sit here worrying, aggravating my chest condition, not knowing where you're at or what you're doing... pray tell, when *exactly* did you get to being so rebellious? You're just that lucky I'm too wore out or I'd tan your hide, and you know it."

Betty held her red shoes behind her back as she slipped by the living room and down the hall of the bungalow, into her room. She tossed the shoes under her bed and lifted the lavender bedspread, slipping a hand under the mattress and feeling around till her fingertips touched her diary. *Safe.* She came back to the living room, where her mother sat in her worn burgundy armchair, still railing.

"Oh, here she is! Where are your gloves?" Her mother held her own hands out as if to demonstrate where gloves go. The woman's idea of ideal society included women in kid gloves and feathered hats and men who wore tailored suits and took the train into the city. Those were the types of people who enjoyed chance meetings that turned into romances worthy of the big screen, played out in penthouses complete with fur rugs and sparkling cocktails garnished with stuffed olives pierced through with those fancy toothpicks.

She'd never gotten the big break she deserved, her daughter still had a shot, and when her chance came, by God, Betty would have pale, soft hands.

"I put my things up in my room already," Betty said. "But Mama, nobody wears gloves any more."

"Is that right? Nobody? Guess you should wear them then." Her face flashed a grimace, as if she'd been slapped. Her voice softened. "I don't care what other girls do, Betty. You wear your gloves, you hear me?"

"Yes, Mama."

Delores leaned to one side of the chair and nuzzled her forehead into the wing, hiding half her face—but carefully, so as not to smash the auburn finger roll. Her visible eye glanced at Betty, then squinted tight with showy anguish. "Oh!" she cried feebly, clutching the collar of her blue sateen robe. "Oh, oh!"

"Mama, do you need your tea? I was going to warm some milk—"

"Yes, I need my tea! Of course I need my tea. Don't I always have my tea by now? But you weren't here."

"I'm not that late, Mama." Betty placed a crocheted blanket across Delores's lap and went to the kitchen.

"I need it, only to keep me alive, that's all. I don't suppose that means too much to you anyhow. Me, who raised you like a flower, like a precious flower I raised you, watching and protecting, I did." She moaned her words, pointing her voice toward the kitchen. "That was me, if memory serves."

Betty set the kettle to boil and gathered mugs, two spoons, and the milk bottle on the counter. Then she reached for Mama's box of tea. She spooned a small heap of the dark, fluttery leaves into her mother's mug. She went to close the box, but then dipped in for an extra half measure. It seemed like Mama might need it tonight. Some nights Mama's thoughts raced until her mind was a small tornado, like the swirl inside her cup as Betty stirred in a single packet of Sweet 'N Low.

When she heard the squeaky floor board in the hall and saw Betty's shadow fall ahead of her in the doorway, Delores tucked her face against the wing of the chair again. She'd seen Bette Davis do it in a movie once, and it was quite affecting, the romantic picture of a tragic heroine. It had broken her heart, seeing her Bette like that, and she affected the pose often.

Betty placed the tea on the little table beside the arm chair and watched her mother's one exposed eye flick open and steal a glance at it. What would the woman do if she knew where Betty had been tonight, the rock and roll show at a tavern on the Westside.

The middle of a street in the dark with a man. A negro man.

Dominicus. Her face flushed. She thought of her hand in his, his face smiling down at her, his smooth voice calling her 'Princess.'

"Mama, I am sorry I was late tonight. Please take your tea," Betty coaxed. She held out the cup, the steam rising to her mother's face.

Delores reached for the cup and was obliged to move her face. Betty watched as her mother drank down to the last drop. Then she led her to the bathroom and to bed, tucking the thin coverlet around her legs and feet the way she liked it.

"Good night, Mama. Tomorrow, we'll make a plan for your birthday, okay?" Betty said.

"My birthday? My birthday! Oh why did you have to mention it? There went my calm state." She pulled the covers up under her chin and stared at the ceiling, glancing sideways at Betty. "What's the point of my birthday? I am on my way out anyhow."

Mama could have been an actress, just like her screen idol. She had two faces, a different one on either side, depending on which way you looked at her. Or which side she showed you. When she needed something, wanted something from you, she turned to the right and dipped her chin toward her shoulder. She was beautiful, precious, blameless. You wanted to do anything she asked. When she was displeased, or needed you to think she was so, she turned the other way and raised her chin, gave you the piercing, raised-brow profile and enigmatic smirk. Was she mad? Was she disappointed? How could you fix it? What could you do to turn her face the other way?

"You are only forty-five years old, Mama," Betty said. Leaning on the doorframe, she looked again at her own hand, probably for the hundredth time that night. Her palm buzzed with renewed phantom energy each time. "Forty-five's nothing. You're not going anywhere."

"'Mornin', Betty!" Junie moved her books from one hip to the other and opened her locker. "See you at practice today?" Her golden ponytail swung with each tilt of her head, and her red and white cheer uniform fit her figure perfectly (her mother had tailored it herself to get it just right). Football season was long over, but basketball season provided a convenient means of regularly reminding everyone, from their class off fifty-seven seniors down to the worshipful little freshman, that she was a cheerleader. She flashed bright, wide eyes at Betty, betraying no sign of their clandestine trip to the Westside two nights ago.

Betty paused with her hand on the dial of her lock. She composed a smile and turned to Junie. "I can't make it. Sorry. Gotta take Mama to her doctor appointment today, soon as I get home."

"Honey, we need your long-legged high kicks to keep the rest of us on our toes!" Junie said. Her voice was like a glass of sweet tea, cool and slick with condensation dripping down the sides. She closed her locker delicately and turned on her heel. She leaned closer with a conspiratorial whisper, "Last time, coach said she's gonna make a rule where you have to be at practice if you want to cheer the game, Betts."

"Well, I did let her know this was coming up. I'll go see her before I leave today," Betty said, hooking her arm into the crook of Junie's elbow. She calculated in the extra five minutes it would take to find Coach Utter and talk to her before she left campus.

"Why can't your mama just make her appointments on a different day?" Junie said. Betty looked down at Junie's face and found her expression didn't match her words. Junie waved her fingers at a trio of boys as they passed by, squeezing her shoulders up to her ears like they were simply the cutest things she'd ever seen.

"Your mama has to start letting you go some time. I mean to tell you, it seems like she knows the time is coming and she's buttering your paws."

"Buttering my paws?"

"Haven't you heard that expression, Betty? I swear, how sheltered are you?" Junie's eyes rolled adorably. "It's like how you put butter on a cat's paws so they don't run off and leave home."

Betty's mouth made a crooked circle and her eyebrows knit together. But she nodded at Junie as if she understood completely.

Walking down the hall with Junie every morning was one of the highlights of her day. Since they were little girls, pretending to be brides under the gauzy sheets floating on Junie's mother's laundry line, Junie had shone like a beacon of what a girl should be. It was a given that she would live a beautiful life, unquestioningly beloved by everyone, her dreams never failing to come true. She glowed with the confidence of these things.

Somewhere deep, Betty held a sort of nebulous, unformed belief that the perfection of Junie's world required a certain kind of behavior from everyone who lived in her delicate crystal sphere, and that if they wanted to remain there, they had to prove they deserved it, had to earn their ring of orbit. As long as everyone did their part, kept her path clear and made the way smooth, everything would stay beautiful for Junie. And if she stayed in step, maybe it would follow that life might be more beautiful for Betty, too.

The pink marshmallows of Junie's cheeks rose with her rueful smile, sending a pang of desperation shooting through Betty's stomach. She was letting Junie down. Junie had been the one to encourage her to try out for cheerleading, told her she just had to do something with those long legs that kicked over her head and split wide in every direction. But she had to take Mama to the doctor. Who else could do it? There *was* no one else to do it.

Mama needed her.

Betty's feet danced nervously inside her stiff shoes. She held her face composed as she locked her locker, as she walked the hall with Junie, as the day wore on.

"*Such a joy to have in class!*" her teachers had always said.

At the last bell, Betty was the first one out of class. She'd packed her bookbag at lunch, including all her textbooks for the second half of the day, just in case there was any homework in those classes, to save the time of stopping at her locker. She walk-ran to the gym and scanned the bleachers.

The basketball team was just meandering out from the locker room on the other side of the gym, passing the ball between them as they walked. Their long socks and small, shiny scrimmage shorts always made Betty laugh. Junie had chided her more than once about it.

Coach Utter sat in her regular spot, precisely in the center of the bottom bench, reading from a clipboard. Her hair was sprayed to the same beauty queen shape it had held since her first swimsuit round at fourteen years old. She looked up and began shaking her head as Betty approached, her self-possessed face morphing as she took in the tall girl loping toward her, not in uniform.

"Now, Betty, I know you are not coming up to me right now to say you won't be at practice—"

"I'm so sorry, ma'am. I really am. But my mama—"

"'Your mama,'" Coach Utter grimaced. "Your mama what? Needs to get off her duff and—"

"Coach Utter!" Betty said. She tucked her chin and glanced around, surprised at the sound of her own voice. She readjusted her hand on the straps of her book bag. It strained pink and white lines across the flesh above her thumbs. "She's ill. She can't help it if—"

"Betty!" Coach Utter said. "The only thing wrong with your mama is that Hollywood never came a-knocking on her door like they were supposed to." Coach Utter lowered her head, controlled her voice. "Now look, Betty. I am sorry I said that, but someone needed to. I know your mama, probably better than you do in some ways. You're gonna graduate soon, Betty, and what are your plans? Hmm? Forget about high school and cheerleading." She waved a lightly-spotted, manicured hand over the room. "Have you thought about what you want to do with your life? Because this is your time, Betty Langdon. This is it." She patted the bench beside her. Betty looked at the giant clock above the basketball net, then perched on the edge of the seat. "Girl, let me tell you something someone should have told you a long time ago. I've known your mother for a long time. Since elementary school. Now, I don't mean to be rude, bless her heart, but your mother is what psychologists call a 'self-centered' person. That means she is the center of her own universe." She paused and clasped her hands for effect, as if she were in the middle of a dissertation. "She will hold on to you forever just to make sure she has someone to take care of her. Is that what you want?"

Betty watched a basketball hit the rim and teeter before swishing through the net. Somebody clapped. "But it's my place. I can't just leave her. She needs me."

"Well, we need you, too! And I really don't want to have to replace you." Coach Utter squeezed Betty's shoulder. "I love having you on the squad. You are such a joy."

Betty stood up. "Thank you, Coach Utter. I sure do appreciate you saying that, ma'am." She checked the clock, wrung her hands. "But I guess you'll have to go on ahead and replace me." Her voice broke, and she turned away. She skirted the edge of the basketball court and pushed through the gym doors. They closed behind her with clattering finality.

That evening, after Mama's appointment and after filling her prescriptions, Betty sat at the kitchen table, pushing the last few SpaghettiOs around the bottom of the bowl with the edge of her spoon. The formica table had been too low for her since she was fifteen and shot up a foot over a summer, so her purple diary served as a convenient riser. She pushed them into pictures of round things—a bunch of grapes, bubbles rising, a surprised face with wide eyes and a gaping mouth, a bunch of balloons on strings scratched into the dregs of the red sauce.

Mama would be wanting her supper soon. Betty set the diary aside and reached for a saucepan. She struck a match and held it to the burner, watching the flame conjure from watery air. Pinching the spent matchstick, she watched the fire, its flames glowing a blue circle with angry red tips. The heat reached her face. She felt her pores expand, her lashes curl upward. Her eyes closed and she inhaled, deep, tremulous. When she opened her eyes, the matchstick had cooled. She wrapped it in a bit of wax paper, it slipped into her skirt pocket. She would enjoy the scent again later.

"We got a spot in a review at the Ritz Theater Saturday." Dominicus leaned back on his elbows and crossed one leg over the other down the porch steps. "Can you come?"

Rehearsal had gone well, but Zeke and Sly were inside the house, teaching O.T. an updated version of The Temptations walk. Betty had arrived late and walked in to find them deep in the working out of harmonies to their cover of "Ball of Confusion." She'd sat in a corner chair of Sly's mamma's dining room, and listened. The lyrics lit her up inside, made her think how lucky she was to be right there, part of a new world.

Now Betty and Dominicus sat on the top step of the front porch. Even the moon looked different, smiled down brighter, it seemed. The air was cool and light, the harbinger of a north Florida winter, and they sat close. Across the street, the nosy neighbor lady they all called Miss Peeks appeared between her curtains and made her usual disapproving face. Even after months of catching occasional glimpses of the tall white girl visiting across the street, she still didn't trust it. Betty wished that lady could see it the way she did, that things were different now. Didn't whites and Blacks live next door to each other on this very street? She flashed a peace sign, and then raised three fingers in a 'W,' the neighborhood symbol that meant "Westside's the Best Side," and the lady disappeared again behind her swinging curtain.

"The Ritz Theater?" Betty said. She clapped her hands and then hugged her skirt around her knees.

"Yeah! The Ritz Theater, in LaVilla. You know, LaVilla? Jacksonville's very own 'Harlem of the South'?"

"Of course!" Betty said. "I've always wanted to see inside The Ritz." Her mind started working: Could she make it back down to town twice in one week? Nevermind, she'd figure it out. "Of course I want to come! I just have to check the bus schedule and let you know, okay? Can I call you at the house?"

Dominicus sucked air through his teeth. "Oh, I don't know...Think you could put a little soul in your voice if Ma answers?"

"Let me see." She held a hand to her ear. "'Oh, heyyy, Ms. Owens! Is Dominicus in?'" Her eyebrows raised. She placed a hand over the pretend mouthpiece and lowered her voice. "How's that?" she said.

"Awful," he said, laughing. "Real bad. You might be the whitest white girl I ever met. Do you know that, Princess?"

"Is that so?" She held out her free arm, turning it as if seeing it for the first time. "But you still like me, right?"

His smile froze. He took the pretend phone from her hand and held it to his ear. "Yes, hello, Ms. Langdon? This is Dominicus Owens calling, and I'd like to speak to your very, very, so-very-white daughter Betty. Might she be at home, pray tell?"

Betty laughed, then cringed as if bracing herself. He reached across her lap and took her hand.

"'Why yes, ma'am, this *is* a social call. You see, the thing is," he paused, holding Betty's gaze, "The thing is, I am very much, entirely, completely in love with your daughter." He smiled and drew her close. "And so if you would be so kind as to get her on the phone, I would just like to let her know that."

He held her chin and brought her face toward his, and when he kissed her, she knew it was all the proof she needed. She was right about the world. It was a new and beautiful place, and they would live in it together, forever.

The neighbor lady was back in the window. Dominicus waved his enormous hand and shouted across the street, "Things are real different out here! Right, Miss Peeks?"

BETTY,
17 YEARS OLD

DECEMBER 1, 1969

Dear Diary,

R eal quick: I went down to see him again today. Watched the boys rehearse and all. Just got back. The bus ran a little late, so I'm late on starting dinner. Dominicus said he wished he could drive me home but I told him no, it's too dangerous. Not worth it. I don't mind the bus. Someone left a DownBeat in one of the seats and I feel bad for keeping it, but man, what luck! It's not the latest issue, but who cares about that?

An agent named Jerry Somebody who saw them perform at The Ritz review really liked them, and he got them a spot in a variety show in Macon. It's amazing news, really out of sight. Domincus said they're going to record some demo tracks at a music studio while they're up there. Things are really happening!

I asked all the boys their birthdays and wrote them down with their last names. The idea of watching a draft lottery on television is making me sick to my stomach. It's inhumane, to have to sit and wait for your birthday to appear or not appear, and it decides your fate. I want to avoid it and pretend it's not happening, and that seems shameful, since these boys can't avoid it.

Mama shouted at me when I got home that she wanted to eat before we watch so she doesn't lose her appetite, but that just means she wants to watch it, too. Mama doesn't have an appetite to lose.

Here's why I'm taking time to write this down right now:

I am going with them to Macon. I don't know how to make that true, but I'm writing it down here because it's all I have in my power to do right now. I can write down those words and look at them to make it real. I am going to Macon with Dominicus.

Diary,

Dominicus' birthday didn't get drawn in the lottery this time. None of them did. Thank God for that.

It felt like watching something unreal, those blue capsules with dates inside, and how they drew them out like they were playing a game of bingo. Mama sat with her family Bible and her address notebook on her lap so she could check birthdays as they read them out. She was animated and talking a mile a minute. This was high drama for her, I could tell. She kept saying, "Oh, I'm in a state! My oh my, am I in a state!" By the time the CBS News special report started, she was very wound up and practically excited, like we were at the movies or something. I was anxious, too, but of course, Mama had no idea who I was praying for the whole time. She acted like she had a son of her own to worry about, she took it on herself so, fanning herself and carrying on with each birthday they announced. But then when they pulled one of the dates, Mama got a queer look. Her face went all white and she didn't want to speak for a minute. When she could speak, she said that was George Henry Latimer's birthday.

Junie's Georgie.

She went to school with Georgie's mother Georgetta, and she thought the world of that boy. When he started dating Junie, she was more happy about it than if he'd asked me out. I know she loves Junie like the daughter she never had, and I can't say I blame her much. I could only dream of being the girl Junie is.

My poor Junie. She must be beside herself. I don't know what I'd do if Dominicus had gotten called up tonight. Mama said not to call her tonight, to leave her alone, wait and give her some time. But I want to run to her, all the way to Gainesville and up to her dormitory door. I wish she would call. I don't know if I can wait till morning to talk to her and to make sure she's okay.

Dear God, please help Junie. And please help Georgie. And all these boys. Dear God, please. I would do anything to help Junie, anything she asked. I would take Georgie's place if they'd let me.

Maybe Georgie won't get called up. They're calling up the nineteen-year-olds first and he's twenty-one. I told her that, but neither of us really understands how the process goes, so we just sat there in that dim living room with the television glowing, sort of eerie. I guess it did seem like a movie after all. Like it wasn't real. They just kept picking those blue cylinders and announcing numbers as if folks couldn't wait to see their sons' and brothers' birthdays announced, like it was some kind of grand prize drawing. They even broke in for Christmas commercials.

I have to call Junie.

TABS AND BLANKS
PODCAST

Transcript
Season 2, Episode 3: Friends and Family, and
Detective Billy John

*Thanks for joining us for another episode of The
Chimney Sweep. I'm Melody Hinterson.*

*Betty's cousin Mark is across the table from me,
flanked by his sister Nora, who is the one who
posted about Betty on our discussion board last
season, and Randell's nephew Paul. Since everyone
had to travel from different parts of town, we settled on a lunch meeting at a Panera Bread. I've
asked them to tell me a bit about how they remembered Betty.*

*On the table in front of us is an array of envelopes
and pictures. Betty as a little girl with pigtails, a
sixteen-year-old in an Easter dress, a shy and very
young bride. There are several of her behind the
counter at the souvenir shop. In each photo, her*

expression is composed and passive, her signature cat-eye glasses perched on the bridge of her nose.

Mark: She was really that person you could depend on. She was quiet, always real quiet, but so smart. We all knew she'd be the one to do something with her life some day.

Nora: She was a few years older than me. I always wanted to look just like her, dress like her, do my hair up like she did.

Paul: She was the girl my uncle married, and I was I think four or five when they got married. I had a little-kid crush on her. Yeah, you know, she was tall and pretty, those nice eyes. Until my daddy said, 'Son, that ain't right. She's your old auntie now, boy'

Talking about Betty seems to bring happy memories to everyone who knew her. Everyone we've talked to so far remembers a sweet, pretty, clever girl. I'm hoping today to get a feel for whether that's a function of her having gone missing, or if this was how people always felt about her.

Nora: But she did change, I will say that. I don't know if you remember that, Mike. Somewhere around freshman year, I'd say it was. She was still so sweet and all, but her grades went down there for a while, where she used to be a straight A student, and she started looking so sad. She didn't want to talk much.

Mike: I was older, played football by then, had a lot going on. I really don't remember that. And even if I did, I probably wouldn't have thought much of it, would have just thought she was being a girl, which I didn't know much about. We weren't so enlightened about our friends' mental health back then, you understand.

Nora: So after Betty graduated high school, her mother got herself a new boyfriend and that's when she moved across the border to Georgia, to be with him up there. After that fellow left her mama high and dry, she relied on Betty more than ever. Betty became her caregiver, basically. I never really knew what her mama's ailment was, but she was always ill. I believe she did battle an eating disorder. Don't think that's a secret. She ended up in and out of treatment and rehabilitation, but she always got out by having Betty come in and promise to live with her and make sure she ate, everything like that. In the years before she disappeared, Betty drove up there every week, early in the week usually, after the busy Sundays at the liquor store. Her last stepdad had died by then and Betty, she'd bring groceries and household things, clean up around the place, help her mother with her bath. Things like that.

Melody: So as far as any of you know, Betty wasn't depressed, or thinking of leaving or hurting herself or—

Paul: Oh no, no no. No. Not that I ever saw. I saw her most every week when she'd come into the grocery store where I worked checkout. She wasn't falling all over herself happy, mind you, but she was, you know, just like the rest of us, I think. Coming in there with her jiffy feet like the rest of us, you know? Life just was what it was.

Nora: Betty would never have jiffy feet, Paul.

Melody: *Listeners, for those of you wondering, 'jiffy feet' is a north Florida colloquialism for dirty feet, inspired by the unapologetically barefoot customers of a local quick stop called Jiffy Food Store.*

Melody: Would you say you all were very close to Betty?

Nora: Oh yeah, I used to call her up all the time, go out to see her every chance I got. But you know, things get busy, too...

Mark: Yes. Well, we weren't close, but we were family. So I kept in touch regular, like we do. Stopped in sometimes.

Melody: Were you all interviewed by Detective Billy John Whitaker?

Nora: Well, no. And that is surprising, isn't it?

Melody: Is it because you weren't around at the time, or…? For instance, when did you learn that Betty had gone missing?

Mark: I mean, none of us, no one was around, per se. They lived out on the highway and we were all, you know, spread further out. But that doesn't mean we weren't close.

Melody: Oh, of course not, no, I got you. So, when did you each hear of her going missing though?

Mark: Oh, I guess I heard about a month after she'd been gone. That sound about right, Nora?

Nora: No, not that long, Mark. I know Loreen had been up there and made those recordings a few weeks after.

Melody: Recordings? What recordings would those be?

Nora: Oh, you ain't heard the recordings? You gotta hear the recordings. Loreen went up there and got Randell on tape, a few weeks after Betty disappeared. She recorded conversations with him."

Melody: And Loreen is your other sister?

Nora: Yes, there were three of us—me, Mark here, and Loreen. Loreen and Betty were closer in age, though.

Mark: The thing that always got me was how Randell never reported her missing. I just couldn't understand what was going on there. It was the shopgirl, Haley or Heather I think, who told a policeman when he stopped in a few days later. Something wrong about that, I always thought.

Melody: Paul, you are Randell's nephew. What was your impression of him after Betty disappeared?

Paul: He was heartbroke, seemed like. Yeah, yeah. Real heartbroke. It was sad to see, really. Made my heart hurt, too, to see him like that.

Mark: But then on the other hand, if he thought she just up and left him, why would he report it? Her mama saw her that afternoon, right? And didn't she say Betty seemed different? I thought I heard that somewhere along the way. Someone said even Betty's mama thought she seemed different, sorta far-off or sad-like. Like Betty knew this was the last time she'd see her mama.

Nora: Yes, I reckon I heard something like that along about that time, too. Someone said the nurse at the home said that, right?

Melody: That detail was in the local newspaper. Although the coverage of her story seemed like barely a blip, we did find a quote to that effect in our research, too.

Mark: Oh, yeah well, maybe that's where I heard it, too. I don't remember. It's been a long time.

In fact, it was a housekeeper at the retirement home who apparently last saw Betty at her mother's residence across the border in Georgia. By word of mouth, her story reached Detective Billy John Whitaker, the lead on the case, several weeks after Betty's disappearance. The housekeeper, who has since passed away, supposedly told a friend that after helping her mother with her hair and fixing up her room to her liking as usual, Betty left the complex by a side exit. She further stated that Betty added a large bag of trash to the facility's roadside bins before driving away. Whether Betty turned south toward home or not, the witness couldn't say.

At this point in the interview with Nora, Mark, and Paul, we are joined by another person. She bustles across the restaurant in a blue Bardot blouse, red cropped pants, and sparkly platform wedges. People turn to watch her pass. She pulls off her giant sunglasses and weaves them into her blonde hair. Her name is June Harris, and she was Betty's best friend back in school.

June: Ooh, sorry, sorry! I'm so sorry I'm late!

Melody: No problem, Ms. Harris. Let's get you set up.

June: Please call me Junie.

I make introductions all around while Dorian gets Junie mic'ed up. Mark stands up and nods. I'm struck by the old-fashioned gentlemanly gesture.

Mark: Oh, me and Nora know Junie from way back. Right, Junie?

Junie: That's right, Mark. How've you been doing? How's Angie? Still baking those delectable pound cakes?

Mark rubs his belly and grins.

Mark: She's fine, and she surely does. How's Walt 'n them?

I get the feeling there's some interesting history here, between Mark and Junie, but I decide to save that question for now. Once they've caught up, I continue.

Melody: So Ms. Harris—

Junie: It's 'Junie,' Sweetie.

Melody: Junie! Right! We were discussing Betty's mindset, her state of mind, around the time she disappeared. You had mentioned you saw her regularly?

Junie: Yes, we were friends all our lives. We didn't live right by each other, but we'd talk on the phone at least once or twice a week, or more. Sometimes I rode up to her mother's with her, and we might get something to eat after, you know. But yes, we were friends since we were small.

Melody: And what do you remember about the last time you spoke to her?

Junie: Well, I do happen to remember it specifically. I was trying to give up smoking, doctor's orders when I got a touch of emphysema, and I said I had some Lucky Strikes she could have for her mama. We always smoked the same brand, you know. She said well, thanks but too late, because her mama no longer favored Lucky Strikes since she read Bette Davis switched brands.

Nora: That sounds like her—

Junie: But our Betty just sounded, I guess sort of tired. Nothing I would have thought much about if what happened hadn't a happened. And so I had to reflect back and think, hmm, how did she sound. But she did sound tired. She always did for others before herself, and I think it was starting to take a toll.

Melody: Tell me more about that. Had she always been that way, or was it more with Randell and her marriage, or...?

Junie: Oh no, she was always that way. And I have to say it, just being honest here, before I was grown and before I knew any better, I was one of those people. I mean to tell you, she would have given me her shoes on a hike through a mud bog if I said I needed them.

Melody: Is that right?

The others nod in agreement. It doesn't seem like just one of those kind pronouncements people tend to make about the departed.

Junie: There was something about Betty probably none of you all knew. Back right after high school, Betty had taken a shine to someone. Before Randell. Yeah. It's true. I was the only one who knew about it, not even any of our other friends knew. She even went off with him to Macon. Mmmhmm. But her mama got real sick and needed her home. Betty's mama always favored me, and Betty asked me if I could help her out, try to talk to her mama, talk her into saying Betty didn't need to come home. Now, her mama *was* sort of a hypochondriac. But I told her no, Betty, I'm not going to do that for you. You got no business being up there with that boy.

Junie hesitates. I think for a moment she's referring to the fact that Betty and this fellow weren't married.

Melody: Why was that? What was wrong with him?

Junie: Well, now. I don't know that I should say. I didn't know him, never met him. But the truth is the young man was Black. Okay? And well, things were different then. It wasn't done. At least not where we were from, and I was not as open-minded as I did eventually become—"

Nora: I had no idea about any of that. Did you, Mark?

Mark: No, Nora! Don't you think I would have said something about that to you, at some point, over all these many years, had I ever heard of that?

Nora: Well. I don't know—

Nora and Mark seem genuinely surprised by this information. Paul appears surprised but highly amused. Junie looks around and puts her arms on the table top. Her charm bracelets jangle and she begins spinning a huge sparkling ring around and around her finger as she speaks.

Melody: So that wasn't general knowledge. Certainly the first we've heard of it in our investigation. Did she talk about it to anyone else that you know of, Junie?

Junie: I don't know. But like I say, that was then. It was a different time. I know we're not supposed to say that anymore, but it was. Betty was a little bit deluded about how things were. She believed all the hippy kumbaya melting pot stuff. I think she really thought that was how it was out in the big wide world. We just wanted to protect her. I don't want you thinking I'm a racist. I'd say different now, obviously.

Melody: Who is 'we'?

Junie: Oh, I just meant...me. And Betty's mama, my aunt, she was an equal opportunity narcissist. She was better than everyone, regardless of their color.

But, listen, I shouldn't have said anything about Betty and that fellow. Maybe you don't have to use that? You can just cut that part out, right? It don't have nothing—doesn't have anything—to do with this. Let's get back to talking about Betty. Did you know she liked to write? And she could sing, too. Had perfect pitch. She was in a special writing group after school. Something the English teacher put together for her better students. Betty had to stop participating because her mama was having health issues. Same with cheerleading, and that was a shame. No one kicked as high as Betty. So I mean, that shows it's true, she really was a wonderful, selfless person.

I'm considering all this when Nora speaks from her corner of the booth.

Nora: You know what? I have to say: I never do understand why people always say that like it's a good thing. Such an awesome, virtuous thing, right? To be 'selfless.' I used to think it myself. Give that woman a prize, a new apron or something, she's so 'selfless.' And I felt badly that I wasn't more like that, like my older cousin Betty.

She pinches a paper napkin around her nose and dabs at the corners of her eyes.

Nora: But I'm an old woman now, and I've seen a lot in my day. A lot of different folks living a bunch of different ways. And I've come to believe that being selfless is actually one of the worst ways to be.

(*silence*)

Melody: Hmm, that's a really interesting perspective. So now, what about Randell? Junie, you say he didn't know about this previous boyfriend? If he had known, or if he found out somehow, would that have been something that made him mad, or—

Junie: Right, he didn't know. As far as I know, anyway. And honestly, Randell was too caught up in his own stuff to worry about what color anybody was. His hotel was never segregated, anybody could stay there, and he never did have segregated rooms or anything like that. There wasn't a pool or public bathrooms, so that wasn't an issue. Money is money and he wasn't going to turn it away. I think Betty may have had some influence in that, though. She was why that place didn't go under completely like others did. Anyway, no, Randell wasn't like that.

Melody: You seem pretty sure.

Junie: I am. I knew him very well and I never knew him to have a problem with Black folks.

The others don't join in, and I'm not sure what to make of that. Are they not sure whether to agree about Randell's open-mindedness? Or are they surprised that Junie says she knew him well? I can't be sure without asking some more probing questions. Maybe now is not the time.

Melody: So thank you all so much for coming out today to speak with us. If I have any followup questions, would it be okay to contact each of you individually?

Nora: Yes.

Mark: That would be fine.

Paul: Sure, whatever you need.

Melody: Junie, can I contact you, or—?

Junie: I'm not sure what else I can add, but sure, if you need to.

Mark raises a hand, then puts it down again. He starts to say something, but then presses his lips closed.

Melody: Hold on please, could you, Dor? Mark, did you have something else you wanted to add?

Mark: Well, I suppose I did just want to make something clear here. Sort of in our defense, if you will. You younger people need to understand something. We—and I'm talking about people our age—

He gestures between himself and his sister, includes Junie, who nods uncertainly, not sure where he's going with this.

Mark: If you think about it, we were basically the first generation to experience what we did. We lived through segregation and desegregation. We grew up in it. I don't know if young people today have an inkling of what that was really like. I'll be honest, the change was hard for all of us, for the Black kids as well as white kids, all of us. None of us knew how we were supposed to feel about it. Many of us went through a hard time at home, when we started to get to know the Black kids in our classes and we liked them, we made friends, and they weren't what we'd been told at all. So then we started to doubt our parents and our families and what they'd been telling us, what we'd heard them saying amongst themselves but where we could hear them. And as a child, when you start to see a disparity like that, between what you think you know because that's all you know and what you're learning is the truth, you can feel like the ground came out from under you. We were on our own if we didn't agree with the elders. There wasn't any road map to follow. And that's the damn truth right there.

So I guess if you want to edit me out, I would hope you can leave in this here: we were the product of our environment. And then we turned into a product of not trusting our environment. But a lot of us did learn better. Not making excuses, just saying. Times change. Understanding changes. I didn't hate anybody. I just thought that was the way it was supposed to be. Separate. Leave each other to our own. Of course, now we know different, know better. Some of us anyway. We learned better. None of us had been outside our little rural area, except Junie's brother Fred when he went to Vietnam, and he came back with a different view of the world. He was my buddy and I learned a lot from him.

Junie has raised her hand.

Junie: And also—

Melody: Yes, Junie?

Junie: Yes. I wanted to add that our Betty, she was ahead of her time. Looking back, I can see it. At least from the perspective of where she was, where she lived, and what you might expect from a young woman her age in that time and in that place. She saw the world like it should be, not like it really was. She was idealistic. She watched Dr. King's speech on television and thought well, that's it. It's fixed now. The world is fixed. She believed in people, maybe more than they deserved. Personally, I think she deluded herself about how things were in the real world.

(*silence*)

Melody: Well, actually, Junie, if you don't mind my saying so, and I don't mean any disrespect, but she had reason to believe it could be so. It sounds to me like she was part of the bigger social movement that was going on at that time, the '60s and early '70s, but in a sort of isolated way. Maybe she wasn't out there marching or demonstrating, but she had a pretty progressive mindset in her own little corner of the world—at least it sounds like she did. It's a very interesting detail we hadn't heard before, and it's very illuminating. And pretty sad, really. That she was made to feel she couldn't be with a man she loved because of his skin color.

-After the break and a message from our sponsor Branches DNA, we'll hear more from our interview with Detective Billy John Whitaker, the former police officer and investigator on Betty's disappearance.

MELODY

2019

Melody and Dorian had been working for hours. The studio smelled of old lo mein and over-heated power cords. Melody couldn't wait to be done recording so she could turn on the AC and get some circulation going. The dining room of Melody's bungalow had slowly morphed into a full-fledged production studio. What had started with two laptops and a microphone bought on Amazon now included acoustic wall panels and strategically-placed light stands, necessary since they'd added in-studio video to the podcast's companion website this season. The room had a wide casement opening with a view through to the living room with its wooden front door, and a smaller doorway on the opposite side of the room which led to the kitchen in the back of the house.

It seemed there were more cords than pieces of equipment to power. They snaked over and under the old wooden dining table which Melody's mother had given her when she moved into the place. The original crystal chandelier still presided over everything, but she and Dorian had raised it closer to the ceiling, bunching its brass chain in loops and securing it with zip ties to minimize strange shadows below. Everything had a slightly temporary feeling. It was a work in progress.

Dorian stood and began to turn off the equipment.

"Sorry, before you do that, should I take that last clip again?" Melody said, stifling a yawn. "My voice sounded tired, or bored, or something, in my head. "Kept thinking you'd stop me any minute."

"We can if you want to," Dorian replied. "I thought it was good. Didn't sound tired." He waited till she motioned for him to go ahead and shut down for the evening, then switched off the monitors. "Thought maybe you were going for a little 'seductive slash mysterious' thing there. No?"

"Ha! No!" Melody's neck flushed pink. "I just stayed out too late last night and my voice is going all 'Lush Life' on me."

Dorian's playful expression dissolved. He stopped wrapping a mic cord and looked at her.

Melody lightly slapped her cheeks and forced her eyes open wider. It only made her yawn again.

"Out late, huh? Who...I mean, where'd you go?" Dorian said, starting to wrap the cord again. Melody's arms stretched outward and she rolled her head, missing Dorian's pointed shrug.

"Just a gastropub near my place."

"Decided not to stay in after all?" His face flushed.

"Hmm?" Melody's shoulders stiffened. "Oh. Yeah! No! I mean, it wasn't like that." *Did that sound defensive?* "It wasn't planned or anything. I was going to skip dinner because our lunch was so late?" She waved an inclusive arm gesture toward him. "But then all of a sudden it was ten o'clock and I was wide awake. And starving."

"Hence, the sexy voice today."

Melody froze. "Is it?"

Dorian ducked under the table. Every cord connection needed immediate and thorough checking.

Melody sighed, then tried to cover it with a yawn. *And here we are again.*

She often wondered what she would have said differently in that moment, that time back in college, when that girl practically accused them of a crime for not being a couple, if Dorian had stopped her from rambling on. She had settled the matter without meaning to, all because she was scared to see him laugh at the idea of being with her. And why could she never let a moment play out without interjecting? Of course they didn't have to be a couple simply because they got along and worked well together. That hadn't been their teammate's point when she asked the question. Her point was that there was something much deeper there, and if she could see it, why couldn't they?

But Melody had gone off on the first tangent that came to mind, just to save herself from the embarrassment of hearing Dorian say, 'What, *me*? And *her*? Are you *kidding*?' She'd stepped in and headed him off.

But what if she hadn't?

It didn't matter. That ship had obviously sailed. In fact, he'd probably start dating their sexy new lighting tech any minute now. Kina Narvaez was a goddess. Plus, she was brilliant at her job, and she found endless reasons to lean and stretch and bend within his field of vision.

What did it matter anyway? She and Dorian had committed to putting the podcast first. Attraction was so fleeting, after all, wasn't it? How lame would it be to ruin their work dynamic? Over what? A silly crush? Working together would have to be enough. They were together, but not together.

Sometimes, being successful at one thing meant sacrificing on another. She had to be practical about this thing. She had to focus.

Focus on Betty.

"You know what I do not want to do?" she blurted. Dorian backed out from under the table, his brows still drawn together from squinting at the mass of cords. Her heart ached from the cuteness. She smiled despite herself and then looked away, looked up at the ceiling instead. "I do not want to turn Betty's story into a melodrama, with the real people involved portrayed as some kind of hokey bumpkins simply because they were rural folks. I don't want us to fall into that stereotype trap, you know?" Melody rocked in her chair, continued. "Do you know what I mean? Like *The Woman Who Went Away* podcast, for example. Even though they cast shade on pretty much everyone along the way, the editing and music all worked to make listeners feel like 'aww but they're just po' country folk. They just go to church and run their farms and their little shops and work themselves to the bone and eat greens for dinner every night till they die'. Like, no. Something happened. Things were happening every day in those decades of marriage before Betty disappeared. Something lead up to her disappearance, whether she was kidnapped or there was a terrible accident, or if she really was murdered. What I'm saying is, whatever happened didn't take place in a vacuum. She and Randell were a real couple living a real life. Life happens to everybody, God willing, and their lives were no different."

Dorian's lips pursed and he nodded along as Melody spoke. A shine glinted at the corners of her eyes and reminded him of a song. He hadn't noticed the exact moment when he'd become such a cheesy romantic. She'd done this to him. It was all her fault.

Melody leaned her elbows on the table, clasped her hands, lowered them toward him. "Maybe that's a hot take? Do listeners expect us to characterize the players in these stories? Or do we owe it to everyone to put these people out there exactly as they are, or were, with no filter? There's a line somewhere between not speaking ill of the dead and glossing over the truth. What do you think?"

Dorian sat across from her. "I think...I know you well enough to know that you won't be happy if this podcast becomes a hit by manipulating the listeners' reactions. In the end, I don't think most true crime listeners want that, either. They want to be part of the journey. They want to feel like they have the same information we do, that we are providing all the details and they actually have a shot at figuring out what happened. Nobody likes a who-done-it they had no chance of figuring out."

"Right! Even if you don't see it coming, you want to be able to look back and realize the truth was there all along." She grinned. "So I guess we need to get to the truth."

"After next week's episode, we'll be in real time," he said.

"That will be fun," she said. "Uncharted territory! We're finally taking the plunge!"

They locked eyes, then each looked in another direction, and she wondered whether he had also imagined leaning in closer.

At least there was a kind of relief in the familiarity of working together in their own shared world. When that clicked, all was well. Hadn't they created everything around them in this studio together? Yes, everything, all of it, from the soundboard settings they'd tweaked until Melody's voice sounded like it came from the inside of an antique viola to the new acoustic panels they added this year when their first ad money profit came through. They'd ripped the old cracking styrofoam egg cartons down with such glee and the cartons had made them both hungry for breakfast food, so they'd made a midnight run to Waffle House. When Dorian sang "Do you wanna split a waffle?" to the tune of the song from Frozen, she had laughed till she almost fell out of the booth. Neither of them could hear the song now without singing that line.

Melody felt light, almost delirious, as if she could float up out of her chair. *This should be enough.* The quietly-circulating studio air hummed against her face, her neck. Her arms still stretched across the table toward him, her hands flat on the surface as if holding the moment down, waiting. He lifted his hands to the table and placed them in front of hers. She looked at them, then up at him, with a small, sad smile.

"Well." She inhaled sharply, lifted her hands and slapped a half-hearted 'ba-dum-pum' on the table. "Great. I'm glad we're on the same page about that." She pointed finger guns at him then clapped her hands together, crossed her arms. "But you let me know if the presentation style starts to seem, you know, flat or whatever." She swallowed, then she smiled again, but it didn't reach her eyes. "Okay?"

He pulled back, rubbed his hands together under the table. "You've got it," he said, his voice low.

"Okay, so what's next?" Melody replaced her headphones. "Should we do the new ad spot for Branches DNA?"

He nodded. As he turned toward the monitor, she watched the back of his dark head, his broad shoulders, his sure and steady arms, and her heart pounded as if it would jump across the table to him. She couldn't stop it, and for the first time she was forced to wonder how the hell they could go on like this.

TABS AND BLANKS
PODCAST

Transcript
Season 2, Episode 4: The Chimney Sweep

What do you think of when I say the words 'chimney sweep'? For me, they conjure up the image of Dick Van Dyke dancing with animated penguins and throwing flirty side-eye at Julie Andrews while singing in a cringey but adorable attempt at a cockney accent.

Betty Van Disson's husband Randell was a real-life chimney sweep, having run a side business inspecting and cleaning out chimneys around the area since he was a young man. His father had once been a fire chief at the local station, his grandfather a mason. He used to say he had soot in his blood.

Detective Billy John Whitaker: Well, yeah, he owned the hotel and package shop in the souvenir shop, but he kept up the chimney sweep business his father started a few years before he retired. Randell said he kept the business going to honor his Dad's memory. Old Mr. Van Disson was the town fire marshal. He took his position very seriously. He'd go around to schools on his time off and teach kids about fire safety, like how to put out your campfire and never to touch your mama's candles, things like that. He'd tell them how important it was to keep the chimney clean and maintained. Weird thing to talk to kids about, but both my kids came home from kindergarten after he visited class, different years, saying why didn't we ever clean out our chimney. I guess he figured if the adults wouldn't listen to his public service announcements he might could get to them through their kids. Good idea, actually, when you think about it.

But Randell told me one time that his daddy had told him about a journeyman mason who worked around the area in the early 1900s. There was a story, a kind of legend I guess, that he came from Sweden and joined up with the local freemasons who were building fireplaces in the bungalows in the Riverside area of Jacksonville. A lot of craftsman came to the area after the Great Fire of 1901, when a mattress factory caught fire and destroyed most of the city. Thousands of people were homeless overnight. But what does that mean? Well this city didn't give up, for one thing. Them folks started rebuilding and of course that meant all sorts of laborers and skilled craftsmen sorts made their way down here to find work in the aftermath and whatnot...

Detective Billie John Whitaker pauses here to take a drag on his pipe. A self-professed local historian, he quotes facts and dates as if from a Google search in his brain.

Billy John: ...and so like I say the legend had it that this mason fellow going by the name 'Nils Oland' just turned up on a job site one day, quoting the builder's name and saying he was there to do some kind of repair to a firebox. He went about his work and no one questioned him or whether or not he was supposed to be there at all till the manager came on sight and raised up a big old commotion about it. Why weren't the men working on the walls, they were on a deadline, et cetera. They point him to the mason who said he had orders to fix the firebox before they did anything else, but by then apparently he was done working because he just -poof- took off, disappeared. Now he might have stayed around in the area, worked under another name, who knows. There was so much construction and restoration going on at that time a good worker was going to find work, no problem. He probably just shaved off his beard, or grew one, and went on with his life. Later on, a lawyer came looking for old Oland, came all the way from Switzerland trying to track him down, saying Oland had been hired to do some work in the home of a wealthy Swiss family, and that he had absconded with an item from their home of considerable value. Now that started a rumor that grew into the legend that Oland had hidden this valuable item inside the masonry of a chimney somewhere down there in Riverside, maybe Avondale or even Brooklyn...

Melody: Ok, so sorry to interrupt here, but I should explain to the listeners that the areas you mentioned are now the historic neighborhoods near Downtown Jax.

Billy John: That's correct, exactly. Are you familiar?

Melody: Yes, I used to live there growing up actually. And so if you imagine in many cities around the country, the big, beautiful old houses, and then the bungalows and cottages, for example, like the ones you see getting remodeled on HGTV and restored to their former glory...we're talking about those kinds of houses, that kind of neighborhood.

Billie John is nodding along, pulling drags on his pipe and swaying languidly as the porch creeks beneath his rocking chair. His wife is bustling in and out from the kitchen to the porch, bringing iced tea, lemonade, and Girl Scout cookies—the cool lemon ones, my favorite. She finally stands at one end of the porch and leans on a railing.

Billy John: That's right. By then they couldn't track down anyone to ask about which house it was. It could have been anywhere in any one of those pretty little bungalows. They've got the largest number of original bungalows in the state right there in Riverside. Or it could have been one of the mansions along the St. Johns River. A lot of them on Riverside Avenue, the mansions on what they called 'The Row' were demolished, though, unfortunately. It could have been one of those.

Melody: Oh no! And for our listeners, The Row was where a lot of wealthy businessmen built mansions on Riverside Avenue near modern-day downtown after the Great Fire. But yeah, most of them were torn down. That's a shame.

Billy John: It is. Anyway, so this Swedish lawyer, damned if he didn't decide to set up shop right here in town so he could keep looking for Oland. A journeyman also with the name Oland died of emphysema just eight months after that, and that lawyer decided that had to have been his man.

Melody: Okay, I see where this is going. So you're saying maybe Randell Van Disson had other reasons for keeping up the Chimney Sweep business. He claimed he was doing it in his daddy's memory, but really he was trying to get a look into every old fireplace in the historic district. Looking for that treasure.

Billy John: That is indeed what I'm saying. Randell told me that his father told him on his deathbed to look for a certain brick with a small Swedish freemason mark on it, just above the firebox at the bottom of the chimney. That would mean the treasure, whatever it may be, was stashed in the wall beside the firebox. Something like that, see.

Melody: And then I guess that homeowner would get the news that their firebox needs some repairs, and Randell was just the expert to do it!

Billy John: Yup. I suppose so.

Billy John Whitaker is a talented—and loquacious— storyteller, and he went on to paint an oral picture of local history that made me think this guy is either a total genius or a talented prevaricator. I guess he could be both. I tend to think it's the former.

Billy John: Now all this being said, I should also add that Randell's father had a bit of a reputation for telling tales. Not lying so much as embellishing. He had a flair for the dramatic, as they say. He loved an audience and once he got you listening, his stories seemed to grow, Paul Bunyan style. I don't know if you're old enough to get that reference.

Melody: Oh yeah, my dad once showed me a picture of a really tall statue somewhere.

Billy John: Right, there is more than one. So yes, like that. He liked to talk and people liked to listen. But Randell was his son, his right hand man, and surely he knew that about his father, on some level. He still believed it could be true and never did stop trying to track it down. He believed some family or young couple or house flipper was in one of those old houses with a treasure hidden right under their noses.

Melody: Do you think Randell's obsession with this so-called 'treasure' might have had anything to do with Betty's disappearance?

Billy John: At this point? You know, I think anything is possible.

He takes a sip of his Arnold Palmer and stares away off the porch.

Billy John: Anything is possible.

BETTY,
18 YEARS OLD

SUMMER, 1970

Betty bought a ticket at the counter and waited in the dim gray terminal for her bus to arrive. Her knee bounced (*Mama would hate that*), making her heel tap a staccato that offered an energetic backbeat to the lethargic human music of the terminal: a harried young woman in a jeans and a crocheted poncho, rocking and humming and begging a whining baby to sleep; a young man in fatigues—eyes dark with fear and jaw set with determination—a giant duffle bag at his feet, swishing his hands in circles on his knees; an industrious man in a newsboy hat, intermittently pointing and shouting, "Hey you! Cab? Hey you! Cab? Hey you!..."

When her mother woke up, she'd find Betty's note on the sun-bleached patchwork blanket beside her.

Dear Mama,

> *I've gone to Macon. There are meals fixed in the icebox, and I got the Chiffon margarine like you had*

asked. I still think you should just eat some real butter. Just a little bit won't hurt you. I got your desserts, too. The store was out of strawberry D-Zerta, so I made cherry since you like that second best. There's a new tub of Cool Whip. Just put a spoonful on top. That will be nice, right?

I'm sorry to go like this, Mama, but I'll be back soon. Loreen said she'd check in on you, and your neighbor Eileen will, too. Maybe you can get out and about with her. She's always asking you to go walking with her. It would do you good. You'll have more alone time to spend with your new man Felix, too!

Betty's stomach churned. Guilt and excitement whirled to a nauseating froth, like a hospital milkshake. But no matter how she looked at it, she had no choice.

"When there is no choice, make the right choice."

Where had she read that? She felt unsure, excited, sick.

Mama had said no, just like that. Flat. *No.* A solid red light. But she had to go. How could she miss that? There was no way. She'd steeled herself, shaking her head against doubts till she imagined them falling out her ears. No. She had to be there. This chance was such a big deal that even Dominicus's mother was coming. Mama Owens didn't take time off work, pack up and go, for just anything.

This was their big chance, Dominicus's big chance. They could be stars! Betty could see it. Next, they'd be on the radio, in the magazines, on television. Maybe

Ed Sullivan would introduce them to his stage some day soon.

Now, waiting outside the Douglas Theatre in Macon, the crowd spilled down the sidewalks and into the street hours before showtime. Boys in shorts and undershirts darted through the crowd, hawking crushed ice and sugar honey-drippers and boiled peanuts for a quarter each. Betty smiled up at the name on the billboard, and then walked a few blocks over to wait for showtime. Dominicus had gotten her name on the stage door list so she could watch tonight's performance from back stage. Until then, she was on her own in Macon.

She'd never been further from home than Atlantic Beach before. The heat of her home, tucked as it was inside a thick forest, was nothing compared to the sweltering heat of Macon in July. Trying to sleep the night before, her chest had felt heavy under the hot, weighted air of her motel room, and as she lay there on the motel bed below a lethargic ceiling fan that did little more than spread hot, sodden air like a wet blanket over her skin, she'd fallen into a fitful sleep and dreamed that Mama stood over her bed, admonishing her for running off and coming down with pneumonia.

Now the streets were hazy with hot dust. She reached a building with a sign that read "Capricorn." As she stared up at the letters, a man passed her on his way to the front door. She turned to continue walking.

"Hey!" A voice said behind her. She stopped and the voice went on. "Excuse me, sorry about that. I think I recognized you..."

Betty turned and had to shield her eyes from the sun. "Hello?" she said. The man stepped closer. He was thin, with long hair hanging close to the collar of his tie-dyed psom. "Oh, my goodness!" Betty said, "It's you!"

"So you know me, too!"

"Yes!" Betty said. "I mean, no. I don't *know* you. But my friends and I saw your band perform in Jacksonville, at Willowbranch Park."

"Is that right?" The man laughed, extending a hand." That must be where I recognize you from."

"Not a lot of girls this tall!" She pumped his hand up and down.

"That is true!" he said, grinning. "Not a lot of girls dressed so fine at a hippie jam, either."

Betty's cheeks flushed. She stopped pumping his hand. "I didn't exactly know where we were going that day—"

"Well, it was a pretty dress," he said. "I remember it. Little fruits all on it—"

"Peaches," Betty said. "It had little peaches..." She almost blurted that the dress was hanging up at her motel room right that very minute, but pressed her lips together instead. He probably didn't need to hear about how she'd made the dress herself in home ec., and that she'd made the one she was wearing now, either.

She looked at her hand, still gripping his, and cringed. She gave a firm final shake. "I'm Betty," she said, and let go. She wondered if that was his playing hand and hoped she hadn't squeezed it too hard.

He pushed lank strings of reddish hair behind his ears. "Well hey, Betty," the man said. "I'm Duane." His eyes crinkled and his scruffy mutton-chops rose up the sides of his face.

Before she could answer, the front door of the Capricorn building swung open. "Hey, Phil," Duane said, "This is Betty from Jacksonville."

Phil looked her in the eye discerningly. His thin plaid shirt was unbuttoned at the neck but tucked in, like it couldn't quite decide on a level of formality. "Well, hello there, Betty from Jacksonville," he said. He extended a hand. "Phil Walden."

Betty mumbled a reply, and stared wide-eyed as the two men began to chat about their plans—apparently they were late for a meeting—while Betty stood there, unsure whether to stay or just turn around and walk away.

"Guess we should ease on down there then," Duane said.

"Well, I'm just gonna..." Betty jerked a thumb over her shoulder and winced an awkward grimace. The men looked at her as if surprised, as if they'd expected her to come along.

"Okay, but hey," Duane said, "what are you doing up here in Macon?"

"Who, me?" She coughed to cover a little snort trying to escape. "Oh! My boyfriend is performing at the Douglas tonight."

"Oh yeah?" Duane said.

"Is that right?" Phil said.

They both gave enthusiastic nods. Betty nodded back.

"That's where the *good* musicians play," Duane said through a warm, crooked smile. Betty hugged her arms around her waist.

They said their goodbyes, and Betty watched them walk away, her mouth falling open now that she was alone again. Only after they'd turned the corner did it occur to her: she should have invited them to the show!

She thought about it as she walked again. A musician's girlfriend had to be quick thinking in that kind of situation. You never knew when you'd meet somebody with connections, someone who might know someone else—a producer or a record company executive, even. Well, there'd be other chances, and she'd be sure not to make that mistake again.

Betty found the place she was looking for, a little diner called H & H. At a table by the window, she sat and drank black coffee, pulling drags on a Virginia Slims while scribbling in her diary. Her leg kicked under the table, hitting the opposite bench in time with the song in her head, and she squinted as her pen flew over the page. The place had been empty when Betty got there, but when she looked up from her diary, it was filling up as musicians broke for lunch and headed out of the nearby recording studio. She turned back to her words, to the rhythm of her own private world where she could store up the moments of her new life for safe keeping. She tilted her head, finding her place while tapping the end of her pen against the table top.

"Whatcha writing there?" Before she could look up again, Sly had swiped the diary from the table and held it above his head, pretending to read from it in a teasing, high-pitched voice. "Ooh! 'Dear Diary, why oh why...is Sly so fly?...'" The rest of the fellows groaned, and Dominicus covered his mouth as if scandalized.

Betty's eyebrows drew together. "Give it, Sly," she warned. She waved an arm, but he held the book higher.

"Cut it out, Sly," Dominicus said. He winked at Betty. She didn't need his help.

"'...he's so-o-o dre-e-eamy!'" Sly squealed, only a little higher than his normal voice. "'How does he get his flat top so smoo-o-o-th...'"

Betty scooted out of the booth and stood up. She towered over Sly and easily plucked the diary from his up-stretched arm. Dominicus applauded.

A woman's voice called from behind the counter, "You boys gonna sit down and order food or you gonna play with that little girl and her one cup of coffee in my window booth all day?"

"Oh yes, ma'am! I mean, no, ma'am! Sorry, Ms. Inez, ma'am!" Sly called back. "That's Ms. Inez. She's my new girlfriend. Ain't you, Ms. Inez?" He conjured his most charming smile, and she snapped a white kitchen towel in the air in reply. His narrow chest puffed, and he nodded with satisfaction when she couldn't keep a smile from lighting up her face.

"What are you all doing here?" Betty asked Dominicus, but Zeke started to answer. He slid into the booth across from her, followed by O.T. They immediately set about studying the menu.

"We're done with the sound check, which was a waste of time since they're gonna change it all for the headliner anyway," said Sly. He got in the booth on the other side and slid to the window. Betty sat back down in her spot and Dominicus pulled up a chair to the end of the table, stretching his legs to the side.

"How do you know how it works so well, Sly?" Zeke said. "Talking like you've *been* on the road."

"He heard somebody else say it and took it for his own, like he always does," O.T. said, flicking the back of Sly's menu. O.T. was still miffed that Jerry had suggested giving his solo to Sly.

"We had a little while before call time, so I thought I'd come find *you*, Princess," Dominicus said. He bent down and kissed her cheek. Zeke and O.T. looked at each other, eyes wide, then glanced around the diner.

"Yeah, *Princess*," Sly teased. "He thought he'd come find you, and drag us along with him. But that's okay, he's buying lunch, isn't that right, Mini?" He rubbed his hands together hungrily.

"Man, what did I say about calling me that in public?" Dominicus said through his teeth. He drew himself up straight, his long legs folding in front of him, and smoothed the sides of his hair with his palm. Betty grinned. How could she have considered missing this?

Hank and O.T. quietly figured out a big food order, their expressions more like exhausted parents than the charismatic entertainers they'd need to be a few hours from now. The waitress poured four more cups of coffee, but O.T. finished his before she'd poured the round, so she filled his mug again. "Thank you," he said in his smooth, silky baritone. She rolled her eyes, but jutted her curvy hip his way as she turned around.

After the men had cleaned their plates, and Sly had his fill of charming the waitress, Dominicus and Betty followed them where blinding sun made the sidewalk too hot for standing still.

"You coming to the barber shop?" Zeke said.

"I'll catch up," Dominicus said.

O.T. cast a glance up and down the road, then caught Zeke's eye. "Okay, don't be too long now," he said.

"Bye-eee!" Sly teased, walking backward and wiggling his fingers, then he turned around and made slurpy kissing sounds while hugging himself, running his hands up and down his own back. Zeke slugged him in the shoulder and O.T. took him by the elbow.

"Come on man, leave them alone," Zeke said.

"Yeah, grow up, would you, Sly?" said O.T.

As they turned the corner, Sly was laughing his high-pitched laugh and playing innocent. Betty and Dominicus laughed, then turned in the direction of the motel.

"Where's your mama today?" Betty said, falling in step beside Dominicus. He walked on the outside of the sidewalk. A real gentleman.

"She was going to see some relations we have up here," Dominicus said. "Probably making sure they all bought tickets for the show."

They laughed together, thinking how Mama Owens was probably 'using her influence,' as she called it, to make sure the entire extended family would be there tonight to fill a few rows at her son's big show. After a few quiet steps, Dominicus cleared his throat.

"Listen, Betty," Dominicus said in a tone of voice somehow both excited and solemn. "Jerry got us a spot with the review tour—"

Betty stopped short right in the middle of the sidewalk and clapped her hands. "That's great news, Dominicus!"

"Yeah, it is for sure. It means we're going on the road, playing the whole circuit." He drew her under the shade of an awning and placed his broad hands on her narrow shoulders. "The thing is, I want you to come along. It's two months. Got dates in Chicago, Detroit, Pittsburgh, then a week recording in Muscle Shoals." Betty's face bloomed with excitement as his voice grew louder and more animated. "You might have to ride on a different bus some of the time— well, most of the time, depending on where we are, you know, but I want you to come. You have to come. You're my good luck charm! So if you can see clear to..."

As he spoke, her mind spun around the details. She'd have to let Loreen know, and Eileen the neighbor, too. She would track Felix down, make sure he kept coming around. It had gone fine the last few days, hadn't it? No emergencies. Maybe this was good for Mama after all, Betty being away a bit. She didn't know. Distance and time had created a comfortable buffer, and the past few days in Macon had felt like living in a dream. She knew she had to go with Dominicus. There was no need, no urge at all, to wait and think about it.

What she *did* need to think on was how to gather the courage to tell Mama. But it would happen. Tonight. When she called home at 5 o'clock.

"Yes. Yes yes. I'm going."

"Yes? You mean it? Oh, Betty!"

"Yes!" Betty said. The conviction in her voice surprised them both. Her mind raced ahead, already on tour. "I'll talk to Mona and the Starlight Girls. They'll get me in on their bus, I'm sure! I'll offer to manage their wardrobe for them. They said they needed help."

This was the world where she belonged. She knew it completely, with the promise of a future of her own becoming real for the first time. In this world, amongst artists whose purpose was the creation of music, the problem of skin color was an outside thing, of another world. They had created their own world, begrudgingly entering the one that trailed slowly behind them only when necessary. In studios, in private, and on stage, these people were painting a picture of what the world should be, and their audiences were starting to reflect the harmony they saw. Seeds were planted at every show, in every town. The chance at a life in *this* world was intoxicating. She'd never felt this particular way before, and she struggled to put a name on the feeling.

Hope. That's what it was.

Dominicus held both her hands, and they forgot themselves for a moment. A passing musician or sound man might go on by without a word, but a local might not. There were many who appreciated the business brought in to town by the music scene, but their benevolence ended there.

All the more reason not to leave it. Not now.

Their bubble was burst by a shadow falling between them and a sudden, muffled holler. It was Dominicus' mother.

"Mama Owens!"

"What the damned hell devil are you doing?" she said. Her eyes darted around, then she shooed the couple back toward the entrance to a narrow alley and calmly blocked it with her wide, solid body. Only when she turned her face from the street did she let her expression show that anything was wrong. She looked them both up and down and then slapped at their entangled hands with her gloves.

"Ma!" Dominicus said. He held on to one of Betty's hands and put the other one on his mother's rounded shoulder. He leaned down to speak softly. "What are you doing out here alone?"

"I wasn't alone, now was I? I was out to lunch with your Auntie Willy. She came all the way down from Atlanta to see us, *both of us*, but I couldn't find you." She held both lace-gloved hands palms-up, then clasped and wrung them hard. "Now I see why."

She tilted her head toward him in a graceful manner. No one watching would know the scolding she was giving her grown son right there in public. She smiled and spoke through her teeth as another pedestrian, a skinny overalled fellow carrying a battered trumpet case, passed them by. "Have you both lost your hell-bent minds? Tell me Mini, did you up and get a hankering to hang from a damned tree?" Martha was a Christian woman, and the only 'bad' words she allowed herself were biblical ones. Still, she usually used them sparingly, and 'hell' and 'damn' weren't usually peppered so liberally, or so close together.

Dominicus smoothly turned both women in the same direction, dipping his head toward Martha. "Ma, it's okay. It's different here."

"Oh, is it now? How's that? How is it magically different *here*?" She looked all around and nodded, the feather on her pink hat punctuating her motions. "Well, I guess you're right, and I certainly do apologize. I did not realize we had all died and gone straight to Heaven!"

Betty assumed a particular gait, one meant to convey that everything over here was fine, while Martha walked between them, her neat handbag hanging from one elbow and her t-strap pumps clacking lightly on the pavement. She kept her voice low, and her words clipped.

"Because of the music, Ma. That's why it's different. It's changing, anyway. Some people don't know it yet, but most of us, my people, we just care about the music."

Martha stopped walking and stamped both feet. "Son, now I love you, but you only see the good in folks. You see what you want to see. Tell me something: Can you and your music friends be out here? Together? What do you think the rest of this town thinks of what's going on in that studio, on that stage? They let you sit together in that diner, but what about everywhere else? *I* know. And it scares me to death." Her voice broke. She swallowed hard and dabbed at her cheeks with the back of her gloved hand, and Betty watched as she then stepped closer to Dominicus and placed a finger gently on his chest. She spoke gently now. "You know, too, if you're honest with yourself."

Dominicus leaned against a chain link fence and looked at his shoes. He knew more than he wanted to know. Hadn't his father been downtown at the plaza on Ax Handle Saturday, that terrible, infamous day, only one decade ago? Fear was not weakness to his mother, but right-headed and reasonable and necessary. Just a year before that terrible event, a new high school had opened on the Westside, named in honor of Nathan B. Forrest, the first grand wizard of the Ku Klux Klan. This was the world his mother knew, the one to which she was supposed to trust her guileless and artistic son.

"It is all well and good that they didn't see color in the recording studio," she told her boy as he leaned against that fence, listening, "but the rest of the world does not have the luxury of another take. The history is already recorded. We don't have acoustic walls around our lives out here. The rest of the world hears every wrong note and feels every dissonant reverberation."

Martha Owens could have been a preacher.

In his mother's eyes, Dominicus saw without knowing, understood without words, the many reasons she believed as she did. And although Dominicus stood firm, in his eyes Betty saw for the first time a blink of doubt.

Delores Langdon sat by the phone. Betty would be calling soon. She leaned her chin on her hand. "I am in a state," she said. Today, she had sent her husband on one of her errands to fetch some epsom salts for her aching joints—well, Felix wasn't her husband, just a boyfriend, but it didn't do to have a 'boyfriend,' so her men were her husbands—and good old Felix did go, as expected. Only this time he didn't come back. They were tests, these errands. And this time he'd failed. Failed *her*. That had not been expected, although given her luck with men, it was no big surprise, she thought. They were good for nothing. They always failed. They couldn't manage to fulfill simple requests. Worse than untrained puppies, they were. Now just like that, her latest husband was gone.

Delores always preferred unattractive men. Ugly men didn't expect much, she said. They were dumbstruck, in awe, couldn't wait to take her out and show her off around town. She would make an effort then, wear her heels and cinch her waist in tight, roll her hair and rouge her cheeks for them, for their friends. Unattractive men put her on the higher pedestals and let their egos puff their chest and couldn't believe their dumb luck. They worshiped her, bought her a steak and a draft beer at the bbq, not the sloppy pulled pork sandwiches and sickly sweet tea the other women got. They were happy to do it. She was a catch. Even if that part only ever lasted for a little while. That little while was the time she lived for. When that time was over, so was the relationship.

She imagined herself a femme fatale, betrayed and wronged in a dramatic twist, at the high point of the script's drama. Her big scene. She rose from her chair and flew around from room to room with the ends of her caftan flapping—glamorously, she imagined—behind her. She stopped to pound her fists on table tops and dressers, grunting and grumbling as she swiped at the air, making high-pitched little exclamations as she swiped at anything unbreakable. She only got one take. Spent, she lowered herself into her chair and was, once again, disabled.

And, scene. Applause, applause, applause. *Quiet on the set, please. Ms. Davis requires quiet on the set.*

She stayed put in that spot, simmering and fussing to no one but herself, compulsively pulling on a lock of hair, winding and unwinding it between her fingers, her eyes flicking as if watching the movie in her mind.

She would wait. She would wait for five o'clock and Betty's daily phone call, all the while practicing the conversation they would have, her lips moving over the words she would say till they were perfect.

At five o'clock that evening, Betty stood at a pay phone, clutching a handful of change. She stood there a while, shifting her weight from one foot to the other, clenching and unclenching her jaw, until finally she grabbed the handset, inserted the coins, and started dialing home.

They were so close, on the edge of a new life, but one that would require unwavering belief that it was possible. They both had to believe they really could walk down the street together—in Chicago, in Detroit, in Pittsburgh. That they could travel together to Muscle Shoals. Betty resolved to be as strong as Dominicus.

Her mother wouldn't understand—she wouldn't see any reason to *try*. And now Betty knew Dom's mother didn't understand either. She didn't trust it. Why would she? The words she'd said to her after Dominicus left them together on the sidewalk still rang in Betty's mind, an insistent warning bell:

"My own daddy was caught up in the bolita raids on Avenue B. Do you even know about that, Betty? He wasn't even involved. Didn't gamble a day in his life. Just went up there to find his friend and haul him on home. They arrested him, and he hasn't been the same man since. We still don't know what happened to him while they had him locked up." Betty leaned on the phone booth and pressed her hand against her heart remembering Ms. Martha's dark eyes welling, her lip quivering as she spoke. "What I *do* know, in my heart, is that my son is going off into dangerous places, as far away as those pastel-colored patches on the other side of a globe. You think things are so different, but *I* see what is *true*. They still segregate the audience, don't they? What do you think *you* are going to do? Change the world all by yourselves? With what? Your music? Your *love*? Betty girl, it's going to take more than that, and until then, you being at his side will only put him in the *wrong* kind of spotlight."

The feathers in Martha's hatband had waved in doleful agreement with the shaking of her head.

Betty's finger hovered over the last digit. Her eyes closed and she was back in the scene of the previous night, watching The Downtown Sound working in the studio: Dominicus's smooth voice, crooning the melody over honeyed harmony, all five huddled around a central microphone; the randomly assembled house band—a freckled good ol' boy with a Gibson Les Paul, a bearded hippy on keys, and a nerd with a Brylcreem center-part on sax—reverentially falling in line around the bass line laid down by a taciturn, monosyllabic man with a gravelly voice and a deep brown skin. The studio drummer's girl had gone into labor and he'd sent a friend to sit in: a fellow they called 'Jaimoe,' with a bear tooth necklace and a sleeveless shirt, round glasses on a hard brown face, and chops like nothing any of them had heard before. She'd recognized him the moment he walked in: the drummer from the Willowbranch Park jam with the hippie she'd run into on the sidewalk earlier, that nice fellow named Duane.

They'd played for hours without slowing down, commemorating each take with slugs of whiskey and passing one small cigarette around and around like brothers. At dawn, someone ran out for sweet rolls and coffee and they ate together, playing and rewinding the tracks, not yet ready to let the night move on to its fate of shared memory.

The song played as if she could hear it, a soundtrack to a slideshow of Dominicus singing, Dominicus laughing, Dominicus winking at her across the studio as he sang: "*...got a penny in my pocket and my girl in front of me, what more do I need...*"

She pressed the last number. Her chest stiffened. The phone barely rang once. Betty hoped the serene Mama would answer. The one who spoke like she was on take three of her big scene. At least, she hoped, let Mama not sound *that way*—the way she sounded when the world could kindly kiss her ass.

"Betty! You have to come home. I mean it now. I need you."

Oh, no. "Mama." Betty's voice caught and the sound that came was strangled. "Mama? What's wrong? Why? Has Loreen come by?"

"I don't want Loreen. I want you."

"What about your man, Mama? Where's Felix?" She gripped the hot phone and pressed it hard against her ear. Her breaths came shallow, her face whitened.

"He hasn't been around since I told him you'd gone. He's left me. It's over." She paused. "And that's on you! He couldn't do for me like you. It was too much to ask. Wasn't right." She added a cough and mumbled just loud enough "...oof, ah, my leg..."

"But Mama, I wasn't planning on being back, not just yet, not for a little while." Her eyes cast about the sides of the little payphone box as if it could help her.

"I got a job, Mama! But it's on the road for a little while."

"Did you now? Well, you're gonna need to quit that. When will you be home? I have a doctor appointment and my pills are low."

"Can't Loreen pick those up for you, Mama? She works so close-by and all." But Betty's voice wavered. Hope drained cold down her body and seeped like life-blood to the sidewalk, pooling at her feet, darkening her shadow. The weight of her mother's self-made burdens descended anew and pressed on her shoulders. Outside the phone booth, the sun sank lower.

Surely it was too early for it to be so dark.

Betty stood just backstage, gripping the musty red velveteen curtain and willing it to hold her up, to hold her right there forever.

The Downtown Sound glided and swayed onstage, only a few steps away, just out of her reach. Those few steps from backstage to center were miles. *How?* Betty blinked at the blinding glow of the footlights. *How do they do that?* It was like being on stage, performing, was as natural to them as singing on Sly's front porch. Betty tried to imagine herself where Dominicus stood behind the microphone, sliding from one foot to the other, eyes squinted as he hit the thrilling high note as the beat suspended at the end of another verse, luring the audience to the edge of a cliff created by his voice, his charisma. Her heart leaped in her throat and she swallowed it down lest it jump onto the boards to be trodden under their shining pointed shoes, shuffling and stomping impossible syncopation. Each move they made, each note they sang, coursed another pulse of energy to the audience who watched from below—men clapping, unable to resist mimicking the footwork, and women swooning, clutching clasped hands to cotton-print bosoms. These boys from Jacksonville had something special.

"*...I've got a penny in my pocket and my girl in front of me...What more do I need?...*"

The audience loved it. By the last chorus, they were singing along as if they'd always known the song, as if their own mamas had sung it to them in the cradle. They'd be singing it as they walked home and humming it as they fell asleep. Men would use those words as they reached for their women and crooned on a breath in their ear: "*...what more do I need...?*" Betty blushed at the knowledge, hid deeper behind the curtain.

Betty had been awake in her bed for hours, worrying over what to do about Mama, how to fix things. Surely there had to be a solution. After hours in the muggy motel room, arranging and rearranging ideas like a puzzle in her mind, she'd fallen into a fitful sleep. Now, there was a knock at the door, an urgent shuffling sound, and a rattle as someone tried the doorknob.

"Betty! Betty, wake up!"

The voice outside in the dark was definitely Dominicus, and his rapping at the door light but insistent. In one swift motion, Betty had switched on the lamp and was out of bed, pulling on her robe as she stumbled across the motel room. She opened the door a few inches at first, then flung it open wide.

"Dom—? Oh, God! What happened?"

Dominicus was stooped to one side, and at first Betty didn't register the smaller person beside him. He held the figure up with one arm as he rushed past her. The man groaned as his back pressed against the chair. Betty gasped.

"Sly! Good Lord, Sly!" She kneeled in front of him and Dominicus stepped aside, catching his breath and darting looks around the room, then turned toward the sink, gathering towels. He ran one under the tap and hurried back.

"Some boys jumped him in the alley by the stage door," Dominicus said. "We waited in the theater till the crowd cleared after the show, then we all left together. Sly went back for his coat." Betty tried to listen as she repeated Sly's name, coaxing him to open his eyes, while pressing the damp towel to the largest wound. "We were waiting on the sidewalk for him."

"Who did this?" Betty hissed. "Did you see them?"

"We saw some men, three I think, run out of the alley. So we ran back there. Found him on the ground. I thought he was dead." His voice broke. "We should have stayed together."

Sly moaned and shook his head. Betty wiped his forehead, streaking a mixture of congealing blood and slick sweat across his skin.

"We have to get him some help."

"Hank said he'd call Levi." That would be Levi Swanson, the variety show tour manager. Dominicus had introduced her to him before last night's show. He was a small, pale man in a baby-blue three-piece suit and purple suede shoes, officious and preening, who always spoke as if slightly tipsy. Betty's eyes grew dry from being wide open so long, and she closed them, hard. She couldn't believe any of this. She needed to think.

Sly slumped lower in the chair. His eyes fluttered open and looked up at her, then they closed again.

He was barely conscious, and his face was shiny with sweat and trails of blood that traced from the gash on his forehead, over his eyebrows, down his face and neck, staining the collar of his white dress shirt.

"Why didn't you call an ambulance?"

"Betty." He blinked, squinting at her as if from across a chasm. "This is faster. Believe me. He's conscious, he's breathing. We can try to help him here first."

Zeke knocked and came in, followed by Hank, and O.T. They each dropped items on the bed, donations hastily collected from the kits and cases of other tour members. "Gauze, rubbing alcohol, cotton balls," Zeke said. "Peroxide, catgut thread, needles, Band-Aids," O.T. said. "And this here's wig glue." All eyes turned to him. He held up the small amber jar, his shoulders raising in a tight shrug. "Jerri said it would help hold the cuts closed." His smooth voice had turned gravely and weak.

Betty shuddered. "Any of you ever sewed up a cut before?" She looked from face to face. Dominicus's dark eyes grew wide and the slight shake of his head said 'no.' Zeke lifted his pant leg to expose a jagged, raised scar. "I tried once. O.T. had to finish it." He wrung his hands over and over each other and O.T. nodded, a grave sickly pallor covering his face at the memory.

Sly began to come around, his moans growing louder. His eyes struggled to open as the flesh around them began to swell them shut. She looked at the thread and needles, the bottles of antiseptics, the bandages spread across the rumpled bedding. *All right, you have to do something. There's no choice.* An image of the school nurse popped into her head, and the poster she had hanging in the infirmary—that's where she'd seen it: '*When there is no choice, make the right choice.*'

Her own voice registered through the pounding in her ears. O.T. pulled the little dining table closer to the bed and Betty quickly organized the pile of supplies. Then she placed her hand decisively on the table. "Zeke. Could you go find some ice?" she said.

He looked at her hand, flat on the table as if to draw strength from its solid surface, then he searched her face. She locked eyes with him and jutted her chin toward the door. He nodded and slipped out the door, grateful for a job. Betty dumped her toothbrush from the single glass by the sink, gave the glass a cursory rinse, and filled it with water. Then she washed her hands and took the deepest breath her tense belly would allow. O.T. added the contents of his pocket flask to the water.

"Here, Sly. Drink this," she coaxed, holding the glass to his split lip while pressing a washcloth to the worst cut, below his right eyebrow. Golden water dribbled to his blue satin shirt. His head turned away, his eyes unfocused and his jaw slack, then he sucked his teeth and grimaced as the cut over his ear spread open and bled anew.

Betty disinfected the needle and aimed the end of a length of catgut thread at the eye. Her hands shook and one eyelid twitched. Sly's head lolled forward, and he inhaled and came to. Zeke returned and wrapped ice in a towel. O.T. turned the chair to face the bed where Betty sat on the edge, holding the needle out as if it were a lit match.

It's just like fabric. No different. Just like sewing a hem. No big deal.

The eye wound bled fresh when she peeled the ice pack away and the towel took the clot with it. She pressed the pack back in place. O.T. stood behind the chair, his hands on Sly's shoulders. Someone added a straw to the drink. "Come on, Sly, you're going to need it." Dominicus' voice roused him, and he managed a long, deep pull on the straw, and then another.

Betty's gaze followed the slumped version of Sly's slight body and back to his face, desperate to see his cocky grin and impish eyes put back the way they belonged, not distorted and bleeding. How hard, how many times, had they hit him? The sight of each cut and bruise sliced through her with a force like the one that caused them. Her eyes pressed closed, self-preserving, but she forced herself to look. She waited for the alcohol to hit his system, then leaned in.

"It's gonna be okay, Sly," she said. "I've done this lots of times. Lots of times." *Those times had involved hems and necklines, but never mind.* Her blood rushed and adrenaline coursed. An image of Marcus Welby's nurse flashed in her mind—*Mama loves that show*—and the actress's confident expression formed like a mask over Betty's tense face.

Sly's head bolted upright and he looked around, wild-eyed. Betty leaned in front of him.

"Look at me, Sly. Just keep looking right here, okay?" He filled his lungs and let the air escape slowly from his juddering chest, holding her gaze.

She dabbed his brow with rubbing alcohol, pinched the two sides of the cut together, and went to work.

BETTY,
18 YEARS OLD

JULY 14, 1970

Diary,

I'm on the bus back to Jacksonville. The bus driver keeps looking at me in his giant mirror. It feels like there's no air in here and this vinyl seat smells like heat and unwashed hair. I don't want to be here.

Every minute takes me a little further away, but my mind is still in Macon, my heart is getting on that other bus, the tour bus they were packing up when I had to get on this one. The road is speeding away under me and I wish I could jump out and run.

Why do I feel like I have to smile when I catch that driver looking? I'm torn to shreds inside but I can feel my face betraying me, trying to look like nothing is wrong and I don't understand why. Why does my face do that?

Everything is upside-down. I'm riding on this bus, on this ground, just rolling down this road and it seems like I'm the only one who sees what's happening, what we're leaving behind. Like I'm in the last car of a roller coaster, riding backward.

Junie said I need to come back, that Mama is in a bad way and it's only right. It's my duty. I wish I'd never called her. I never should have told her my plans. I should have hung up the moment she replied, "Oh." I could hear it in the way she said it. "Oh." Not "Oh!" No smile in her voice. So flat, so discouraging. Like she was hoping I would have had a change of heart since my conversation with Mama, but now it fell to her to deal with me, to make me see some sense. I knew from that "Oh" that Mama had already spoken to her. I can't believe the rest of the things she said to me. It makes my mind spin.

Every time I close my eyes, I see Ms. Martha's face. Her words and the fear in her eyes on the sidewalk when she saw her son with me out in the broad daylight—she was so scared. Her face was all I could think about while I pulled needle and thread through Sly's skin. People can be so cruel to each other. I've been so sure about how the world is changing, how Dominicus and I could be together if we got out of our small corner of the world. But she doesn't see it that way. What if she's right?

I'll go home. I'll make sure Mama is set up with help or even better, get her well enough not to need help. And then once she's set I'll find out where Dominicus is and meet him there. It's just a delay, that's all. I'll get back to him, back to my life.

<u>Soon.</u>

TABS AND BLANKS
PODCAST

Transcript
Season 2, Episode 5: Dry County, Wet Sundays

Welcome to Episode 5. I'm Melody Hinterson.

We are driving down a county road off Highway 17, a few miles southwest of the Maryview Motor Inn. Pine trees, palmetto fronds, and dark bracken wound with clutching kudzu vine line the two-lane road and give way to fields and pastures before picking up again, thick and lush. A person could get lost in there.

*We've passed at least three possums who've recently met unfortunate ends. But the scenery really is beautiful out here, and it's a little hard to believe we're only about thirty minutes out of Jacksonville city limits. But as locals love to tell you, owing to the consolidation of Jacksonville in 1968, Jacksonville **is** the biggest city in the contiguous United States. In square miles, that is.*

We pass big and small houses both, the grand and the humble, the old and the newer, well-kept beside dilapidated. A few random shops dot the landscape—a garage, a beauty salon, a brand-new Dollar General. American flags flap against their poles with that familiar clink. Political yard signs are posted like talisman. Yard signs seem to be a big thing out here. They are everywhere—"Georgia Peaches," "Local Honey," "Notary Public." There are "Gators Football" signs, "Go 'Noles!" signs, "Georgia Bulldogs" signs.

Dorian: That's a good one—'He's a Gator, She's a Seminole: A House Divided.'

Melody: Uh oh!

At the front of one picket-fenced yards, there seemed to be one of those inspiration signs you might find in Kirklands or Hobby Lobby stores, the ones that state the rules of the house in flowery fonts, like 'In this house we believe in love, prayer, and chocolate chip cookies.' But on closer inspection, this one turns out to have a different take. It reads:

"In this house,

we believe in your right

to stay the hell off our land."

On this day, we drove down a road you'd easily miss from the main highway. Like entering another world, we pushed back a galvanized gate and the attached wild blackberry vines to meet up with Heather Stoates.

Heather worked for the Van Dissons at the snack bar and souvenir shop in the lobby of the Maryview Motor Inn. Randell Van Disson bought the place before he and Betty married, but she managed the place.

Heather: "Well, at that point I hadn't seen Ms. Betty in about two months, because I'd been out to visit family near Gainesville. Betty had gone off, you know, disappeared before, but only for a day or two, and then she'd be back behind the counter when I came in for work after school like nothing had happened. She'd be humming and baking cookies for the snack bar or fixing sandwiches. I did ask where she'd been, but she never did say. I heard she had a real old sick mother across the river so I figured maybe she got tied up over there.

Melody: So do you remember anything she said the last time you saw her? Anything different that stands out to you?

Heather: No, nothing different, so to say. She was behind the check-in watching one of the morning shows. I said bye and gave her a kiss. She patted my cheek and told me to quit smoking. She was like that—real motherly and caring, and my own mom couldn't a cared less where I was or whether I smoked, so I appreciated Ms. Betty. The news was talking about the anchorman getting fired or quitting or something, and she seemed interested in that. She said she'd see me when I got back, said 'drive safely now' and the like, and I left. Next time I came to work, it was about a week later because it was spring break and my family all went up to South Carolina to see my mom's people, and when I came back Mr. Van Disson was running the snack bar. Well, I say he was running the snack bar, but he didn't know what he was doing. Had some bologna sandwiches and bags of chips all lined up on the counter.

Heather: Ms. Betty was the one who knew how to run things. She had all the ideas to try to keep the business going, even after most everything else shut down on this road. She used to joke that she only married Randell for the neon signs. She loved those glowing signs, and when the business started to slow down and everything started to go downhill, and those signs stopped working one by one, it was like the light in her eyes dimmed right along with them, so to say.

Heather puts a shoe box on the coffee table and sits down beside me on the couch.

Melody: Oh Payless Shoe Store! That brings back memories!

Heather: Right? I know. I miss that place. Mother hauled all us kids there a couple times a year. Christmas, school about to start, Easter...

Melody: Yes! Easter was the big one. Then we had to put them straight back in the box and only wear them for church until the first day of school that next fall.

Heather: Yeah, but when school did start the next fall, my momma would be surprised when we'd outgrown the shoes over the summer. Every year! Like, really mother?

Melody: I remember Payless because it was the only place to get wide-width shoes for cheap.

We laugh over our shared memories of a now-defunct American retail icon from our childhoods. But soon enough, we both remember why I'm actually here, and we settle in to talk about her former employers Betty and Randell Van Disson.

Local real estate records show that Randell bought the four acres on the east side of Highway 17, just before the St. Mary's River that marks the border between north Florida and south Georgia. At that time, there was a low-slung building just off the highway and one outbuilding. Both buildings were designated as commercial property, but the Van Disson's built out one room of the motel just off the main lobby to use as their residence after they got married. A house, a beige bungalow with graying cedar siding, stands on the southern edge of the clearing now, but it was built a few years later.

It's less than a two hour drive from here to the setting of one of my personal-favorite Florida books— The Yearling. I can't help imagining Jody Baxter and Flag in these woods, which are largely unchanged from how they were in the time of that book's setting. On the edge of wide scrubland, tall pines provide a canopy over palmetto palms and fern. Bear and deer do still make this forest their home.

Folks still stayed in the Maryview Motor Inn, and business was at least good enough to keep it open, but by the time Betty moved in, records show the liquor store was the main business. Theirs was one of several along the stretch of rural highway locals and some regulars called The Gauntlet.

Only nine years before Betty Van Disson disappeared, another woman had disappeared from this same area. Nellie Olfort's case was a mystery for years, and it bore striking similarities to Betty's. Although she was a bit older than Betty when she disappeared, Nellie was also the wife of a state-border liquor store and motel owner—the Riverside Motel and St. Mary's Liquor—located less than a mile up the road from the Van Dissons's establishment. In both cases, the woman disappeared without a trace. In both cases, the husband refused to allow a search of the acreage behind their businesses.

And in both cases, the women had seemed to have lived relatively isolated lives. Neither had children, and both spent most of their time tending to the motel customers who came and went in smaller and smaller numbers, and liquor store customers who, by the time of their disappearances, mainly turned up on dry Sundays.

Nellie Olfort's husband Knud vehemently refused to allow his property to be searched for clues, and the case grew cold. His lack of cooperation led locals to believe he had something to do with her disappearance, and he died with a cloud of suspicion over his head five years later.

Two years after his passing, in 1999, during military diving exercises being conducted near the blue bridge in the St. Mary's River, a car was discovered submerged just off shore on the Florida side. The car was pulled from the murky waters, and Nellie's remains were found on the driver's side, still strapped into the seat belt. It appeared that she'd mistakenly driven off the road just before the bridge, driving straight into the river, and drowned.

Questions remained: How could we know whether she'd been conscious when she went into the river? Did Knud push her in there to get rid of her body? Could she have committed suicide? If Knud had nothing to do with his wife's disappearance, why wouldn't he allow a search of his property?

No evidence of foul play was ever reported after her body's recovery. And the general consensus was that if Knud had indeed killed his wife, he had no reason to proceed to put her in a car and drown her body. So could it have still been a murder? And if so, could Betty's disappearance be connected?

There's no explanation for Knud's adamance regarding his property, but in light of Randell Van Disson's similar behavior, perhaps it reflects the pervasive local attitude of this rural area. A staunch belief in other peoples' right to stay the hell off my land.

Melody: Heather, did Betty know Nellie, that you know of?

Heather: Not that I know of. I know she knew who she was, of course. Similar business, obviously, right up the road like that. They were competition. But since our place was on the other side of the highway, some people preferred to go the little extra distance just to turn right instead of left. People around here are creatures of habit. We have our 'druthers.'

Melody: Gotcha, like, "I druther do this" or "I druther have that."

Heather: Exactly.

(*laughter*)

Melody: What did you make of Randell's refusal to let the police search his land? Especially after what had happened with the Nellie Olfort case nearby? I know her car was also gone, but I've heard speculation that it could have been stolen, if someone came by the motel and found it empty, for example. So many 'ifs,' but they're credible possibilities, so—

Heather: Yeah, I get you, but honestly? Personally, I didn't read anything into that whole thing with Mr. Van Disson at all, so to say. If you look out there, you'll see there wasn't any way Ms. Betty could have gone out into the woods behind the motel. Even back then, there was no way in. It's not some magical forest like in a fairy tale, you know? It's thick with underbrush, saplings, vines, all that. It was mostly choked with kudzu then, just thick with it. I don't know if it was the principle of it, but I don't remember him making a big deal about not letting them search. It was more like, 'You can't search because you literally can not search.' I mean, it was too wild and thick to get more than a few feet past clearing.

Melody: Do you mind if I ask how you know that? You worked in the lobby and the shop, not on the property, right?

Heather: Right, but I used to go back there on my breaks sometimes, to smoke usually, and I'd walk the perimeter out there. There weren't any paths into the woods or anything like that.

Melody: Got it, okay. Sounds dangerous, smoking near a thick forest?

*(*laughter*)*

Heather: Maybe it was. You know what, probably not the best choice. But it didn't feel like it was. Dangerous, I mean. I've lived out here my whole life, and smoked for most of it—got the gravelly voice and smoker's abs to prove it—and never started one forest fire, that I know of.

*(*laughter*)*

Tourists coming into the state had long ago abandoned Highway 17 in favor of Interstate 95, and liquor could be had easily at any number of burgeoning exits along their way to points south of Jacksonville, a town that seemed boring and unnecessary when the state offered places like Orlando, Miami, and Tampa Bay. The city struggled to tempt visitors to stop at Florida's "First Coast" on their way through. "Hey, wait!" it seemed to say, reflecting in rearview mirrors, "We have a river! Look! It flows north."

By the time of Betty's disappearance in 2001, Jacksonville was taking its place as a 'big city,' having lured an NFL team franchise to town and some big names to the popular Jacksonville Jazz Festival. As an aside, locals may remember that 2001 was also the first year the festival didn't happen. Try as it may, the "Bold New City of the South" just couldn't get any respect.

To put the timeframe in perspective, it's important to note that Betty's disappearance took place less than two weeks before a terrible day in America— September 11, 2001. Local FBI saw their focus shift from anything non-essential to the investigation of this crime and the implementation of security measures for the country. Local law enforcement everywhere hit pause on many cases as they trained and implemented new protocols for a scary new world. This certainly would have affected the subsequent investigation of Betty's case.

Heather had one more thing to add:

There were two things I made sure to let the police know. I always thought they might possibly mean something or help somehow. I told the investigator, Officer Billy John—

Billy John Whitaker was a police officer back then. He became a detective later on.

The first thing was that when I came back from that trip, the painting from behind the check-in counter was gone. It was one of those Florida Highwaymen paintings of a tree with red leaves or flowers all over it and some water. Betty had told me Randell bought it right off the wall of the motel where they stayed on their honeymoon. She always said it like it was silly, like it showed something about Randell that he would do that just because she said she liked it. Like, what was he trying to prove, or whatever. But anyway, it was missing, or it was gone, when I got back and I asked Randell about it. He just looked up at the empty space and shrugged his shoulders, like he didn't know.

Melody: Interesting. Wonder what happened to it. What was the other thing?

Heather: Right, the other thing was, it was probably nothing, but whenever Betty would be away for the day, like when she went up to help her elderly mother, and I'd be covering the motel lobby, oftentimes she would come back with a couple of shark teeth.

Melody: Shark teeth.

Heather opens the shoe box, removing the lid she has decorated with scraps of felt, small beads and sequins, and the words "Ms. Betty" written in silver glitter.

Heather: Yeah. She always just said she 'found them.' She'd drop them in a jar she kept under the desk. I guess Officer Billy John didn't think it was important, or maybe he did look into it, I don't know. But my uncle used to look for fossilized shark teeth out in the creeks, and I know it can be kind of rugged. Some folks drive out to Fernandina

Beach and out near the fort to find them on the beach, but he had his certain secret spots where he'd hunt, like I say, in the creeks and swamps. I knew better than to ask a fossil hunter where their secret spot was, but now I wish I had asked Betty. I really wish I had.

Heather unpacks the shoe box in which she has saved mementos that remind her of Ms. Betty, her former boss. There is a birthday card signed in Betty's florid hand, a pair of ladies' gloves she loaned her for a Halloween costume, a pack of gum which she explained Betty gave her in an attempt to help her quit smoking. There's a cassette tape with "Songs For Heather" neatly printed on the label. Heather explains that Ms. Betty loved music of all kinds.

Heather: She kept a blank tape in her boom box under the counter so she could quickly press the record button when she heard a song she liked on the radio.

There's a picture of Heather on her first day of work, standing in front of the shop's magazine rack.

Heather: Ms. Betty took that picture. Boy, did she love that magazine rack. Couldn't wait for the delivery guy to refill it every week. She especially loved the music and entertainment magazines. *Rolling Stone, Variety, People, Spin, Billboard, Downbeat.* I remember once some British rock band came through on their way into Florida for some shows. They were impressed by the selection we had. Wouldn't expect that at a little Southern highway motel liquor store, I guess. Especially looking at Ms. Betty, you'd never expect it, never guess that little country lady in the cotton dress and apron would be keeping up with pop music, R&B, funk, disco. *(*laughter*)* There was a lot more to Ms. Betty than meets the eye, so to say. And she always made sure those magazines were on our order. She made *sure* of it.

When you look up the St. Mary's River and the area around Highway 17 in particular, you learn some very interesting things. There is a unique phenomenon that occurs around this point, after the big bend that takes the river east all the way to the Atlantic Ocean.

This natural occurrence isn't unique to the St. Mary's River by any means, but it does provide a bit of information that could hold meaning for our investigation. The river banks change several times a day here, rising and lowering in a call and response with the ocean some fifteen miles away, an ocean you cannot see from there but who keeps her powerful hold from a distance like some unassailable monarch far-removed. ˙

In light of Heather's statement about Betty and her habit of collecting shark teeth, and knowing the tragic outcome of Nellie Olfort's missing person case, the possibility that Betty could have drowned in the river seems a reasonable possibility. Betty was a lifelong resident of the area and must have known, or at the very least been aware, of the constant changes the tides create along the river. But is it reasonable to think she may have stopped to look that day without thinking about a high tide? Could it be she simply stopped alone for a quick search, which according to Heather was something she sometimes did, and she misjudged a recently-flooded river bank? Is it possible the sodden soil gave way and dragged her in, pulling her down with the sucking pluff mud to be overwhelmed by the brackish water?

I called Detective Billy John Whitaker to ask him about all this.

Melody: So, do you think that's a possibility? Was that something you looked into?

Detective Billy John: I did. Now, Heather never told me that, about the shark tooth thing, that I recall, but I'll tell you what, you can't investigate any kind of crime in this area without it coming back to the river some way, somehow. There's always some reason to take a look at the river.

Now if Betty used to go to the riverbank down there, either the Florida side or the Georgia side, whatever her spot was, she would have known at least the basics about how the banks change. That rising and falling is something you keep in mind when you're a fossil hunter around here because each time it does that the water can reveal something new. That's part of the fun. My buddies and I used to always be on the lookout for all sorts of teeth and bones, the black ones are the old, fossilized ones, and sometimes you'd find an arrowhead or some pottery. But when you know the river, you also know the tide stain, so it follows, at least in my mind, that Betty would have known it.

Melody: The 'tide stain'?

Detective Billy John: Yeah. That's the high water mark, or the strandline, left behind after the water rises and then recedes. It'll be right there at the top where the water reached at its highest, where it backed off and left its mark behind. There might be debris there. It's just a natural, visible indication of where the water reached at high tide, and you have to be careful below that on a riverbank in case the soil is drenched. You could step on a spot that looks solid and it could give way and take you with it, in some places there's the pluff mud which can suck your feet in like quicksand, only worse. The more you struggled, the deeper in trouble you get. If you don't know what you're doing you can easily find yourself getting pulled against your will right into the water. It's a scary thought. Probably why quicksand used to be the plot twist of choice in the action adventure shows back in my day. When you want to understand where some old fogey is coming from, just remember he grew up with the fear of quicksand instilled from a young age.

*(*laughter*)*

Melody: So, what about what she said about the edge of the property, and how it was too thick for a person to go into the forest?

Detective Billy John: I guess I wouldn't know, since he didn't let us back there. I know we tried to look around back there, but he said no, she's not out there, it's no use anyway.

Melody: So did he refuse, or did he say you literally couldn't get into the forest?

Detective Billy John: What I remember is being told he said no to us investigating back there.

Melody: You were told? By...

Detective Billy John: By the officer who went out there.

Melody: I see, okay. We didn't see that in the case file.

*(*silence*)*

Melody: So...

Detective Billy John: So, yeah. That is an interesting piece of information Heather gave you. I do wish I'd known it, could have looked at the tides that day in a different way, checked to see if a reverse flow from an incoming tide matched up with when she should have been heading back home. No witnesses came forward to say they'd see anyone, but that doesn't mean anything. She could have been on her way back and thought hey, maybe I'll make a stop today.

(*silence*)

Detective Billy John is quiet for a few moments. It's very unlike him.

Melody: Detective?

Detective Billy John: Yeah, I'm still here. Just thinking. You know it's not a good feeling to be so far removed from an unsolved investigation and get new information that makes you look at the whole case in a new light. What can I do with it now? Yeah, not a good feeling at all.

Melody: Well, I'm sure if you'd had the information, you would have done whatever you could with it.

Detective Billy John: I would have. I surely would have. I've thought about that poor lady a lot since y'all brought it all up again. It's the not knowing that's hard to accept.

"It's the not knowing that's hard to accept." That is so true. And it's why we at Open Mouth Productions do what we do. Knowing that there has to be an answer out there. People don't just disappear. Something happened and the truth exists, even if it's hiding, known only to the creaking forest, or the weeping river.

MELODY

2019

Melody gave a thumbs up, and Dorian gave the all clear. As Melody unclipped her mic, Detective Billy John Whitaker rose from his arm chair, pushing off against the armrests with a grunt, and leaned toward the tabletop mic. In a cheesy '70s game show host voice, he announced he was going to the bathroom. Melody rubbed her temples.

"I'm starving," she said.

"I brought a whole freezer bag of my Lola Maria's lumpia," Dorian said, cocking his head toward the kitchen.

"Bless you. And bless Lola Maria."

Melody checked her notes. The detective had been relatively forthcoming. She was pleased with how the interview had gone. He'd answered more of her questions than she thought he would.

"What do you think?" Dorian asked. "Enough for an episode?"

"It's good. He's a character, that's for sure. Speaks in headlines. Every other sentence is quotable. I have to fact-check before some of this goes in the show notes," she said, and lowered her voice, "but he's believable, right?"

"Sure. It's been a long time since he was on the case, but he seems legit to me," Dorian said.

"Still, it doesn't go in my official fact folder until I know it's a fact, Jack," she said.

Dorian shook his head, a smile reaching the corners of his eyes.

"I want to end the group interview episode with what you said about Betty. That was good stuff," he said. "Ms. Junie didn't know which way to look."

"Thanks," Melody said. "It just came out." She'd been struck by Junie's ability to say the ugliest things in the prettiest of ways, and frankly disgusted by how when Junie hadn't liked the direction the questions were going, she'd automatically turned a conspiratorial eye to Mark, as if calling on some allegiance, some loyalty, owing to a secret between them. She'd put him on the spot, and she'd been obvious about it, as if she wanted the rest of them to wonder. To wonder what? Maybe the 'what' didn't matter. The act was a means to elicit some reaction. And he had reacted. The man had shrunk back as far as one could possibly retreat in the hard back of a restaurant booth. Perhaps he'd been sucked in before.

Melody pulled her hair into a topknot and tucked the ends in, watching the back of Dorian's head as he worked. Glancing toward the door, she listened for the bathroom lock. She leaned over the table, speaking low.

"The way this guy smirks..."

"Right?"

"...like he thinks he's charming the pants off you with that drawl and that little twinkle-eye thing he does..."

"Guess it must have worked for him at some point." He yanked at a tangle of cords as if they had purposely plotted to tangle themselves.

"I guess," Melody whispered. "Ugh. That George Clooney smirk." She paused, waited for Dorian's laugh. Instead, he remained facing his screen, barely cracking a smile.

"So," she said, "what is up with you today?"

Dorian's chin jerked down. "I don't know...what do you mean? I mean, I'm just," he shook his head. "I'm just working, like usual. Doing some on the fly editing on this interview."

"Okay." Melody sucked in the flesh behind her bottom lip and held it resolutely between her teeth for a moment. "What I mean is, something is up with you. Like, something is definitely different. Are you mad or something? Did I do something?"

"No, no. Nnn-nope. All good. I don't know what... why you'd think anything is wrong? I'm just, like I said, I'm trying to work here. So..."

His jagged protest hung there, ringing hollow. Melody wavered, then fought the urge to push. Dorian's still shoulders and the determined knit of his brows implied she should leave it alone. But she knew when he was upset—just like she knew when he was happy, when he was hungry, tired, frustrated, elated. At least, she *thought* she did.

The boundaries used to be clear. Once the unspoken decision had been made—that they were friends, a great team—she'd convinced herself it would work. All they had to do was keep it professional. Everyone knows you don't mix business and romance, right? It's an established, tested recipe for disaster. So if she thought she'd caught him looking at her a moment too long, with a gleam in the center of his warm eyes that for all the world resembled unabashed longing, it must be all in her head.

In their work, she had always known in her gut when to push a subject with him and when to drop it, when it was right to lean in and when it was not appropriate. But lately, she couldn't trust her gut. She couldn't trust *herself*. Her voice would ring in her own ears before she realized she was speaking. It was disorienting. The tension was becoming visible, insistent, like a warning light. And it meant that more and more often, she ended up going with the latter choice, the confounding one, the one meant to calm the awkward moments and keep the two of them on opposite ends of their constant friendly tug of war. But that choice did little to break the tension. Instead, it only added to the inconvenient desire to give the rope that one final, satisfying pull.

Detective Billy John came back around the corner. "Y'all're out 'a terlit paper," he drawled.

Melody jumped in her seat and swiveled toward him. She forced a smile. "We're not recording, detective."

"All right, all right, I gotcha," said Billy John, dropping the overblown accent. "I guess I am getting a little full of myself, with this newfound fame and all. My Twitter account is blowing up!"

"Twitter, huh?" Melody said. She looked at Dorian as he went about starting his shutdown checklist. His face was red and the line between his dark brows stood out. "Well, we appreciate you coming in again like this, detective. Your insight was...invaluable." She forced a smile.

Detective Billy John puffed up a little, gathered up his notes, and headed toward the door. Melody followed, opened the front door and held it for him, but the puzzle table caught his eye. He veered away from the door and posted himself beside it, hands behind his broad back. "These must be the famous tabs and blanks," he said, leaning over the table. "The *titular* tabs and blanks, I should say." He exploded with laughter.

"Nothing gets past you, sir!" Melody said. The sarcasm was completely lost on him.

"Thanks again, detective!" Dorian shouted from the studio. Melody held a polite smile and pulled the front door open wider.

"Any time you need me, let me know," he said. "I'll be happy to come back in. Any time."

"Thanks so much." Dorian waved as Melody closed the door.

She came back to the studio and leaned against the doorframe. Her arms vibrated with unspent energy. She crossed them and tucked her hands away. Finally, Dorian shut off his monitor, stood and looked all around, everywhere except at her. She cast about in her mind and thought of something.

"Did you want to work on the puzzle for a while?"

"I wish I could, but I've really got to head out. Maybe tomorrow?"

"Tomorrow."

"For sure."

"Yes. Good."

"Okay." He swung his bag over his shoulder.

They'd been so careful. Every step of the way, they'd been deliberate and cautious, protective of their friendship, their partnership, from supporting each other through demanding school projects to the joint television news internship to starting the podcast. They'd built this production together and nurtured it from the ground up, learning as they went. Now it had grown into a commercially successful multi-media branded product with advertisers clamoring for space and outlets requesting interviews—interviews with *them*! The New Yorker, Vanity Fair, E TV. All along the way she'd thought they'd had between them that unspoken understanding. *We both get it: this works so well because we work so well. We agree not to do anything to mess it up.* But something was wrong.

Maybe it had never really been right.

Maybe it had been bound to happen, the inevitable product of denying their other feelings — stuffing them down, down, down. It had seemed imperative to set the possibility aside, right from the beginning, not to fall into that old trap of giving in to a romantic relationship only to have it go bad and ruin everything. But maybe the very thing they'd avoided for the sake of their partnership was finding a way to wedge in anyway. A tight little pain grew in her chest and spread up her neck, gripped her temples. Finally, he looked at her, but they didn't speak. He held her gaze and his sad smile was a mirror of hers.

BETTY,
18 YEARS OLD

DECEMBER 1, 1970

Dear Diary,

I think sometimes that I don't belong in my own life. I wonder, was I dropped down in the wrong place somehow? God doesn't make mistakes, so that can't be. Then I wonder, was I adopted? But that can't be, either. I favor my Mama's side too much for that to be true.

It's like I understand a thing one way, and I think that's how everyone else understands it, but then something happens that shows me I don't really understand anything at all. What feels like the right choice to me always turns out to be wrong one way or another. Everyone, I mean every one, knows better than me.

There's a kind of desperate, hungry feeling in my stomach all the time. It feels like every minute, and every second inside those minutes, is time wasting. And I'm a frugal person, so it bothers me even deeper.

I'll never be able to gather this time back up. It's just gone. There's another minute gone, just writing this down.

If I wasn't meant to leave here, why did He let me meet Dominicus that night? Maybe it was a test. I should never have gone back there again. Then I wouldn't be in this mess.

I can't say it anywhere else, so I'll only say it here:

I love Dominicus. I love him so much and I'll never love someone else like that. How could I? And I know he loves me. It's not like it used to be. It's not illegal anymore. But Mama, our families, this town, just everybody would rather I give him up and for them not have to hear about it. They don't want to hear that I love him. They'd consider me fallen somehow, just for <u>thinking</u> I love him. Imagine if they knew the truth of it! I can't imagine it. That's partly how I know I'm not living the right life. My right life has gone on ahead without me and I can't even imagine it clearly anymore.

He's out on the road now, and really I am so happy for him. Of course I am. But I should be there beside him. He wanted me there, on the bus with him and the others, traveling from town to town. When I saw their name up on the marquee that first night in Macon, I thought I might faint right there in the street, right in front of the theater! All those lights flashing around their name: 'Tonight! The Downtown Sound.'

We were going to see the country together. Things are changing so fast out there. And I was so close to being a part of all of it.

They're going to make it, that I know. People will love them. Just give it time. They'll be on top of the music charts and everyone will know how great they are. The Allmans and the Van Zants got out of this town, didn't they? And they're making records now. Dominicus said Ray Charles was from around here! So it can happen. It will happen.

I should be there with them, with him, when it happens. Maybe I can still get things settled here and go join him. I have to try, don't I?

I remember one time when Junie brought her Mama's diary to school, one she kept back when she was in high school, around our age. Junie pointed out different parts and laughed, all the most embarrassing things her mama had written down in secret, and I admit I joined in. I'm ashamed to say, but I did. Junie said her mama's diary showed that she was just like we were, probably worse. It felt like she wanted it to be so, to justify all the trouble <u>she</u> wanted to get up to herself. And she wanted me along. I will own to my part. I wanted her to want me along more than anything. But now I wonder if she wanted me there for some other reason, maybe for security. Like the bumper on a bumper car. I see now how maybe I was only there to cushion the blow. She could go merrily along at full speed, ramming into things and causing all kinds of wild chain reactions, and still be okay, so long as she had me to take the brunt.

I hate to think like that about her, I really do. It makes me feel sick and cold inside. But now that I'm back here at home, after how she did me, I can't help it. Why couldn't she take my side? When I called her that night from Macon, told her Mama said I had to come home, Junie said if Dominicus hadn't been Black, maybe she could have been on my side, that she would have helped me deal with Mama. Now I'm looking at those words I just wrote down and I can hardly believe them. How did I never see that was how she was? Thinking back, I suppose we never did talk about things like that. She said it never occurred to her I'd want to 'run off with a negro'. I said it never occurred to me she would say a thing as ugly as that. And that was when I saw the truth of it—that Junie never knew me at all. She never cared to try to know me. I assumed the best of her because I thought I knew her, and I could never think badly of her. Not Junie. All that time, I had just been happy she let <u>me</u> know <u>her</u>, and that had been enough.

Stupid, stupid, stupid.

Wasn't she the one who always said I shouldn't have to take care of Mama all the time? I feel badly even saying that, even in private in my own journal. I just wish someone could tell me if this is normal. If this life I'm living is what it's supposed to be or if I am wrong for wishing for something else. Something for me.

That sounds so bad. I never thought I was selfish, but you know what? Maybe I am. Maybe I'm supposed to be learning some kind of lesson from all of this. Something to put me on the right path and make me contented and selfless and good. Make me think about simple things and a simple life, not riding around on tour busses with my boyfriend from city to city. Who do I think I am, anyway? I should focus on what's real right now.

I did have a good trip to the grocer yesterday, found all Mama's needs and some baking things so I can make a pie for the Calvary bake sale. They had a good deal on D-Zerta. I went ahead and got six strawberry so we don't run out. (Mama was mad as a wet hen last time.) Picked up a fresh carton of Lucky Strikes for her, too. But on the way home, I saw those signs again on the side of the highway, the ones for the new fruit stand. The ones that say "Peach's" and "Strawberry's" and "Onion's" and "Tomato's." Why, oh why, do folks here use apostrophes like that all the time? Did they all have the same bad English teacher? Or did all the English teachers have the same bad English teacher before them? Thank the Lord for Ms. Connor and her red marking pen. I may not ever write a book, but I sure as heck won't ever use an apostrophe to make a word plural, that's one thing for sure. For the life of me I can't understand who would go to all the trouble of painting signs by hand without checking somewhere first to make sure you're writing them correctly. Just another in the long list of things I can't understand. But I swear it is going to drive me nuts. Oh, well. There's not much I can do about any of it.

I pray for Dominicus, for all of them, every day. I think about them out there on the road and I pray their bus doesn't break down. I wonder how Mona and the Starlight Girls are faring without me. Mona sure appreciated how I fixed her dress when that sequined appliqué popped off the bodice. Right before they went on stage! What a commotion that was, me trying to sew it back on off stage with the footlights nearly blinding me and her shouting out loud enough for the front row to hear when the needle barely grazed her bosom: "You better watch it with those long pale fingers, Betty!" I never did poke her, blinded as I was by those lights. She told everyone the story later and made the whole event so much bigger than it was, like I had saved the show, and I was proud. It is funny how it's grown in my mind the more often I remember it, filling in and expanding like a balloon till now it's even bigger than her tall tale. It's one of the good memories.

I guess Sly should be all healed up by now. Probably has a nice scar over his eye where I sewed him up. Of all the places a person could get a scar, Sly just <u>would</u> get one in a spot that doesn't ruin his good looks. One that girls would notice and fawn all over, like a soap opera star. They always get injured in the most glamorous way possible. I can just hear the girls now. "Oh Sly, what haaappened? How'd you hurt your pretty face?"

If they ever find out who did that to him, I swear I'll find them and, well, I don't know what I'd do to them, but it would be really bad. I would figure something out. I'd corner them in an alley like they did him. Times are changing. It's supposed to be different now. Some people don't know it yet, and I guess some people don't like it, but too bad for them. I am just so sick of things never being fair. How some of us get to roam the world free while some of us are just always going to be stuck. No matter where we are. Stuck. Like some sad old bobcat dragging her snap-trapped hind leg around. You can't get far like that.

Who am I kidding? I couldn't do a dang thing to get even for Sly. Not a dang thing.

I sure wish I could know where they are right now. I hope they're seeing lots of new places and being safe. I also wish Dominicus could see my new blue jeans. He wouldn't believe it, me in blue jeans. I tried to hide them, but Mama saw. She said they're vulgar and a lady wouldn't wear such a thing as a pair of blue jeans. Said all they're for is showing the world the shape of your behind. She said did I think Bette Davis would have been caught dead in a pair of raggedy blue jeans like that? I don't know why she's so stuck on Bette Davis, and I finally told her so once and for all. I had just had it that day, I guess. I asked her did she realize Bette Davis was born in Massachusetts and not right here on the blessed and holy Florida-Georgia line? And she said, in that high and mighty way of hers, "Well, yes. Of course I do know that, Betty. But I don't hold that against her."

I'm keeping the jeans.

The tour must be almost half over by now. Sure do hope the recording sessions went well out in Muscle Shoals. Imagine hearing them on the radio! I remember Dominicus said they might do "Princess Betty Lou" on the B-side of "Penny." How appropriate. Feels like my life is a record that got flipped and just kept on turning, and now I'm <u>living</u> on the B-side.

Wow. Aren't I just that dramatic? But that really is how it feels. I think about it and I feel nauseated. I feel nauseated a lot lately.

All there is to do is pray. I'm going to keep on praying for them and praying I can make it back to them, to Dominicus. For now, I'll try to think about how some day (maybe soon!) I might hear Dominicus sing my song to me through the radio.

BETTY,
19 YEARS OLD

1971

B etty sat at the kitchen table, trying to chew quietly. The early morning sun through the blinds drew white spaces across the table's dull, dark surface. It reminded her of the staves on a page of sheet music. She picked up the salt shaker and placed it on one line, then she put the pepper shaker on another, humming the interval. She moved the pepper and hummed again.

"I guess you're not concerned about what those things are doing to your figure, hmm?" Mama glanced at her face but didn't wait for a reaction. Betty jumped sideways from the dining chair, her arm half-buried in a bag of Doritos. She licked the orange powder from her lips.

"I thought you were back in bed, Mama," she said.

"I see that," Mama said, waving a dismissive hand in Betty's direction. She shuffled across the kitchen, pink hospital socks drooping around her ankles. She went straight to the screen door and watched the mailman come up the walk.

"Morning, Frank," Mama said.

"Morning, Ms. Langdon. Here you go." He handed the small stack of mail and sales circulars to her.

Mama had taken to watching for Frank every day and came out to meet him at the door. She never missed a day. Sometimes Betty wondered if Mama was sweet on Frank or something. Mama would shuffle through the stack, drop the bills on the kitchen table, and clutch the rest to herself as she carried it back to her room. She reminded Betty of a squirrel, always shuffling off to her room holding something to her chest. Betty had seen her once or twice over the years, kneeling on the other side of the bed where Betty couldn't see what she shoved underneath.

Lately, when Mama scurried—if she could call Mama's motions these days 'scurrying'—it summoned vague childhood memories, appearing like wispy vapors that dissipated just as quickly into the pressing, needful present. A pretty new paper doll dress, missing from its box; the purple barrette she'd traded for with the girl next to her in class, lost from where she left it on her bureau; the shark tooth she'd found that day her father came to see her, "misplaced," Mama said. She should be more careful with her things. A slow shrug, the end of a pink sateen robe following Mama into her room, the door closing. She recalled a resignation, a childish understanding that God must take things He thinks you shouldn't have, things you covet or love too much.

This morning, Mama stood in front of the fridge, looked pointedly at Bette Davis, ever present, ever watchful, then she opened the door and retrieved one two-inch piece of celery from the jar which Betty had just refilled for her earlier that morning. She breathed a shallow, shuddery sigh.

When was the last time Mama ate? Betty watched her mother rewrap the front of her robe and tie the belt with a weak but determined tug. The ends of the belt dangled almost to the ground. There was almost nothing left of her these days as she slipped like a phantom up and down the long dark hall to and from her room. The sounds of her emptying her hollow stomach in the bathroom then opening the mouthwash bottle—swish, gargle, spit; swish, gargle, spit—twice this morning already, gave Betty an empty feeling of her own.

Mama filled a glass at the sink and sat down on the other side of the forest green formica table, still clutching the mail and the portion of celery. The rings under her eyes had become dark hollows and her clavicles jutted out like fingers grasping for nourishment.

"Do you want your protein shake, Mama? Or a D-Zerta?"

Mama shook her head. She lifted the water, but had to set it back down. She put the mail facedown in her narrow lap and picked up the glass with both hands. Her wrists shook and the pale blue-green veins seemed to have retreated deeper under her translucent skin.

Betty's heart pounded. *She has to eat something.* She got up, tugging at her own robe. It barely reached around her middle now. "I'll make you an omelet, Ma. Egg whites and a spoon of onion was okay last time, remember? You liked it. You kept it down, didn't you?" She'd mastered the art of cooking egg whites on a non-stick skillet since Mama wouldn't eat oil, nor butter. You had to set the burner on low and let the pan heat up gently first. She put the pan on the stove and turned the knob. The lighter click-click-clicked, and the fire hissed into a watery blue circle.

Mama raised her head and fixed her gaze on Betty. Her eyes narrowed and her papery forehead crumpled, watching as Betty duck-walked back to the fridge and thoughtlessly pressed a maternal hand to her aching lower back.

"No," Mama said, her voice sliding down an octave.

"Yes, Mama," Betty said, "A little food—"

"No," Mama said again.

Something different pulsed in Mama's tone, a low icy note on the edge of her voice, and Betty froze with one hand on the refrigerator door. She dropped the other hand from its comforting spot, let it hang limp at her side, and glared pleadingly at Bette Davis.

"Mama," she said, not turning around. She'd known of course that Mama would have to notice some time, that she wouldn't stay quiet when she saw the swelling of her unmarried daughter's belly. The inevitable moment had come.

"Betty. No." Mama said. "You cannot keep it." Her voice was a gavel.

The finality of it took Betty's breath. A hundred arguments jostled though her mind, shot down one by one before they reached her lips.

The fan hummed in the corner and a gnat landed on Mama's water glass. She watched it walk around the rim. Then she pushed her chair back and stood.

While she waited for the dizziness to subside, pride preventing the appearance of a swoon. She raised her shoulder and tilted her chin—reaffirming her power, dominating even in weakness. She pressed her palm to the tabletop until the sparkling darkness passed, then opened her eyes and swiped feebly at a nonexistent crumb. She'd left the celery warming in a bright strip of sunlight, a barline to end Betty's tabletop melody. At the kitchen door, she paused, put a hand on the door frame. A shot of unreasonable hope poked Betty's chest, and she raised her head. Mama cleared her throat.

"I'm in quite a state now, Betty," she said. "I'll take those eggs in my room."

BETTY,
19 YEARS OLD

FEBRUARY 8, 1971

Hi Diary,

For some reason, I've been thinking about my father a lot lately. Guess that's not so strange, things being how they are. I keep wondering how everything might have been different if he'd been around. And well, it's late and I can't sleep and I might as well write it all out.

One time, he came to visit me. I remember it so clearly. I think I was four or five and Mama put me in my best dress and my patent leather church shoes. She shoved me in front of her when he came to the door and said, "This here's Levi Maurer. He's your daddy. He's just taking you out for a movie and ice cream." I remember the shot of excitement. Ice cream! Then she said, "One small scoop, in a cup, no cone." After she closed the door behind us, he winked at me, and I understood him right away. I could get more than one scoop. And probably a cone.

We rode in his little baby blue car all the way into town. I always remember the tan leather seats and the matching dashboard, all shiny. I touched the dashboard and my fingertip glistened like it had baby oil on it, like what Mama used when she laid out in the sun. I wondered if my daddy was trying to make the leather darker, too. He laughed at that and patted my head.

I don't remember watching the movie because I was busy drinking all the Coke and eating as much popcorn as I could fit into my mouth. So buttery and salty! And that sweet soda to wash it down. Mama didn't let me eat those things. Said I'd grow up fat and wouldn't be able to find a man. There was a glossy magazine picture of Bette Davis stuck up on our fridge, with her pretty hands on her tiny waist, gazing down at me with a warning about whatever I supposed I might sneak from the fridge. Well, Mama wasn't there, neither was Bette Davis, and right then I didn't care about my waist or getting some man. What would I want a man for? I only cared about how much soda I could drink before my stomach exploded.

The music is what I do remember of that movie. It filled that whole theater. Now I know it's called a 'soundtrack.' The movie was *A Star Is Born* and the man who was supposedly my daddy loved it. He couldn't take his eyes off of it. He even cried. I remember I thought it was because I didn't leave him any popcorn but he said, no, no, that he didn't eat greasy foods. He was watching his 'waistline.' He said it's just like Mama and I thought, well, I guess Mama's right about men and waistlines.

I clearly remember looking down at my belly, the light from the movie screen flashing on my dress, blue and amber. Then in the car, the seat belt was stretched out just a little and so was my dress, and I crossed my arms over it. I tried different ways of laying them and ended up stacking one above the other like a shield.

What's funny is I never did stop doing that, even when there was nothing there to hide.

After the movie, I told my father I didn't want to go for ice cream after all. I was so mad at myself, that I'd filled up like that, and now I was losing my chance at a whole scoop of strawberry in a cone. And Daddy said, "Well if you're sure, but then we have some time before your mama wants you home. How about instead we go down to this spot I know and I'll show you how I look for shark teeth?"

Shark teeth? Seeing as how I was only a little kid, I was afraid. I spent the whole ride over there shivering in my Mary Janes about how a person is supposed to get a tooth away from a shark. But I didn't want to seem like a scaredy-cat crybaby, not to my dad who I'd only just met and who probably already thought I was greedy and fat—and sassy to boot, since I'd made that remark about his oily car.

We drove back the way we'd come and then past our street and on up to the St. Mary's river. He sang along to the radio and he knew all the words to every song.

"Do you like music, Betty?" he asked. I nodded, forgetting my belly momentarily. "Me, too! So what's your favorite kind of music?"

On the radio, a man was singing something exciting and bouncy. "I like this one," I told him.

He reached out, his hands were long and narrow with neat nails that shone like the insides of shells in the sun. He turned it up. "This here? This is Chuck Berry. Saw his show in town at The Armory. Oh, you should have seen it! He danced this funny dance up there on stage while he played this very song here."

Then my father sang along while I sat beside him, watching. His face changed, contorted as he sang, like neither could he understand why old Maybellene couldn't be true. I tried to imagine seeing the singer from the radio singing in person on a stage right there in front of you. I had seen singers on television, but to see them in person? I thought, wouldn't that be amazing?

He said it sure was some show, and then I remember his face changed and he stared off out the window. He said they had stretched a white rope down the middle of the concert hall, and the white people had to sit on one side and the colored people on the other. Then he smiled. He said at the end of the show, damned if everyone didn't rush to the stage together. That's the moment I remember feeling close to him, like he must really like me, right then when he said the word "damned." Even then I understood you only curse in polite conversation if you're really close with someone. He gave me a smile, like he knew I was there. Like he was glad I was there. And then he patted my head again and looked back out the windshield and said, "They can't stop it, Betty." I didn't know what he meant then, but I always remembered how the side of his face looked, sort of amused—and now I realize it was also defiant—when he said that: They can't stop it.

He pulled off the road and parked, and we tromped down a little ways till suddenly the water was right there at my feet. There were trees and bushes on either side, but that little clearing was like it was made just for us to stand there. At least that's how I remember it. He took a little shovel from a bag he kept in his trunk and dug a scoop of heavy wet dirt, then he dumped that in the strainer and sifted it around at the edge of the water. He did that a couple times, showing me each time, then dumping it out and starting again. Each time he dumped it, he said, "patience."

I have no idea how much time passed, while he scooped and sifted, showed me what was left behind, scooped and sifted some more. I waved my hands in the water at the shore and it felt like warm soup, my hands stuck closed when I squeezed them and made a sucking sound when I tried to open them again. Eventually he looked at the sky and said, "Well, it's getting late, just one more scoop." His voice sounded like he was singing all the time, high and sweet. He looked into the strainer and his face lit up. A little black point stuck up from the layer of rocks and sticks. A shark's tooth.

"That tooth right there belonged to a shark millions of years ago, Betty," he said, and I was amazed. I didn't know how long a year was, let alone a million, but it sounded amazing, the way he said it.

I'm still amazed every single time I find a shark's tooth. To think how long it's been hidden in the ground, since this whole place was the bottom of an ocean. No highways. No motels. No liquor stores or souvenir shops or produce stands. Just teeming with giant sharks swimming around free, losing teeth. That spot where my daddy took me that day is still my favorite. That clearing on the St. Mary's, not far from the base of the blue bridge.

At one point, we took a break and my daddy held my hand and we walked to the edge of the forest for the shade. He struck a match and curled his hand around the end of his cigarette as he lit it. I still remember the wonderful smell of the match and the curl of smoke, like a question mark, rising above him. He stretched out on the ground with one arm behind his head, looking up at the sky through the tree tops. I lay down next to him to see what he was looking at. All around us, the skinny pines and cypress looked like roots, upside-down like that, like they were reaching for the sky for their sustenance. I remember thinking: maybe there's another world underneath us, under the ground. Like the air was the soil and the ground we lay on hid the real world, the one I couldn't see.

Boy, I tell you what, Mama was M-A-D mad when she saw me. Daddy had rinsed my hands with water from a canteen, and he had cleaned off my muddy shoes the best he could before we got in the car, but there was nothing he could do about my dress. She yanked it over my head right there at the front door, making a point, and he said, "I can take it to the cleaners." And she said, "No, that would mean you'd have a reason to come back."

When I go to that spot now, I can't help thinking how those trees spring from that dark mucky ground and try so hard for so long till finally they can't do it any more. A storm comes, no stronger than other storms they've survived before, but this time they give up and that muck pulls them down, down, down, down, till they disappear completely. The trees my daddy and I laid under back then aren't the same trees anymore. The ground is just waiting for them, impatient and grasping, and a little bit welcoming, too. It must be a relief when they can let go, just go down.

Diary, remember when Dominicus and I went out to the beach that time before Macon? I remember his eyes when we sat on that blue towel watching a dark gray cloud to the south to see if it was going to miss us, or if we'd have to run for it. I was so happy as we sat there together, looking at my pale pink arm leaning against his dark brown one. "Looks like a vanilla sundae with fudge," he said, licking his lips. And I pointed to my freckles and said, "with sprinkles!" and oh, didn't he laugh! The way he laughed, from somewhere deep down below his heart, it made me lose my breath.

He kept on looking out south even after the cloud passed. We both saw some of the looks we got. I guess I thought it was just that it was still a little new to folks, to see two people like us together on this particular beach, one that used to be segregated not that long ago. Dominicus told me how his uncle had been what they called a 'wader' on a beach further south, near St. Augustine. The waders went out on white-only beaches and waded on into the water.

Sometimes they'd go to segregated pools. There was pride in his eyes when he talked about it, and I felt proud for him. And now there we sat together on a towel. I think now, I had no idea how naïve I was. Not everyone thought like me, thought how great it was that things were changing. Man, how foolish I was! I wonder if Dominicus saw that about me and thought I was naïve, too. Because now I know better, and now I know that I didn't know anything then. All I knew was I loved him. He would just smile at me and smooth his hand on my face.

I told him then about my daddy and the time he took me to look for shark teeth. I showed him how to search for little black triangles among the shell beds and along the wash up line, and we looked for a while together. I told him how I hoped some day I'd find a big old tooth, a megalodon, that was my goal. I was so excited when I found a little black tiger shark tooth, but he took one look at it laying in my hand and got a confused expression, kind of disappointed. He took it and made like he was going to throw it back in the ocean before I stopped him.

He said, "Come on, Betty. You're happy with this little, old, sad tooth?"

"Well, yeah. It's still something, like, a million years old! It's good enough," I said.

"Princess," he said, and he took my hand and tilted his head down to look me in the eyes, that way he did. He said, "We don't settle for 'good enough', you hear?" I can still see him holding that little tooth up in the sunlight between his thumb and forefinger, squinting at it and shaking his head disapprovingly. "We take sad little million-year-old teeth like this one right here, and we throw them right back to the ocean. We let that ocean know that <u>we</u> know it can do better. Now come on," he said. He put the tooth back in my hand and waved his arms toward the breakers. "Go on!"

I knew he was just teasing me, and so I called his bluff. He was completely shocked when I ran to the water's edge and darned if I didn't throw that tooth!

"I know that's not the best you've got, ocean!" I yelled. Dominicus gasped. He splashed into the tide, searching around for that "sad little tooth" after all.

"I thought I was supposed to make that ocean do better!" I said.

"Well, yeah, but that's still a million-year-old tooth!" he said. We laughed till I thought I'd faint dead away.

Later, we lit a little campfire, and he started singing. Song after song, and he wasn't shy at all. People gathered around as it got dark, drawn in by the music and the crackling fire, both seeming to add warmth to the slightly chilly evening air. The sun was setting behind us and the clouds turned purple and orange and then silvery gray. Soon the little crowd was calling out requests.

As one song ended, Dominicus went right into another, s sort of impromptu medley. *My Girl* turned into *The Dock Of The Bay* and segued into *Beyond The Sea*, then *I Wish It Would Rain* flowed into *Pennies From Heaven*. Someone passed beers around and he took a sip here and there. Amber droplets shimmered on his lips as they formed the words of the songs. People clapped, snapped their fingers, moaned when he hit a sweet high note, cheered when he growled one down low. They dabbed tears and held each other close and hung their heads low when he sang *Handsome Johnny*.

They said things like "Man, what are you doing hanging around this town?" and "Where can I buy your record?" and "Righteous, man. Really righteous." Then he sang *Hey, Jude*—like Wilson Picket did it, only even better, in my opinion—and left them all flat in the sand.

I miss him so much. He was the best I'll ever find.

How I wish my daddy had been around. I wish he was here now. I know he would have helped me. He would have known what to do.

TABS AND BLANKS
PODCAST

Transcript
Season 2, Episode 6: New Activity

Hello, Listeners! We had a call to our information hotline that we felt warranted a short midweek update episode. Today, we'll hear from a new voice.

Will Brantley stayed at the Maryview one weekend and was a frequent visitor to the Van Disson's liquor store. According to Mr. Brantley, his wife didn't know he'd been there, and he never came forward after Betty's disappearance, but since his wife's death last year, podcasts became his favorite pastime.

Will: My wife was a very religious woman, you understand. I want you to know, she was the finest woman you ever want to meet. And back then, well, let's just say I didn't deserve a woman like that, you get me? I used to head down over the state line after church most every Sunday. Said I was going fishing. And I did. I did fish out there many a time.

Randell said he was thinking maybe Betty killed herself by jumping off the bridge up the road. He said he looked all over there by the woods to make sure she wasn't out there hurt or lost, but he never found anything. That's what he told me, anyway. Pretty sure.

Melody: You spoke to Randell? To Mr. Van Disson?

Will: I did. A couple months after.

Melody: Did you stop by there, or call him, or—

Will: I stopped by.

Melody: And how did he seem to you?

Will: He seemed like...well, he seemed...sort of lost? It sounded like he was at a loss, didn't know what to do next.

We did some digging and found that Will Brantley was one of many area men questioned at the time of the disappearance of the woman from another Highway 17 motel, the woman named Nellie Olfort. You'll remember from previous episodes that her body was eventually found. Sadly, it seemed she mistook the road to the bridge and drove her car into the St. Mary's River. Mr. Brantley was questioned but never under suspicion for Nellie's disappearance. However, he told me he felt the suspicion on him until the day her car was pulled from the water. And regarding the disappearance of Betty Van Disson, he feels it still.

We'll hear more of our phone interview with Will Brantley after a word from Branches DNA...

MELODY

2019

Last season's show, a series on a missing child case out of Key West, had seen a huge rise in downloads since this season of the *Tabs and Blanks* podcast was blowing up. Total download numbers grew exponentially every day. Branches DNA had just re-upped their sponsorship, new advertisers were buying up all the available spots, and the windfall had financed some quick and much-needed upgrades to their studio setup. They'd darkened the room with new sun blocking curtains and then added light back with a flattering ring light and a new set of professional studio cans. This week's behind-the-scenes footage for the website would be positively theatrical.

The new intern's expertise had already brought up the video quality. Kina Narvaez, a recent graduate from NYU film school, had moved back home to Florida to put her expensive education to use as a barista at the most hipster coffee house in Riverside. When they first met her, getting some decent coffee after an early interview at a different coffee shop, Melody had been so enthralled by Kina's shoulder tattoos, which Kina coolly mentioned were done by Kat Von Dee herself, that she almost didn't notice when Dorian asked to photograph them. Almost.

"It's going to take a while to get used to all this luxury." Dorian searched under a desk for an outlet and popped his head up, following a cord back to its device.

"So fancy." Melody spun around in a new cushy office chair. "I don't know how to act." The chair turned smoothly with no squeaks, no sound at all. She ran her hands down the cushioned armrests. "We're moving up in the world."

We must be doing something right.

"I got an email about a sale on those Sprinter vans. Maybe we should upgrade." They'd bought the current van from the news station where they interned when the station had sprung for a shiny new fleet.

"Oh, I don't know," Dorian said, his voice muffled by the table top. "I kind of like the news-mobile."

Melody smiled to herself. The van had been part of their podcast team from the beginning, and Dorian's loyalty to it was adorable.

"When is Kina supposed to be here?" she asked, checking the time. "I have to run over to my mom's house real quick this afternoon." She clicked on the podcast website, checked for new comments. "Apparently, I need a wash of red to look less like a zombie on camera." She pushed her cheeks up with her fingertips. "She said I looked 'low-key sad' in our video posts." She made air-quotes and shook her head.

"Is that what she said?" Dorian sat up. He gave a quizzical grin, but Melody frowned, and he pushed the corners of his mouth back down. "She's the lighting expert, but I thought you looked..."

"What?" Melody said. "You thought I looked what?"

"Fine! I thought you looked just fine on camera." He cleared his throat and turned away.

Melody used her phone to check her look. *Fine.* She wasn't into makeup or trying out the latest TikTok hacks on her hair. She liked her simple look, especially when she was working on a story. She appreciated the freedom to get up and go without a lot of fuss and loss of precious minutes of sleep. Usually, 'fine' was good enough. She'd check the mirror on the way out the door or before hopping out of the van. She didn't shoot for better than 'fine'. But right now, 'fine' sounded awful coming from Dorian's mouth. She gathered her fluffy hair to the top of her head, twisted it into a fat rope, wrapped it into a bun, and crossed her arms.

"Everything okay?" Dorian asked.

"Yup." Melody's knee bounced, but she turned a fake smile on him.

"You sure? I only meant—"

"What? Meant what?" She uncrossed her arms and shuffled papers unnecessarily.

"About the lights—"

"What about the lights? Why are we still talking about the lights?"

"Because you asked when Kina was—"

"Oh right, we're talking about Kina..." Melody pulled her bag from the chair beside her. "Again..."

"N-n-no, I wasn't. I was...I hadn't answered your question. She'll be here in about fifteen minutes."

"Cool, cool, cool." Melody dug around in her bag.

"Are you sure?" Dorian jammed his hands on his waist.

"Yup," she says. She extracted a tinted lip balm. "It's fine." A tight smile pulled across her lips. *That word again.* "I mean come on! I look 'low-key sad'?" Again with the air quotes. Dorian stared at her. She was in it now. She heard herself speaking, hated her own strident tone, but doubled-down. "I mean, I love slang, in general, but only if it's clever. Love me some clever slang. But like, 'low-key sad'? It's so...I don't know...lazy? Or something? Right? It doesn't say what it's trying to say, you know?" *Good grief, am I still talking?* "I'll have you know, several subscribers have professed undying love for me this week alone." *Stop talking. Close. Mouth.*

"Oh, really?" he said. "Well, can't blame them for having good taste." Dorian turned back to the refuge of his soundboard. He connected his field equipment to the main and began organizing the sound files from the family interviews.

His words had just entered her ears when they were overtaken by voices from the soundbite track.

Betty's cousin Mark's voice filled the studio, saying "*Randell would never hurt anybody,*" followed by Nora's voice chiming in, "*Mmhmm, nope. Never.*"

"Oops, sorry!" He fumbled with the volume. He hadn't meant for the track to play, but the timing was impeccable. He glanced at Melody. She was smiling into her hands. "I had to keep reminding myself not to take everything those people said at face value just because they're old," he said, nodding toward the speaker. "It's hard, though. I have a soft spot for old faces."

Melody leaned back in her chair. Dorian leaned back, too, and went on. The flush began to drain from his cheeks.

"You know what I mean? Old people have obviously had more opportunity to commit dastardly deeds, AND more opportunity to learn how to cover their deeds up, just by virtue of the longer time they've spent on the planet. But it's those soft wrinkled cheeks, you know? Those hangdog eyelids, the wrinkly old hands. Gah! Makes me feel like a jerk to think they could've ever done anything wrong."

"Not me," Mel said. "I think everyone is up to something at all times." She set her bag back on the floor. "Maybe it's bad or sad. But I don't believe a word most people out there say." She paused, shook her head at her own disappointing attitude.

The front door opened and in jogged Kina Narvaez. The tinkle of the door alarm seemed to announce her arrival like a Disney soundtrack. She waved at Melody and Dorian from across the room and raised a finger, then leaned over in slow motion, slapping her hands against her thighs, which were encased in cropped black leggings with generous panels of mesh fabric on either side that went right up her hips. As Melody stood and stared, Kina straightened up, then leaned a toned arm on the puzzle table and bent over, taking in the half-finished scene Melody and Dorian had been working on while arching her lower back in a catlike stretch.

She rubbed the backs of her calves, the muscles flexing under her skin and reminding Melody of pulled toffee. A set of tanned abs glistened in the space between her low-folded waistband and a hard-working sports bra. She looked over the puzzle, and Melody thought for a moment she might actually touch it, but Kina put her hands back on her hips and walked in a circle, breathing at the ceiling. Loud panting breaths filled the room until she took out her earbuds and heard herself. She gave an apologetic smile, then turned serious as she inspected the earbuds, frowned, and rubbed them with her thumb.

She bounced into the studio, dabbing at her forehead with an Adidas towel. "Okay! Soy aqui, soy aqui!" she said, already catching her breath. "What do you need?"

Dorian reached under the studio table and grabbed a bottled water, tossing it in an arc that Kina intercepted perfectly with a catlike swipe. "Really just the lighting for Melody," Dorian said. "We want to offer full video of this week's episode on the website."

"Right," Kina said. "I think we talked about adding the red gel to an upper can." She glanced at Melody, then up at the lighting tree. "You don't need much. Just a punch to keep the life in your skin tone, so you don't look so washed out and dreary." She made a long face to demonstrate. Melody doubted it was possible for Kina to ever look "washed out and dreary."

Melody reached across the table and wiggled her fingers. "I'll take a bottle of that water, too," she said. "For yoga class—practice!" She shook her head in several directions and nodded, "Yoga *practice*." A high-pitched little laugh escaped, and she cleared her throat to stop it. "What are you supposed to call it? I should know *by now!*" Dorian looked surprised, but pressed his mouth closed. Melody raised her eyebrows at him, then closely scrutinized the water bottle label.

"Ooh, where do you practice?" Kina asked, her face lighting up. "Yoga Loft? Namaste Yoga? What else is around here...Oh! The one at the brewery..." She snapped her pretty fingers. "Hops and Poses?"

"No, no!" Melody looked left, thought fast, dragged her words out. "It's-uhh...It..is..a...Youtube channel." She nodded in agreement with herself. "Yeah. So good! Very—" she coughed and rolled her eyes upward in a pious manner, "—zen! Very zen." Her voice rose at the end so it came out more like a question. She pressed praying hands against the water bottle till it crackled, then set it down and crossed her arms across her belly.

Dorian gave her a bemused look and stood, leaned a hip against the table. "Yeah, Mel's been raving about it. Maybe I'll try it, too, huh Mel?"

"Sure. I'll send you a link." She spun her chair and dropped into it. "Maybe we should get started on the lighting, though, huh? Right?" She set the water bottle on the table and it tipped over. "Yeah! Need to get this episode up. Advertisers don't pay those big bucks for no content!" She righted the bottle and drummed her hands on the table. "Ready. To. Go!"

Kina worked on the lighting, adjusting the positions of the cans and trying various angles against Melody's valiant face. She added the red gel sheet and checked the effect on Melody's skin tone in the monitor over Dorian's shoulder. Melody wasn't allowed to move until they had it right, so she watched helplessly as they worked together, side by side, both of them scrutinizing her image on camera and looking back and forth between parts of her face and the screen, pointing and scrutinizing.

"Don't clench your jaw," Kina said. Melody let it drop like a marionette, then clenched her hands instead.

Dorian glanced over at her and smiled as the two of them discussed highlighting her 'gorgeous mouth,' and she responded by crossing her eyes.

"Melody doesn't need fancy lighting to look good," Dorian said.

Kina gave her an appraising look, then nodded affirmatively.

"Thanks, Dor," Melody said. The blood rose in her cheeks and she turned away.

Kina fussed a while longer, leaning close to Dorian as they worked. Melody held a tight smile till her cheeks burned. Finally, Kina was satisfied. She tucked her phone in an impossibly sexy pocket in her leggings and headed for the door, stopping again at the puzzle table. She poked a few pieces around before waving at them over her shoulder and jogging out the front door.

After Kina left, and the door shut behind her in a shimmering wake of sleek shininess, Melody scooped her notes into folders and jammed them into her tote.

"Kate Spade would not appreciate how you're handling her bag," Dorian said. "God rest her soul."

"Just in a hurry," Melody said.

"To get to yoga?"

"Oh, shut up." She picked up a stapler, examined it from different angles, and shoved it in the bag.

"What did I do?" he said innocently.

"It just came out, okay?" she said, rearranging her space unnecessarily. "She's so freaking perfect."

His expression flickered and he looked toward the front door. "You think so? I guess she is pretty fit, and very good at her job. I don't know about perfect." He sat down across the table, his hands clasped beneath the wooden expanse between them. "You are—"

"Being a butt, I know!"

"Not what I was going to say. At all."

"It wasn't?" she said. "What were you going to say then?" A flash of dumb hope coursed, and her stomach punched her heart for it.

Dorian stood. "I was going to say you're just as... even more...you know..." He started to carve an hourglass shape in the air, then crossed and uncrossed his arms and shoved his hands in the pockets.

Melody stood, too, swinging her bag over her arm. She attempted a careless laugh, but it came out as a snort as she slugged him in the shoulder. "What was that?" she said, mimicking his hands drawing in the air. "Are you trying to call me a snowman? No? An ice cream cone then. I'm shaped like a double dip from Baskin Robbins, is that it?"

"That's not what I meant and you know it," he said.

"Okay, okay," she said, letting them both off the hook of what was getting dangerously close to sexy banter. "I've got to head out. My mom's expecting me. You'll lock up when you leave?"

"Sure."

"Unless you're still here when I get back..."

"Yeah."

"Okay, bye," they said in unison.

Dorian followed her to the living room. She stopped at the puzzle table and checked to see what pieces Kina had moved, moved a few stragglers back to their color groups. Dorian opened the door and held it for her, closing it behind her with a soft, indecisive click. He leaned his forehead against the door while on the other side, Melody did the same.

BETTY,
23 YEARS OLD

1975

Betty downshifted her little green Dodge Dart and turned down the radio, but she kept humming along to the Minnie Riperton tune as she dug around in her tapestry carpet bag. She tried one more time to sing the last few bars of the chorus, after the 'lalalalas' and 'doobie doos,' but it was too high. She shook her head.

"I don't know how she does that," she mumbled, shoving her journal to one side of the bag and hooking a finger through the red plastic thermos cup handle, the thermos from her old Flintstones lunch box.

The song faded as the dj's low, nasal voice rose over the outro: "The number one hit from coast to coast on this week's American Top 40 countdown, Minnie Riperton, and 'Loving You.' I'm Casey Kasem, and until next week..."

She poured a cup of water and gulped it down. The thermos was a handy way to take cold water along when she ran errands, but she kept it in her soft woven bag, under other things, so store clerks and the check-in girls at Mama's appointments wouldn't see it and give her that quizzical look. What was so weird about it anyway? Didn't they ever watch cartoons? And anyway, it was a perfectly good thermos.

She'd woken up that day agitated and cross, and every moment since further exacerbated her raw mood. The night before, after getting Mama settled, she'd spent the evening in her room glued to the radio, scanning the dial. Just once, could she land on a channel and hear a Downtown Sound song right from the beginning? Not halfway through the second chorus, or worse, almost over? It would be like a sign, a message from Dominicus, that he thought of her. That even after five years, maybe he still remembered. She sent him messages over the airwaves all time. *Where are you? I wish you could hear me. There is so much I need to tell you.*

She'd fallen asleep with her ear close to the little speaker and woken up in the early morning to the last bars of "Penny In My Pocket" fading, giving way to the first bars of Tony Orlando & Dawn professing "He don't love you… `1" Her forehead was pressed against the edge of the bedside table, and she winced as she peeled it away. She'd slapped the radio off, and that had hurt, too. She tried to cancel them out by rubbing the sore line on her forehead with the stinging fingers, which only increased the discomfort of both.

Her prickly mood spilled into the rest of the morning. She'd hurried through her morning routine, making sure Mama was fed and settled with the bare minimum of what she needed to start her day in front of the television. Then she'd taken the shopping and errands lists off the refrigerator, scowled bitterly at Bette Davis, and left the house.

On the way back home, she passed a familiar row of signs advertising the roadside fruit stand. She'd passed these same signs hundreds of times before, announcing fruits and vegetables, each with their matching misplaced apostrophes. Peach's. Strawberry's. Mango's. Why did she care about those stupid apostrophes? *This is what my life has come to: badgering innocent people trying to sell fruit on the road-side over their grammar.*

She'd driven by and turned around, driven by once more, turned around again. Too bad the number one song in the countdown wasn't something more rousing—something with some zing, something like that Charlie Daniels one about southern rock. That would have helped. Instead she'd sung along to the sweet love song while trying to work up the nerve to stop.

Love songs used to feel like stories that were possible, used to fill her with a dreamy longing for what she knew could be hers too, one day. It didn't seem that long ago. Five years since she'd seen Dominicus. The stretch of time felt like nothing, but also like a lifetime. This was it. This was life, as it was right that minute it always would be. If she let herself dwell on it in the daytime, she couldn't get through. She'd heard on a local radio show that this Minnie Ripperton song was written in Gainesville, only an hour away. She leaned her head on the headrest and closed her eyes. Could those vibes still be in the air, could they reach her here in her car? That voice—like an angel singing about that ideal love—it set off a desperate little fire in her chest, a familiar flame that would flare up and catch in her throat before settling like ashy embers.

Betty's green cotton shirt dress stuck to her legs when she got out of the car. She slammed the door, taking a big breath and clenching her jaw as she took in the fruit stand. On her list today was a resolution to speak to the owner about his signs once and for all.

The tables and shelves were covered with a bounty of fruits and vegetables, ripe and fresh, with good Florida-Georgia soil still clinging where it could. Suddenly she was very thirsty again.

She didn't see anyone around until she heard a sound from behind the farthest table. A small television was perched on a barrel. Betty eyed the trail of mismatched extension cords that ran off behind the stand toward the building and across the parking lot toward the motel that stood beyond. The Brady Bunch was on. Bobby was saying something cute, and then Cindy said something even cuter, followed by canned laughter. A fold-out chair creaked and a man stepped out of the shadow into the blaring sun.

He was the most average man she'd ever seen. Average height. Average face. Nothing notable, but nothing terrible either. Middle-aged, she figured, by the looks of his middle and the thin white stripes of his crows feet. She stopped in front of the tables. He was peeling an apple with a pocket knife, but stopped when he looked at her.

"Afternoon, ma'am," the man said. He touched the brim of his straw hat with the knife, then pointed it toward her. That's a nice one you've got there," he said, drawing a circle in the air. She bristled, looked where he was indicating, on her chest, then relaxed. Her hand went to her necklace.

"Oh, the shark tooth," she said. "Yeah, I found it. Up there on the river bank." She said vaguely, "but listen, did you realize—"

"You found that?" he said. "That's a real nice find."

"Yes," she said, a bit deflated. "Thank you." Maybe she shouldn't say anything about the signs. They didn't seem to bother anyone else, given how long they'd stood there, unashamed of themselves, just as wrong on this side as they were on the other. Standing there looking at them from this angle, her resolve returned.

"You do know your signs have a little grammar problem, don't you?"

"My signs?"

Betty nodded toward the road. "Your signs there."

"Ah."

"Yeah." She smiled apologetically and picked up a Georgia peach from its basket. She raised it to her nose.

"Yeah." The man turned, grinding a heel in the dry roadside dirt.

"Your produce is fine," she said, loud enough to be heard over a passing car.

"Thank you. I get it twice a week from the fella who stocks my shop," he said.

"Your shop?"

"I own that motel and the shop there." He jabbed a thumb over his shoulder, then shoved his hands in the pocket of his overalls. The gesture sent a regretful pang through her belly. *What kind of mean person makes a special stop just to correct some stranger's grammar?*

She picked up a short brown bag of tomatoes and gave them a sniff, raising her brows as if very impressed. "I'm sorry I was so blunt about it. It's just that...well, you have a fine stand here, don't you?" She gestured over the tables, smiled at a cantaloupe. "Those signs are your first impression to folks driving by this way." The man clasped his hands behind his back and tromped back to the side of the road. Betty inspected a pint of strawberries. "I did wait a while, to see if they'd be fixed." She called, by way of apology.

The man shuffled his boots in the sandy dirt. He was tall, tall as she was, and might have been handsome a few years ago. He'd smiled when he said hello, and his eyes crinkled the way nice people's eyes do.

A small cloud of gnats took flight around him, but he stood firm, ignoring them with great purpose till he was forced to swat one away from his eye. His gaze drifted down the road over his row of signs. "I've been meaning to fix...that." It came out a bit like a question.

"Oh! Well, that's good to hear."

"Oh yes." His face reddened. "It was my buddy painted those and I, well, I didn't want to say anything to him, you understand. Wouldn't want to seem ungrateful now, would I?"

"Of course not. Especially not when he was so good to do that for you. Maybe he wouldn't mind, though? It's an easy fix, really."

"How would you suggest I go about that?" he said. She came to stand beside him and looked in the same direction. Another car passed, kicking up a haze of hot reddish dust. "I mean, I know how I would do it." He let that trail off. She didn't reply, so he went on: "But you are the customer! 'The customer is always right', and all that." He laughed. He inhaled a gnat and coughed.

Betty pretended she didn't notice. "Well, I think it will be a simple fix. Just paint over them and fix the endings. That's all they need."

"Paint over them?" His voice rose. "Well then, what good would the signs be?"

"Not over the whole sign. Just over the apostrophes." Her head tilted. "And then fix the endings. No need to repaint them completely. Unless he wants to. Couldn't hurt to freshen them up."

"Right, right, that's just what I was thinking, too," he said.

"Good," Betty said. She handed him a thin stack of dollar bills.

"What'll you do with that okra?"

"Oh, probably pickle them for my mama."

He nodded, his voice and expression greatly relieved. "Best thing for 'em," he said. "You got a recipe?" He worked out her change. A gnat flew around his face, swooping to avoid his hand every time he swiped. Gnats were one thing that could infuriate Betty and she wore a dab of peppermint oil behind each ear in the summer to keep them away, but this guy barely reacted. He went on talking. "I have my daddy's prize-winning family recipe for pickled okra. It won the blue ribbon at the Duval County Fair."

"Did it now?" she said. She took a step closer, genuinely interested, and his eyes grew wide. She clapped once, checked her hands, and showed him the smashed gnat on her palm. He touched the brim of his hat. She dusted the bug off on her skirt and accepted the handful of change. "But yessir, I do have a recipe." She squeezed her plastic change purse and dropped the coins in then dropped it in her bag. "My mama only will only eat them a certain way."

"Oh, well, her loss, I say. But to each their own."

"Yes," she turned to leave. "You have a good day now."

"Will do, and you do the same," he said. His mouth opened, then closed again.

She placed the produce on the scalding hood of the car to dig for her keys, trying not to look back toward the stand as she maneuvered her bags. He was watching, she felt it, and she wondered if she could possibly appear any more awkward.

"Miss?" His voice grew closer along with the sound of his boots in the dirt. Betty resolved to refuse help, then realized he may have decided not to let her comments on his signs pass quite so easily. She shut the passenger door and took a step backward, keys in hand. He stopped a few yards away, put his hands back in his pockets.

"I have some of that pickled okra put up," he said, "if you've a mind to try it."

Betty strode around the back of her car to the other side in a few steps. She lifted her door handle. "That's quite al lright, sir." She slid into the seat and fumbled the key into the ignition. The man shifted from foot to foot but stayed in his spot.

"Oh, I didn't mean right now," he said, a little louder. She drove the few feet to where he stood and he spoke through the closed window. "I can bring them out here to the stand, for next time you stop by."

Betty smiled, her shoulders relaxed. "I'd love to try them, sure. That would be fine." He gave a thumbs up and stepped back from the car.

She started to drive away, but stopped and put the car in park, reached over and rolled down the passenger window. "I'm Betty, by the way," she said, reaching a hand out.

He took his hand from his pocket, dusted it on his pant leg, and stretched it through the window, leaning down so his face was framed in the open window. "My name's Randell," he said. "Randell Van Disson."

BETTY,
23 YEARS OLD

APRIL 12, 1975

Diary,

Took Mama to her appointment with the new doctor today. There were so many forms and they had to be filled out in triplicate. Who doesn't have a Xerox machine by now? Or at least carbon paper. He was the oldest doctor I've ever seen, and the nurse at the front desk may have been older than him. I asked for a Kleenex and you would have thought tissues were on ration, like 'Save a Tissue for the Troops.'

The radio was on in the waiting room and they played 'Free Bird.' I closed my eyes and I guess I swayed my head a little too much during Allen Collins' guitar solo at the end, because when I opened them again the nurse was staring at me over her little glasses, all puckered up like she was sucking on a lemon.

I pointed at the speaker in the ceiling and said, "They're from here."

"I know," she said, "that's the only reason I don't turn it off." What a pill.

This doctor's office is close to downtown, right off the freeway that cut a whole new path through here. It's like what was here before never was here. If you didn't know, you'd never guess. I only know because Dominicus told me about it once. Come to think of it, I always did want to write down the things he told me about his family. At first it was too hard to think about it, to remember our conversations and those good times getting to know each other. After a while, it seemed easier not to think about it. Let me go ahead and give it a try now.

His grandfather was named Lucius, I think that's how you'd spell 'Lucius,' and that was his mama's daddy. He came from Gullah Geechee people who've lived here for generations. He was a deacon at an AME Church. (That stands for 'African Methodist Episcopal.') He helped found a bank for the African American community, and he helped finance new neighborhood businesses and support the older, established ones. He practiced law with a firm that had an office in the Black Masonic Temple, and I think Dominicus said he was on an advisory board at Edward Waters College. Or maybe that was another relative. His family was very active in the community, I know I remember that part. Both sides of his parents' families had owned homes on 8th Street in Sugar Hill, which was Jacksonville's finest African American neighborhood, but most of it was demolished to make room for the new stretch of I-95. And the new hospital, which is the thing that brought me there today. He said that after that, the neighborhood on the other side of the freeway went into decline, the family moved out around the city—further north and to the near Westside, like Sly's mother did.

I had never heard of 'red-line neighborhoods' until I met Dominicus. Now I read the newspapers whenever I can. I don't want to be in the dark anymore. Don't want to be blindsided ever again. There is no safety in idealism.

Dominicus's mother was born in his maternal grandfather's fine family home, a red brick two story house with a big porch and balconies upstairs. I saw a photograph of it once. It was beautiful. His mama's auntie was a well-known midwife and the story went that she got to the house just in time to catch the baby, she was that ready to get here. I always thought that was a dear story.

There. Now I've got that down. I'm glad coming out here reminded me of all that. The longer I'm away from Dominicus, the more it seems like it was all a dream. Mama got no new answers from this doctor, but now coming out to this doctor's office wasn't a complete waste of time. Maybe Ms. Owens was born right where I was sitting today waiting for Mama to get her stomach looked at. Or maybe I drove right over the spot.

While we were in the waiting room, a song came on that I remembered from somewhere. It was driving me crazy trying to remember, but finally it came to me. It was on a variety show I used to watch with Mama when I was a kid. Come to think of it, I should have been in bed, but Mama never did bother about a bedtime, and I used to watch The Tonight Show. I guess I was about twelve years old. That night, the show came on late because they were showing a recap of the March on Washington. I remembered all that because of that one song that played on The Tonight Show.

I sat up watching that show with Mama. I remember she fell asleep in her chair in front of the TV and I took advantage. Her cigarette was dangling from her hand, kind of precariously, so I slid it from her fingers. I snuck a few puffs before I stubbed it out in her amber glass ashtray (that was my first taste of nicotine), and then I stayed up watching till she snored herself awake. The Tonight Show was back on by then, and the musical guest played that song I heard on the radio today. I can't get over how that works. How hearing a song can trigger a whole avalanche of memories. Like a snowball on top of a mountain, it grows as it rolls toward you, unstoppable. Uncontrollable.

That man Randell from the produce stand came in while we waited. That was a coincidence. I almost didn't recognize him out of his overalls. He said 'hey' and met Mama and all. She said I should talk to him. Once she heard he owns a motel and a liquor store, not to mention the produce stand where I got that okra, she acted like he was Prince Charles or something, bowing her head and calling him 'Sir.' I swear, she almost curtsied. She asked him right out if he was there with his wife, and he looked embarrassed and told her no, he wasn't married. Mama elbowed my rib so hard I yelled out, "Ow!" and the nurse gave me another dirty look. I told mama, "Why don't <u>you</u> talk to him?" She said, "See if I don't, if you pass on him. Maybe even if you don't."

When the nurse called us in, he stood up. For a second, I thought he meant to come in with us. But he cleared his throat like he was about to make a speech.

"Miss Betty," he said, "I did bring out some of my daddy's pickled okra, like I said I'd do."

"Oh, yes?" I said. "Well, I'll be sure to stop by your stand next week."

"I was thinking, if you didn't mind, I'd just as soon bring it out to you," he said, "to your house." His earnest expression was like a little kid practicing his manners. Mama drew herself up straighter and clasped her gloved hands as if he were asking for my hand right then and there.

"I guess that would be fine," I said. "You can come around on—"

"Tomorrow," Mama interrupted. "We'll be home all day tomorrow. Betty will make a nice supper."

Randell looked from Mama to me, and I nodded. "Fine, yes. That will be just fine, Randell. We'll see you tomorrow then?"

The nurse shuffled the pages on her clipboard and made a huffing sound.

"Tomorrow it is," Randell said.

TABS AND BLANKS
PODCAST

Transcript
Season 2, Episode 7: On The Trail

Welcome back to The Chimney Sweep! At this point, listeners, you are caught up to where we are in the investigation. From here on out, I'll be reporting each week more or less in real time. We have some interviews lined up in the coming days and a few leads I'm running down. We've gotten a lot of questions on the boards over on our website, and we appreciate them! Rest assured that we are running down every lead and following every rabbit.

I want to take a minute here for a word from our sponsor. Branches DNA is offering our listeners a special discount if you use the code: CHIMNEY. I sent in my sample just last week. It couldn't have been easier.

Just go to www dot BranchesDNA dot com and enter the code...

BETTY,
24 YEARS OLD

1976

Betty pulled at the scratchy lace collar of her ivory wedding dress and avoided looking at her new husband. She watched the sawgrass and palmetto rush by the passenger side window. The wedding had been a simple affair, despite Mama's sequined red gown.

Randell took A1A—he avoided I-95 as a matter of principle—down to St. Augustine for their weekend honeymoon. They stayed in a motel that looked a lot like the one that would soon be Betty's home, only shinier and without harboring the impression of trying to hide in the trees. Across the street, the Matanzas River rippled dark and slow like mercury under a blue-smoked sky.

So this was it. She looked around at every item individually: a yellow ceramic lamp with a brass base, gold curtain panels tacky with humidity and the leavings of other people's hands, a dull burgundy bedspread with plastic thread quilting, its surface and lurid gold tassels dangling provocatively from the corners. This was where it would happen. Her wedding night.

Betty's mama had sent her off with her version of a blessing and a declaration that Randell Van Disson was "not a bad catch." Not bad at all. He owned that motel and that liquor store, didn't he? And all that land. Enterprising fellow, setting up that fruit stand when the liquor sales went down. If she hadn't been so unwell, she could have had him for herself. But Betty getting him was good enough. Surely these two would eventually stop behaving like polite brother and sister and get over their obvious lack of chemistry. What mattered was that she and Betty were set now, no doubt about it.

While Randell washed in the motel bathroom sink, gargling while scrubbing with a washcloth at his armpits and at his neck, Betty turned on the radio. She edged the volume up just loud enough to drown him out and then fiddled with the dial, flicking forward over a nasal voice giving the local weather report, a low-toned conversation on how to keep your squash plants from dropping flowers, a sermon on the evils of drink. A string of country music stations, and she paused to hear the end of a Wanda Jackson tune—*that woman has soul*—then kept scrolling. At the sound of a five part harmony, she stopped, adjusted the dial.

'*...I've got a penny in my pocket and my girl in front of me, what more do I need...*'

A deep voice resonated from the speaker, inches from Betty's face: "Here it is for you! The one you all've been requesting. 'Penny In My Pocket' by our own Florida boys The Downtown Sound..."

Betty closed her eyes. *Never fails.* Her stomach tightened as her heart lurched to her throat.

Randell spat out the mouthwash. "Thought I heard that ol' Hank Williams' song. How about turning on back to that?"

She hadn't realized he could hear over the running water and the gargling. "Which one?"

"That ol' 'Love Sick Blues,'" he said.

"It wasn't Hank," Betty said, turning the dial back. Randell's back stiffened. He turned off the taps and looked up, drying his ears and talking into the mirror.

"What was that?" His voice was a tap on a tin can. Betty looked away from his reflection.

"Just that it wasn't Hank." She settled the dial back on the song. "That's Emmett Miller."

"Oh, yes?" He tossed the towel in the sink. "Well, yeah. Sure enough. I hear that now." His face had gone red. Betty's lips drew in between her teeth. *Shouldn't have corrected him—what difference did it make?*

"I heard some Wanda Jackson. Want me to find that?" she said. *No problem. Everything's fine.*

"No, never mind that now," he said. He pulled an undershirt over his head and sat on the bed to put on his shoes. "I'm fixin' to go find us something. Some Cokes, maybe." He walked by her and stopped with his hand on the knob, his back to her. She wished he'd hurry if he was going to go. "I guess you like Coke?"

"Oh, yes!" she said, trying to sound like a bride—bright, fizzy. "I love Coke. And thank you."

He lowered his head and ambled out the door.

Betty spun the dial back to the spot. The dj was speaking over the end of the song. "Well now, there you go. That's a mighty fine track! Next up, a little Wilson Picket, with his smokin' cover of "Hey Jude…"

A small flame lit in her chest with a churning feeling, warm and thick. Beads of sweat formed above her lip and a chill ran down her neck, down through her limbs, like ice water, finding the warm, dark places and turning them to cold, coarse sand paper. Her mind went back in time, and she was in the outbuilding behind the school, eighth grade, in the auto shop, where boys learned to work on car engines while girls took home ec in the kitchen next door. The lunch bell rang. She walked out with the other girls, but turned around and went back. She'd left a book behind. Mr. McCoy asked her to come in to the garage, could she help him with something in his office real quick?

It had been painful, terrifying, his rough hands stained black with grease in the creases and around his fingernails, his mustache like a scrub brush against her face, her neck, her chest. She couldn't get free. Her eyes fell bleary on a poster on the wall, some black words on a yellow background—'right choice,' or 'wrong choice,' maybe it had said 'no choice'?—the words had floated, defying order. He pushed away from her after, pulled a small black comb from a chest pocket embroidered with his name in a silly cursive font, and dragged it across the top of his head, smiling. She'd vomited at his feet, splashing his shoes before running away and he'd shouted something after her, unafraid of being heard.

If she hadn't left her composition book, or if she'd decided to just leave it, for goodness sake, or if she'd kept up with Junie and the other girls and gone on to lunch. If she hadn't let herself been caught alone. Afterward, she'd found her friends in the courtyard outside the cafeteria, huddled around a transistor radio hidden in Junie's purse. Junie kept her hand inside with her finger on the volume control in case a teacher came by.

Junie had taken in Betty's disheveled hair, her crooked blouse collar. "What's eating you, Betty?" she'd said. Betty's mouth wouldn't move just then, though she tried to force her lips to form words. Her stomach lurched, like the moment you lose a balloon. Then Georgie had driven up in his dad's new Firebird, and Junie jumped off the bench and bopped away squealing, her perfect ponytail swinging in the sunlight, her world still perfect.

Even though she shouldn't—especially not tonight—Betty let herself think of Dominicus, their one night together in Macon. There was no pain that night, only love. Perhaps it would be like that. Maybe not like that, but it could be fine. She breathed deliberately—in slowly, then out. In slowly again. The sweat began to wick away, down to the small of her back, and she shivered. Now the radio played Aretha, "I Never Loved A Man." She knew, couldn't help remembering even in this moment, this record was recorded in Muscle Shoals.

She could have gone with him to Muscle Shoals.

The key was in the lock and the door knob turned. She changed the station.

"Oh, yeah!" Randell said. The soda cans clanked on the table top and he dropped his wallet and keys beside them, did a little shuffle. In the whole one year they'd been keeping company, she'd never seen Randell try to dance. "My daddy loved him some Hank Williams."

Betty smiled. "Me, too. I like him, too."

Soon she'd know how Randell was, if he would be gentle and kind, or rough, taking what he wanted from her. She'd know once and for all what her life with him was going to be like.

Randell carried a flat package under his arm, wrapped in brown paper and twine. He set it on the floor in front of his legs and leaned it against his knees, dusted his hands and put them on his hips. "Well, I got you something. Here it is," he said. "Here you go."

"What is that?"

"Well, I suppose since they wrapped it, you probably ought to open it."

Betty walked the small patch of rug between them. She waited but he didn't pick it up, so she reached for the sides of the package, turning her head as her face got close to his waist. She turned to the bed and laid the package down, gave a grateful smile. She began to recognize the size and shape. "Is this—"

"Open it and see." He had already turned and gone back to the sink. He poured a glass of water and leaned against the counter, watching in the mirror. When Betty looked over at him, he looked away.

"In the lobby mensroom, they have a barber shop pole up on the wall as a light. That's pretty smart, huh? Do you think that's smart?"

"Yeah, that's a clever idea."

"Maybe I should get one for the motel."

"Maybe."

"Why don't you open the package?"

"Right." Betty pulled at the end of the twine. The twine fell away and the paper came open slightly. She pushed the folded ends away and lifted the edges.

"It is," she said. Her eyes flicked over red flowers on a windblown poinciana tree with a curving beach cove and palm tree beyond. She grasped the frame, her thumbs rubbing the rough-carved grooves in the wood. "It's the painting from the lobby."

Randell nodded. "You liked it when we checked in, so—"

"That's very thoughtful."

"I thought it would look good in our lobby."

"It will."

"Yes, I think so."

"You're right." Betty folded the crackly paper back down and smoothed it over the painting. She tied the twine back into a neat bow, lifted the package off the bed, and leaned it against the wall. Then she sat at the foot of the bed, and waited.

BETTY,
25 YEARS OLD

OCTOBER 20, 1977

Dear Diary,

I got this little blank book today from the delivery fellow who stocks the card rack. It was free! A gift for being a loyal customer, he said. That's a good idea. Maybe we should offer some free gifts to loyal customers. How many of those do we have? Four? Haha.

Such a pretty little journal! So fine. And all the pages are so clear and white. Just flipping through them makes me want to write and write. There are so many words inside of me every day and I feel like I just swallow them back down over and over until they jumble up and get clumped up. Constipated. I suppose I could take some ExLax. (There I've gone and written something gross in the very first paragraph.) Instead I think I'll write in here when I'm bored or lonely, like I used to do.

Randell doesn't like when I say things like 'gross' and 'out of sight.' Asks me how I know all this 'slang talk.' I put him off by pointing out the magazine rack right there in his own shop.

Today's my wedding anniversary.

I really shouldn't get bored. There's plenty to stay busy with. The rooms always need dusting, at least, and I'm never done vacuuming it seems! It's a good motel. It is a little further down from the border, sure, but I think our mattresses are nicer and I make sure our package prices are a dollar less than up at the St. Mary's. Have to get them in how we can, Randell says, especially now folks prefer the interstate for getting to Orlando. We still get a good dry Sunday crowd from Georgia, and folks who came through with their parents when they were kids on family vacation, they want to take the same route now with their own kids. That's sweet, I guess. Nostalgia holds things together around here, in lots of ways.

I gave the shelves a good cleaning today and helped some folks find their purchases. Well, I guess I do every day. Someone left this fine pen I'm using in one of the motel rooms. I brought it up here to the lobby for safe keeping, but I don't suppose it would hurt for me to use it just to write in here. Maybe they'll never even realize they lost it, and if they do, maybe they won't know where. Anyway, no sense having it just sitting there, and I just got this little book and all.

Oh, looks like somebody's pulling up outside.

I'm back again. Junie just stopped by and made me turn on the TV. I can't let myself think on it. I just can't. Lynyrd Skynyrd's plane crashed in Mississippi. It's just too awful. Junie was crying and carrying on like she knew them. Not as upset as when Duane

Allman crashed his motorcycle, though. She always says Randell looks like Duane if he'd have cut his hair, tells him he should grow his hair out. She really had a thing for that hippie guy with the guitar. The boy sure could play.

But I can't let myself think about the plane crash. Or that motorcycle crash. I hope Dominicus doesn't fly in little planes. Or ride motorcycles.

Junie thinks it's strange that Randell and I don't sleep together. I don't know what made me tell her, but now that I have, and seeing her reaction, maybe it is strange to live this way. After our honeymoon, when he was done in two minutes and fell asleep, it was like "well, I guess that's done." His face was so red, like he had a job to do and was embarrassed at his performance. And he never came to me again. That was fine with me. I suppose it has seemed like we just have a different kind of marriage. There are different kinds of marriages, right?

Junie doesn't think so. She got this strange look in her eye, the look she gets when there's a challenge, or a dare. Maybe she thinks she can figure out a plan for me to change things. The thing is, even if she comes back with some sort of advice, I don't know that I'd want to take it. I'm fine with things between Randell and me staying just as they are, if that's how he wants it. I know he's not a real husband to me, but Loreen says there's different kinds of husbands for different kinds of lives. This is my kind of life. It is now anyway. He's a different kind of man, that's all. And this must be a different kind of marriage.

Well, I felt bad for using the pen. Put it in the lost and found and got this plain old pen from the cup on the front desk. It's not so nice and smooth to write with, but it does fine.

My goodness but don't these days get long sometimes. Randell is out on a call to service a chimney near the city. He specializes in those old chimneys, it seems like. Drops everything for a service call down in Avondale or Riverside, especially. Guess he just likes those old brick ones. He lets me come sometimes, if we have help in the shop or if the motel is empty. "They don't make them like this anymore." That's what he tells the owners of those old houses. Big grand ones and little bungalows, too. They have those old, solid, brick chimneys that stay standing even when a hurricane takes everything else down. Guess I can understand why he likes them.

When folks call the number on his business card, it's me they usually get on the phone. I book his jobs and tell him right away if the address is one of those old ones. Boy, does he rip those ones out of my hand and jump on them! Never thought I'd be all right with a man being like that, so short and a little rude if you think about it.

Something I noticed is how Randell's interest in the chimney sweep business grew after his daddy died. Ninety-three years old and the man still kept that business up with Randell's help. When his father passed, Randell said he had to keep the business, in honor of his daddy, the fire marshal who thought it was so important to teach the community about home fire safety.

Well, okay.

That's what I said to him, too. "Well, okay, Randell. You go on ahead and keep up the chimney sweep business." He said he promised his daddy on his death bed. I saw the old man whisper something in Randell's ear the last time he saw him. Maybe he was making him promise to keep it going.

Someone is pulling up to the fruit stand, be right back.

Hope they don't want to talk about the plane crash.

December 12, 1977
Dear Diary,

Okay, I'm back. Sorry it's been a few weeks, though. There was a story I wanted to get down in here. I've been reading *Little Women* again, and it made me want to try writing a story out of something that happened to me, like they say Louisa May Alcott did with Jo March? I used to get really good grades in English back in school. Anyway, here goes a story about what happened to me the other day:

Choir Practice
by Betty Van Disson

Yesterday at choir practice, Brother Willard was in one of his high-key tizzies. He'd had the tuner come in to work on the piano that afternoon, but he said the dang fool had dropped his tuning hammer on the concrete and couldn't finish the job.

"And me without my pitch pipe!" Brother Willard lamented.

A voice came from the choir. "If it helps, Brother Willard, I can find middle C in my head." It was Betty. Betty stood on the top row of the risers, on the end, next to the wall. She was so tall, her head was practically in the rafters.

"Oh, can you now, Betty?" Brother Willard said, pinching his pointy nose between two fingers. "Can you, indeed..."

"Yes, sir," Betty said, trying to sound confident.

"You have perfect pitch, do you?" He gave her a dubious look. The ladies of the choir either shifted their gazes down, flipping pointlessly through their hymnals as if the correct pitch might lay in there somewhere, or else they turned in place to look right at her with challenging eyes.

"Well, yes, I suppose if being able to find middle C without the piano means perfect pitch, I do have that," Betty said.

Brother Willard sighed. "Oh, well then by all means, Sister Betty. Be my guest." He swooped his hand as if to say, "The stage is yours."

Betty started wishing she'd kept her mouth closed, but it was too late now. She closed her eyes and listened in her mind till she could hear it, then started singing.

"*Carry on my wayward son, there'll be peace when you are done.*"

"Sister Betty, what hymn is that?" Brother Willard said, a little alarmed.

Betty held up a finger. "I'm-not-there-yehhht..." She sang her reply on the same note where he'd interrupted her:

"*Lay your weary head to rest, don't you cry no mooore,*" Betty sang. She sang the last word, went down an octave, and held the note. Eyes wide, she pointed to her mouth, nodding.

"Are you saying that is middle C, Sister Betty?" Brother Willard said, incredulous. He looked like a big old bass fish.

Betty stopped holding the note and swallowed. "Yes, sir."

A high voice spoke up from the front row. One of those diva sopranos, as usual. "Why, Brother Willard! Brother Willard! That song ain't no hymn!"

"What's that, Sister Carol?" Brother Willard said.

"That song she's singing! It's evil!" Sister Carol said, her mouth contorting. "It's a *rock song!*"

Brother Willard looked as though his red face could fly right off, it shuddered so much.

"Is that true, Sister Betty?" he said. His jowls jiggled with righteous indignation.

"It is true! It is!" came a chorus of agreement from the choir, starting 'pianissimo' and rising to very 'fortissimo.' "It's the devil's music! And she brought it in the Lord's house!"

Betty looked over all the permed, hairsprayed, indignant heads. She looked at Brother Willard. As he stared at her, his face growing redder by the second, his arm raised and his fist opened up so he could point at the door.

"We won't be needing you in our choir any more, Mrs. Van Disson," he said.

The whole choir nodded and murmurs passed between them. They made a path for her to step down the risers.

"Well, all right then," Betty said, mainly to herself. Her face burned. She gathered her handbag and her scarf, then she turned back to face them. "But isn't it interesting that you all knew the song so very well yourselves." She smiled, then she sang the guitar riff right at them: "Bah dah dah DAHHH," she turned on her heels, "bah dah dah DAAHH."

Then Betty raised her chin and marched out of the church, leaving a tableau of dumb shock behind her.

THE END

Well, that's my story, loosely based on real-life events. Story Betty handled it better than Real Life Betty did. Real Life Betty prayed she'd get raptured right off the risers and through the ceiling.

Guess that's the end of my church choir career.

Anyway, somebody's pulling up in the lot. I'm so glad to have this diary. I'm not much of a writer, but like I say, I do have a lot of words stuck in me.

TABS AND BLANKS
PODCAST

Transcript
Season 2, Episode 8: In Studio with a Private
Investigator

This week on The Chimney Sweep:

"She had all this evidence, hours of taped conversation and her own observations as a close relative, and basically they didn't want to hear it..."

We're in the studio with a guest who has been looking at Betty Van Disson's case, and she had uncovered never-before-heard recordings made by Betty's own cousin just weeks after Betty went missing:

"Why would they not want to hear what I had recorded—straight from Randell's mouth?"

Last week, we got a call in the show's message hotline:

"Yes, this is Rebecca Dowe. I'm a private investigator and I looked into the case of Betty Van Disson a few years ago. I have some information you might be able to use..."

Private Investigator Rebecca Dowe runs her own legal investigations firm in Lake City, Florida. She has worked on some of Florida's highest profile missing person and murder cases, and she agreed to come to Jacksonville to meet with us in our new studio.

Melody: Thank you so much for driving in to speak with us today, Rebecca. You are our first guest in the new digs!

Rebecca: Thank you for having me. This is nice. Very high-tech. I have no clue what all these gadgets and devices are. So many little lights!

Melody: That's okay, neither do I! That's all Dor. I mean Dorian! He's the sound genius.

Dorian: Aww shucks.

Rebecca: I'm honored to be the first. I'll add it to my resume.

Melody: 'Guinea pig for upstart podcasters, 2019.' That would look great on your LinkedIn profile.

Rebecca: Right? Hollywood will be knocking at my door.

Dorian: Oh, tell them I have a screenplay!

By the way, listeners, we'd love to hear how you like our new sound design. Drop us a line wherever you listen to podcasts, or on our website.

Melody: So Rebecca, you were looking into this case, you said, a few years ago, correct?

Rebecca: Right.

Melody: And in your research and talking to people who were around the Van Dissons at the time, folks who lived in the area—and I think you said you spoke to some customers—you ended up speaking to one of Betty's cousins. Could you tell us about that?

Rebecca: Sure. I don't know if I should use her name.

Melody: That would be Loreen, is that right? Mark and Nora brought up the existence of some recordings when I interviewed them also. They said we needed to contact her, and we have done that. We hope to interview her soon.

Rebecca: So yes, one of the family members I spoke to recommended I get in touch with Betty's cousin Loreen. So, they were saying the same back then, too. They said Loreen had recordings of conversations with Randell taken just a few weeks after Betty went missing, and that maybe the recordings might have information that could have lead somewhere.

Melody: Now I noticed you said 'could have led somewhere.'

Rebecca: Yes, and that's because when Loreen tried to share the recordings with authorities, while the case was still relatively new, she said they didn't take her information seriously.

Melody: And why do you think that was?

Rebecca: I really couldn't say. I tried to speak with the detective—

Melody: Detective Billy John Whitaker.

Rebecca: Right. And he said he couldn't comment on that. He did go ahead and say what he thought about the person who had made the recordings, though. So my feeling was that he didn't trust whatever was on the tapes, or maybe didn't necessarily believe they were real. That's just the feeling I got. I wouldn't say I'm necessarily right about that.

Melody: But you are a private investigator. You have pretty good judgment on this type of thing.

Rebecca: Sometimes, yes. A large percentage of the time.

Melody: Gotcha. So you met with this person—and for the listeners, we have reached out to them and we're in the middle of a game of phone tag, but we hope to have the chance to interview her here on the show as well—but you met with them and... what happened?

Rebecca: Well, it was really interesting. There are recordings of several conversations made over a weekend. She, I guess I can say 'she,' went to the property, and Randell sat down with her. She brought casseroles and pies for him, stocked his fridge as Southern people do in bad times. This was very soon after Betty disappeared, so it has the value of being close to the event itself, and Randell did not know he was being recorded.

Melody: Maybe that's why Detective Billy John didn't want to hear it.

Rebecca: Maybe. But still, I would think as the lead detective he'd at least listen to see if it might lead somewhere. Whether or not it was admissible later on, if Betty were alive and perhaps in trouble, or if any little thing sparked a line of investigation that lead to finding her, it would have been worth it at the time.

Melody: Absolutely. And you heard the tapes, so can you share what he was saying about Betty's disappearance?

Rebecca: Yes, I did listen to them. And mostly Randell just waxed philosophical about his marriage, about his life with Betty, what he thought might have happened to her. He seemed to believe that she just got tired of living out there and running the motel and liquor store, and she took off.

Melody: Really.

Rebecca: Yes. He said he'd always been afraid she'd eventually get tired of it, and he guessed she finally had. But it was hard to discern from just listening whether he was being honest or being cautious.

Melody: I should say here for our listeners that this is all hearsay, of course, but Rebecca is a licensed private investigator, and the fruits of her investigation are details that could be taken as testimony in court.

Rebecca: Thank you.

Melody: There was another disappearance in the area only about, what was it, eight years before this, correct? Another woman, a bit older than Betty but still, a mature woman, who disappeared from another motel and liquor store not far from

Randell and Betty's Maryview. What, if any connection was there at the time?

Rebecca: Yes. That was the missing person case of Nellie Olfort. The cases had striking similarities. Both motel and liquor store owners on the same stretch of highway, both women just disappeared, both husbands refused to let police onto their land to search. It was looked into, and Randell and the husband in that case, one Knud Olfort, did know each other, knew of each other in any case. I think Betty's case would have helped reopen Nellie's, and maybe investigators would have been able to piece things together and perhaps determine whether there were any links between their cases, if not for what happened so soon after Betty's disappearance.

Melody: Which was...?

Rebecca: Which was September 11, 2001.

Melody: 9-11

Rebecca: Right. It's obvious from FBI files alone that Betty's case was basically dropped after that date. FBI bureaus around the country went on high alert, but especially here in Florida. People don't realize the role Florida's FBI units play in United States security. There just wasn't the bandwidth to deal with the disappearance of a rural woman when it was 'all hands on deck' somewhere elsewhere.

Melody: So Betty's case got pushed to the back burner, and ultimately nothing came of it. It was not that long after the body of the other missing woman from the area, Nellie Olfort, was actually found, basically by chance during some military diving practice. Maybe that made it easier for officials to write off Betty's disappearance, too. Like, maybe something similar to what happened to Nellie also happened to Betty. Since they didn't have the manpower, her case languished.

Rebecca: That's right. It happened all over the country at that point. Many cases were put on hold, some would say 'understandably.' But it's still very sad.

Melody: It is. Moving forward, where does that leave us? We're looking at it now, and we're not going to let it drop this time. You've probably had access to more documentation from this investigation than any other single person. What do you think happened to Betty Van Disson?

MELODY

2019

Melody pulled off her headphones and pushed her chair back from the table. She glanced at Dorian and they locked eyes, nodding silent agreement. The interview with the private investigator was a wrap.

Rebecca seemed in no great hurry to take off her headphones. She'd brought pages of quotable sound-bites along to the studio, and she was only half-way through them. When Dorian gave the two-minute signal, she checked the time and seemed genuinely shocked that two hours had passed. She took a gulp from her water bottle and leaned back, tilting her chair and shooting a bemused expression back and forth between Melody and Dorian.

"Great stuff," Melody said. "Thanks for doing this."

"No problem, thanks for having me," Rebecca said. "I'm sorry I couldn't do more…"

Dorian glanced at Melody and registered tension in her face.

"No, no! It's okay. I was just caught off guard," Melody said. "Wasn't prepared to hear it like that. On the phone, you seemed less sure."

"I know, but the more I thought back on it...I really do think the most likely thing is she jumped off that blue bridge and took her own life."

Melody had tacked Betty's photo to the studio wall—a sepia-toned moment when Betty had stood outside the Maryview, her arms crossed over her waist. Melody looked up at the photo, as she'd done so many times each day since the start of this story. She raised her gaze to the composed, unsmiling, yet pretty face. Betty was beginning to look familiar, taking on the specter of a long-lost face from a childhood memory. Her photo looked down over the proceedings in the studio with ironic interest, as if waiting to hear one word about her that might approach the truth.

Rebecca had opened the podcast website on her laptop and was scanning the comments. "Look at this! This person says 'Melody is 'hot, *all be it* a little fluffy.' It's 'albeit,' Genius!" She shouted, backhanding the screen. Dorian winced. "On the other hand, Melody, you'll be flattered to know that they *do* go on to assert that they would, and I quote, 'still hit that'."

"Ugh, can I block him?" Melody said.

"I think it might be a 'her' actually, Melody," Rebecca said. "Way to make assumptions. That's how you get yourself canceled, you know."

Melody reached in front of Rebecca and took over the keyboard. As she clicked through the posts, her mind went back over replies she had posted on the boards recently. How often had she assumed genders? She never even thought about checking pronouns. Her stomach churned as she scanned the threads for negative replies.

Rebecca leaned back in her chair. She watched the two young hosts of one of America's fastest-rising podcasts, and she shook her head. Melody had noticed her teasing expressions during her interview.

"It's cute how you blush when she calls you 'Dor,'" Rebecca said, and her expression went from curious to amused. She pointed a red fingernail back and forth between them.

"So what *is* going on here?" she said.

Dorian's face froze. Melody shot him a surprised look before her own face went awkwardly slack.

"What do you mean?" she said, at the same time as Dorian said, "We're not dating." They looked at each other again.

"Uh huh," Rebecca said. She jabbed the arms of her sunglasses through her frosted helmet of hair and smirked. "Okay."

Melody coughed. "He means...we just...people ask us that all the time," she said, the gift of gab thoroughly abandoning her.

Dorian made a complicated show of shutting down production for the day. He peered at buttons which urgently needed pressing and lights that required immediate, up-close inspection. His forehead was red, the pinched lines colliding in the space between his brows.

Melody felt him glance at her. He'd caught her smiling, and smiled even wider than her. She suddenly felt as though she were on a ferris wheel, round and round, up and down.

"But anyway, he's right. We're not dating," she said.

"Well, why the hell not?" Rebecca said, eyes wide as the Botox would let them. "I don't see any rings on those fingers. You're both hot. And you obviously make a good team." She delivered her pronouncements with utter confidence.

Melody tried to reciprocate. "Well, Rebecca, I don't know," she said too loudly, "I don't know 'why the hell not'."

Stop! She didn't know where to look. She turned to Dorian, but her mouth kept moving. "Why the hell not, Dorian?"

What? Why?! Stop talking! She wished for the ability to inhale her own words, some sort of supernatural recall button. Rebecca had put her on the spot, and that spot was a tender one.

Rebecca leaned back, a self-satisfied look on her face, with all the annoying confidence of a woman who knew when seemingly-smooth places could stand some roughing up. When it came to intuition, her track record spoke for itself. Sure, sometimes she was wrong, but only about things that didn't count. It would be a shame to miss an opportunity to be right. She crossed her legs and pressed on.

"Well, Dorian?"

He looked around the floor under his feet as if hoping it might open up and swallow him. It did not cooperate. He was trapped there, behind the computer monitor, cords dangling around his legs, his back against the wall, and Melody had a sudden, powerful urge to protect him.

"We're just—we're coworkers. And she's great. She *so* great." He held up a shaky finger and took a gulp from his water bottle. Then another gulp. He lowered his finger. "Wouldn't want to mess that up. Right, Mel?"

Rebecca peeled her delighted gaze off Dorian and turned openly to Melody. Melody clenched and unclenched her hands. "Right, Dor!" she said, the pitch of her voice was unfamiliar, like a brand-new kindergarten teacher. Rebecca's unabashed grin was really starting to irritate her. Heat rose in her throat. She forced her voice down an octave—*"Well, thank you so much for the fantastic interview, Mrs. Dowe"*—but now she sounded like a pubescent prank caller. At least the flattery succeeded in changing the subject.

"Oh, my pleasure! Very exciting," Rebecca said. "This podcast is everywhere lately! I know it might seem like it's big here because it's local and everyone's into it. But my people in Missouri, Ohio, Virginia, they're all talking about it." She waved her phone in Melody's face. They say everyone's listening. How many downloads are you at?"

"We're close to hitting a million total downloads, over both seasons so far. Growing fast lately with this one getting so much attention. I don't want to get obsessed with the count, so I've been trying not to look at the numbers."

"*I* look at them. A lot," Dorian said. This topic was much more comfortable. "Probably hitting that million total episode downloads soon, in the next day or so." He grinned and jabbed his hands at his waistband, changed his mind and crossed his arms.

Melody smiled. She was so proud of their work, their teamwork. That's what this warm feeling was.

It didn't have to mean anything else. Their professionalism and diligence was paying off. The success of Open Mouth Productions must prove they were on the right track, that their working partnership was worth protecting.

"Very cool, very cool," Rebecca said absently, "cool, cool, cool." She aimed a suggestive smirk at each of them, then at a granola bar packet she'd pulled from her bag, while Melody strolled encouragingly toward the front door. Rebecca stayed seated, leaning her elbows on the table and pulling open the crackly foil granola packet. "I hear it's becoming quite a mania. Seems folks around here are staring up their chimneys like they're waiting for Santa!"

"It's a phenomenon, for sure." Melody said. Her hand dropped from the front door knob and she slumped back into the studio. She pressed her fingertips against the tabletop, her hands forming little tents. "Thanks again for the interview, Ms. Dowe. I'll let you know when it's going live."

Rebecca smiled up at her, gathered her things, and stood. "Well," she said, "you are more than welcome." She waved at Dorian. "You'll let me know?"

"Will do," Dorian said.

"Cool, cool, cool," Rebecca said, and sauntered out of the room.

Melody shut the door behind her and locked it for good measure. Her eyes squeezed shut tight and she braced herself, clenching her fists as she went back to the studio. He looked up expectantly when she entered. She held her breath.

"Not trying to be ageist or anything..." he said.

She exhaled. "Uh oh."

"...just hear me out here, okay?" He held a hand out in her direction, and she pressed her lips closed. He went on. "Just want to make sure we're on the same page here, so...I *will* need to edit out some of her 'cool, cool, cools,' right?" He looked genuinely concerned. "Didn't it feel just a *little bit* anachronistic?"

"What are you saying?" she feigned alarm and looked around as if worried he may have been overheard. "Are you *trying* to get canceled?" He smiled, then zipped two fingers across his lips and raised his palms. "Anyway, I don't know," Melody said. "Didn't her generation actually popularize the term?"

Dorian looked up and rubbed his chin. Melody watched his silhouette and grinned with relief. He had known what the moment needed and stepped in right on time. It was like they'd made up their own dance, and it was one they always did when they didn't want to face the music—one of them would simply hit the fast-forward button and jump to another spot, to a track where they knew all the words. Just like that, they'd create time to inhale the awkward space and exhale a fresh atmosphere. One would act like it never happened, the other would go along with it. Good. Simple. Melody hugged herself. "Maybe we are actually too young to say it."

"Ahh!" Dorian tapped his head, nodding. The heat began to recede down his neck, and he gave her that smile that made her question everything. "Maybe you're right."

TABS AND BLANKS
PODCAST

Transcript:
Season 2, Episode 9: "What Do You Think Happened?"

(*soundbite*) Voice of Cousin Loreen: I kept asking where Betty was. When Betty's mother passed away up in Georgia, there was a funeral and no way Betty would have missed it. Huh-uh. Just no way.

This is The Chimney Sweep. Welcome to Episode 9. Where Did She Go?

In the Maryview Motor Inn lobby, behind the welcome desk, hung a Florida Highwayman painting. A scene not unlike the view just outside the motel itself: a tree covered in red blossoms framed by the graceful branches of a live oak, blowing sideways in the familiar, lilting pose of Florida foliage, in a Florida breeze, against Florida skies, with the Florida coast in the distance beyond.

The Florida Highwaymen were artists in the early 1950s to 80s. The artists traveled up and down the east coast highways selling their pieces to hotels and restaurants for $25. According to Betty's cousin Loreen, during Randell and Betty's honeymoon weekend in St. Augustine, Betty fell in love with a piece hanging on the wall of their hotel lobby, and Randell, inspired by his new marriage and wanting to impress both the hotel manager and his new bride, offered to buy it right off the wall. The manager of the hotel accepted his offer and they took the piece home and hung it in the lobby of the Maryview Motor Inn. It hung there for years. Promotional pamphlets show Betty and Randell proudly posed behind the check-in desk, in front of the painting.

Loreen: The thing about it is, that painting disappeared right after Betty did. When I came up there to talk to Randell, when I made those recordings, it's the first thing I noticed. I said, 'Hey Randell, what happened to that painting you had hanging right up here?'

Melody: And what did he say?

Loreen: I said 'Well now Randell, you know what I'm talking about now, come on. The landscape y'all got on your honeymoon, the one Betty liked so well.' I mean to tell you, that gave me a little shaky feeling right away when he acted confused about it, because we all knew the story of him buying that for her. But then he said something like: 'oh, well we moved that last year, was going to put it in the living room after Betty got done painting in there. I don't know where it is now though.' I really wanted to look around, in the garage or something, because something about it being missing, with Betty just gone a few weeks at that point, it got to me. I really wish I knew what happened to that painting, boy, I tell you what.

Welcome back, Sweepers. On today's episode, we're visiting the home of Betty Van Disson's cousin Loreen Hastings for an interview. You'll recall from our interview with a few members of Betty's family that one of them, her cousin Mark, mentioned we needed to talk to Loreen, who was Betty's first cousin and close friend.

Loreen lives closer to the city now, in a beautiful home in the upscale Deerwood area of Jacksonville, Florida. She grows and shows orchids, and her living room is full of them, tall spikes covered in big, bright blooms. A few of them have orchid show medals displayed in front of them.

Melody: You'll have to give me some tips on taking care of these before I go. I got one for Valentine's Day last year and the poor thing...let's just say it doesn't look like these!

Loreen: I'd be happy to.

Loreen gives us a little tour on the way to the dining room where we'll set up for our interview. Pictures of her husband Jerry hang over the sofa. He wears his navy uniform and poses in front of the flag. Loreen points out his medals, looks lovingly at this photo.

Loreen: He passed away two years ago now.

Melody: I'm so sorry to hear that.

Dorian: We sure do appreciate his service.

Melody: And yours, too, Miss Loreen. Spouses sacrifice a lot, too.

Loreen settles into a dining chair while Dorian finishes setting up the video equipment on the table. We'll be sharing video clips from this interview on the Chimney Sweep Podcast website.

Loreen is a vibrant and energetic woman, silver hair perfectly set and tinged with just a touch of pink. She's a licensed cosmetologist, and her nails are seriously fabulous. I shake her hand and shove mine back under the kitchen table where we're sitting down for her interview. I'm wishing I hadn't dressed like a podcaster today. Loreen's got style. And she's got something else.

Melody: Well, Miss Loreen, we're all set up here. That's the mic right there.

Loreen: Well sure, I guess I can see that right there.

Melody: Yes, so thank you for speaking with us today.

Loreen: This is a whole lot fancier than my set-up was, I tell you what. Mine did the job, though.

Loreen is referring to something we're going to hear all about in just moment.

Melody: Loreen, before we get started, would you mind explaining what you have to share, what we are about to listen to here?

Loreen: I don't mind at all. After my cousin Betty had been missing for several weeks, and nobody seemed to give a hoot to do anything about it, I decided to go up to Randell's, up there at the motel, and just, you know, have a little talk with him.

Loreen's sugary southern accent adds a little shiver to her words, like the chill of an ice cube in your sweet tea.

Loreen: I watch too much crime dramas, spy movies, and such. So I went out to the spy shop over here on Southside Boulevard and got myself this recording device.

She points to the antiquated piece of technology on the table. It must have been high-tech back when Loreen sashayed into the local secret agent supply store.

Loreen: So before I went in to see Randell, I put that down in my...well, my girdle, if you must know, and then the wire came up under my bra and the little microphone sat right there, right between.

She points to her chest. She blushes, but I'd say she seems pretty pleased with herself.

Melody: And now, what made you feel like you should do that? How did you come to decide, 'Hey I know, I'll go see him and record the conversation?' Was there something he said, or was he acting a certain way?

Loreen: Oh, yes, he was acting a certain way. I thought he was anyway. Actually, no. I take that back. It was more like he *wasn't* acting a certain way. He just wasn't acting like a man who was distraught over his wife disappearing without any word, no trace, no note, nothing.

Melody: Because if she had just run off of her own volition, maybe with the intention of leaving Randell and starting a new life somewhere, you think she would have left a note or let someone know, right? She would have let you know?

Loreen: Exactly. Yes, she would have. She never would have left town with no word to me. Or to her mama. Everyone said, 'Oh, leave it, Loreen! Betty's mama was too far gone by then to know what Betty said or didn't say.' I didn't believe that, either. And then all these years with no word? But even back then, even when it had only been a few weeks with her gone, I knew something wasn't right. So why didn't *he* know that, too? If he hadn't done anything to her, then why didn't he act like it didn't make sense to him, either? The old bas—

Melody: Miss Loreen, how would you describe your feelings toward Randell before Betty's disappearance?

Loreen leans back in her chair and looks at her hands in her lap. Her brows pull together and she glances up at the kitchen window behind me and squints as if seeing something going on out there, over my shoulder. Then she shakes her head.

Loreen: At first I didn't think anything bad about him. He seemed fine enough. He had her out there on that nice property, owned his own business. I don't personally like the alcohol thing, you know—how Georgia folks got around their dry laws by slipping down over the border to his place, and the other places along the highway like his. But he wasn't breaking any laws. He was giving her a nice enough life and she seemed happy enough working there, far as I could tell. She liked being the lady proprietor and whatnot. So I guess I liked him fine. It was just how he got after she turned up missing that started to change my mind toward him, my feelings toward him. I thought I detected something suspicious. Made me anxious, in my heart.

I took all this to Billy John, Detective Whitaker. He didn't take me seriously, and when I called the station later on to check how things were going, nobody even knew who I was.

Coming soon, on The Chimney Sweep:

We're bringing you an interview with independent private investigator Rebecca Dowe.

Melody: So the question is, Ms. Dowe, what do you, as an experienced private investigator with dozens of solved missing person cases to your name, think about the evidence in Betty's case?

Private Investigator Rebecca Dowe: I've read the police report. All her things were there. Randell says he thought she might have gone to her mother's that day, but her mother didn't remember seeing her. Randell says he 'can't remember' the last time he spoke to her. I mean, come on.

MELODY

2019

Melody touched her phone screen. "Call Mom," she said.

A photo popped up on the screen and Melody smiled. It was her favorite picture of her mother, her head tilted back and her body arched backward as she belted a note into the microphone, her dark curly hair lit like a halo in the spotlight.

"Calling Mom," the phone said. It rang one and half times, and her mother answered.

"What do you want, why are you calling me, I'm extremely busy."

Melody grinned. "Okay, bye."

"No, no, no, wait. I was kidding," her mother said. "Can't you even take a joke? Gosh."

"You are nuts."

"Yeah."

"Are you at home? I'm in the area and I need coffee and—"

"And what?"

"And...a hug?" Melody swallowed hard.

"Get over here then," her mother said.

Melody pulled up beside her mother Belinda's old craftsman bungalow. Only last year, this had still been her grandparents' bungalow, but now that they were both gone, passing away within months of each other, Belinda had moved back into her childhood home.

Melody's shoulders relaxed. She leaned against the headrest and closed her eyes for a moment. Even outside her mom's house was better than the inside of most places.

Belinda Hinterson waited at the door when Melody pulled up the gravel driveway. She wore a fitted purple tee and flowy pants with a bright flower print all over. Her hair was pulled up in a puffy ball on top of her head and tied with a pink silk scarf. She strode to the front of the porch, barefoot as usual. Melody felt better just seeing her standing there.

"Hey, Mom," she said. She stopped on the step below the porch and let her mother wrap her arms around her shoulders. She was six years old again.

Melody trailed into the house under her mothers arm, kicking her shoes off under the foyer table. She smiled at a picture of her grandparents sitting beside the day's mail and a curvy brass lamp. She remembered finding that lamp at a yard sale years ago and how her mother had recovered the shade and polished the metal till it gleamed like gold. She exhaled through pursed lips as the door closed behind her. Her mother let her lead the way, and Melody headed straight for the multicolored chintz arm chair in the golden yellow living room. That chair had always been her favorite, with its jewel-toned flower and emerald vine print. It had gone with them wherever they lived. She tucked her back against one corner, pulled her feet up under her, and took a shuddery cleansing breath.

Belinda had been a foster child. She'd moved from home, usually in the middle of the night and with only a pillowcase full of belongings, thirteen times in her first eight years. Finally, she was adopted by Bill and Linda Hinterson, a couple who, upon meeting the little girl, instantly couldn't imagine their lives without her. Even her name, sounding like a combination of their names, seemed to confirm that she had been meant for them. They'd let her pick a paint color for her own room. They'd learned to comb and braid her thick, curly hair. They had given her a microscope in case she was into science, dug a garden for her when she said she liked flowers, bought a whole set of Encyclopedia Britannica so she could look up anything in the world right there in her own living room. The dolls arranged on her little pink bed each day looked like an all-female UN meeting.

Bill and Linda recognized and eagerly encouraged their daughter's musical talent, and she'd attended the same magnet school Dorian later attended—Douglas Anderson School of the Arts—to study musical theater and vocal performance. She loved to tell people how she once sang on a track on a friend's jazz album, and the drummer had been none other than future heavy metal drummer John Otto of Limp Bizkit. She'd sung with that group on the main stage at the Jacksonville Jazz Festival, and she'd thought the eruption from the crowd at the end of her performance was for her, only to turn around and see world famous trumpet player Chuck Mangione, his famous hat down low on his brow, stepping on stage behind her for his set. All her singing stories were like this, stories of brushes with greatness. But she told them with humor. Once Melody came along, her daughter's happiness and security came first. Her vocal career began its journey from the front burner to the back, then it chilled in the fridge, and finally it got stuck in deep-freezer. Nowadays, she only sang occasional karaoke, and only after a great deal of prodding and a few margaritas.

Bob and Linda Hinterson were not only Melody's grandparents. They were her heroes. And her mom was her favorite person in the world.

Belinda Hinterson's bright, eclectic living room had a welcoming, comfortable feel. It was not quite elegant, not quite shabby chic, but somehow perfect. Overstuffed chairs and a bright red velvet couch welcomed visitors to get comfortable and stay a while. Melody's 4th grade Mother's Day art project, a ceramic bowl with black and white piano keys around the rim, was always full of Jolly Ranchers that glowed like gems in the soft sunlight through the gauzy white curtains. Melody was sure her mother was trying to single-handedly bring back brass as a home decor trend, stubbornly using brass candlesticks and brass sconces and brass anything else regardless of what the host of her favorite HGTV shows might say.

Photos and awards hung on the main wall, across from the bright front window. There were framed shots of Melody from childhood to the present and clippings and print-outs she'd pinned to a cork board. In the middle of the collection was a new page

Belinda had printed recently, straight from the *Variety* website, showing Melody and Dorian smiling from a collage of thumbnail photos over a headline that announced "The Top Ten New Podcasts You Do Not Want To Miss!"

Among the many photos were shots from Belinda's musical career, shots from live performances at bars, private parties, weddings, and festivals. Another was a wider-angle of the same show as the photo Melody had on her phone but this shot included more of the whole stage and the band behind her as they performed at The Jacksonville Jazz Festival in Metropolitan Park. Promo photos, some black and white glossies and some full color depending on how the bands' finances were doing at the time, showed Belinda surrounded by musicians through the years: a pop and R&B lineup in sequins and lamé from the '80s, a Latin group in identical red guayaberas and jaunty straw fedoras from the early 90s; a jazz quintet with each musician affecting serious musician expressions that Melody always found comical. Belinda loved coming up with band names. She dubbed the 80s band 'Microfiche,' the Latin group 'Coconut Champagne,' the jazz quintet 'Skoville Scale.'

The gallery served as a sort of yearbook, immortalizing the many hairstyles Belinda had tried over the years in her quest to tame her unruly curls. (Those were the days before she learned to embrace the pouf.) There was a shiny Jheri curl gathered to one side in a sequin scrunchy, a bob that had been dangerously pressed flat with a steam iron, a severely slicked ponytail, a pixie cut lacquered to her forehead with pomade. "I'm so happy for these little baby mixed-chicks coming up today," she'd say. "Everybody wishes they had hair like mine now! Who woulda thought?" Melody considered her own hair her best feature. It was thick and wavy, dark with random auburn strands, and not too silky. It held up to the careless way she yanked it tight in her heavy-duty hair bands. Since she hadn't known her father, Melody had no idea where she'd gotten that hair from, but she was grateful for it nonetheless.

There were record covers and reviews scattered throughout the haphazard arrangement, but in the center of it all was Melody's college graduation portrait, which Belinda had had mounted in a huge, glittering frame.

"What's up with this music?"

Belinda cocked her head toward the speaker on the mantel. "'Four Walls of Raiford,'" she said. "Lynyrd Skynyrd."

"Okay. Not your normal house jam."

"I'm learning some new stuff. Some guys from that wedding band I used to sing with are getting a new group together. They want to work up a full set of songs by Jacksonville musicians. Didn't I tell you about that?"

"You didn't tell me about that. You're gonna work with a band again? That's awesome, Mom!"

"I'm actually pretty jazzed about it. Wasn't sure I could pull it off, but we jammed here last night and, you know what? The old girl's still got it." She jiggled her shoulders.

"Shut up, you are not old. That's exciting! When's the first gig?"

"Oh, we're not quite there yet." She sat on the edge of the sofa. "If we decide to play out, I'll let you know."

Melody nodded. She let her head rest on the back of the chair. The song ended and another one on Belinda's study playlist started—Tom Petty and the Heartbreakers' "Gainesville."

"That's not Jacksonville," Melody mumbled.

"Close enough," Belinda said, her palms rubbing together. "But don't worry! 'Sweet Home Alabama' and 'Midnight Rider' are on the list. We're not trying to get pelted with beer bottles. We want to do some unexpected stuff."

"Well, if that's the case, you should do 'Loving You.' Dorian said Minnie Riperton and her husband wrote it in Gainesville. Did you know that?"

"I did know that."

"Of course you did."

They made matching mocking faces at each other.

"So," Belinda said. She leaned forward casually.

"So," Melody replied toward the ceiling.

"You and Dorian dating yet?"

"Oh, good grief, Mom."

"What? That's what this is about isn't it?"

Melody rolled her eyes in a thoroughly teenaged manner, and Belinda responded with an obdurate look. Even as she shook her head and her gaze landed on a picture of her mother, standing under a tree with her own mom before Belinda's high school prom, she knew it was a superfluous gesture. She knew exactly what was causing her stomach to stay in constant knots and her head to pound with the effort of trying to discern what she should do. What would her subscribers think if they could see her right now, huddled deep in the recesses of an armchair in her mommy's living room? The woman her listeners thought they knew would get out there and find a solution to her problems—with clear-eyed focus and the perfect efficiency of words. She crossed her arms over her belly and jutted her chin at her mother.

"How do you know? How do you always know?"

"I'm your mom." She shrugged, her strong broad shoulders pushing at the thin fabric of her t-shirt. She reached for the candy, jiggling the bowl in front of Melody first. "We know stuff."

"Yeah, but you don't have to be so..." Melody said. She begrudgingly plucked a green piece by one end of its twisted wrapper.

"What? I 'don't have to be so...' what?" Belinda said. She closed her eyes and picked a candy, pulled the ends of the wrapper and popped it in her mouth, then rubbed her hands together. "Mmm, strawberry." she mumbled.

"You don't have to be so..." Melody looked up helplessly at the shining brass chandelier, "...so freaking *right* all the time."

BETTY,
32 YEARS OLD

1984

The morning had been bright and clear, but steely gray clouds were already gathering on the horizon for summer's afternoon rain. A tropical storm was threatening, but they seldom actually hit Jacksonville, and everyone had already stocked up on bread and batteries.

Betty followed close behind, keeping pace with the car in front of her, one foot hovering over the brake pedal, in the long procession to the grave site. The line extended beyond her field of vision ahead, while behind her only a few more cars trailed through the cemetery gates.

Earlier, back at Shiloh church, a joyous congregation had celebrated the life of deaconess Martha Arleta Owens, better known as the mother of Dominicus Owens, the iconic lead singer of The Downtown Sound and now world-famous solo artist in his own right. Betty sat in the back pew. She giggled into her handkerchief when the pastor joked, right there in church, about how many of the congregation had probably gotten 'in the family way' to one of Martha's son's songs. The hour was filled with fiery music and brimstone messages, interspersed with storied memories of Sister Martha.

"Who else has a word to share about sister Martha?..."

Betty strained her eyes over the multicolored sea of church hats. He would be in the front row, with his family. She could tell from the way the crowd turned at the mention of Martha's famous son that he was in the middle of the front row. But he was too far away to catch a glimpse.

Until finally, the reverend called for Martha's son to step up and say a few words.

And there he was. The round back of his head appeared as he stood to his full height. she'd almost forgotten how tall he was, and then he turned and gave a small smile to the congregation.

He climbed the few steps to the pulpit, his arms and legs moving with smooth, practiced grace. Before he turned to the congregation, he clapped his hands together softly and the room went silent. He knew how to take a stage.

His voice came through the speakers and jolted her. His mouth, familiar but inevitably changed, formed the words, but at first she heard nothing he said. Like cool water to parched earth—droplets absorb one by one, but a deluge floods the earth before it can take it in. She breathed short, sharp breaths in the back of her throat, clenched her arms across her stomach.

What would she have said, if she'd had the chance to walk up to that podium? How would these people think if she stood up and walked to the front, the mousy white lady in a predictable black polyester Dillard's dress. *Oh, my. What have we here?* Maybe they'd think she'd been one of Martha's many English students, or some looky-loo who somehow made it past security. She bit her lip and hoped she was hiding it well, prayed no one would read it on her face, how Martha was more than that to the pale woman in the back. People filed up to the pulpit, taking their rightful chance to tell the world how Martha was like family, like family, like family. They couldn't know that for Betty, she really was family, even if Martha never knew it.

"Yes, I am married, and he's a good man," she said. Car doors were closing at the head of the line and Dominicus held up a finger to his driver. There was no time, but so much to say. She tried to condense her life, to distill the story to the crystalline poetry of a sad love song. "We're not like that, like man and wife, he doesn't know my other life..."

BETTY,
32 YEARS OLD

NOVEMBER 21, 1984

Dear Diary,

I need to write quickly today. After I get chores done around here, I'll get ready real quick and head out.

The funeral is on the Northside, so not too far. I hope it's okay me being there. But I did know her once. She was Dominicus's mother, and I wouldn't feel right about it if I didn't pay my respects.

We've got nobody staying at the motel. I think we'll be shutting down the motel soon, actually. But I'll write about that another time. It's just no use keeping it up when hardly anyone stays here anymore. The only people we get are kicked-out husbands and running wives. They stay too long and leave in the night. We're still the closest convenience store for folks out here, so I told Randell we'd do better to focus on that.

Right now my hands are shaking. I'm trying not to think about seeing Dominicus. It's been so long. I know he's married.

Diary, I'm back from the funeral. He was there. I can't think straight right now. Don't know how I drove home. Don't remember the drive.

I told him. So now he knows. I still see his face when he realized what I was saying. It's burned in my brain like staring at a lightbulb. It's not how I would have wanted to tell him such a huge important thing, standing by my truck in the funeral procession line with his limo waiting ahead, and his mother's body freshly in the ground. It came out. As soon as he walked up to me I knew it was going to come out of my mouth. Like saying it would bring all three of us together in that place, just for that moment.

He told me he wrote to me. He said he wrote to me every week and sent postcards from every town they played. How could I have doubted he would write? I never saw one of them. He called, and she told him not to call there any more. She lied, told him I had a beau, that I was so happy and he should leave me alone. She warned him off. And then he came here to try to talk to me, but she turned him away. How did I never suspect Mama would do things like this? It's like something out of a cheap soap opera. You wouldn't believe it if it wasn't your own life. All that time I thought she was trying to flirt with the mailman, she was really intercepting his letters. That's stealing. She stole them, and so much more, from me. I wonder, did she save the letters? Or did she throw them away? I took care of her house, helped her move, surely I would have found them? Maybe she burned them.

My chest feels like it's full of hot sand. Like quicksand.

There's something I haven't thought about in a long time. Quick sand. I used to be scared to death of it, thought it must be everywhere. Couldn't hardly watch a tv show or a cartoon without somebody getting mired in quicksand and dragged down to their neck till only their head stuck out of the ground. Turned out it's not really everywhere. I guess I let my guard down. Now here I am with my feet out from under me and the ground pressing in. If you fight, it drags you quicker. If you stay still, you might manage to keep your head out a little longer till help comes. It doesn't matter if I struggle. No one is coming for me.

His wife wasn't there. He said they're splitting up. But a new lady was waiting for him at his car. He said he has a solo album coming out. Might release a duet with Diana Ross. Isn't that something? Diana Ross.

I let him take my hand. I know I shouldn't have, but I did. He called me 'Princess,' just like he used to. He remembered that. He looked the same, but different. Like a polished-up trophy version of my Dominicus.

I'm back behind the desk and it's like this morning was a dream. Like maybe it never happened. Did it really happen? Did I really see Hank and Zeke and O.T. again? They looked incomplete without Sly, like a record player missing its tonearm. I'm looking around this lobby and asking myself: Was Dominicus really standing right in front of me just a few hours ago?

There's a big storm heading this way. The clouds are dark and angry and whipping in the sky. I understand them. Feels like I could fly up there right now and join them, just blend right in and be a part of them. No one would notice.

Suppose I'd better go ahead and start taping up the windows.

Betty took off her apron and washed her hands. Her back ached, but not as much as her chest. She needed a shower and some sleep. Had the funeral really only been this morning? This might have been the longest day of her life, and she'd had some very long ones.

Randell stopped her as she headed from the lobby toward her room. So close.

"Listen, when you're done with your chores and all, I need you to reorder some supplies for my kit," Randell said. He shuffled through a pile of mail and dropped it on the front desk. Her eyes stayed focused on her hands. He tapped the worn surface with a finger outlined in black creosote. "Okay, Princess?"

Betty froze, her fingertips pressed the tops of her thighs. *What did he just say?*

She had to hold it together. She reasoned with herself. None of this was his fault. The man didn't even know the things that ate her up inside, and whose fault was that? He wasn't mean. He wasn't cruel. She couldn't let herself imagine it was like some old Loretta Lynn song. He didn't do her wrong.

She lowered her head and closed her eyes.

After the funeral that morning, she'd driven up to see to Mama and found her in unusually high spirits.

Delores looked forward to her daughter's visits, mostly because they meant she would get to soak in the tub rather than suffer the indignation of a bed bath given by some nurse with cold hands.

"Betty! Oh, Betty. Did you hear? That song I like so much, 'Bette Davis Eyes'? Well, damned if it didn't win the Grammy! I saw it on Regis and Kathie Lee. I tell you, I know good music. I don't usually care for that particular sort, but I can make out talent, and I said when I heard it, 'Now that's a good song, right there!' Ask anyone, they'll tell you I said that. I love that part about how the woman's got Bette Davis eyes. Mama had sung it while sitting in the bath, repeating the same line over and over, her voice breathless and gravelly from years of nicotine.

"That was over two years ago, Mama."

Something about her mama's voice, and the splashing of the bath water, and watching from afar as Ms. Martha's coffin was lowered into the ground, and being so near to Dominicus only a few hours before...it all conspired to move her mouth like a ventriloquist's doll. "You know what, Mama?" she said, her voice half there in the bathroom, half on the 3:42 flight to Los Angeles out of Jacksonville Airport. "An old friend of mine was actually at the Grammy Awards that night, when that song won. Can you imagine that?"

Mama had stopped singing. Betty's hand shook as she dipped the washcloth in the bath and rubbed it on Mama's bare, boney back. She saw the wasted muscles under the thin blanched chicken skin suddenly go tense. Betty got up from the bathroom floor, lowered the toilet lid, and sat.

She'd closed her eyes, leaned back against the tank till it creaked, her own voice unrecognizable when she asked:

"What did you do with the letters, Mama?"

She had driven home somehow, her insides vibrating and the blood pulsing high-pitched in her ears. *Gone. All Gone.* And now Randell stood beside the table, staring expectantly at her. She still hadn't answered him. *Mama singing in the tub, Ms. Martha in the ground, Dominicus on an airplane flying away. A big, dangerous storm blowing in.* Betty heard that same unrecognizable voice.

"Don't call me 'Princess.'" Her fingers pressed harder through her skirt, into her flesh. The hairs on her neck shivered.

Randell stopped pulling at his dusty boot. "What was that?" he said.

Betty's heart sped. She tried to soften the edges of what had come out of her mouth.

"I just...if you don't mind...could you not call me that?" she said. A smile pulled across half her face and she pretended to look at the mail. "I'm probably, you know, a little old for that nickname, don't you think?"

Randell looked at her for a beat longer, went back to pulling his boot.

"Well, I do apologize. Perhaps you've ascended to 'Queen', hmm?" He rubbed his hands on his knees. "My apologies, Your Highness."

Now she'd insulted him. *Ungrateful little thing.*

She bit her tongue till she tasted salt and tried to bring a smile up to her eyes.

I am so sorry, Princess. So sorry.

She had to try harder. It wasn't his fault. She was the one who was lying, going off to see her old boyfriend in secret. It wasn't Randell's fault. It wasn't his fault he wasn't Dominicus.

TABS AND BLANKS
PODCAST

Transcript
Season 2, Episode 10: Randell Van
Disson on Tape

This week, on The Chimney Sweep:

Betty Van Disson's cousin Loreen visited Randell shortly after Betty's disappearance in 2001, ostensibly to discuss Betty and talk about their memories of her. Loreen encouraged Randell to talk about his missing wife, and she asked him what he thought might have happened to her. She also recorded these conversations.

The recording was turned over to the police immediately after Loreen obtained it. Since Betty's case is technically ongoing, I asked Detective Billy John about them:

(*soundbite*) I did listen to Loreen's tape. There just wasn't anything there. Absolutely nothing of any worth. Listen, I understand her wanting to help, 'playing spy' and all that. But you go on and listen to it yourself, let your listeners hear it, too. There is absolutely nothing there of relevance to Betty's case. Play it. But you're gonna hear the same thing I heard: either Randell is as innocent and clueless as he sounds, or else he's a world-class sociopath.

Here's what Loreen had to say about the circumstances surrounding her recording of Randell:

Melody: Did Randell know you were recording him?

Loreen: Well, no. At some point, I think I may have said to him something like, 'Well, would you say that on tape?' And he said, 'Well, yeah, I suppose.' He said, you know, 'Go on ahead and record me if you want to,' or something to that effect. Why would he care, if he was innocent of any...what do you call it? 'Wrongdoing.' That's it. Why would he care if he was innocent of any wrongdoing? For two days I just kept talking to him. And it was eye-opening, to say the least.

He talked about how he couldn't see running things without her. The motel business was basically over by then, he just hadn't accepted the fact. But the chimney sweep business had been going pretty well, he said, and that sort of kept them afloat.

And next, we will finally hear from Betty's husband Randell Van Disson...

(*soundbite*) Right before my daddy died, when he was deep on morphine and had one foot and part of his leg in heaven, he started talking again about a treasure. 'The chimney treasure, the chimney treasure...' He just kept on repeating that.

The following is from the recordings Betty's cousin Loreen made of her conversation with Randell Van Disson.

Voice of Randell Van Disson: ...but you know, she hates bridges. She always hated bridges, Betty did. Didn't even like for me to say the word 'bridges.' Nope, no way, no how. Thing is, it wasn't for the reason you might think. She wasn't scared of crossing them or driving over them. No. It was something else. Something else, you *(*inaudible*)*

We apologize for the sometimes garbled audio. Remember, the microphone wire was buried in Loreen's bra. But here Randell pauses, seems to be waiting for Loreen to speak. She doesn't, and you can hear a certain strain, a hesitation in his voice as he goes on:

Randell: Well, I don't know how much you know about it. Guess it doesn't matter much now if I tell.

Y'all had a shop teacher back in school, name of 'Mr. Bridges,' didn't you? You remember a guy by that name?

Loreen: Yes, Randell, I do remember that man. I surely do."

Randell: Okay well, I don't know if you know... (*inaudible*) what he done to Betty, how he bothered her—"

Loreen: Oh my God, Randell! What on earth are you talking about now?

Randell: Well, now, I don't know how to come out and say it, do I? After I always kept it secret for her (*inaudible*). She was ashamed, you know what I'm saying. But the man wasn't right, see? Come on, now. She was abused, Loreen. Right there in the shop behind the school, inside one of those donated vans they used to use to teach boys auto mechanics. That's what she told me. And when she tried to stay away, he went to threatening her. She told me if she didn't come out there at lunch, he'd come up into the school to look for her. One of his buddies was the vice principal, you remember Mr. McCory? Yeah, big round guy. I knew him from the liquor store. Yeah, she said he would come into Betty's class sometimes and call her out for a special 'office assignment' or a job in the library. There weren't no job in the library. Just so she could go out to the shop, he did that.

She hated vans, too, for that same reason. VW vans. Made her skin crawl. I wished I coulda said something to you when you rolled up here in that VW van, the one Oren had you running around in a while back? Betty was a strong-minded woman, but when it came to that, it could set her to just ruminating on it like junior high school was yesterday.

Loreen: Damn, Randell. I had no idea that happened to her. How could I have no idea about something like that? Betty and I were like, we were like sisters almost. You know that. I wished you'da told me.

Randell: I don't know. Wasn't my thing to tell. She barely told me, and I was her husband...am her husband. *(*inaudible*)* ...so when she comes back you can ask her yourself, how about that?

Oh. I keep remembering this. How the first thing Betty wanted to do when she moved here with me was she wanted to paint the front door of the souvenir shop out there. That's why it's blue. 'Haint Blue,' she called it. Said where her daddy was from, they paint the door that blue color to ward off spirits. They called the spirits 'haints.' *(*inaudible*)* ...and I said, 'Go on then, paint it if you want to.' I had heard something about that myself, only it was that folks painted the ceiling of the porch that blue. Just different people, different superstitions, y'see.

Loreen: Yes, I know about all that, too. Between my mama's side and my daddy's, they were painting everything that gawd-awful shade of blue. Betty's momma didn't like that, though. She was high-minded, Aunt Delores. Said a Christian had no place messing with superstition.

Randell: Well, I say amen to that.

Loreen: Mmm hmm. So Randell what is this, huh? What do you think happened to Betty? I mean, my heart is just breaking to think of her...

Randell: Well, she took off, right? I'd say that's pretty damn obvious. She played like she was the lady boss of this whole compound out here, but I knew some day she'd have to get tired of it. She finally did. Must'a had enough. All I know is she's gone from me. Gone from me.

Loreen: But at her age, Randell? You think she waited all those years to go find herself a new life? Come on now.

Randell: My grandmama left my granddaddy when she was fifty-five. Just up and took off. And what do you mean 'at her age'? Betty wasn't that old, was she? How old was she...is she? She could still do what she always wanted to do.

Loreen: And what was that? What did she always want to do? I'd love to know, so why don't you go on and tell me?

Randell: Well, for one she always said she could have been a Rockette. So that's one thing she might'a run off to try right there. She always did have real nice legs.

Loreen: What in the dern hell are you talking about, Randell? A Rockette?

(*muffled laughter*)

Randell: Now you listen here, Loreen, I won't have you coming in Betty's home and disparaging her, you hear? Now I don't want to be ugly, but no ma'am. We might not have had the most romantic of marriages, but that's still my wife you're laughing at. You trying to imply my Betty couldn't'a been a Rockette if she'd've wanted to?

Loreen: I'm not saying that at all, Randell. Now just calm down. She could have. Certainly she could have been a Rockette, if that's what she put her mind to.

Randell: You're damn right, she could have. Wouldn't be surprised if we see her on the damn Macy's Day damned Parade come Thanksgiving. Let's just you and me wait and see about that. *(*inaudible*)*

Loreen: Seriously, Randell? Is that what you're going with here?

Randell: Well, I don't see why not. She's just a little young thing.

(*rustling*) (*silence*)

Loreen: All right, Randell. We'll watch for her on the damn Macy's Day damned Parade. We'll just do that.

MELODY

2019

Melody lifted a limp Phalaenopsis orchid from the out-of-the-way spot where it had languished for well over a year. She blew on the dusty leaves and turned it from side to side. "Loreen said I need to look at this thing's roots," she said. She pulled the plant up from its pot and frowned at the dry lump of moss tangled through with gray, alien-like roots. "Pretty sad."

Dorian looked up from the puzzle and side-eyed the leathery yellow leaves. "Are you entirely sure that's even the same kind of plant Loreen has?" he said. Melody mimicked his sardonic expression, but Dorian was unrelenting. "Because, I'm no expert, but I'm pretty sure hers was, like, green? And I'm almost positive that stick is supposed to have flowers coming out of it."

"Okay, okay, that's enough, Martha Stewart, thank you very much. I *have* watered it." Melody said. "I think."

"Got that for Valentine's Day? Last year? I don't remember that." Dorian shrugged out the words. "Who from?" He shrugged again.

"That guy Reggie at the TV station. Remember him? About forty, super-pale from living that troll life in that control room?"

"Oh, okay."

"What does that mean?" She lowered the plant and turned to face him.

"What? I just said 'okay'."

"Right, but what does that *mean*? 'Oh, okay'? What *wouldn't* have been 'okay'?"

"Nothing. Nothing wouldn't have been—"

Melody walked over to him. "Dor?" She waited until he looked up at her. "What's the deal, Dor? Is something wrong?"

She didn't need to ask. She knew him, knew every nuance of his expressions. She knew from the way his jaw tightened and his lips moved silently in sync with his tongue, forming shapes that produced no sounds. She waited. He started to speak.

Her phone rang. She pulled it from her pocket and clicked to ignore the call, holding Dorian's gaze as she put the phone down on the table beside them. He started to speak again. Her phone rang again. It was Loreen.

"Just answer it, please."

She crossed her arms and let it ring. He couldn't stand letting a call go to voicemail, and she knew it.

"Come on. Please." It continued to ring.

"Will you talk to me after the call?" she asked.

"Yes! Now please answer it."

"All right, all right, sheesh…" She tapped the screen and answered the phone, still watching Dorian. "Loreen!" she said, keeping one eye on Dorian. I just checked those orchid roots, and I'm afraid it's a pretty tragic scene."

She stopped talking and listened. "Oh no. Well, what happened? Uh huh." Dorian made a questioning face and she held a finger up to him, mouthing "It's Randell!"

"Hold on, Loreen, let me put you on speaker." Dorian leaned closer.

"Did you want to record this?" Loreen asked. Melody and Dorian looked at each other and nodded. He thought fast and started the voice recording app on his phone.

"Loreen, we're recording. You were saying, about Randell? Where did they take him?"

"He's at Shands Hospital now. Like I said, the hospital told the nursing home he came in complaining of chest pains."

"Shands?" Dorian says.

"Yes, on 8th Street?" Loreen said.

"Right." Melody said, then covered the phone to speak to Dorian. "UF Health. Used to be called Shands." Dorian nodded and clicked a key on his keyboard. The monitor's blue glow flickered and he started a search for the website as Melody went back to Loreen. "So what happened? Did the retirement home transport him there?"

"No, and I am not trying to sound like this is funny, but apparently he downloaded an app and called himself a taxi!" Loreen's voice rose in pitch till she stopped mid-sentence, took a breath, and started over. "I missed a call from the retirement home this morning, letting me know the hospital called them. He got himself checked into hospital before I even knew he was out. The hospital won't tell me anything over the phone except that he's admitted."

Dorian fiddled with the audio. Melody paced, hands on her lower back. "How did he just leave? Did someone check him out?"

"No, no one signed him out. He's on camera just walking out the front door and getting into the car! But I called the taxi company. The manager said he'd talk to the driver about pickups at nursing homes, and that's all well and good, but too little too late if you ask me."

"Uber wouldn't have picked up a senior citizen from a nursing home." Dorian mumbled. "Just saying."

"Loreen, thanks for the information. Let me get right on this, okay? Buh bye." She rang off and peered over Dorian's shoulder at the hospital information page.

"We need to get in there and see him," Dorian said.

"Yes," Melody said. They exchanged a look, and both thought, "...before it's too late."

BETTY,
33 YEARS OLD

1985

The mailman was late, and Betty waited by the front door of the lobby. She peered out the window, alternating rising on tiptoes to see over the bushes and hunching down to see through them, trying to get a glimpse of the mail truck coming down the road.

Then finally, it was here. The mailman had placed the small box with a Service Merchandise logo directly into her hand. Within a few minutes, she'd unpacked the box and loaded up the new Walkman with two fresh AA batteries. She fumbled with the earphones, untangling the long wire behind the front desk in case someone came in and she had to shove it away. Her pulse raced with secret excitement—her own personal music player.

She looked around. No one seemed to be heading to the lobby. Who was she kidding? No one was ever heading to this lobby any more. She took the new device into the storage room.

On a bottom shelf, she moved aside cleaners and cans of touch-up paint to reach a file storage box labeled "Receipts." She lifted the lid and shuffled some papers aside. Under a thick manilla folder was a row of cassette tapes.

Her fingers walked across the spines, a small collection she'd accumulated over the years, stopping on a purple and black one with a groovy font in gold: The Downtown Sound. Funny how the group's first album could already look outdated next to their newer ones. There was their second album *Sugar Hill*, which was nominated for album of the year, and then all the albums since then till the row ended with the most recent one. Made after Dominicus's mother passed away, the group had put aside their differences for one more album and festival tour—Betty had saved all the news clippings in the manilla folder. The cover of this album featured a black and silver design with a silhouette of a top hat against a glittery moon.

The cassette deck in her car had given up the ghost months ago, and Randell had dropped the portable one she kept behind the front desk the week before she got this newest album. She'd stored it safely with the rest of her cherished collection, but now that this amazing new Walkman was here, she could finally listen to it.

But first, she wanted to hear something old. It still gave her a thrill to look at that first album, to hold it in her hands. She set the new album aside and pulled out the oldest one. She carefully opened the case, removed the cassette. Instinctively, she put her pinky into one of the reels and turned, drawing the tape taught inside its black plastic case, then she popped the cassette into the new player. One press of a button and, like magic, Dominicus was right there, in her ear. *"I've got a penny in my pocket and my girl in front of me...what more do I need..."* Quickly, she turned the player over, searched the labels looking for the right button, and clicked it off.

It was too much.

She gathered herself. She removed the crinkling cellophane wrapper from the new album, opened the case, and pulled the cassette out, turning it over to take in both sides and all the edges, as if it might hold a secret message. When had the print on these things gotten so small? She pulled out the five panel j-card, unfolding it carefully. She loved being able to follow along with the lyrics. She put on her glasses.

She always looked for their albums, in every record department she came across, just to see them there, in their rightful place. She bought cassettes instead of records—they were more compact and easy to store in this single box. Any time, she could come back here and pull one out, look at Dom and the boys, smile at the changing fashions and hairstyles, know that the space they always left when they posed for pictures was where Sly should have been standing.

The row of cassettes in their special storage box represented The Downtown Sound's entire musical evolution, from their unique Southern strain of the Motown Sound to their 'psychedelic soul' phase, then disco, and the latest, full of the love themes and ballads the public couldn't get enough of. To run her finger along the spines was to keep a grip on the other life, the one that had gone on without her.

She checked the motel lobby again and closed the door, leaned against it and slid down, crossing her legs in front of her on the floor. The linoleum was cool against her skin, and the closed door behind her back felt secure, comforting. She inserted the new tape. Then she leaned back and closed her eyes, set the player on her lap, and pressed play.

Dominicus's voice, but more mature and somehow even more soulful, filled her head again. She listened as he started to sing the first song, and her eyes grew wide as the words began to tell a story. She pressed the earphones to her head, her breath growing shallow.

Then room filled with the sound of her gasp.

BETTY,
41 YEARS OLD

1993

Dear Diary,

I haven't been very good about keeping up a diary, have I? This is my first entry this whole year. I'm not sure where the year went, but it certainly has gone.

Randell's away on a couple of chimney jobs. Just today, I've had four calls for chimney service. If it gets any busier, I might have to start going out on some of these jobs myself. Randell is running himself ragged. He can't seem to say no to any of them. And he's not charging them much, I know because I keep the books for him. Sometimes when I go out on the jobs with him, I have to remind him to get paid before we leave.

Lots of word-of-mouth business in the historic district, Riverside and Avondale, especially since I ordered some of those magnetic signs for Randell's truck. It's a mobile advertisement now. Probably folks see his truck outside the neighbors' houses and think,

"Hey, do we need <u>our</u> chimney cleaned? And then they just write down our number.

I designed the magnet signs myself. They say:

Randell Van Disson
Traditional Chimney Sweep
Specializing in Historic Homes
Minor Masonry Repair
A Clean Chimney Is A Safe Chimney!

It's got the phone number on it, and I even made a page on the World Wide Web. Randell didn't want to, but I got us hooked up. It only takes about fifteen minutes for it to 'dial up,' and it makes a big racket like a dying robot while it does that, but then you're on the Web!

I wanted the business page to have basic information, but Randell said to make it where people can read about his dad and how Randell still does chimneys in his Daddy's memory. So I did it that way, like he wanted. Didn't take him long to have an opinion on the Web Site he didn't want.

There is a Web Site where you can ask a Magic 8 Ball questions. Sometimes I ask it questions for an hour or more instead of working or doing the books. I keep on asking it questions till I get a reply I like.

Once I asked it if I could have been a Rockette. I know—how dumb is that? It kept saying 'ask again later' or 'cannot predict now' or 'don't count on it.' I think that last one is kind of funny. One time it said 'Concentrate and ask again.' So I ran in the back and hitched up my dress and made sure I could still kick as high as I used to (I almost can. Hips aren't what they used to be, though.), and then I asked again. That time it said 'better not tell you now,' which is probably good because I wouldn't need much encouragement to pack up and head to New York City! Ha ha! Can you imagine? They should have a special show where they let scrawny old biddies like me dress up and do a big-old saggy kick line just once before we pop off.

Heather's shift just ended a little while ago. It is nice having help now. She doesn't mind helping clean rooms, dealing with customers, stocking shelves in the package store, doing inventory. She's so grateful for a job and I'm certainly grateful for the help. Randell thinks it's a terrible waste of money, having an employee, and can't see why I would want it. That's because he has no idea how much I do. It's a big help, and it makes it easier for me to focus on the things that bring in some money. And anyway, it's good to have another soul around here some-times, besides the birds and squirrels and whatever God-only-knows-what lives back there in the forest, behind that ugly chain-link fence.

Will Brantley has been by more and more often lately. I had to put up a sign, 'Shoes required' because of him, always coming in here in his jiffy feet. He just picks up whatever random thing he sees first, a bag of chips or a pack of jerky, then he leans against the counter and settles in for a chat. I try to be hospitable, but finally I have to say: 'well, I suppose I need to get on back to my work now'. Then he acts embarrassed. But he comes back and does it again a few days later. Now that Heather is here, he comes by less, but it seems somehow Heather is never at work when he does come in. I hope that's in my mind, or a coincidence. Otherwise, it sounds like the plot of one of those horror movies.

My brain sure gets to racing off with itself, doesn't it? Sometimes I catch myself in the mirror while it's going, and I don't look at all like I feel. I'll be going along thinking, if anyone saw me right now, they'd wonder why I have wild eyes and why my neck is straining so. But in the mirror, turns out it's just a calm smile. Like Mona Lisa. Just that peaceful and benevolent. And kind of creepy.

Next week, Randell has to take a trip to Macon to meet with a supplier. I wouldn't let him tell me I didn't need to come this time. Told him I'd amuse myself sight-seeing while he had his meeting. I never did get a picture outside the Douglas Theater, and I really could go for some of Mama Louise' and Ms. Inez's fried chicken, with a side of okra and tomatoes, at H & H. I wonder if they'd remember me. Anyway, I'm going. Heather can hold things down for a few days just fine.

When Junie came by today it was right as Randell was leaving, so she caught a ride into town. That worked out well. I wonder if Randell will get a real haircut before his meeting. He never lets it get below his ears, says his daddy would have beat his butt if he tried to let it grow, but the back is getting really long. When he was getting ready to leave, I saw him stop to check it in the lobby mirror. He tossed his head like a rock star. It was hilarious and I had to duck in the back so he wouldn't see my face crack up.

1993
Diary, I'm back. I'm gonna quit apologizing for the long lapses.

The police just came by here, about an hour ago now. Nellie is missing! Nellie Olfort, from the St. Mary's Inn down the road. They say she's disappeared. God, what could have happened to her? The policeman seemed to think she and I would have been close friends, being that we both run motels along this highway and probably have some of the same customers. He looked doubtful and I felt guilty, the way the one officer kept asking. We've met, of course, in passing at the grocery store, places like that. I know we have some of the same suppliers. They asked me about regular customers, folks who come by this way all the time, anyone acting strange. Had to tell them about Will Brantley, but I also told them he seems harmless. He's just bored and lonely. If they think somebody kidnapped her, and oh I can hardly bear to think of that, but if that's what they're thinking, then they should be looking for a transient passing through just as much as a local. I would think so, anyway. Maybe they are. I don't know how the police work.

I'm going to keep the lobby door locked from now on, at least for a while. That's what the police suggested. Never occurred to me until now, but I'm a sitting duck in here. Sitting behind this counter waiting for any old stranger to happen in. And when they do, I just smile and speak to them like they're old friends. They're not though, are they? Lord, I pray they find her soon, safe and sound. Maybe she just took off for a while. I've considered it myself a time or two. Maybe she's taking a little vacation and she'll be back wondering what the fuss is about.

Okay, so I locked the front door. Feels so strange to do that. This is a motel! Who locks the lobby of a motel? I'll have to keep an eye out on the parking lot. Maybe put up a sign to knock for service? Went down the service hall to the liquor store and checked that lock, too. Now I'll just sit here, I suppose, till Randell gets back.

Diary, it should be easier by now, but it's not. I don't think I will ever understand this world.

BETTY,
43 YEARS OLD

1995

Dear Diary,

He still thinks I don't know. And after a lot of thought, I'm going to keep it that way.

I want to hit him in the chest and kick him in the head and smash up his car. Then I want to go to her work and slap her without saying a word and walk back out. Then I'd like to set this place on fire and sit across the street and watch it burn to the ground.

Instead I'm going to keep this knowledge just for myself. I have never in my life been this steamed. My brain is on fire but I won't let them see it. It's nice to have something of my own.

Looking back now I am realizing it's been going on for a long time. After Junie's last divorce, she started calling on Randell a lot to help with this and that. And he said he was helping her out, doing it all on my account. But after what I saw today when I came home early and there they were, coming out of room six—her clawing after him, and him grinning like an idiot—after seeing what I saw, I know. Her cloying voice saying his name: "Ran-dehhhhl." I'm going to be sick.

Even if she hasn't succeeded in seducing him (yet), for him to have an emotional affair? It's WORSE! If they have that, what exactly do I have?

I should tell her she could have had this life if she wanted. All she had to do was ask, and I would have handed it all over on a silver platter. With a piece of parsley on the side. Here you go, Junie! Enjoy! When did I ever keep anything from her? From the first time she said my name that day in class, she's been taking from me.

I remember like it just happened. I was sitting in the back row of class and she was sitting in front of me, like she always did from that time on. The second week of sixth grade. I had just gotten my first bottle of nail polish and when the teacher left the class alone, I took it out of my bag. I think I wanted her to see it, to impress her.

She said, "Ooh, give it here. Can I see?" and I handed it over, just like that. Then she painted a thick layer on each one of her pearly pink fingernails and wiped it all off. She used my nail polish to take off her own polish, all the while giggling with Sadie.

What I should have done was stand up right then. I should have said, "Give it back right now, Junie." But I didn't. The bell rang and she shoved the bottle in her bag with her other things. I followed them down the hall to get it back, and so I happened to be standing with them when their boyfriends stopped us. One of them invited me to a birthday party that weekend, just because I was standing with her. I never did get that polish back.

I didn't say anything then, and I never did all the years we've known each other. She takes what she wants, and I'm supposed to feel lucky she wants it.

So maybe I share the blame. I'm the one who let her think she could take anything she wants, that what's mine is hers. All she had to do was take it. Well, I wish she would have just taken <u>him</u> a few years ago when she decided she wanted him.

My imagination is running wild. I've run through it all in my head already—how I wish I could find them together, doing whatever weird things they do, because God only knows. Probably Junie puts on her old cheerleading uniform and sashays around while he whips his grimy new mullet side to side till they both fall asleep. I would slam the door to wake them up and then sidle up and make them wait for what I was going to say until their stupid cheating mouths were hanging open, and then I'd point my finger in both their doughy faces, one at a time, and smile real sweet and say, "Go. Straight. To. Hell."

It's no use confronting him with it. He would just do that quick-talking thing he does and assume I don't think fast enough to keep up with his jive. I do keep up. I always have. I just don't tell him so. I've always let him talk and talk and walk off all self-satisfied. I don't <u>care</u> enough to argue with him. How about that? She can have him. Good luck getting that yuppie life you've always wanted, sweetie!

Wonder how long till the romance of a sexless marriage will get old for her? Or maybe she does something for him I didn't. I've learned to live with it, our relationship never was like a man and wife anyway. It's gotten to the point where I look in the mirror and think, "That slightly turned-up nose, these dishpan hands, this neck, these breasts, this womb, it's all been a waste. It's all going to be dust some day, and for what? What was the point of all this? What was the point of my life? I was loved once. I've loved, too. But I gave it all up. Gave up more than I can ever know. I came back here because Mama needed me, and because Junie said so. She conspired with Mama and got me back here, not for me. For them.

After a while, I suppose I can see it now, my mind unplugged, and my body gave in. And gave up. It accepted its fate and the unneeded, unused parts just went to sleep.

Well, I tell you what. I bet with some changes of circumstance, they could wake the hell up.

TABS AND BLANKS
PODCAST

Transcript
Season 2, Episode 11: In-Studio Discussion

Although this is a truly fascinating story and we at Open Mouth Productions knew it was one worth telling, we never could have imagined the way it has blown up in the last few weeks. Thank you, thank you. To each and every one of you, our listeners, for downloading, sharing, leaving reviews...the community on the website is growing every day, and you guys seem to love the comment section! We especially want to thank the new subscribers who moved the podcast into the 'Most Downloaded' category on iTunes last week. Yay! Around here, we've started lovingly referring to you all as 'Sweepers.' We love you, Sweepers!

As we move along in this story, with the interviews we know we have coming, the names might start to get confusing. But not to worry: we have a page on our website with photos of most everyone I mention here along with biographies to help keep you on track.

While you're on the website, check out the information from our sponsors. And when you shop with them, use our code CHIMNEY for exclusive discounts.

Melody: Welcome to a special episode. Today we're in the studio, and we're going to take a breath, right, Dorian? Yes, he's nodding yes, we are.

Dorian: Sorry, I forgot I'm allowed to talk for a second there.

Melody: I know! This is such a treat.

Dorian: For sure. Hopefully you won't regret letting me off my muzzle.

Melody: Okay, okay, they don't have to know all that, Dor. *(*laughter*)* Don't forget your non-disclosure agreement.

(*laughter*)

Melody: This in-studio episode will let us step back, take a breath, assess everything that's happened so far in this investigation. Today Dorian and I will take some time to go over some key things we've learned so far, and just talk more about what we've heard from people who were there the last night

Betty was seen. Here are a few compelling quotes from our interview with former St. Mary Motel employee Heather Stoates:

"...I do think Betty was outgoing and friendly. She could hold her own with all these men, and women, who came for the liquor and stayed for the congeniality. But she was also very private. She didn't like people in her private business, so to say..."

"...Yes, I did see Ms. Betty getting into the car mad one time, slamming the door and driving off, not speeding off but you know, raising some gravel behind her. Randell was real quiet mostly, but he had that look in his eyes that you knew you didn't want to cross him..."

Dorian: Mel, I know you looked at the case file and there was no request for a warrant, or at least not one that's in the file. Detective Billy John told us there would have been no use asking for one. But gosh, doesn't it seem like someone, a family member or somebody, would have just come up there and demanded to look around the property?

Melody: I agree to a certain extent, Dor. We know from our interview of some of the family and friends that none of them tried that. But, I have to say—we've seen the property ourselves. Listeners might remember from Episode 2, "Legend Tripping"? It's huge. Like, vast.

Dorian: We should mention that we did do a drive by after listening to Loreen's tapes of Randell.

Melody: Right, right. Seeing the property really puts some things in perspective. Like, it's easy to say 'why didn't they search the wooded area.'

Dorian: But if there's literally no way in to the wooded area...

Melody: Right! And if it was as heavily forested and overgrown with underbrush at that time as it is now, which Heather did state it was, well then I can see how it would have seemed useless to do much more than walk out to the end of the clearing, maybe into some more open and accessible areas, to look. But beyond that I can see how it might have seemed silly to try to go hacking their way further in. She couldn't have gotten far into the forest. It would have been obvious, she would have left some sort of trail, if she had gone beyond their fence. She would have had to jump a chain link fence, and *then* literally clear the land as she went, like with a machete or something, to go off into those particular woods, the Van Disson property.

Dorian: I guess that makes sense. And not to be callous about it, but it's the truth: there would have been buzzards circling over the area if she had died there, or if she had been buried out there. Unfortunately, that's the reality out there in such a rural area.

Melody: Right. And we don't think we need to be coy about it. It is what happens, and that's something searchers look for in missing persons cases where the person may have gotten lost in the woods. It's just a natural fact, and we know that buzzards have helped find bodies in many missing person cases.

Dorian: I do wonder about the shark teeth, though. Heather said Betty had that jar where she dropped in shark teeth she found. She said Betty would sometimes go off for a day or even two, and she didn't know where, thought she was probably up caring for her mother across the state line, but when she'd come back she'd drop a couple of new teeth in the jar. We don't know where she used to look for them, but it's safe to assume if she was looking in that immediate area, that it would have been on the banks of the St. Mary's. We did confirm that people find these fossilized teeth and other fossils around the area. It's a popular hobby.

Melody: Yes, and so by extension, it isn't far-fetched—you can't help but wonder—did she go searching that day and have an accident? Maybe she slipped and hurt herself, fell into the river? We've been out over there—over the blue bridge on Highway 17—several times now, and it's pretty remote. Doesn't seem far-fetched that Betty could have had an unfortunate accident and disappeared under the water.

Dorian: Right and Detective Whitaker confirmed that was in his mind as he had to put her case on the back burner after 9-11. He let himself believe that was a big possibility even though they couldn't prove it. But something I find fascinating, and sad, is how little coverage Betty's story actually got at the time. I mean, we know 9-11 happened soon after, but even in the days before, when her disappearance was new, there were *maybe* three articles I could find on the story from the time.

Melody: It just shows a lot, that lack of coverage. I feel like it would be different today, almost twenty years later. There would be more urgency, maybe a silver alert? The Silver Alert program wasn't activated in Florida until 2008. But the lack of coverage of her story, to me, is crazy.

Dorian: It is.

Melody: Then there's the Chimney Sweep business. Betty helped with that business, and that opens up a whole other line of people she came in contact with. Like, a whole other world that was mostly Randell's, but that she had a foot in by the fact that she was basically running that business for Randell.

Dorian: By the way, Mel—and I promised myself I wouldn't get you off-topic today, but oh well—I don't know if you've looked at the message boards lately? On the website? You would not believe the pictures that are coming in over there. Listeners are sharing on the boards, sharing to Facebook, posting on Instagram, tweeting and retweeting, all with the hashtag #thechimneysweep. People who live in the Riverside Avondale area here in Jacksonville are posting pictures of the bricks in their chimneys, in their fireplaces, the areas around their fireplaces…it's crazy. Everyone is searching for that special brick, but no one really knows what they're looking for. I'm actually afraid that some people might start hacking at their fireboxes with pick axes. I'm thinking, let's just state something right now, right? Like, "PSA! Don't destroy your fireplace!" Right?

Melody: I would hope people don't need to be told something like that. Our listeners are smart people. Surely they're too intelligent for that.

Dorian: Right, Mel. I would agree, but look at these pictures! These cool old houses…like, don't destroy your hundred-year-old fireplaces, folks! And if you do, don't blame us!

Melody: I bet there will be a run on those, what are they called? You know what I mean, those tiny cameras on a long bendy thing that let construction people see inside walls and stuff?

Dorian: Inspection cameras.

Melody: That's it.

Dorian: Yes! They're probably selling out everywhere.

Melody: Before we ended our interview with Betty's Cousin Loreen, I asked her about the legend of the treasure hidden behind a fireplace down in Riverside. Do you happen to have that clip?

Dorian: I do happen to have that clip.

Melody: Would you be so kind as to play that for us?

Dorian: As you wish.

"...I never heard that story, except from Randell. Just what you heard there in the recordings. If he really did think he might find some treasure some day, I don't suppose he would have been spreading it around, do you? But you heard those tapes, Melody. You tell me. If you ask me, Randell was full of shit. He had delusions of grandeur. Here he is running a crappy roadside motel and package liquor store, and he thinks he's a secret treasure hunter, like Indiana Jones or something. You know what treasure I think he should have looked for? My cousin Betty, that's what..."

So what do you think, Sweepers? Was Randell, The Chimney Sweep, on to something in his search for stolen Swedish treasure hidden by a mason during the time of reconstruction after Jacksonville's Great Fire of 1901? Or was he following a flimsy legend, unable to let go of a tall tale perpetuated by his father, who locals say was a big talker, a story teller, a fabulist, all the way to his death bed?

Dorian: You know, one thing I thought of regarding the whole treasure hunt thing is: we don't know how Randell's interest in finding this treasure may have affected Betty. Detective Billy John said Randell was, and I am quoting here, "obsessed." I don't know why, but at the time that reminded me of something I read about Michael Jackson in his last days. His tour manager said Michael didn't want to go to sleep because God was speaking to him and giving him ideas, and if he went to sleep, God might give the ideas to Prince.

Melody: Oh my gosh, seriously?

Dorian: Yeah. It's sad, and a little funny. But also it just illustrates that mindset when someone becomes obsessed, and when that obsession stems from a formative—or at least highly influential—relationship. Strange things begin to make perfect sense to the person who is suffering from the delusion.

Melody: Interesting. And of course, we're not doctors and we don't know Randell's mental health status at that time, but you're right. If his obsession had gotten that deep, it certainly could have been a factor in Betty's disappearance. Maybe she got tired of him spending all his time on it. Maybe she issued an ultimatum. That's not far-fetched at all. And I'll have to look up that story about Michael Jackson. Your mind works in mysterious ways, Dor. Very mysterious.

Dorian: I know, I don't know why I put those two things together. Maybe because everything comes back to music for me, one way or the other.

Melody: (*singing*) Like the Blondie song?

Dorian: Yup, like that. Exactly like that.

(*laughter*)

(*silence*)

Melody: Switching gears now, we also wanted to talk about the recordings we heard a few weeks ago. Our focus needs to remain on investigating the mystery behind what happened to Betty Van Disson. She was a wife, a daughter, a sister, a well-known member of the close-knit rural community of northeast Florida and southeast Georgia. We have a clip queued up from our interview with Heather Stoates, the Van Dissons's employee in the time just before Betty disappeared. We didn't use this anecdote in the episode where we featured Heather, but I think the listeners should hear it. It gives you such a picture of the real woman at the heart of this case. Betty was a real person. She could be any of our mothers, our grandmothers, our sisters. Heather was describing one of the last times she saw Betty, and I mean, ugh! My heart! Here, let's go ahead and play that for the listeners right now, Dor.

Heather: So I came in to work a little early and Betty was in the lobby with some headphones on. I'd never seen her with headphones! She had this sad little old Walkman in her hand. She was wearing one of her cotton work dresses with the little flowers on it and the lacey collar—just the cutest little southern country lady you ever saw, though she was pretty tall—but anyway, here she was dancing around like she was in a rap video or something! Just sticking her bootie out and shaking. I mean, she had the moves down! I went back outside and made a little commotion with the door, didn't want to embarrass her. But when she saw me, she pulled the headphone plug out so I could hear what she was listening to. Damned if it wasn't Mary J. Blige! '*Family Affair,*' you know? '*No More Drama*'? I've never been so shocked in my life, I tell you what.

Melody: I mean, come on. What a cool story. It shows another part of Betty a lot people we've spoken to didn't seem to know about. I mean, no one else in any of our interviews said, 'Oh yeah, and she was a big R&B fan.' It really reminded me that Betty was a real person. Not that I needed reminding, but you know what I mean.

Dorian: Yes, I know what you mean. I felt the same listening to that while I was editing. Had to stop the playback just to sit back and think about it. It made me smile. You know I'm a big music fan myself, love the history and the way it brings people together—like nothing else does. That image of her dancing to a song no one would have expected? It's kind of adorable. Makes me wish I could have met Ms. Betty.

Melody: In that previous episode, we listened to Betty's cousin Loreen Davies's recordings of several conversations she had with Betty's husband Randell a few weeks after Betty went missing.

Dorian: Fascinating stuff. I mean, just the fact that she had the presence of mind to do that right then, so soon after her cousin had gone missing. Brave, too.

Melody: Yes, it was amazing really. Many listeners have written in on the boards to comment that Randell didn't sound like a person concerned about his missing wife. We've all heard ad nauseam how everyone reacts to these things differently, everyone grieves differently, et cetera. And I do think that it's dangerous to impose onto a narrative our own opinions of how a person 'should' act in any given situation—

Dorian:Right.

Melody:—but at the same time, we do get impressions, we get a feeling, just from our own experiences as people, as human beings. We can't help that. I know it's greedy to say this, given that these voice recordings of Randell, speaking candidly in the privacy of his home at that time, are a goldmine of information, even just to be able to hear his voice and to get a feel for his mindset, but honestly, listening to those recordings makes me wish so hard that there was video, too.

Dorian: Oh dang, can you imagine? Man. But you're right, for what we're doing here, trying to go back in time basically and uncover some unturned stone, to find a path that hadn't been explored yet, those recordings are just...priceless.

Melody: And real quick, as always, we want to remind all of our listeners out there, anyone who might have knowledge about the disappearance of Betty Van Disson to please, please reach out to us via our website, The Chimney Sweep dot com, or on our dedicated phone line.

Melody: We're going to talk more about our impressions of the voice recordings after the break. But right now, I do want to update listeners on some exciting news from our sponsors, Branches DNA.

I recently had the opportunity to try Branches new DNA testing services. It's an easy, quick test you can do from the comfort of your own home. Just swab your mouth, insert the sample into the pre-serving tube, drop it in the prepaid envelope, and mail it in! It's so simple. Within a few weeks, you'll have your results, which can be sent to you via their amazing Branches DNA app. On the app, you can find out why you have those hazel eyes, or where your great-grandmother came from, or even con-nect with branches of your family tree you never knew you had. Go request your test kit now and don't forget to use our code to receive that Chimney Sweep fan discount.

MELODY

2019

The dining room studio had grown dim around them as Melody and Dorian spent the last hours of the afternoon hunched over their keyboards. Earlier, they'd puttered with the puzzle during a lunch ordered from the local ramen place, but they weren't making much progress. A piece was definitely missing, and another missing piece was the last thing either of them needed right now. They'd both given up, placed their bowls in the sink, and gone back to working on the next episode.

"Maybe Betty was restless, regretted her life choices," Melody said now, breaking the silence. The blue light of her laptop screen reflected a mirror image of Betty Van Disson's winsome face. "Never gave up her dreams of going off to the city to be something great, or at least someone different. She could have been bitter, wishing she'd gone after those things instead of spending her days cleaning a motel and selling liquor and keychains to tourists and down and out locals. Maybe she just couldn't take it any more and she just...blew."

Dorian made an explosive sound, puffed his hands out beside his ears.

"I'm serious, Dor. Regret and bitterness can make people do crazy things. Imagine being her age and looking back on your life and realizing you've spent it all and maybe you don't love how you spent it. What if you never took your shot?"

Dorian nodded. He knew exactly where she was coming from, and what had brought on her introspective mood. He was right there with her.

"This case has me all in my feelings, too," he said. "I can't help imagining myself when I'm old, and in my imagination I am lot like my grandpa, balding and with a round belly, a mole right here on my liver-spotted scalp topped with a single, solitary silver hair, and it bobs dejectedly with every bite of my lonely dinner of stale cheese puffs."

Melody held her stomach and laughed. "Wow," she said incredulously, trying to catch her breath. No one made her laugh like Dorian did, and more than that, he knew precisely when she needed it.

"I see a single recliner positioned directly in front of a blinking television. Wait. Why is it an antique RCA, complete with those buggy antennae?"

Melody took a deep breath, trying to stop laughing. "Come on, Dor. Can't you see what that might have meant for Betty? What it might have led her to?"

"What are you saying? You think maybe she committed suicide?" he said.

Melody winced. Though she'd never met the woman, she *had* spent months thinking about her, studying her, trying to track her life. She saw Betty's face when she closed her eyes, dreamed of walking into the deserted Maryview Motor Inn and finding a smiling Betty behind the counter. Last week, she'd imagined the wizened checkout clerk at Winn Dixie could have been her. She'd actually done mental math while the woman scanned her groceries, trying to figure out whether it was possible. She couldn't let herself imagine Betty taking her own life. It was too much.

"I feel like maybe we're avoiding talking about it." The words formed in her mind and came out of her mouth before she realized it was out loud. At the sound of her own voice, her stomach dropped.

"About...?" Dorian's chair swung around, his feet planting when he faced her, his hands clasped between his knees.

"What I mean is..." Melody said quickly. She forced her eyes away to stare at the crack of light between the blackout curtain panels, "...starting out on this investigation, we didn't know exactly what we were getting into. It was a good local missing person story, and that's why it won out for this season's topic. But now that we're deep in it, at this point we should have an opinion of what we think happened, right? Even if it's too soon to share in the podcast?" She tightened her ponytail. "I know *I'm* starting to have a feeling. You must be, too. Are we just avoiding talking about it?"

Probably. Seems like we do a lot of that lately.

Dorian studied his hands. "Maybe."

Melody pulled the sleeves of her hoodie down and gripped the wristbands in her palms, crossing her arms like a hug. "I wanted to believe she ran away. I wanted to find out she saw how Nellie Olfort's case went cold and thought nobody would look for her."

Dorian nodded. "Me, too."

"That's not what happened, though, is it?"

"Probably not."

"And we still have to present this story as if we think it might be possible."

"We don't have to," Dorian said. Anything to wipe away the despondent look on her face right now.

"Maybe we shouldn't have switched to real time. Maybe we should have had it all planned out to the end. Maybe the interviews should have been done and laid out nice and neat ahead of time." All those 'maybes' brought the lyrics of a song to both their minds simultaneously. They exchanged sheepish smiles.

One of the first secrets they'd shared in college was their mutual love of Sick Puppies songs, a fact neither of them would have admitted to anyone else, at the time. When they attended the Welcome To Rockville concert festival downtown especially to see them, they did it under the pretense of supporting Shinedown, the hometown band, like everyone else.

"We decided we hate that, though, right?" Dorian said. "We didn't want to give our listeners that feeling that they were being manipulated to think one way or another. Because we hate that." *'We, we, we,' all the way home... Could I say 'we' more times?*

Melody uncrossed her arms. "You're right. We did it this way for a reason. Maybe it's because this one's local," *that word again*, "I don't know, but it's definitely affecting me differently. Last season was a whirlwind and a rush—our first podcast!—and all I cared about was not being a big flop."

"This year is different."

"This year *is* different."

They looked at each other, holding a fearless gaze for the first time in a long time. Dorian's lips parted and a syllable escaped before he was cut off. Melody's phone rang.

"Sorry," she said.

"No, check it," Dorian said.

She checked the caller ID and declined the call. When she looked back at Dorian, he had turned back toward the computer monitor, the spikes of his black hair backlit by the glow.

Melody's jaw clenched. She leaned in to her laptop and clicked through to the listeners' discussion boards. Nothing like the comment section under a new in-studio discussion episode for a dose of distraction.

"What's the deal with Melody and Dorian? Are they a couple or what?"

"It's so cute when they call each other 'Mel' and 'Dor.' Ugh, sooo cute."

"I am shipping Mel and Dor <u>so hard</u>. Their babies would be so adorable!'

"Anybody else downloading the transcripts? I read them at night lol. Thinking of starting a fan fic story on Wattpad all about 'Mel and Dor' and their torrid romance."

"I'd read that!"

"Why don't they just admit it already. It's so obvious."

"Maybe they'll read this and put us out of our misery."

Melody glanced over the top of her laptop. Dorian sat in front of the main computer. The splash banner of their website's discussion board spread across his screen. He was reading the same posts, and he kept cocking his head one way, then the other. His fingers thrummed on the mousepad, and the sides of his bright red cheeks glowed almost violet in the blue light.

BETTY,
49 YEARS OLD

SEPTEMBER 2, 2001

Diary,

Well, I guess I'm starting a new journal, since my others were stolen. I'm writing this one like a letter, though. Might as well, since I know you're probably going to read this, too, Randell! You want something to read so bad? Well, here you go. I don't even want to but it's all I know to do. I'm so angry right now and I have no one to talk to about it. You made sure of that, didn't you?

Even writing feels wrong now. It feels like someone is inside my head with me. I can't be alone in my own mind.

The walls of this motel lobby may as well be bars. It's like I haven't looked at them clearly all these years, just putting my head down and trying so hard to make a good life. For both of us, Randell. Just make the best of it, I kept telling myself. All these years. I put aside what I wanted and keep on trying to be grateful for all I have. I have tried. But this is too much for me.

You took my diaries! My private journals. The only thing I had of my own all these years, out here living in a motel on the side of a country highway other people only use for a detour. But you didn't only read them, you took them. I feel I'll explode from wanting them back.

So you're mad about what you read. I suppose that's why you never should have read them! I'm here, aren't I? I've cared for this place and made it into something when all the others have gone under. You've never been a husband. You act more like a teacher, always knowing better than me, or like my father. Even parents get in trouble for reading their kid's diary these days! I can't even act like the woman of my own house. You act more like my boss than like a husband. Like I'm some kind of on-call secretary. My mama wanted me to be an old-fashioned kind of wife, and I guess you know now: I never did want to be that. I wasn't brave enough back then. Mama needed me and I was obligated. So I chose a different life from the one I wanted. I tried to believe I should have wanted this life from the beginning. You've shown me over and over how little you think of me, Randell, except as someone to keep your home and your motel and book your chimney sweep jobs.

Well, guess what? I'm not doing it any more.

Here's all I have left to say to you:

I know you and Junie are seeing each other.

Tell me what you did with my diaries.

And don't ever call me Princess again.

TABS AND BLANKS
PODCAST

Transcript
Season 2, Episode 12: Holy...

On this week's episode, a stunning discovery. This new information doesn't really affect the case. It affects me, your host, Melody Hinterson.

(*soundbite*) "So Melody, your ancestry results are in. You're not going to believe this. You probably should sit down."

My interest, my connection, and my emotional investment in this case just went from curious local journalist—

Dorian: Look right there, Melody. Whose name is that in your family tree?

—to family historian.

Melody: Okay, wait. Let me understand. So Betty Van Disson's cousin Loreen is related.

Dorian: See right there? She is your blood relative.

Yeah. That happened. Let me back up.

A few minutes ago, Dorian and I were getting ready to do some office stuff, because behind the scenes at a podcast is a lot less glamorous than you might think, and all of a sudden Dorian says, "Ooh, Mel, there's an email from Branches DNA." I looked over at him and his hand hovering over the mouse. He said, "Want me to open it?"

I said, "Yeah, go ahead," like, 'Duh, sure I want to see the results,' and I went on about my business, just watering my sad orchid and willing it back to life.

Dorian is quiet for a minute, and then he says, "Oh my gosh, Mel." He looks up, and his face is drained. Like, pale. So I come to look over his shoulder, thinking maybe it says I'm related to Hitler, or some other awful thing I'm not sure I'm ready to know.

Dorian had the presence of mind to start recording. I read the results. And here we are.

Melody: Okay, fire up the equipment.

Dorian: I already did.

This week, Betty's disappearance becomes much more personal.

Dorian: The best I can tell, one of Loreen's kids did a DNA test through this site. And the two of you are matched, says "likely close relation, perhaps second cousin."

Melody: I never understood what all that meant. Like, third cousin once removed on your daddy's side? What even is that?

We can see a general outline of my family tree, just a line map that shows how I'm related to Loreen, on the website, but basically her son Michael Jack submitted his DNA to BranchesDNA.com*, the popular site that lets you track down your family tree and find out where you came from, and also our podcast's biggest sponsor this season. This site also sponsors the wildly popular reality television series "Roots and Branches" on the cable channel AFN, where celebrities get help from genealogists at Branches to find out about interesting, and sometimes problematic, people way far up their family trees. They usually focus on the least-desirable leaf, if you know what I mean. Makes for dramatic television. It's always a good time and a hoot to watch those famous faces fall when they find out that seven-times granddad Jebediah was a slave-owner who had seven kids—four with his wife and three with the daughter of his long-time foreman.*

As you can imagine, I'm pretty blown away by this news. This case originally stuck out to me out of our list of potential Florida cold cases because of the proximity to where I grew up, and because I was amazed I'd never heard of it before in all my years as a resident, and as an aspiring journalist. I'm so grateful to Nora for posting about her missing cousin Betty on our discussion board last season. The story of Betty Van Disson had somehow just disappeared in the backwoods, settled somewhere high in the canopy, got smothered by new growth.

But, trust me, listeners: I am more determined now than ever to shake every tree till the truth comes falling down.

MELODY

2019

Melody pushed open her mom's front door with her hip and walked through the bungalow to the kitchen. Paint cans and brushes covered most of the small countertop.

"Hey Ma, I'm here!" Melody called. "Brought you your favorite!" She pushed a can of Painter's White aside with her elbow, set down a Publix grocery bag, and pulled out the contents. "Flamin' Hot Doritos! Your favorite!" She shook the bag as if calling a puppy for treats.

"Okay, okay!" her mother's voice came from around the corner, "What do you want?" There was some pressing and beeping of buttons, then the sound of water gushing into the washing machine.

"Nothing!" Melody said. She washed up and slid onto a bar stool as her mother appeared, pressing a fuchsia kiss onto her daughter's cheek then rubbing at it apologetically with her thumb. Melody grimaced and hugged her around the waist.

"How're you doing, sweetie face?" Belinda said through puckered lips.

"Good, good," Melody replied. She inhaled sharply. She hoped her mother's reassuring eucalyptus spearmint scent might calm her. "I got some crazy news, and I think you're gonna find it pretty interesting, too." She patted the barstool beside her.

"Something you had to tell me in person?" Belinda's light brown eyes narrowed.

"Well, yeah," Melody said. "I wanted to tell you before you hear it on the podcast."

"Oh, intriguing," Belinda said. "Give me one sec." Belinda gave up trying to perch on the barstool and settled for one leg up, one on the floor.

"Whatever. Leave me alone." Belinda smacked her daughter's behind. "Now, what is this mysterious news you have to tell me?" An unexpected pause and a change passing over her daughter's face made Belinda's brows draw together. "Okay, Melody, what is it?"

Melody turned to face her mother, placed a hand on hers. "Well, you know the lady whose disappearance we're investigating this season?"

"Yes, of course." Belinda relaxed. "Betty Van Disson, the second lady to disappear from a motel she ran on Highway 17. All my friends have taken turns driving up there and snapping pictures of the place. They text them to me. They all think they're 'legend trippers' now." She made little air quotes. "What about her? Oh!" She slapped the counter and gasped. "Did you solve it?"

"No, no. It's not that. But I did find out something really interesting. From a DNA test." Her hand moved to her mother's shoulder. "It's pretty big news Mom."

"Okay..." Belinda watched Melody's hand slide down her arm, then looked questioningly at the cautious look on her daughter's face.

"It looks like we're related," Melody said. "To her."

Belinda's jaw went slack and her lips parted slowly. "Related to her?"

"Yes. Listen, I know it's a lot, Mom, but it seems to be true. There was a DNA test."

"DNA?" She slid her leg off the stool and wandered to the other side of the kitchen island.

"Yes, it's a close relationship. Her cousin Loreen— you remember, the one from the podcast with the recordings?—one of her kids submitted their DNA to Branches, and apparently we matched. It showed that I'm definitely related to her on my maternal side."

"Maternal side."

"Yes, Mom. Maternal." Her elbows rooted to the counter and she pressed her palms together. *Slow down.* "I'm so sorry if this is a shock. I hope this is ok, how I told you."

Belinda leaned against the counter and gripped the edge. "Of course." Thoughts raced through her mind and over her face. Her hands rose to her cheeks. "Of course it's okay. More than okay," she said, her eyes shining. "It's amazing."

TABS AND BLANKS
PODCAST

Transcript
Season 2, Episode 13: Black Freemasons

This week, we're taking a little detour into a world we never imagined we'd enter, at least not in our pursuit of Betty Van Disson. What does the Jacksonville order of Black Freemasons have to do with the disappearance of a little old white lady, you may ask?

The unexpected story of Randell Van Disson's obsession with the idea there may be some valuables, some sort of 'treasure,' hidden in the fireplace of a historic home certainly kicked off a bit of a frenzy around here, to put it mildly. People are searching their fireplaces and chimneys in our city's historic district, there's been a run on those inspection cameras that let you see inside the walls, and property owners have taken their houses off home sharing sites like AirBnB till things calm down. Apparently, they don't want treasure hunters booking their houses in the historic district for fear they'll tear up the masonry. To all those who have been affected by the excitement, we can only think of one thing to say, and that is 'wow.' On so many levels, just wow.

We had no way of knowing this was coming when we started this investigation, but it's taken on a life of its own. And that's why this week, we have a different kind of episode for you. I think you will find it eye-opening.

It is 8 AM. We are standing on a sidewalk in an area called Lavilla, near downtown Jacksonville, Florida. We're waiting for today's esteemed guest. He is not late, mind you. We were just very early.

One thing about this city: if traffic is even a little bit bad, it can take an hour just to get from one side of town to the other. Did we mention Jacksonville is the biggest city in the country? Biggest in square miles, that is. Never mind that most of those square miles seem to be forest and water.

Lavilla has a storied and rich history. There's a middle school for the performing arts here now which feeds into the city's performing arts high school. Our engineer Dorian went to school there.

Dorian: Told you I knew my way around this area. But I never knew this building's history.

The sun is already sucking the dew from the grass and hanging it like wet laundry around our heads. We're decked out with all our gear, but we're also both wearing heavy rubber boots—brand new—as instructed by the assistant who set up our meeting.

We are standing in front of a beautiful old building, six stories of sharp red and beige brick and smooth limestone. Light glints off the eastern front-facing windows as the city wakes up around us.

Deacon Ezekiel Fullman, Jr. appears at the top of the sidewalk, waving. He's carrying his boots in a bag. Smart. Dorian and I give each other a sheepish look. We both feel pretty ridiculous standing here in the heat wearing ours.

Melody: Mr. Fullman! Hello!

Ezekiel: Ms. Hinterson! Hello, hello. You can call me Ezekiel.

Ezekiel Fullman has the walk of a man who knows people watch him, as if there are eyes in the windows above us following his procession up the walk. He is tall and narrow, with a slight hitch in his step that might be a slight set-in limp, or might be an extension of his personality. I tend to think it's the latter since I started to see that the little skip doesn't actually happen on every left-footed step. It happens when he turns his head and shoulders as one unit, looking around with a wave at the ready for the inevitable moment when someone recognizes him. Sure enough, a car driving by slows down and a hand reaches out. Ezekiel steps off the curb to slap the hand and grasp it warmly. We wait while he speaks to the driver. The sun blares off his windshield. It's going to be a hot one.

Ezekiel: Your mama and them all right?

Driver: They're good, you know. Can't keep Mama down!

Ezekiel: Haha! Hey, man, I know that's right. Listen, I got this appointment here. But we'll see you this Sunday, right?

They slap hands again, and Ezekiel beams a blinding smile after the car as it drives away. Then he smiles toward our boots and leads us up a walkway to the imposing building's grand front doors.

Mr. Fullman is a high-ranking member of the Masons and a knowledgeable historian. His encyclopedic knowledge of Jacksonville's African American history is truly impressive. I learned more in my five minute phone conversation setting up this interview than I could even absorb. We had to meet him in person.

He has agreed to meet us here today and give us a tour of this rather majestic building, The Masonic Temple, Most Worshipful Union Grand Lodge

PHA, also known as The Black Masonic Temple. Designed by former mentees of famous local architect Henry Klutho, the building has a rich history which tells the fascinating story of distinguished people whose contributions helped build this city.

We follow him through the front door. Inside the long lobby, it's as though we've literally stepped back in time. The long marbled space is still decorated with ornate woodwork detailed with crosses. Ezekiel has shared some of the amazing history of this place and its members, and we will have more of his interview on the podcast website. Right now, Ezekiel is leading us down a steep set of stairs. Yes, I said 'down.' Because even though we are in Florida, this building sits on top of a cellar space. Even more surprising? That cellar space has tunnels that lead under the streets and alleys. Underground tunnels, right here in Jacksonville, that most of us locals have never even heard of. As we move along, Ezekiel is giving us some history of the LaVilla neighborhood around us.

Ezekiel: ...worked for the railway, the turpentine industry, the docks. A lot of the people here were Gullah Geechee people. My people. By about 1870, there were colonies of freedman in this area—former Union soldiers, freedmen—from as far as South Carolina, they came here. Because what do we have here? The river, that's right. And plenty of other natural resources. By 1920, the community was the largest Black metropolis in the Lowcountry.

Did you know the Gullah Geetchee neighborhood of LaVilla boasts the first documented performance of The Blues?"

Dorian: That I knew!

Ezekiel: Good. That's good. More people should know what this place means to the city. The new courthouse is that way.

Ezekiel points above our heads ostensibly orienting us, but personally, I'm hopelessly turned around. The "new courthouse" Ezekiel mentioned actually opened in 2012, but it still hasn't entirely lost the moniker. We follow Ezekiel's pointing finger all around the space.

Ezekiel: So over here, this tunnel used to go under Broad Street, all the way across to where the Richmond Hotel used to be. When Black politicians, preachers, musicians, people like that, came to town, they could use the tunnel as a passageway between buildings. But it was also there for the community, if trouble broke out.

My curious journalist mind instantly wants to research the Gullah Geechee people, and maybe even find a story for the next season of this podcast. Although theirs may not be my stories to tell, they are stories we should all know. As we tromp through the damp underworld of the city, I imagine familiar

Broad Street above our heads. Until now, it was just another road into downtown. Little did I know...

The smallest sounds echo in the dank, cavernous space, and I confess to enjoying a shiver of thrill at the hollow return of my own voice.

Melody: So as you know, I've been looking into the old story of a missing lady up near the Georgia border, and the funny thing is that led us to a legend about a stolen Swiss treasure. The story is that it could be hidden inside or behind a chimney or a firebox in some old house in Avondale or Riverside, which is right near here.

Ezekiel: Oh yes.

Melody: Yes, Riverside is nearby? Or yes, you've heard about the legend?

Ezekiel laughs.

Ezekiel: Yes, I've heard about the legend. Of course I have. It's well known in certain circles around here. I'm not telling you any big secret when I say, yes, I've heard of the legend.

Melody: Is there anything you can share about that?

Ezekiel pauses, seems to be sizing me up anew.

Ezekiel: Only that it could be true. *(*laughter*)* The story goes that a mason came to town for work after the Great Fire of 1901, and according to oral history, he did hide something behind the masonry of a firebox or a chimney he worked on with the plan of going back for it when the trail cooled behind him. What I've heard is that it was a piece of a fine music box, you know the kind they're famous for making in Switzerland? The old folks used to say it was a special custom-made cylinder with a song the man of the house had commissioned from a fine music box artisan as a gift for his dying wife. It wasn't necessarily that valuable on it's own, but to the family it was a treasure, and they offered a huge reward for its return.

The story grew, like these things do, and the legend said that only a person who had known true love was supposed to ever be able to find that treasure. The legend also said the mason may have learned somehow of these tunnels here under the Temple and used them to escape the Swiss authorities when they turned up looking for him. Anyway, I hadn't heard about that legend for a long time until you asked me about it.

Melody: That's amazing. You've really shed a whole new light on the legend for us. Now these tunnels, I'm a little embarrassed to admit it, but I never realized there used to be a lovely neighborhood right there where the freeway runs through the north end of downtown. When were they demolished?

Ezekiel: You know, there is a historic appropriateness committee for every little thing people want to do to their homes in Riverside and Avondale. But when it came to our houses, houses in Sugar Hill owned by African American doctors, lawyers, business owners, et cetera...well, just tear those damn things down, right? Those were mansions, some of them. I'll show you the pictures. It's a damn shame how they were just lost forever, and they were just as historic, fine examples of architecture and workmanship, built at the same time as the ones the committee falls over itself protecting. And I'm not saying they shouldn't be protecting those old homes, you understand. What I'm saying, what I'm asking, is how was **that** neighborhood 'declining' and razing it was justified, when the other one just like it must be saved at all costs? It was because it was a prosperous community of African Americans, and some people could not abide that in their town.

To answer your question, there was a beautiful neighborhood, a park, a library. All built by that community. All gone. And the neighborhood went to seed after that. They were demolished in the fifties.

Melody: And they would have been built after Jacksonville's Great Fire of 1901, the same time as the Riverside and Avondale homes were being built?

Ezekiel: Basically, yes. That's right. Many were built before the fire, but then the ones that were damaged would have been worked on after, rebuilt and restored.

I'm struck by a new idea.

Melody: Ezekiel, about the legend again: Is it possible that the stolen item—if it were real and the legend is true, that is—is it possible it might have been stashed in a chimney in one of the mansions in Sugar Hill?

At this, Ezekiel stops short. It's clear I've hit on something—I can almost hear the 'clink'—and a controlled smile raises the corners of his mouth.

Ezekiel: Well...

Melody: Of course it is! So—thinking out loud here— if that's the case, and those houses were razed long ago, the hidden treasure, that priceless music box song cylinder, would be long gone, wouldn't it?

Ezekiel is smiling. He touches the tip of his nose and taps repeatedly.

Ezekiel: Ding, ding, ding!

So, Dear Listeners, how's that for a twist?

We climb the damp, molding stairs and reenter the main lobby. Ezekiel gives us a tour of the upper levels, including the breathtaking, fifth-floor auditorium called the Grand East where dignitaries have addressed the honorable assemblage for well over one hundred years. Too soon, we are stepping back out of the Black Masonic Temple and into the blinding light of mid-morning. After a few more minutes, Dorian and I begin to realize what we've really stepped into. We have been treated to a history lesson from a master story teller, a griot of Jacksonville's disappearing history. Ezekiel goes on, in the throes of inspired recollection, and we are loathe to interrupt his flow.

Ezekiel: I love to come to this part of town and just... soak. Just let it seep into my pores. Even though it was born from the times—it existed because of Jim Crow laws—the community that was created was rich. It was a place that birthed and nurtured ideas that became part of the fabric of American culture, and that's not over-stating it.

Feels like I can close my eyes and the ghosts of old LaVilla come to life. It was bustling here. Black business, hotels, theatres, shops. Houses of ill-repute, and bars, too, with music everywhere. Hollywood Record Store, The Colored Airdome, Frank Crowd's Bijou that became The Globe Theatre—that's where Clara White Mission is now.

We nod at him, wide-eyed. We're familiar with the Clara White Mission, had no idea what was there before.

Ezekiel: They used to call this area right here The Harlem of the South. Isn't that something? The first published account of the performance of blues singing, April 16, 1910, was right over here, at The Globe Theatre. Blind Blake's song *West Ashley Street Blues* mentions that street right over there. Patrick Chappelle started here. 'Ma' Rainey herself shouted and stomped here.

A. Philip Randolph lived and worked here. James Weldon and J. Rosamund Johnson were born here, right here in LaVilla. Think of that! They performed at Little Savoy Theatre, which was up here on West Forsyth, before leaving Jacksonville for New York City. Most folks around here have heard of James Weldon, who wrote what some like to call the "Back National Anthem" *Lift Every Voice and Sing*."

Melody: I'm familiar because I went to Stanton.

Ezekiel: Yes, Stanton High School. He graduated from Stanton School and came back to his hometown after college to teach there. He became the principal and is credited with making it the state's first high school for African Americans.

Stanton College Preparatory School is now one of the top high schools in the country, with its magnet program attracting some of the top students in the city. I am a proud alum.

Ezekiel: So he's a well-known native son, but not as many know of his brother Rosamund, who actually wrote the music to his brother's poem, and they did it right here in LaVilla. Rosamund went to New York and was a big success on Broadway, wrote and starred in his own productions. He was in the original cast of *Porgy and Bess* and in the first ever all-black production on Broadway. He went on to write music that elevated the topics allowed for black performers.

He paused and shook his head here. We're all feeling the weight of history around us here in this place.

Ezekiel: Sorry, I'm getting off topic, as usual. We're still pretty proud of the Johnson brothers.

Dorian: As we all should be.

Ezekiel: That's exactly right. Until we all see each other's community history as part of our *own* history, we haven't really solved our problems, am I right?

Dorian: Agreed.

Melody: Right.

Ezekiel sniffs deeply. He remembers something else and his eyes go wide.

Ezekiel: Ray Charles! He lived here in LaVilla, after he left the Florida School for the Deaf and Blind. He joined the Local Union 632 musician's union. He played piano over there at the Ritz Theatre, and up at another well-known place on Moncrief called The Two Spot. That's gone now. Hey, are either of you old enough to remember when Gregory Hines came to town to help save the Ritz Theatre?

I wish we had more time to explore this place and hear every story stored up in Ezekiel's whip-smart mind. It occurs to me that he and Detective Billy John could really hit it off, talking about local history. I absolutely have to come back and talk to him again, probably more than once. But for now, we have to get out of these boots and get back to the studio to get this episode out on time, on schedule as promised.

You can find links and photos of the beautiful homes of Sugar Hill that were indeed demolished to make way for the interstate through Jacksonville back in the 1950s on our website. You can also find links to information on LaVilla's rich history and the mind-boggling connections it has to America's musical and theater history. There are shots from our tour of the Temple, too, so a visit to our companion website is well worth your time this week. While you're there, don't miss Dorian's perfectly-timed photo of Ezekiel's reaction to my suggestion that the treasure—if indeed a treasure existed—could have been hidden in a mansion in Sugar Hill.

(***Transcript Update:** Since this episode aired, the photo mentioned has been removed at Mr. Fullman's request.*)

MELODY

2019

Melody and Dorian dumped their mucky boots in the back of the van. Melody swung into the passenger seat and slammed the van door. Her knees bounced as she waited for Dorian to get in. She tightened her ponytail a little too hard and winced.

"So. This is crazy. What if the treasure was hidden in a house in Sugar Hill?"

"It could have been buried when the house was demolished and then scooped up to a landfill for all anyone knows."

"Do you think they would have saved the bricks from fireplaces? I'm sure the nice fixtures were removed and sold, or taken, to be used in other buildings, right?"

"Right. I guess it would depend on the house and the circumstances. If they just wanted to knock the houses down and be done with it, maybe they wouldn't have bothered salvaging the bricks."

"So if there ever *was* a treasure, and if it were hidden in a house in Sugar Hill, it's probably gone forever."

They drove in silence for a while, Dorian's fingers thrumming the steering wheel while Melody stared out the window at the passing downtown and imagined the beautiful lost neighborhood of Sugar Hill. How had she never even heard of the neighborhood, of the name 'Sugar Hill'? She grew up right here, only a few miles from it. She'd gone to a magnet school literally on top of the area that used to bear the name. But it was as if it never existed. She'd never heard anyone mention it. All she ever heard were warnings: *It's rough up past 8th Street. Don't ever find yourself lost on the Northside. Avoid certain roads altogether.* The 'bad' part of town. Rarely a mention of the circumstances that helped it turn 'bad.'

Her cell phone buzzed under her leg.

"Miss Hinterson. It's Ezekiel." His voice has transformed, his voice shaky, unsure.

"Mr. Fullman, hi! Is everything okay?"

"Yeah, yeah. Everything's okay. It's just that..."

"Mr. Fullman?" Melody said, pressing the phone harder against her ear. "Ezekiel?"

"Yeah, I'm here. Listen, I just got off the phone with my father, Ezekiel Fullman Senior. Told him about my morning with you both, and well, I think you might want to talk to him."

"Okay, Ezekiel. Certainly." Melody waved a hand at Dorian and he pulled into a shopping center parking lot. "Should we head back over to you or—"

"I can meet you at his place actually, if you have time."

"Sure, we can do that."

"We should probably keep this off the record for now. You can ask him about recording when we get there. You're not recording right now, right?"

"That's right, I'm not recording," Melody said. "Can you tell me what this is about? What does he want to share?"

Melody listened for a minute. Dorian watched her face.

"Wow," she said. She repeated that a few times: "wow....uh huh...wowww." Her jaw went slack.

She turned toward him, eyes wide. She mouthed something and he tried to decipher it. "What?" he mouthed back. "Get going?" he whispered, and put his hand on the gear stick. She shook her head. "Put it on speaker," he said. She held up a finger and gave him an apologetic look.

"Ok, Ezekiel, thanks. See you there." She hung up and looked at Dorian. "Let's roll. He's sending an address. We're going to talk to his father." She kept her eyes on him, excited to see his reaction to what she was about to say, but searching for the words.

He put his seat belt back on and started to pull away from the curb. "Okay, why? What's going on?"

"I don't know exactly what he's got for us, but you will not believe this. It turns out Ezekiel's father was a founding member of The Downtown Sound. Can you believe that?" She shook her head.

"Wait, what?" Dorian said. Melody clicked on the address Ezekiel had sent and snapped her phone into the mount as they stopped at a small intersection. Dorian took the opportunity to swig a gulp from his water bottle as Melody continued.

"So get this," she said. "Apparently, we need to track down Dominicus Owens."

He choked on the water. "Dominicus Owens?" he said. Water sputtered on the steering wheel and he dabbed his chin with the back of his hand. The light changed and someone behind honked immediately. He had to drive. "*The* Dominicus Owens? 'Penny In My Pocket' Dominicus Owens?"

"The list goes on, but yes, that one." Melody googled his name and scanned the results. "A record one hundred three charting songs over his illustrious career, yada yada, 'Penny In My Pocket' with The Downtown Sound got them on the map, yada yada... Oh, here's a discography!"

"Did you just 'yada yada' The Downtown Sound?"

She read down the timeline, throwing out names of songs they both recognized despite their age. "Boy band Orlando Sound sampled the bridge of The Downtown Sound's 'Penny In My Pocket' on their 1994 hit 'Carry Me'..." She read on down the search results, then she stopped.

"Dor?"

"Yeah?"

"There's a song on the reunion album, never released as a single..."

"Okay."

"It's called 'The Chimney Sweep.'" She held her phone out toward him, like unearthed gold. His face transformed into map of question marks. "It's called 'The Chimney Sweep,' Dor." She clicked her screen to download a sample clip. In seconds, a haunting electric violin intro began to play, followed by a soulful, raw voice:

> *He's a hardworking man and he does what he can*
> *He never would leave her alone*
> *At the end of the day, he's the one who gets to say:*
> *'Sleep tight, baby' and 'It's all right, baby'*
> *And he keeps the fire burning, keeps the wheels turning*
> *Keeps her safe and warm*
> *At the end of the day, he's the one who gets to say:*
> *'Come over here, baby' and 'You're beautiful, baby'*
> *To the one that got away, the one that got away*
> *She's a road that leads away from home*
> *And she's the only way back*
> *She's a home fire lit by wild fire*
> *She's the ember on a match*
> *When the day is done*
> *and the fire is gone*
> *He's there to watch her sleep*
> *He's the Chimney Sweep*

While the clip played, Dorian pulled off the road and into a gravel parking lot. He and Melody stared straight ahead out the windshield, not seeing the white sunlight streaming through the old live oak trees and dappling the ground. Oblivious to the outside world, Melody and Dorian couldn't hear the sounds of cars tooling by, their passengers oblivious to the axis tilt taking place inside that strange, recycled news-mobile.

Twenty-five minutes later, they pulled up to the front of a two-story brick house. The front double door sparkled from the diamond glass panels and flower boxes overflowed with multicolored petunias and sweet potato vines both upstairs and down. A young man met them at the front door.

"Melody and Dorian? Come on in," he said. "I'm Malik, Mr. Fullman's assistant."

They wiped their feet and followed him into a cream and gold foyer with a marble floor.

He led them through into a vaulted living room. A floor-to-ceiling fireplace took up one full corner and a baby grand piano took up another. As they passed, Melody realized the statue on a marble table beside the piano was a Grammy. Dorian paused. "May I?" he said, raising his camera. Malik nodded. He snapped a photo of the wall covered in gold records and plaques from the American Music Awards, Billboard, BET.

"You'll have to ask him about using them, though." Malik said.

Ahead was a wall of windows looking over a sloping lawn that led down to the river glittering beyond. A large wooden table surrounded by a dozen chairs sat in the middle of the lawn under a gazebo draped with magenta bougainvillea. To their right was a set of French doors, and inside an old man with salt and pepper hair, both on his head and shaved to a jaunty point on his chin, sat at the head of an enormous dining table.

He was in a wheelchair, and an oxygen machine stood nearby, the tube snaking around the arm of his chair and up under his shirt. As they entered, he cleared his throat loudly and pushed himself up by his elbows, then he settled to leaning an arm on one of the armrests, cool as can be. He gave Melody and Dorian a once over and began singing.

"Hello, young lovers, wherever you are..." His voice was surprisingly strong, his eyes clear and piercing.

Melody cleared her throat and smiled crookedly. She glanced at Dorian, who was busy trying—and failing—to hide the fact that he was completely star-struck. They shook hands with Zeke, and he gestured to the ivory upholstered dining chairs on either side of him, still humming the song.

"We're not—" Melody cut a look at Dorian, who hadn't taken his eyes off Zeke for a moment, even as he unpacked his equipment. Zeke raised one eyebrow and smiled mischievously to himself. Disarmed, Melody let it drop. Why protest? Sometimes old people see things younger people don't. And arguing an idea she wasn't even sure she disagreed with any more felt disingenuous.

As Melody settled into a chair beside him, the old man looked more closely at her. His brows crinkled together and his lips puckered out curiously. "Have we met before, young lady?"

"Oh, no, sir," Melody said. "Pretty sure I'd remember that!"

He cocked his head and looked at the ceiling.

"Will it be ok if we record our interview, Sir?" Dorian said.

"Yep, sure, go ahead on," Zeke said.

Melody produced a legal pad and clicked a pen open against it. Zeke watched with keen interest as Dorian unpacked his remote audio recording equipment and set up the camera. "So, Mr. Fullman, did Ezekiel Jr. explain about our podcast, about what we're working on?" she said.

"My son explained, yes. Said maybe I should talk to you two, and he doesn't do that often. Usually he's the one turning interviews *away* for me, see. So if he says maybe I should talk to you about your investigation, I guess I will." Something caught his attention and he turned toward her.

Melody arranged her things on the table in front of her, placing everything just so, and then tucked a coil of hair behind her ear. Zeke squinted and rubbed his chin. "You're sure we haven't met before?" he asked.

"Yes, sir," Melody said, "I'm positive!"

When Dorian was ready, Melody recorded a quick introduction and started the interview.

"We have the huge honor today to speak with Zeke Fullman, one of the founding members of The Downtown Sound Band! I have to say, this is a huge treat for us. Right, Dor?"

"Yeah, I still can't believe this is happening," Dorian said.

Melody continued. "Mr. Fullman, could you tell us about yourself? How did you go from Jacksonville musician to singer in a legendary vocal group?"

"Well, how The Downtown Sound got started was with me and Sylvester, he went by Sly. Our daddies knew each other from the Brooklyn Royal Social Club,"

Dorian gave Melody a look. Zeke noticed.

"What was that? You two heard of it before?" Zeke asked.

Dorian nodded. "We happened to pass the Brooklyn Royal building just this morning."

"Yes," Melody said, "and I was telling Dorian that a friend of my mom's, a musician friend, got married there. It was a surprise wedding. The guests didn't know. We thought it was just a big birthday party. They had swing dancing. It's such a cool space."

"Your mom is a musician?"

"Yes, sir. She was, is, a singer. Jazz and pop, some wedding cover band stuff. She's very good. Even if she weren't my mom, I'd think she's amazing at what she does."

"Is that so? What's her name? Maybe I've heard of her."

Melody told him about her mom Belinda and rattled off a list of the groups her mother had performed with over the years.

"Now, I think I've heard of that last one," he said. "Think they might be the cats who played at my niece's wedding. Jacksonville's music community is a close-knit one. Kind of incestuous, meaning everybody has played with everybody else at one time or another." He laughed loudly, then coughed. Malik came in with a wooden tray and three glasses of water, passed them out, then disappeared again.

"So, anyway. Sly and I spent some good times at Brooklyn Royal with the older folks. I don't know if you want any of that history?'

"We'll listen to anything you want to tell us, Mr. Fullman," Dorian assured him, his eyes wide and shining. He'd actually fumbled his equipment on the smooth mahogany dining table.

"You asked for it!" He laughed his throaty laugh again. His hands moved through the air as if he were spiriting them back in time. "So, they had their social club, and they used to have concerts to raise money for charities in our community, see. Some well-known early gospel quartets came out of this town, and one in particular. A singer by the name of Caleb Ginyard joined the Brooklyn Royal Social Club, and he and some other fellows formed the Royal Harmony Singers. Later on, they became The Jubilaires. Guy by the name of Charlie Newsome managed them, and he helped the Dixie Hummingbirds along, too. The two groups were sort of rivals, you know, even though they were gospel singers. Can't take the competition out of harmony singing, you better believe that. Doesn't matter if you are singing for God. I bet when I get to Heaven, the choirs of angels on high will be low-key competing."

Dorian slapped his knee, then clapped his hands together. Melody shook her head apologetically and grinned at Dorian, who replied with a look that said, *Is this really happening?* A lump rose in her throat. Zeke's chest puffed, a consummate performer responding to a rapt audience, and he continued.

"Anyhow, Sly and I saw them perform when they came back to town one time, and of course we wanted to be just like them." He snapped his fingers to music in his mind and swayed in his chair. His feet shuffled on their metal footrests as they remembered dancing on stages around the world. "We used to mess around with harmonies, added our little moves, when we were real young, just little kids, but when other kids played stick ball and keep-away, we'd be up on the that old rickety roundabout merry-go-round thing, making like it was a stage, with sticks for microphones. We'd make up smooth steps, we thought so anyway, pretending we knew how to sing harmony. We did learn, eventually." His stiff fingers snapped and fluttered, ready as ever to indulge the audience with one more song. He gave an ironic smile and an expertly-timed pause, just long enough to let Melody and Dorian imagine him as a young boy.

"Later on we met Hank and O.T., in school, see. We thought we were pretty smooth, but we needed that one more voice, and it had to be somebody really fine, all the way around. We knew that. Nobody we tried fit the bill, but we knew if we could just find that one last piece, we'd be golden.

"Then one day we were hanging around the Edward Waters Campus, in Centennial Hall—we liked to sing in the stairwell, had good acoustics—and here comes this tall, lanky dude, see, coming down the stairs above us. Good looking, had the style and those shiny shoes. He looked like a star already. I remember that now like it was a scene from a movie.

"He joined right in the song we were singing, just found his part and jumped in like he'd always been there. Just a'snapping his fingers and smiling that big old smile. And that was it, man, just like that, that was it. We had our fifth man. Dominicus Owens."

Dorian shook his head. "Incredible," he said. He beamed aimlessly around the table.

"The rest is history, right?" Melody said. Zeke bowed his head, and Melody realized he must have told this origin story hundreds of times before, though his twinkling smile made them feel like they were his favorite audience of all time.

"Well yes," Zeke said. "It was us five till we lost Sly in '83." The web of lines around his eyes tightened. He pressed his lips together then opened them again. A micro-movement, but Melody noticed. She moved to ask more about Sly, but Dorian spoke.

"What happened to Sly?"

Zeke inhaled a sharp breath. "Simple version is he was messing around with somebody he shouldn't'a been messing around with, and the other man didn't like that very much. Sly was shot while he was fast asleep, naked in the wrong bed. I hate that's how he's remembered. He was my friend. He was beaten senseless once in a theater alley by some ol' KKK boys. He was caught up in the last draft, and he fought for our country, and he made it through a stint in 'Nam. He was a founding member of The Downtown Sound. A legend. In the end to go out like that..." He pinched the bridge of his nose. "Still can't talk about that, though. I'm sorry." He pressed a large knuckle between brows.

"We understand," Melody said.

Zeke shook his head, lowered his gaze, then he inhaled a big hit of oxygen. He brightened a bit, and looked at Dorian. "So that's when we got us our little Irish boy tenor."

"Skip McKee," Dorian said, snapping his fingers into two pistols.

"That's right! Old Skip," Zeke nodded and made the same hand motion, his finger guns pointing back at Dorian. "For the life of him, Skip could not do a jazz box step and turn without ending with those pistol hands. Pew pew." He laughed. "We used to make him keep his hands on top of his head during rehearsal to try to break him of it. Funniest thing you ever saw. I'll tell you what, bringing in that little white boy set some tongues wagging, but we didn't notice. Nor did we care. It was the music that mattered. We heard 'Oh, the white folks won't like it,' 'The black folks won't like it.' The sky was falling up at our record company. But our fans—the real ones, the music lovers—they loved us even more for it.

"Makes me think. All that most people out there have done the last fifty years, seems like, is talk-talk-talk about learning from the past." He waved a hand toward the front door, toward Jacksonville, toward the world. "Seems to me nobody's learning anything except history. 'My people did this, your people did that.' We still don't know how to be all one people. History is important, do not get me wrong, and we've got to remember, but it helps very little unless you learn from it, let it change you going forward. *That's* where music has *always* been ahead of the game, young people. Musicians recognized early on that we need each other, that the spark of a creative soul is a piece of God's light right here inside us. It's not a Black spark, it's not a white spark, it's not any one color. It's light. All colors. It can live in any body, whatever color skin it happens to be wrapped up in. Musicians want to get to that spark, and touch it, and pass it around. When we do that, like the kids say, 'It's fire.'"

Dorian sniffed, turned his head. Melody tapped away droplets from the corners of her eyes.

"When Skip passed last year it was like losing a brother," Zeke said. "No, not 'like.' It was exactly that. Couldn't tell me any different."

The room fell quiet. A sound from across the house brought Melody back to her questions. "Mr. Fullman, we've been looking over your discography on the way over—not that we didn't know all your many hits already, of course!—but we noticed one song from an album in the '80s. It wasn't released as a single. Called "The Chimney Sweep," and written by Dominicus Owens."

"Yes, Mini—we called Dominicus 'Mini,' just not in public!—so Mini wrote that one himself. It was after his mother passed. We all came down here for the funeral. Something happened then, and I think that may be why you two are here. After Junior talked to you two this morning, he remembered some things and put them together, see, and he called me up to ask about it." He pressed his mouth closed, opened it wide, then closed it again, tilting his chin as if unsure how to proceed.

"Right. Why does he think we need to get in touch with Mr. Owens?" Melody said. Zeke clasped his hands and stared at Melody. "It's okay, Mr. Fullman," she said. "If you say anything you'd rather we not use, we will edit it out." She reached out and placed her hand on the table between them. He looked down at it, and again his brows drew together. He searched her face, and she smiled encouragingly.

"It's kind of funny, because I've been wanting to get in touch with Dominicus again myself. See, he has my prize copy of Sugar Underwood's "Davis Street Blues," with "Dew Drop Alley Stomp" on the B side. He *claims* he saw it first, one day when we were browsing the old DJ's record store on Edison Avenue. But no, sir! He did not."

Dorian shook his head in wonder.

Melody brought the men back to the subject at hand. "You were saying Ezekiel Jr. remembered something from a funeral?

"Oh yes, that's right. My son got to thinking about Dominicus's mama's funeral, something he remembered from the cemetery. He was a kid, and he had minded through the whole church service, just on his very best behavior. I don't know if you know how our memorials go. Everybody sings and talks and prays, and sings some more, and folks get to carrying on. And it tends to go on a little while. Well, his mama had promised him ice cream if he was good, and he figured he'd been good enough for long enough, and he wanted to get going on out of there. But they couldn't till Mini got back in his limo. Junior remembered Uncle Mini held up the procession to go talk to a lady by her car.

"We went up to check on him, Hank and I did, and it turned out to be an old friend of ours from way back. The girl was named Miss Betty Langdon."

Melody covered her mouth, though she made no sound. The blood rushed from her head for a pulsing, ringing measure of time, then it turned around and rushed back up. The dizzying sense of falling was nauseating, but she realized she should comment—for the recording, for the podcast. The only sound that would come out was a dry "oh." She glanced at Dorian, whose mouth had gone slack. She fought an inappropriate urge to laugh. Zeke continued.

"Betty was a dear friend to us. She and Dominicus had a thing right before we made it big, see, and she was supposed to go out on the road with us, on our first circuit tour. But something happened back home and she had to go take care of it. She was supposed to join him in Muscle Shoals when she got things settled, but we never saw her again after she left us in Macon." He stopped and inhaled deeply from the oxygen tube at his nose. He took a sip of water, and Dorian and Melody quietly did the same, scared to break the spell.

"Dominicus pined for that girl something awful, wrote her every week from every town. It got bad for a little while. Here we were rising up the ranks on the tour, our name higher and higher up the marquees. We were recording, releasing our first singles, and he was still looking for Betty. Girls were everywhere, all wanting a piece of him. He didn't even see them. We thought he'd never let it go. He'd send her our schedule so she could write ahead, but she never replied, not one time. He tried calling, but either the number was changed or her mother said she wasn't around. Every time he tried to plan to go home, to see what had happened, something else would come up with the group, some show or interview or whatnot, and we had to convince him, like look, man, she's not replying to your letters. Maybe she changed her mind. We need you here, see. The group needs you.

"Our first hit *Penny In My Pocket*, we wrote that song about her. The night she and Dominicus met, we were practicing outside on Sly's mama's porch. I remember that house had recently become our regular rehearsal place since Sly's family got 'relocated' (he drew sarcastic air quotes without raising his hands from their armrests) in reality, they were pushed out from Sugar Hill when they put the new freeway right through the neighborhood. I remember how his mama had somehow lost her prized dining room rug in the move, but she used to make out like it was some kind of divine providence. Like losing the rug was meant to be, just so we'd have better acoustics when we practiced in her dining room."

As he paused for breath, Melody tried to remember the questions she wanted to ask him. Even if she could have brought them to mind, she wouldn't have dared interrupt. Zeke's eyes had taken on a nostalgic gleam.

"That night we were on the porch. It was a fine evening. Betty had wandered over from this old saloon down the road, to listen to us, and Mini—woo–oo! I swear he seemed to float right off the porch toward her. Like he had no choice, almost. They were drawn together like magnets. She spilled her purse and all her change fell out in the street. There again, I remember it like a movie, those two beautiful young people standing under the streetlight, her *so* light and him *so* dark, and there was something beautiful about that. They were staring at each other while those pennies rolled around at their feet, in slow motion. It was one of those moments you remember, man."

Melody pretended to take notes, but wheels were spinning. They seemed to spin in different directions. She struggled to focus on listening now, thinking later.

Dorian spoke up. "That is amazing. So our Betty, the woman whose disappearance we've been looking into, might be your old friend, and Dominicus Owen's one-time girlfriend?"

"Junior thought so. Ah, here he is now! The man himself," Zeke said. His face lit up as Ezekiel Junior entered the dining room. He patted his father's back and stood behind him with an expression like a teapot about to whistle.

"Yeah," he said almost breathlessly, "I wanted you guys to talk to Dad first, but after I left you this morning, I checked out your podcast website out of curiosity. I could have sworn that old picture of the missing woman was the same lady I saw at the funeral. I was eleven or twelve, and I could be wrong, but I generally don't forget faces."

"Seems like you're not wrong, Junior," Zeke said. He took a deep drag on his oxygen and leaned back in his chair, the leather seat punctuating his statement with a soft creak.

"Well, what do you know about that?" Ezekiel finally said.

Zeke gripped the armrests. He looked past them, seeing a moment in time predating his young guests' lives, but that he remembered better than yesterday. "Did something bad happen to sweet Miss Betty?"

348

Dorian gave a sad smile. "She went missing in 2001, sir," he said. "We're trying to find out what happened."

He glanced across at Melody. She was looking the other way, out the dining room window. Shattered light from the diamond glass panes turned her eyes to kaleidoscopes.

"What a small world," Ezekiel said, shaking his head.

Melody spoke to no one in particular. "It's getting smaller every minute."

The conversation went on while Melody tried to put the pieces together. What did this information mean, if anything? Could Betty have been depressed, maybe all her life, over the loss of her relationship with Dominicus Owens? How did Junie not know the man Betty left behind in Macon went on to be a superstar? Did no one know Betty well enough to know this part of her past? Did they not care enough to know? She would find out, but in the meantime, none of this could go on the podcast. No matter how tempting it was to upload the raw interview right now, finding out the truth for Betty Van Disson had to come first.

When she came back to the conversation, Malik was walking into the room carrying a guitar and Zeke was speaking. "That there is a guitar played by none other than Duane Allman."

"No," Dorian said. Malik held it out reverently and Dorian wiped his hands on his jeans.

"Yes," Zeke said. "Yes it is. Duane messed around on that ax when he came into the studio in Macon. It belonged to a studio musician, and when he passed he left it to me. We were up there working the same time as them, our careers took off from there." He grinned, showed his expensive white teeth and straightened his collar. "Hometown boys did good, didn't we?"

Dorian reached out and accepted the worn old dreadnought like a priceless relic. He looked at Zeke, who nodded encouragingly, then he propped the body on his knee and cradled the neck in the crook of his hand. He strummed a chord, then played a lick. Zeke looked from side to side, raised one eyebrow and one shoulder. "All right, Dorian, all right! You got some skills," he said. Dorian wiggled his fingers. He'd earned a 'stank face' from a legend. Emboldened, he played the first chords of *Penny In My Pocket*.

"Awww, man! You've done it now!" Ezekiel warned playfully, and his father's fingers began to snap as if involuntarily. When Zeke sang his part, the others could see him as he used to be, on stage in some circuit theater, the footlights casting a magical wall of wonder between him and the multicolored sea of faces looking back, ecstatic, adoring.

Melody watched as Dorian talked to Zeke, his words trailing off into riffs like parts of speech and back again to words, sentences ending where sweet chords and deft licks proved the best choice of phrase. She pressed her hand to her chest, pressing at the swelling beat that threatened to burst through, and closed her eyes. He sang the melody with Zeke singing harmony, holding out the last note till Melody thought she couldn't take it any more.

"*...what more do I need?...*" When she opened her eyes and looked at Dorian's face, he was looking back at her.

"I knew you could play," Melody said, "but I didn't know you played like that." "Yeah, well," Dorian said, "I'm full of surprises." He held the guitar tenderly yet firmly, his hands cradling the neck, his fingers moving deftly over the trembling strings.

Ezekiel and Malik clapped. Melody tried to catch her breath and a wash of sparks spread from her center to her neck, her fingertips, her toes. Surely everyone could see them, shooting out, betraying her with their brightness.

She hid her reaction behind a tearful round of applause.

TABS AND BLANKS
PODCAST

Transcript
Season 2, Episode 14: Quick Update

Hey, Sweepers! We love that you all have embraced that nickname for yourselves, by the way. Coming to you today with a quick update, just to let you know we're working on an exciting new episode! As you know, after the first several episodes this season, these episodes are being produced in real-time, and sometimes that means we have to delay the release of a new episode in order to bring you the latest.

Dorian and I will post the new episode as soon as we tie up an exciting loose thread. It will be worth the wait, we promise. For now, let me just say that we will be bringing you a big, big interview very soon. Make sure you have push notifications turned on for this podcast, stock up on popcorn and your beverages of choice, and in the meantime, please visit the website to download transcripts, view photos, and join in the discussion.

Don't forget to visit our amazing sponsors, BranchesDNA and enter the code CHIMNEY for exclusive discounts.

MELODY

2019

Despite the AC's valiant efforts, it was swelteringly hot inside the van. The black vinyl seat burned through her good interview pants and the panel below her window burned her elbow when she forgot for a moment and rested her arm. She pressed her toes into the floor to raise her legs and rested her hands on her knees instead.

"So we'll hold off on using anything from Zeke's interview until we know more." Melody watched old houses go by.

"Right," Dorian said. "I'm putting out feelers to contact Dominicus Owens. Zeke said he has a condo near his son in Atlanta, but his agent was out of office when I called. They said they'd email him."

"We might have a road trip in our future?" She smiled to herself at the prospect.

Riverside Avenue was tonier than she remembered. "Hey, I used to live off that road," she said as they passed over a street anchored on one corner by her childhood library. And my mom used to bring us to this park!" She looked for the park sign. "Yup! Right there! 'Willowbranch Park'!"

"Wait," Dorian said. "Willowbranch? *That's* Willowbranch Park?"

"Yes. We used to shoot hoops right there and I'd ride my bike around and around that playground. It was the only place my mom would let me out of her sight for two seconds. We used to play hide and seek behind these trees."

"Willowbranch?" Dorian flipped on the blinker and turned right at the next road.

Melody raised her eyebrows and nodded mockingly. "Dang, Dor! Yes." She said it slower. "Wil-low-branch. What are you so excited about?" Dorian's face had lit up, the same expression he got when he'd tracked down a story lead or killed a phantom buzz in the studio—one of her favorite Dorian faces.

He turned onto a residential road that bordered the park and pulled the van into a narrow parking space. "Mel," he said, "do you know what happened here in this park? Do you have any idea?"

Melody thought of the news story a few years back, about the elderly man who was stabbed walking his dog in this park. He lived down the road and could trace his ancestry back to the Mayflower. Awful story. She'd thought it would be an interesting one to cover on the podcast. But that couldn't be what Dorian was referring to. Not with that expression on his face, like a little kid seeing Disney World for the first time. She raised her shoulders. "Um, nooo."

"This is where The Allman Brothers played! They would play here on Sundays right after the band became a band." He pointed out the windshield. "The first iteration of the Allman Brothers gave free jam session concerts right there!" He stared across the wide green space as if he could see it now. "Imagine that. Duane Allman, Greg Allman, Jaimoe Johanson, Butch Trucks—out here just jamming. Nobody knew that hippy guitar player was the guy who'd talked Wilson Picket into recording 'Hey Jude,' and played on the track. Or that he was the guy who would come up with that guitar lick on 'Layla.'" He ran both hands through his hair.

"I can't believe I grew up right down the road from here and I never knew that!" Melody said. "How is that even possible? The city needs to make a bigger deal about it. Right? Claim its music history."

"Fans already make their own pilgrimages here. I got sucked down a Reddit rabbit hole the other day researching Riverside houses for the treasure hunt update. There's a whole long subreddit of people from around the world who stop in Jacksonville just to track down the music sites. The Gray House where the Allman brothers actually *became* The Allman Brothers Band should be a few blocks that way." He pointed in the direction of the north-flowing St. Johns River a few blocks away. "Ray Charles lived and played piano in LaVilla; Lynyrd Skynyrd members grew up on the Westside; The Downtown Sound used to practice harmonies on a porch right down the road from a tavern where Skynyrd played sometimes—"

"Amazing."

"Hell, even Pat Boone lived here." He unlocked the doors and hopped out.

"Pat Who?" Melody said, sliding out the passenger side.

"A singer from the '50s. My grandma had a big crush on him."

"Your grandma?" Melody said. "Not your *great* grandma?" Her laugh carried across the park as she fell in step beside him.

They walked between two redbrick pillars flanking the park entrance and past an old playground and basketball court. On a baseball diamond to their left a little girl took batting practice with her earnest young dad, and to their right a pickup basketball game was getting serious. Melody's beloved library stood on the corner across the way. Dorian stopped in a clearing between tall oak trees, lush green grass rolled in every direction. He inhaled, taking in the scene. "Does the park look the same as it did when you were a kid?"

"I remember a bunch of big oak trees were blown over in Hurricane Matthew, but other than that, pretty much, yeah."

"Those concerts were right here, Mel! Probably right here on this spot! Fifty years ago." His gaze fell far across the field. "But somehow it feels like I just missed it. Like they just finished a fantastic jam session, packed up their gear, and headed back home to The Gray House."

In that moment, Melody wished for the power to turn back time, just for him. She would take him back to one of those balmy Sunday afternoons, watch his eyes light up as they both listened to the band, maybe they'd share a picnic...

She watched him take it all in with a squeezing feeling in her chest.

Kina came by the studio that evening, bringing new bulbs for the studio lighting. Melody watched her, wondering how she managed those big lighting cans and unwieldy light stands without breaking a single nail.

When Dorian left the room, Kina leaned in. "You know you don't have to wait around for him to make a move, right?" she whispered, raising her impeccable brows. "I mean, what year is this?" Her sleek ponytail bounced, punctuating each word. She reached for the red can light and tipped it down a quarter inch, following the soft beam with her eyes to the recording chair where Melody was stationed, stiffly holding her head the way Kina had positioned it.

"No, yeah," Melody said with a circular nod. Kina held up a warning finger and Melody snapped to attention. *So I'm going to talk about this—with Kina?* "It's not that. It's more about, like, what if I made a move, and then he actually isn't interested?" She shuddered. "I don't want to lose our friendship. And yes, I do know how lame that sounds, but it's true."

"Have you ever considered the possibility that your friendship just adds to the long list of reasons you *should* be a couple? I mean, how many other guys are you friends with like that?"

Melody opened her mouth and closed it again.

"Stop that. You look like a sea bass."

"Well that's not nice."

"I'm blunt."

"You are," Melody said, "And that works for you, I guess?"

"Usually."

Melody glanced toward the doorway. No sign of Dorian. Kina went on. "But seriously, you need to own what you've got. Look at you, girl!" Kina said. "You're a badass yourself. Don't get it twisted. Who built this famous podcast that's tearing it up out there? What's it up to, a billion trillion downloads?" She raised a hand, thwarting Melody's attempt to interrupt. "You're smart. You get things done. You've got that 'nerdy hot' thing going on, the messy bun with the pencils sticking out or whatever." She waved her hand model fingers around Melody's face. "And Dorian wants you. He one-hundred-percent wants you. He's probably got the same lame reason for not telling you. Like, 'Oh, but our friendship. Our precious fragile friendshiiiip.'" She motioned a finger down her throat and made a gagging sound.

Melody shook her head. "I don't think you're supposed to make that gesture any more," she said. Kina looked confused. "Not P.C., super insensitive to bulimics," Melody said.

"Are you serious?"

"That'll get you canceled," Melody snapped her fingers, "like that."

"Thanks for the heads up," Kina nodded like a wide-eyed marionette, "but you are avoiding the subject."

"I am."

"Well," said Kina, fanning her fingers as she slapped her hands to her hips. "You need to stop it. The guy has it bad for you, and you obviously want him—"

She held up her hand as Melody started to object. "Yes, you do. You look at that man like he's a whole tres leches. Honestly. I'm embarrassed for you." She laughed, and then put her warm hand over Melody's, her teasing expression suddenly turning compassionate. "Seriously, though. Trust me on this. You two need to deal with each other before your feelings cause a lot of unnecessary damage."

TABS AND BLANKS
PODCAST

Transcript
Season 2, Episode 15: Interview With Randell
Van Disson

Listeners, this week I'll skip the long introduction and get right to the interview we know you are all here for.

Dorian: Is it okay if we record this?

Dorian is back for another shot of sanitizer from the dispenser on the wall. Dor hates hospitals.

Randell is struggling to push himself up in the bed.

Randell: I suppose, if you want to.

Dorian sets a mic on the bedside table and carefully drapes the cord away from Randell's web of tubes.

Randell: I hear your podcast show is doing real well. The nurses say I'm famous.

Melody: Well, yes, I guess that's true.

Dorian pulls a chair up beside the bed for me.

Randell: Hear folks are all excited about the treasure.

He looks from Dorian's face to mine and back again.

Randell: Any sign?

Melody: Nobody's had any luck so far. But yes, it's been quite a phenomenon.

Dorian's pinning my mic on and I sit beside Randell's bed. His snow-white hair swoops from his forehead, a wispy shadow of the pompadour I remembered from his old photos. Randell has recently had a heart attack and bypass surgery. He seems very tired, but he is engaged and alert.

Randell: Well, I guess I hope someone finds it anyway, before I go. At least I'll know it was real.

Melody: That would be something. Actually, we've been wanting to ask: What is the mark folks should be looking for when they look at the bricks in their chimneys?

Randell: Well, I don't know for sure, but my daddy had said it might be a circle with an infinity symbol, or it may be an embossed star (*coughing*) with rays from the points. (*coughing*)

Loreen: So I guess we're related somehow?

Yes, listeners, that's Loreen's voice. She happened to be visiting during our scheduled interview. She's not mic'd, so we apologize for her audio.

Loreen: Should I call you cousin Melody?

Melody: I guess so!

Dorian: What are the chances of that?

Dorian's not mic'd, but this coincidence has got him very excited.

Melody: Around here? Pretty good chances, it would seem.

(*laughter*)

As you can hear, we shared an inappropriately loud and awkward laugh.

Melody: But more than the treasure, of course, we want to find out what happened to Betty, right? I did want to ask, Mr. Van Disson, you and Betty didn't have any children—correct?

Randell: Right. We didn't have any.

Melody: Was that a conscious decision for you both, or—?

Randell: Not really, no. We never discussed it. She never came up pregnant, and it didn't matter to me either way, to be honest. Although as I got older, I did sometimes think how it would have been nice to have a son to pass the chimney sweep business down to, like my daddy did for me.

Melody: You wouldn't have wanted to pass it to a daughter?

Randell: Or a daughter. Sure. Why not?

Loreen shifts in her seat, inspecting the rings on her fingers.

Melody: Loreen, did Betty ever express to you a desire to have children?

Loreen: No, she did not.

Melody: Is that something she would have spoken to you about? I mean, did you have that kind of relationship?

Loreen: Early on we did. Later, after she was married and busy with the motel and all, not so much. Randell, I'll leave that explanation to you.

She is obviously uncomfortable with my question about children. I'm not sure why. Yet.

Melody: So what can you tell us about that, Mr. Van Disson?

Randell: Well, now, you know, I suppose there are *some* things I could tell you that no one else could.

So back then you couldn't just talk about a thing like this, but I suppose it doesn't matter now. It's not going to hurt anyone but me, and I'm an old, old man now. I don't know that I care to keep it like some sort of secret any more. That's the thing these days, right? *(* laughter*)* The thing is, I just never had the—well, the same desires that other men do. At least not in the same way.

Melody: Do you mean that you're gay, Mr. Van Disson?

Randell: No, it's not that. Of course, that's what folks would have thought. But it's more that I just... never had any *use* for any of it. I guess I'm saying I didn't really have the desire 't'all. Just never did know what all the fuss was about. I had my interests, and my work, and that was just my life. Then I got Betty for a wife, a partner really, but it wasn't really fair to her. Even the one time I went outside our marriage, that woman did her best, if you get my drift, but she didn't succeed. Not like she wanted, anyway. But I'm getting off track.

Melody: Why don't you just start wherever you'd like to start and we'll go from there, ok?

Loreen has uncrossed her legs and leaned in, her elbows on her knees.

Randell: Before she disappeared, we had a fight. Believe it or not, it was our first real fight. All those years, first real fight. Around then I would be gone from the motel for days at a time, getting myself in more and more of a frenzy to find that damned treasure. It was really whipping me up. I'd come back, get clean clothes, and go back out.

That day of our fight she had been up to see her mother and I'd come home like that. When she got home I started saying how I knew she wasn't happy. She was sort of shocked, me talking like that. She said, well yes, it was true she'd had dreams for her life, but she was fine. I asked her, 'Like what?' And she said, 'Just dreams, you know. Just like, girlhood dreams.' I guess I pressed her on it and she finally said, 'Well, for one, I wanted to be a Rockette.' And I said, 'You're out of your mind if you think you could have been a Rockette.' I laughed at her. He grimaced and turned away, blinking hard. And then I said, 'I know now why you're not happy, Princess.'

She looked like she'd been hit by a hot poker. She yelled at me not to call her that. 'Don't call me princess, don't you call me that.' She ran to her room and looked under her bed. She knew.

Melody: She knew what?

Randell: I remember my face getting hot, like a boiled turnip. I said to her, 'I beg your pardon?' She was looking under her bed and then she raised her head and looked at me. I followed her and said again, only louder. 'I beg your pardon?'

She said, 'I said, I'd prefer if you don't call me that, is all,' Each word came out louder than the last one. Her voice was getting away from her. It was sort of fascinating, seeing her like that. Like I was meeting her for the first time. She said it again: 'Don't call me princess.'

I didn't understand her. Hadn't I taken care of her all these years? Had she wanted for anything? I worked hard. And hadn't I had dreams, too?

Right then she stopped looking under the bed and said to me, 'I know you believe you've done what a husband's meant to do for his wife. But I could just as well have been any other woman and it wouldn't have made one whit of difference to your life.' Then she stood up and asked me where her diaries were. I was stunned. Shocked. Because we'd never talked like this before.

Melody: Randell. Her diaries?

Randell: Yes. I found her later on sitting in a clearing on the edge of the property.

He pauses and looks out the hospital room window, far down the St. Johns River, as if he could see north all the way to the thick forest behind the Maryview Motor Inn.

Randell: She was just sitting there holding her knees. I stood beside her and she started talking, so kind and gentle again, it about cut through me. She said, 'It's not your fault, Randell. I'm not what you thought you were getting. I'm not a natural wife, any more than you're a natural husband. I've tried, for so long. I take care of this place and these customers and all those rooms. I clean the toilets and wash the bedding. I try to smile and make everyone so comfortable, Randell. But I'm not, she said it like that. 'I'm just not.' Flat like that. She said, 'I haven't felt comfortable my whole life. All I had of my own were those diaries, and now they're gone. They're gone, Randell.'

Melody: Randell, I'm sorry, what happened to the diaries?

He looks surprised and turns away from the window as if he had forgotten we were there.

Randell: This is the part I have trouble saying. There's a shed on my property where I put her things. It's not much, just a few boxes. I did something I'm not proud of, and I never told anyone all this time. But the truth is it might be what drove her away from me. I don't know.

Melody: And what is that, Randell?

Dorian and I are on the edges of our seats. Loreen looks as if her face might crumble like an avalanche. Randell's fingers curl tightly around the siderails of the bed.

Randell: The truth is, I *had* found the box under her bed, the one she was looking for. When I called her that, she knew. We pretty near always kept separate beds, at first because she said she was shy to sleep beside me, and then it just became our way, y'see. But that day when I stopped home, I was looking for something, a missing tool or something, I don't rightly remember. Betty was up with her ma, and I never should'a done it.

Melody: Done what?

Randell: I never should have looked inside the box.

Melody: Go on.

Randell: Well, she'd hidden all these books in there, y'see, up underneath some old dress and some old magazines, like she meant to hide them. And I opened one, just to see what it was. That's when I saw it was a diary. And I went to put it all back the way it was, but a couple hours later, I'm 'shamed to say, I had read all of them.

Melody: Oh, I see.

Loreen has covered her mouth. Her eyes are closed. I wait for Randell to continue.

Randell: I learned some things from them I don't suppose I was supposed to know. And she knew it that moment I called her 'Princess.' She was so angry, flying around the house, looking for her things. Saying how I had no right, how I was a worse than a thief. I'd never seen her like that, not once in all those years. And I slunk off that night, but I wouldn't tell her where they were. I was going to, mind you. I never did plan to keep them from her. But she was gone before I could make it right.

Melody: And so you said you found her out on the edge of the property?

Randell: Yes, she'd gone out there to check the fire pit, to see if I'd burned the diaries. She thought I had burned them, and I didn't tell her otherwise. I never did get to tell her I had them safe and sound in the shed, because she was gone.

Melody: And you think that may have made her upset enough to leave?

Randell: I wouldn't blame her.

Melody: Well, Randell, I have to ask: Why didn't you turn them over to the investigators?

Randell: I didn't think it would do any good. They wouldn't have been any help finding her. There was nothing in there that would help them. It was too personal, and I'd done enough to hurt her. I didn't want to hurt her memory, too.

Melody: So you've read them all.

Randell: I have.

Melody: Can you tell us anything you remember from them?

Loreen: Randell…

Randell glanced over at Loreen here, then lowered his head. Loreen shifted in her chair, agitated, her gaze fixed on Randell's face. We all wait for his response.

Randell: I think it will be best if I just tell you where they are, and you can go read them for yourself. Then you can decide what to do.

At this point, Loreen got up and left the room. By the time we wrapped up the interview, she had left the hospital. She has not answered our calls since.

It would seem that the elusive treasure for which Randell searched so prodigiously and with such single-minded determination did ultimately come to a fruitful end. What greater treasure could we ask for than the diaries of Betty Van Disson?

Sadly, the day after this interview, Randell Van Disson suffered a massive heart attack and passed away. He was 82. Our thoughts and condolences go out to his family, wherever they are.

MELODY

2019

Dorian and Melody rode up I-95, taking the last exit before the border and heading west toward Highway 17.

"Any thoughts on Randell?" Dorian said. "What did you think of him?"

"Of Randell?" Melody said. She stopped jotting in her notebook and flipped it closed. "Seemed believable. He doesn't seem like a murderer, for one thing."

"That's true. But then what does a murderer seem like?"

"I don't have a clue," Melody said. She had to admit, the deeper they got into this story, the more she felt she was losing the thread. "I feel like I can't trust my instincts lately."

The GPS chirped loudly in its know-it-all tone.

'*Continue straight for two miles.*'

Melody bristled. Shouldn't GPS be smart enough to take a quieter approach in certain situations? I felt somewhat inappropriate for the voice to sound so smug at a time like this. A little note of understanding, a bit of a conspiratorial '*come on, guys! Let's go find this place together'* attitude, might be nice. The moment they reached the highway, Melody punched the 'stop' button and shut it off mid-sentence.

"Yeah thanks, girl," she mumbled. "We got it from here." She clamped her hands between her thighs to keep from thrumming them on her knees, but the energy just switched to her legs. Her feet bounced against the floor mat and her knees bounced fast, as if surely they could outrun this giant tortoise of a van.

"Doing okay?" Dorian asked. He took the turn onto the highway then glanced over. Her jaw tensed and relaxed, then tensed again.

"Sure, I'm fine." Her words came out with a squeak and she cleared her throat, tried that again: "I'm fine." She turned to flash a strained smile, then turned back toward her side window. Her knees went back to bouncing.

Smokey clouds, out of place against the otherwise clear blue overhead, blotted out the sun as they headed north and approached the Maryview Motor Inn. Rounding a curve in the county road, a wide field opened in front of them, deep green and sprinkled with multicolored wild flowers.

"Hey, that looks like our puzzle," Dorian said. After they finished the current puzzle, they'd have to decide whether to re-up their membership in the club or let the membership end. "I still can't find that last piece. But I'm sure it'll turn up. And then, I guess... we'll be done." He glanced at her profile, the small smile she gave as a reply, her jaw muscles working. He turned his gaze back to the field, then to the road.

They pulled into the parking lot as a breeze blew across the gravel, lifting yellow-gray dust into a swirl that rose up the front of the building and dissipated into the rustling canopy.

A dark afternoon cloud thinned and pulled apart, revealing the sun and bringing up the lights on the motel façade like a scene from a movie.

"Right on cue," Dorian said.

"Yeah!" she said too loudly, offering a crooked smile while peering side-to-side out the windshield. Something about this situation felt big. Randell's information could be everything they'd been looking for. Or it could be nothing at all. Her stomach twisted in tangled knots.

They drove around the side of the motel, down the dirt road between it and the Van Dissons's tiny bungalow, and turned behind a cement outbuilding. There was the garage-style metal door Randell had described to them after their interview, on the broad side of the building facing the forest behind. There was the padlock, hidden behind a row of cinder blocks at the base of the door. Dorian pulled them away and cleared the white dollar weed runners that tangled through the chain while Melody spun the dial and arranged the numbers to match those on the slip of paper Randell had pressed into her hand.

She pulled on the lock. It didn't open. She spun the dial and tried again.

"Maybe it's rusted," Dorian said. He reached over and tugged on to no avail, then picked it up, chain and all and dropped it hard against a cinder block. Melody spun the dial one more time and tried the numbers. She closed her eyes and pulled, and the metal loop gave, pulling free and spinning away. She jumped off her knees and hugged Dorian. "Ugh, I love you!" she shouted. Dorian flushed, but he cleared his throat to reply as she bent down, pulling in vain on the door handle. "Give me a hand," she grunted. They counted off and pulled up in unison, sending the rusty metal door creaking up its track and crashing into the stopper.

There was a rustle on the roof as squirrels took to nearby branches. They stopped to watch, chattering protests from their safe perch. Dorian snapped a photo and followed Melody into the building.

Melody pulled a string hanging from the ceiling and the space lit up with dull fluorescent light. The concrete floor was bare in the middle, and neat stacks of boxes and plastic storage bins lined the walls. To one side, cardboard Office Depot boxes were piled up, each one labeled 'Taxes' followed by a year. Next to that were plastic bins, the lids brittle and the sides worn and etched, with labels: 'Light Bulbs,' 'Rags,' 'Fruit Baskets.' Each label had an apostrophe before the final s which someone had attempted to cover with Wite-Out.

The back area seemed to have been devoted to the chimney sweep business. A long table lined the wall, and a pegboard hung behind it, covered in tools on hooks with small yellowing labels above them: "Creosote Scraper," "Chisel 1/2 Inch," "Chisel 3/4," "Wire Brush #1," "Wire Brush #2"... Tacked in the middle of the pegboard was a half-page ad for "Randell

Van Disson, Classic Chimney Sweep, Specializing in Historic Homes."

On the middle shelf of a storage rack was the Davison's Department Store cardboard box, just as Randell had described.

Melody's breath caught in her throat. A low hum in her ears twisted and spiked to a single high-pitched note sustained in the space between her and whatever truth that box might hold. She stepped closer, Dorian close behind, and lifted the box from its resting place.

The diaries were stacked neatly in the box under a faded blue calico dress and a stack of music magazines and clippings. Each little book was covered in a different feminine design, but all were in shades of pink and purple. The perfumy scent of face powder mixed with aging leather and tangy metal, the aroma of things that used to be precious, emanated from the long-closed time capsule, a treasure in its own right.

Dorian recorded as Melody carefully picked through the box. She drew out one leather-bound journal and ran a hand over the embossed surface before opening to a middle page. Dorian kept an eye on sound levels, ensuring capture of Melody's reaction should she come across anything new or relevant.

She read an entry, following the lines with her finger. She paused, realizing the weight of responsibility. The private thoughts of a mysteriously missing woman, years of them, were at her fingertips. It was important to read only for information.

But as she read passages, scanning for any new clue, Betty's existence came to life in full color and rich sound, and it seemed to Melody like the type of story that could keep her up all night, unable to stop turning the pages. But this wasn't fiction. This was Betty's life—in her own words, in her own voice, unfurling like some enchanted vine. The story unfolded, wound around Melody's heart, and squeezed.

Her eyes roamed the pages and she forced herself to keep moving through them though she wanted to savor each word, each revelation. Her mouth dropped open repeatedly and she looked at Dorian each time, handing one open book after the other to him. "Look at this," she whispered, pressing a plum-colored volume into his hands, "and this," and before he'd finished reading it, another one: "Read that."

Dorian gave up squatting and sat down on the dusty floor beside her, following her finger as it trailed over Betty's neat, precise script. They read in silence, speaking only to assure each other they really were seeing what they were seeing.

"So she was..."

"Yeah..."

"And this is before she got married..."

"Yes, according to the dates..."

"Wait, what does that say?..."

"Oh, man. Poor Betty..."

"...wait, they *never*...?"

Melody's finger stopped moving over the words and Dorian's mouth formed a soundless 'whhaa'. They looked at each other.

"A baby, Dor. There was a baby..."

BETTY,
19 YEARS OLD

MARCH 4, 1971

Diary,

I'm empty. She's gone from me. The day came and went and everyone is going on like nothing happened. But it did happen. She happened.

I wish I could have kept her inside a little longer. When she was part of me, that's when she was still mine and there was still hope. But she was ready.

I will write down everything here so it won't ever be lost. Because, like I keep telling myself, I won't see her again. And I'm so afraid her little face will fade from my mind.

She came a little early. So she's at least a little like me, always early. She was so small, but I heard her holler. And I heard them say, "She's good. All's well."

They took her away so fast, I barely got a chance to hear her cry. But I saw her face for just a moment when the nurse turned out the door. Just the side of her peaceful little face, relieved to be finally out and free, I imagine, one arm raised up and her fingers curled out. Like she was waving goodbye.

I keep praying for God to just go on ahead and bring me home. Maybe I'll be blessed with a short life so I don't have to grow into an old woman still aching like this. The least He can do is cut my suffering short. If He won't change my life to one that lets me keep our baby, then at least He could take me out of this life altogether. I surely don't belong here.

MELODY

2019

Melody nodded and shook her head as she read on, her head moving in a continuous, delirious circle.

"Dorian, if she had a baby, and if I'm her blood relative..." She knew exactly what it meant. But somehow the circumstances, the crazy coincidence of it all made the obvious fact bounce off her head like a rubber ball each time she tried to catch it. There must be something else she wasn't seeing. Or she was seeing what she wanted to see and not what was really there. It had to be.

It couldn't be.

Dorian closed the diary he held, keeping his place with his thumb. "Mel?" He waited for her to pull her gaze away from the looping chains of deep blue script, her eyes narrow with confused questions. Her bloodless cheeks went slack in the dusty swath of sunlight that reached from the dirty window like a drunken slap. He placed his hand on her knee and fought the urge to lean across the stack of diaries between them and wrap his arms around her, to prop her up as she seemed to soften and melt in front of him.

"Mel?" Her eyes had dropped back to the page.

"Dor?" Her voice was shattered glass, sharp and falling. "What do I do?"

TABS AND BLANKS
PODCAST

Transcript
Season 2, Episode 16: Treasure Hunt

Hi Sweepers! Today's special episode is a return to Riverside. You may remember, from our episode about the legend of the possible treasure hidden in a fireplace of one of the houses in Jacksonville's Historic District of Riverside Avondale, that the mystery of some sort of valuables stolen from a wealthy Swiss family at the turn of the last century was never solved. Well, that might be about to change.

This is a part of our investigation we never could have anticipated.

We've just arrived at the home of Martha Claire Beakman. The house is a beautiful, historic colonial in Avondale, pale blue with a bright red front door, just a few houses down from the St. Johns River. Though it's lovely and well-kept (it looks almost unreal with its climbing Don Juan roses and storybook façade) it's actually the smallest and most modest home on this oak-shaded lane.

Melody: So Mrs. Beakman, you called in to the podcast hotline just this morning to say you may know something about Randell and Betty Van Disson, is that right?

Martha Claire: Yes, I called. Well, my son told me to call. He listens to your show, your cast pod show or...

Melody: Yes, ma'am, our podcast—

Martha Claire: Right, well, he wanted me to talk to you because he listened to your most recent episode—the minute it came out last night—and I guess you were interviewing your missing lady's husband? My son said the husband was a chimney sweep years ago?

Melody: Yes, Ma'am.

Martha Claire: Well, my son, he remembered one autumn when I had convinced my husband, his daddy, that we needed to get the chimney cleaned out properly before the winter, so we could use it and not kill the children with carbon monoxide poisoning. I had seen a story about that, you know, on the news?

Melody: Hmm, yes, good call. And do you remember when that was? What year?

Martha Claire: I don't remember the year off hand, but I keep records of everything so the invoice has to be somewhere. I got the boxes out after I called you. I'm getting ready to look through them right now.

Mrs. Beakman is referring to several file storage boxes set out in a bright sunroom. She seems nervous, wringing her hands and shaking them out.

Melody: Mrs. Beakman, we really appreciate you speaking with us. Your home is beautiful.

Martha Claire: Thank you, thank you. We've done a lot of work on it. It's pretty different than it was back then. Would you like to come on in?

We follow her down a little hall stopping on the way while she retrieves a pair of scissors and a Rolodex from the desk in a sunny office full of books and paintings of magnolias, and into a bright sunroom. Some folks around here would call a sunroom a 'morning room,' and since we're here in the morning, I can see why. The sun is streaming through an east-facing wall of windows, forming long golden stripes across the heart pine floor. It's the perfect spot for Mrs. Beakman's adorable shih tzu Sugar Bear who lifts her head only to see if we came bearing gifts, then lays back down, disappointed.

The plaster walls and crown moulding are gorgeous. These old homes have atmosphere and character you just can't find in newer houses. I realize that's not exactly an original proclamation to make, it is said about thirty times a day on HGTV alone, but that's because it's true.

We settle into wicker armchairs and Mrs. Beakman takes the lid off a file box.

Melody: Mrs. Beakman, could you go ahead and tell us what you remember about the day you had your chimney serviced?

Martha Claire: Yes, of course. Like I say, I had been trying to convince my husband we should hire someone to clean the chimney so we could use it that winter. I had tried one of those creosote cleaner log things, and after I burned that, I had gone outside to the clean-out to brush out the ash. I had looked in there, you know, dusting it all around with a little brush, and I noticed there was a brick in the side of the firebox that seemed like it was a little bit loose. I didn't want to fool with it, you know, I was afraid the whole chimney might cave in if I did! My neighbor came out and asked me why I was doing that myself, said those creosote logs do more harm than good.

Mrs. Beakman slits the tape on another file box and lifts the lid. She begins flipping through files as she talks.

Martha Claire: So I called the chimney sweep service. My neighbor said all the other neighbors had used him and recommended him. She gave me a business card. It said they specialized in old houses and small masonry repairs and the sort. It should still be in the Rolodex.

Melody: Oh, good. So you called the chimney sweep your neighbors recommended—

Martha Claire: I called the number. A lady answered. She said she set appointments for him. I told her I wanted to go ahead and get the chimney cleaned by a professional. And I told her about the problem with the loose brick in the firebox. She asked me some questions about that, and she said they were usually able to make that kind of repair. She said not to mess with the brick any more, that I was right to leave it alone like I did. We set an appointment for first thing that Monday morning, which was the next day. I specifically remember that because it was my husband's birthday, and I thought I'd have a fire going for his birthday dinner, let him see how nice it was to use to the fireplace. It was ridiculous since it's nowhere near cool enough for a fire in September, but I figured I'd cut the AC on real low. I do that pretty much every year when I get tired of waiting for fall. *(*laughs*)* So that was September 3rd.

Melody: September 3rd. And you are sure about that date?

Martha Claire: Oh, yes. I'm positive, because of my husband's birthday. But we can check the invoice when I find it. Where is that dang thing...

Melody: And Ms. Beakman, how did the service visit go?

Martha Claire: Well, I believe I'd say it went fine. I was a bit taken aback when I answered the door, you understand. But she did a fine job as far as I could tell. I let her in there and left her to it.

Melody: I'm sorry, you said 'she'?

Martha Claire: Oh, yes. That's why I was surprised. I was expecting her husband. It didn't matter one way or the other to me, mind you. She seemed capable enough, a bit older to be doing something so...well, it's quite a labor-intensive job, wouldn't you say? She was a tall woman. She was wearing a coverall and a hat, and I remember her glasses— that cat eye style? With the points? So she seemed youthful, energetic. She was older than me and I remember thinking, "I hope I'm that spry when I'm her age." Which I supposed I am now, coming to think of it.

Anyway, she had a bucket of tools and whatnot. Showed me what she'd use to fix the loose brick, laid out a cloth to keep the area clean while she worked. Seemed like she knew what she was doing, and I got the feeling she didn't need me hanging around while she worked, so I left her to it. She climbed her ladder to check out the chimney at one point, I remember that, because... wow! Anyway, after about an hour or so, and when I came in to offer her an iced-tea or something, she was all done.

Melody: What was she doing when you came back in?

Martha Claire: She had her tools all packed up, back in her bucket. When I came back in, she was wrapping up the drop cloth, rolling it up, I suppose to keep any ashes from flying around. I appreciated that, of course—

Melody: Certainly, yeah. And then what did she do?

Martha Claire: She tucked that cloth in the bucket and dusted off her hands and said she was all done and she was leaving now. I said, 'Well, wouldn't you like to get paid?'

Melody: Right.

Martha Claire: And she sort of paused. She looked, I don't know, surprised or caught off guard? She said, 'Oh! Well I suppose so!' And we both laughed at that, and I gave her a check, and she left.

Martha Claire is pulling files from one of the boxes as she speaks. She continues to shuffle through what seems to be a collection of every receipt or invoice she's ever received.

Melody: So she seemed in a hurry then?

Martha Claire: She did, a bit. But the other strange thing was that the check was never cashed. After a couple of weeks, I called the number on the card and left a message. When I didn't hear back, I called again the next week, left one more message. Then I forgot about it. Ah! Here's the blessed invoice!

Martha Claire smooths out the old paper on the coffee table between us.

Melody: Did the woman give you her name?

Martha Claire: She may have, but I don't recall.

The invoice doesn't contain the service person's name.

Melody: The date of service is September 3, 2001.

(*Dorian*: The same day Betty went missing. Let me see!)

Martha Claire gets up and walks to a tall secretary desk. She returns with the Rolodex and flips through it.

Martha Claire: But I would have made the check out to the name on the business card. Ah!

She skims a finger over the information on the card.

Martha Claire: Ah! There you go. 'Randell Van Disson, Specializing in historic homes.'

If there is one thing an investigative journalist should never be, it is 'speechless.' I have to be honest here and admit that at this point, I had a hard time putting words together.

Before we leave, Mrs. Beakman takes us to have a look at the chimney clean-out. Around the side of her living room, at the base of the chimney, there is an access door. It's a solid cast iron door, about one foot square, maybe a little bit bigger, with a little handle. Mrs. Beakman twists the handle and pulls it open.

Inside, we can see straight through the firebox and into the living room through the glass door on the other side. She demonstrates how she likes to brush the ash out of the opening to avoid making a mess inside the house, then she explains that Betty had looked at the clean-out when she arrived, but that she'd done most of the work inside the house. Then Mrs. Beakman reaches in to point out the brick that had seemed loose before she called Randell's service all those years ago. She pokes at it and it doesn't move at all. Then she steps aside to make room for me and points to the middle of the brick.

Martha Claire: There. You can see right there.

Melody: What am I looking for?

Martha Claire: See? Right there. It has a different mark than the rest of the bricks.

I lean over to peer where she's pointing. Dorian shines a light inside over my head. And then I see it.

Melody: A star, with some lines coming out...

As we drive away from Martha Claire's home, we can barely contain ourselves. What does this new information mean? If Betty found the price-less music box that day, what happened next? Did Randell find out? Or did Betty keep it from him? If so, did the rightful owners find out somehow and come for her?

It's the first we've heard of anyone else who might have seen Betty the day she disappeared, and we've certainly never heard the possibility that she went anywhere except over the bridge, over the border to Georgia to see her mother. I give Detective Billy John Whitaker a call to share what we've just learned.

Melody: It was her, right? Betty must have taken the call. We have no way of knowing why she took the job instead of Randell. But the fact that this service call happened the day she disappeared? What do you make of that? I mean, had you ever heard anything about this before?

Det. Billy John: I had not. That is definitely news to me. If that was Betty, well, of course that's huge.

Melody: It is. Wow. Dorian, can you believe this?

Dorian: I mean, wow. What in the actual...wow, wow, wow.

Melody: Right? It still hasn't fully sunk in.

When we got the call from Mrs. Beakman this morning, we had no idea what we were going to hear from her. All we knew was that she lives in a historic home in Avondale and she used a chimney sweep service during the time when Betty disappeared. She was available right then, so we got in the van and drove out to her place.

Melody: But Detective, what about those phone messages Mrs. Beakman says she left? Did you ever hear anything about them? Did your team check the phone messages?

Detective Billy John: We did ask Randell if he'd had any contact from Betty. Any messages or a letter, or the like. He said he hadn't heard a thing from her.

Dorian: But the two messages from this customer were left two to three weeks after she disappeared.

(*silence*)

Melody: Detective?

Detective Billy John: I'm here, I'm here. Yeah, I'm thinking back and no, I didn't know anything about those calls. They wouldn't have meant anything to our investigation, unless they mentioned Betty, anyhow. But no. I can't say as I remember anything about phone messages after our initial investigation.

We know the investigation basically came to a grinding halt, or was set aside and ultimately went cold, after the terrorist attacks of 9-11. All these years, this seemingly trivial bit of information, this clue and potential line of investigation, sat uncovered and unexamined. It was just sitting there, hiding right out in the open, where it would have remained if not for this podcast and the various unexpected ways it has touched this community.

So, what does this mean? Did Betty find the treasure that day? If so, what happened to it? If not, did she tell Randell about the call at all? How would he have reacted to that news? Would he have been angry to learn she took the job when she knew there was a loose brick? Is it merely a coincidence that the service call to Martha Claire Beakman's house occurred right before Betty disappeared?

Is there such a thing as a coincidence? Or does the passing of time connect the dots between otherwise unrelated moments? If only we had known this information before we met and spoke to Randell, we could have asked him. Maybe his answer would have helped us find answers.

On the other hand, maybe not.

MELODY

2019

The van rolled down a quiet stretch of A1A and slowed, coming to a stop under a row of palm trees, their long, husky trunks bent in matching unison, shaped by ocean breezes and passing storms. Dorian put it in park and held on to the steering wheel a little while longer before getting out and coming around to open Melody's door.

She gripped the seat and checked the mirror, again. She threw the reflection a thumbs up and flipped the visor. Everything made sense now. The last week had been a dizzying blur of revelation, one that forced Melody and Dorian to make hard, fast choices they couldn't have imagined when they read the post on the podcast discussion board, when they picked this obscure local cold case from so many possible stories. What were the chances?

They had a plan. It was time.

"Are you ready?" Dorian said, offering a hand as Melody stepped out.

"Ready," she replied. She'd *been* ready since the phone call from Dominicus Owens's manager.

Today, the cameras would not roll. Dorian's equipment was packed away deep in the back of the van. Melody reached into the footwell and picked up a box from the floorboard. Dorian took it from her and carefully closed the door. Melody offered a look of solidarity, Dorian gave the side panel door several decisive pats, and they made their way up the sidewalk.

The house stood partially hidden by giant azalea bushes and palmettos, down a stamped gravel driveway, behind a double iron gate. Beyond, the Atlantic Ocean glimmered like shattered glass. They'd glimpsed the water in blinding snatches as they'd passed houses and patches of scrub beach and the sawgrass dunes that lined the Fernandina Beach shore. Private lanes hid certain properties from the road while rows of smaller, stilted homes filled in between. Unique ocean-themed mailboxes punctuated the roadside: a leaping dolphin holding a box in his mouth, a flamingo with an opening under its pink chest feathers, and several fish—carp, bass, kingfish—with their eyes wide and their mouths agape, ready and waiting to swallow the daily post.

Out here, where the Florida sea coast meets the Atlantic with a friendly yet cautious hand, a person could hide if they wished. They could disappear in plain sight, left alone by others who wished to do the same.

The house was at the end of a hidden, private lane. A security camera hung in a beautifully gnarled juniper tree, and the gate swung open as they pulled up to it—someone was watching, waiting for them. The front door opened before they could ring the bell.

A tall, narrow woman stood inside, half hidden by the door but nearly as tall, and Melody inhaled a soft gasp at the first sight of a shock of grayish gold hair held back with a purple velvet headband. Dorian waited. Melody stepped across the threshold, her hand held out, but the woman raised her lanky arms and wrapped them around her.

"Ms. Betty." Tears pressed behind Melody's eyes, contained by the tingling grip of utter amazement. On the woman's face was a reflection of the familiar, enigmatic smile Melody had grown up with—the demure, sweet smile that simultaneously managed to be open, generous, dazzling. She recognized it as the smile that had lit up her own mother's face, the one she loved to see every day of her life.

Melody realized in that moment that in all the time she'd been looking at Betty's photos, not one of them had shown her smiling. If they had, she would have known the truth right away. Wouldn't she? She pulled away reluctantly to search the woman's face again. The old woman reciprocated, her eyes filling with tears as she smoothed Melody's hair behind her ears and held her face in between her palms. As if reading Melody's mind, she moved one hand from Melody's face and pressed it to her own. "My cheeks hurt from smiling!" She sniffled. "Let's go sit down, okay?"

Melody nodded, held her grandmother's hand and fell in line, trailing behind her.

"Yes, ma'am," Dorian said. He glanced at the security pad beside the door, each button—"Back Door," "Kitchen Patio," "Gate"—carefully labeled in large print. He followed behind the women, holding the package away from his shirt front so as not to crush the curling froth of ribbon.

She lead them through the foyer, past an inviting dining room and a bright sunroom office, toward a living room that opened at the end of a hall. As she walked, she pressed a palm to her left hip, turning back toward them with an apologetic smile and saying, almost to herself, "I did one too many high kicks."

The living room was furnished with soft chairs and a lavender sofa covered in violet cushions. Stained glass windows on either side of the fireplace cast sprinkles of colored light around the room. A painting hung on the wall above the mantel, and Dorian remembered editing music to fit over Melody's description: "A tree covered in red blossoms framed by the graceful branches of a live oak, blowing sideways in the familiar, lilting pose of Florida foliage, in a Florida breeze, against Florida skies, with the Florida coast in the distance beyond."

Melody and Dorian stood while Betty lowered herself to the edge of her arm chair. There was a sound from down the hall. "Oh!" Betty said, "here he is now."

They all turned toward the open French doors that lead back to the hall. There was a stomping of feet on a mat, the rustle of grocery bags, then footsteps. He called to Betty, "I'm here. Got your favorite!" He spoke as he came down the hall then appeared in the doorway, holding up a bag of Doritos. "Well, the driver actually *got* them, of course, but *I* told him what to get, so I get the brownie points, right?" He rounded the corner. His eyes went wide when he saw them all sitting there, and he stopped. "Ah," he said. He removed his hat and sunglasses, and his famous smile spread across his face. His gaze fell on Melody, and his eyes glistened with instant recognition.

"You are here," he said, coming toward her and extending both hands. "I am so very happy to meet you. I'm Dominicus Owens." His face crumpled as his voice broke. "I'm your granddad."

Melody reached for his hand and gently pulled herself toward him. His hug felt like home, and she hugged him back, spilling tears onto his shoulder. Dorian found a box of tissues and extended them around to the sniffling trio, then they all sat down, gingerly, as if not to break the moment, around a gleaming coffee table. Melody set down her bag beside the couch while Dorian placed the package they'd brought with them, bright pink with a purple satin bow, on the table.

Dominicus squeezed Betty's hand. "Doing all right, Princess?" he asked.

Betty blushed, and a transformation passed over her face. There was the young woman from the old photos Melody and Dorian had pored over and posted to the studio wall. The young woman from the diaries, standing on a dimly-lit street outside The West Tavern, drawn down the road by the lure of sweet, perfect harmony.

"Ms. Betty," Melody said, "we brought you something." She slid the box over.

Betty pulled the ribbon and carefully tore the paper, recognition registering even before she lifted the flaps of the box.

"My diaries?" Her voice was a tremor.

She pulled out a volume and placed it on her lap, spreading her hands flat on its dusty, velvety surface. Her eyes pressed closed and she lowered her head as if remembering the words she'd written in that book long ago. Her voice came softly.

"Does she know about me?" Betty whispered.

"Yes, ma'am," Melody said. "She knows."

"Does she want to meet me?"

Melody reached over and placed a hand on Betty's.

"Of course she wants to meet you," Melody said, laughing through tears. "She wants to meet both of you."

"Oh!" Betty's other hand went to her chest and she looked upward. Dominicus came to her side, lowering himself to one knee beside her chair and covering her hand with one of his.

"We all just wanted to make absolutely sure it was what you wanted," Melody said.

Betty and Dominicus both looked at her, incredulous. "Yes!" they shouted, in harmony.

Melody and Dorian exchanged a quick glance as the old couple embraced, and Dorian left the room, taking his phone from his jacket pocket.

Melody imagined her mother waiting where she said she'd be, a few miles away at Main Beach. She'd be sitting in the driver's seat of the news-mobile waiting for Dorian to say the word. Her freshly manicured fingers would be blanched as she gripped the steering wheel. She'd been so excited, and scared, for today. She'd be passing the nervous time by watching the kids at Kona Skate Park confidently dropping the tips of their skateboards and stepping on before careening down into the curvy cement bowl. Over and over—drop, step, ride…drop, step, ride… She'd probably have the window rolled down to hear the music they played. Melody knew her mother well enough to know that if they didn't call her soon, she was likely to take up skateboarding herself. She wished she could see her mother's eyes widen as she looked at her phone and saw Dorian's call come through. She would probably be humming "Skater Boy" and would stop mid-chorus to take the call.

Melody felt a surge of love for her brave, bold mother. This was all so unbelievable, so wonderful. Her life was about to change forever.

"I can't believe this is really happening," Betty said.

While they waited for Belinda, Dominicus and Betty led Melody and Dorian on a tour of the house, starting at a hall off the main room. It felt like a gallery, with photos of Dominicus's kids mixed with photos from his career—some black and white, some color—backstage, on tour buses and in offices, in booths of both upscale restaurants and grimy roadside diners, behind velvet ropes, on red carpets and on shag rugs. There was Dominicus with Booker T and the MGs, Jay and the Techniques, The Temptations, Phil Walden, Jerry Wexler, Rick Rubin, Charlie Daniels, Aretha Franklin, Wilson Pickett, Duane Allman and Jaimoe Johanson, Smokey Robinson, Miles Davis, Percy Sledge, Michael McDonald… There were photos of

Dominicus's mother Martha, always in a fabulous hat and with the same arched brows and strong jawline as her son. Several older photos included Betty, with her demure smiling eyes peeking out from under rolled bangs. In one, she stood with a group of unlikely-looking session musicians on cement steps outside a recording studio, wearing a cotton shirtdress and pumps, and in another she leaned against the side of a winged Cadillac in dark sunglasses, legs crossed at the ankles and holding the collar of her coat closed while smiling wide, upward and to the side, like a movie star.

"Those were taken in Macon. We didn't know whose car that was," Betty said. "Sly told me to act like it was my ride and he snapped that picture." She slid a finger down the wooden frame.

"I would have known if I'd had this photo of you to go by!" Melody said. Betty watched her profile, wonder sparkling in her eyes. Dominicus squeezed Betty's shoulder, pulling her closer, then they looked at each other and smiled.

"What is this?" Melody asked, pointing to another, smaller frame.

"That's the penny," Betty said.

"*The* penny," Dominicus said. "Betty gave that to me the night we met."

He sang the famous line from "Penny In My Pocket" with a touch of remembrance, yet as if composing it for the first time.

Dorian and Melody shared a glance. *This is incredible.*

"Come on in here, you'll like this," Dominicus said. Melody and Dorian followed him, Betty right behind them, into a room off the hallway, an office with a wide desk and walls covered in memorabilia. "This here is what I call my 'Hometown Wall',, Dominicus said, waving his long arm toward another frame-covered wall. Hanging there were pictures of musicians going back generations, groundbreaking musicians from Jacksonville and performers the city claimed as their own: Ray Charles, Lynyrd Skynyrd, Blind Blake, The Allman Brothers Band, Classics IV, 38 Special, Molly Hatchet, Pat Boone, Gram Parsons, Hoyt Axton and his mother Mae, each neatly labeled like a museum gallery ("Mae Axton, co-writer of 'Heartbreak Hotel'"). Under that row was a row representing another generation of local bands: Limp Bizkit, Red Jumpsuit Apparatus, Yellow Card, Shinedown. ("My little cousin went to school with some of those boys," Dominicus said, tapping the glass.) There were old advertising posters for concerts by The Jubilaires, Jelly Roll Morton, Patrick Chappelle's "The Rabbit Foot Company," Ma Rainey, Florida Playboys. And behind his desk, a framed print of a photograph—James Weldon Johnson sitting at a piano with his brother Rosamund Johnson standing beside him, both looking over a piece of sheet music.

"It's important not to forget where we come from," he said. "It's a cliché because it's true."

Dorian nodded, but couldn't speak. His eyes roamed the walls, moved over to a bookshelf, and then fell on a record, a single, in a yellowing paper sleeve and held up on a little easel. It had the record company name "Victor" emblazoned across the label, and Dorian realized he was looking at the Sugar

Underwood recording of "Davis Street Blues," the tune named for a street in downtown Jacksonville, Zeke had told them about—the one with the disputed discovery story.

"We were naïve, back in the day." Dominicus looked across the wall of photos, but his eyes were on a time far away.

"Looking back, I can see it now in a way I didn't see it then. Those early days in Macon, then in Muscle Shoals, then starting out on that first tour... we were insulated, in some ways. Change was coming. It was there, like you could almost reach out and touch it. And we felt we were part of it, part of making it happen. Every stop, every town that seemed to welcome us, every show with Black people and white people together on stage and the audiences loving it, loving us and what we were giving them...I didn't realize then just how different things were for us, because of who we were. I knew what came before, of course I did, but that made it even more tempting to pretend. We were doing it better. Our generation knew better. Music was the answer. So for musicians? Man, that meant we could lead the way!"

Betty nodded along as Dominicus spoke. He placed his hand on hers, and they shared a look that spoke of innocent idealism, a look of regret for chances not taken, for time lost. Melody watched as he squeezed her hand, almost feeling the strength that passed between them in that one simple act.

"That sounds like what Zeke told us," Melody said. "He said, 'That the spark of a creative soul is a piece of God's light right here inside us. It's not a Black spark, it's not a white spark, it's not any one color. It's light. All colors.'"

"That's what we believed. I guess I *chose* to believe what we had on stage reflected what was going on out there, outside the theaters. All the world's a stage, right? If only. If only the world worked like we did in the studio, together. We saw color and it didn't matter. Education didn't matter, politics, who you slept with, how you wore your damn hair, none of it. Others had broken the ground and laid us a new groundwork, a different path for us coming up behind them. It was like..." his long fingers spread in the air "...like we floated along in a magic bubble. All kinds of craziness still went on around us, but we were just there floating along together, just so happy inside our bubble. Out on the road together, in the studio, we all had a voice. Hell, the white boys wanted to *be* us! They wanted it so bad it was funny!" He pointed at a framed news clipping with a photo of a grinning man with a sharp flat top. "It was when we lost Sly, in '83, that our bubble really burst."

Melody followed his gaze to a studio headshot of a young man with an impish expression and an impeccable flattop.

"See that little scar above his eye?" Betty said. "That's where I sewed him up after he was beaten up outside the theater in Macon. I stitched it with a needle and thread, in a hotel room, no less!" When she looked from the photo to Melody's face, the young woman looked back at her as if disbelieving.

"The day I left Randell, I'd been to see my mama one last time, and I was just overwhelmed. I realized

I was older than she was when she started *acting* old, like her life was over. I was just...struck... that's the word. I was struck. By the tragedy of it. What a beautiful woman she was. Smart. Healthy. So much potential—all wasted. Literally wasted, in pining for another life. She could have had a different life, too, if she weren't so scared. If she'd seen she could have done it for herself. If I think on it too much it makes me sick inside, that I didn't have the courage to say no to her, to defy her. She told me a story that day about how her own mama, my grandmother who passed when I was small, kept her from the man *she* loved, because he was Catholic. Can you imagine that? She sent him off without Mama ever knowing. Didn't find out the truth until he came back to town to care for his own sick daddy—came back with his wife and two children." Betty laced her hands, smoothing the parchment skin of one with the tarnished thumb of the other. Her eyes begin to glisten. "So you see, I can't blame my mama, not really. Good or bad, we can only do what we know to do."

"Do you ever wish you'd known sooner? That Dominicus had tried to reach you?"

Betty tilted her head and tucked her chin, looking at Melody as if watching a baby discover grass under tender little feet. "Whatever has happened, darlin', it happened how it was supposed to," she said, shaking her head. "Wishing takes time, and I'm not wasting any more time."

Her words rang like chimes, and everyone paused while the reverberations reached the corners of the room, then Dominicus answered, "Amen to that!"

Melody and Dorian glanced at each other and then away, moving as if the air were suddenly heavy, their faces frozen, and their eyes returned to roaming the wall of images. In the center was a candid black and white shot of a smiling Otis Redding, standing in front of a large recording studio microphone, head tilted back, eyes squeezed shut, mouth open wide. The photographer had caught him singing full-throated and mid-belt. Melody's ears rang with this first life lesson from her newfound grandmother.

Dominicus was talking to Dorian. "You see, it all connects in one way or another, forward or backward, whichever way you look at it, right straight to Otis Redding," he was saying, drawing invisible connecting lines in the air. The two men looked at the photo reverently.

Back in the living room, Melody brought the conversation back around. It was time.

"Could you tell us more about when she was born?"

"Well, she was born early, but she was so perfect. So beautiful. Only five pounds. So much curly hair and those light brown eyes, just like her daddy." Melody glanced at Dorian.

Dominicus pressed his lips together. He rubbed the gray stubble at his jaw.

"The church charity downtown said they'd find her a loving home. They said I was doing the right thing. I was scared, and if I'm being honest, I was weak. I've wished I could know how she was all these years. All I wanted was her and Dominicus, for us to be a family. But it couldn't be. It seemed like it just couldn't be." Betty's eyes filled with tears.

Melody leaned closer, handing Betty a tissue before pulling out two for herself.

"I guess you read my diaries, so you know I found out I was expecting pretty soon after I came back to take care of Mama, after that trip to Macon. I just laid low and wore big dresses. Maybe people knew, I don't know. Mama never said anything until it was obvious. She said, 'You know you can't keep it.' That's all. Just like that. I begged, said I'd move away somewhere where people wouldn't care so much." She held the tissue to her lips.

"I used to look for her in every young woman I saw. Looking for those eyes. See, Dominicus?" She turned to him. He looked down at Melody, her face a reverberation of the love between the two of them, and nodded. "If I'd have seen you on the street, I would have wondered if we were related somehow, would have done the math. It never left me. I celebrate my baby's birthday every year. All these years, I've looked deep into every face I passed, wondering if that one or this one could be her."

"Betty didn't know I'd been writing to her," Dominicus said. "I would have come for her, for both of them. So many things could have been different."

Melody lowered her head. Dorian placed a hand on her shoulder.

"When I left, Randell had taken my diaries, and I was so...it was like I was outside myself, looking at myself from the outside. Looking at myself that way, I realized, 'I don't know that woman.'" Betty's shoulders shook, a small moan escaped from somewhere very deep. "All we can do is try to grab ahold of the good before it passes by." Fresh tears ambled down, streaking her soft, powdered cheeks. "So when I found the treasure in the lady's chimney, the very next day, I knew. It was a sign." She wiped her tears. "With the internet, it took me all of an hour to find out who to call. I accepted the reward, but made them promise to keep my name out of it."

"Why did you go on that chimney sweep job alone?" Melody asked. Her listeners might not get the answers they hoped for, at least not this season and not until Betty said so, but the journalist in her had to know.

"I hadn't told Randell about that call before I found my diaries gone. So I went myself." She dabbed at her eyes. "Even after I got the reward, I didn't want to go far. I wanted to stay close to where I had my baby." Saying the words broke her composure completely.

"Oh, please don't cry, Ms. Betty." Melody reached out and put a hand on Betty's knee. "Sorry about that."

Betty wiped her eyes. "Please, if you're comfortable with it, I'd love for you to call me Grandma," she said. "I know you must have lovely grandmas already, but..."

"I did," Melody said. "They were wonderful women. They're both gone now."

"I'm so sorry," Betty said. "I can tell just by knowing you a little while, they *must* have been wonderful."

Dorian's phone buzzed. "She's here," he said, smiling broadly as if he were part of the family reunion himself. He hurried through the house to the front door and watched as Belinda stepped out, straightened her dress, slammed the van door needlessly hard, winced at the noise. She fidgeted the job of dropping the keys in her bag, fiddled the straps on her shoulders. She stood beside the van until he waved her over. Her shoulders lowered, and she leaned in the direction of the house as if caught on a lasso, pulled along by something strong and inevitable. When she got close, she straightened up and hurried the rest of the way, not stopping till she was through the front door and halfway down the hall. Dorian followed, then led her the rest of the way. He placed his hands on Belinda's shoulders and gave a supportive squeeze while she caught her breath. They nodded at each other. Then he stood aside.

She stepped into the doorway. Melody stood. She looked from Betty to Dominicus and back again.

"Grandma, Grandpa," she said. The words felt natural on her tongue. "I'd like you both to meet Belinda Hinterson—my mother," Melody said.

The room went quiet in the presence of overlapping revelation, washing away the years. Dominicus took Betty's elbow and they stood. They faced their reflection standing in the doorway in stunned silence. In unison, all three lifted and extended their arms as Belinda came closer, mother taking in daughter's eyes, her hair, her skin, every part of her, for the first time since she'd watched her soft silhouette float away in the arms of a nurse. Their long arms wrapped around each other in a messy, perfect tangle.

"Oh, my baby." Betty said, over and over. "Oh, my baby. Oh, my baby. I can't believe it's really you."

She stared at Belinda, then covered her mouth, removing it only long enough to make more little exclamations, and Belinda could find snatches of words only when it was necessary to reply, a call and response bridging distance and time.

"You're so beautiful—"

"—*You* are so beautiful."

"I can't believe this—"

"—I can't believe it either."

"Is this really happening—"

"—I don't know, is it?"

Dominicus stood beside them, his arms around them both. He tried to speak and failed at first. Then from above the huddle came his low, melodic voice.

"My girls."

"I can't believe it. Thank you, Jesus. I just... Look at you!" She touched a shining coil of Belinda's hair. "Oh—" Her eyes filled again. Her hands ran up and down Belinda's arms, grasped her shoulders. She lifted her daughter's hands and looked at them, then held them to her chest.

Melody felt Dorian's arm raise beside her and drape naturally around her shoulder. She wanted it there, wanted him there. In the days they had been planning this trip, the idea that he might not need to come had not occurred to her once. Of course he had to be a part of this moment. He was her person. He rubbed her arm as they looked at the scene in front of them, and he leaned closer. "You did that," he said. He began to regret their decision to leave his equipment in the car. He took out his phone, held it up.

"Do you think I could take a picture, for posterity?" he asked. "We won't post it, promise." Melody held up her hands and looked at Dorian. *We promise.*

Betty and Belinda laughed, and Belinda leaned her head close to her mother's. Dominicus pressed in, saying, "I'm gonna put this at the top of my Jacksonville Wall!" and Dorian snapped a photo.

Tears shone on Dominicus's face as he leaned his head back to get another look at his daughter. "You look just like us," he said.

At that, they all looked at each other and pulled apart, and as if the same thought had occurred to each of them simultaneously, and all three turned their gaze to Melody. Her mother and grandmother waved her over and made her stand in between.

"You have your grandmother's smile," Dorian said, and at that Betty and Belinda and Melody all gave that same demure, enigmatic smile — sweet, yet somehow slightly out of place on the faces of such strong, bold women. But through the lens of Dorian's cell phone camera, with all three of them together, smiling that same smile, it looked like the last piece to a beautiful, complicated puzzle.

MELODY

2019

D orian's expression had turned pensive. Melody put her phone away, deep in her pocket, and leaned against the van beside him. He looked toward the house where, unable to pull herself away, Belinda continued the joyful reunion with her birth parents.

"It makes you think," he said. "You think you have so much time, nothing but time. But it's not true. You only get one life—and you only get a *long* one if you're lucky."

"They seem content." Melody nodded in the direction he was looking. It was true. Betty and Dominicus had gotten their happily ever after, hadn't they? Eventually.

The thought made her stomach twist.

"Right, but it could have been so different."

"Yes," Melody said, considering. "But if their story was supposed to go another way, don't you think it would have? I mean, don't you think they would have made it happen? Or fate would have stepped in? Something?"

"No." Dorian said. "No, I don't actually. I think we get opportunities and it's up to us what we do with them. Sometimes people miss their destiny because they choose wrong." He squinted at the sun setting in the distance with a spectacular final show, then turned his head to look at her. "I don't want to choose wrong."

"Don't you think there are hundreds and thousands of possible ways your life could turn out that could be just as good as any other possibility?"

He stared at the sunset. "Not for me," he said. He swallowed hard against the tightening in his throat, his shoulders tensed, and as driven by a surge of adrenaline turned his body and he stood there in front of her, teetering on the precipice. "Not unless they include you."

Melody went still. The color rushed from her face. She didn't speak, so he went on, his voice growing more resolved, more urgent.

"Here's the thing, Mel," he said. He moved closer, holding her gaze, "I've looked at it from every which way. I've tried—so hard—to be careful. To not screw things up and lose you in my life completely. But I know you value the facts, and so I have one for you. Here it is. Here it comes. I am absolutely, totally, completely, hopelessly in love with you." He clapped his hands certainly, at the inevitability of it all. "You can write that down and put it in your precious folder." His arms dropped and shrugged, helpless. "It's a fact, Jack."

The color returned to her cheeks and a longing slipped over her gaze as he stared at her with an open directness that sent a shudder through her center. He stood inches away, his hands clasped as if to keep

415

them from following his eyes on her cheek, her lips, her hair, her neck. His voice grew deeper. "I don't want to waste any more time. You are it for me, Mel. I've always known it. And if you feel that way, too..."

He loosened his hands and touched her cheek, then her hair. The strands slipped between his fingers, somehow both silky and coarse, but exactly as he'd imagined they would feel. He drew her face closer until she had to look at him.

Her hesitation lasted only a moment, then she nodded. The kiss was like a key clicking home. One turn and the door to the place where she kept her feelings—out of sight, safe, compartmentalized— would open wide. She let it happen just a little longer, melting into the gentle strength of the kiss. Golden fireworks went off behind her eyes, filling her head with a shower of glittering stars.

She shivered. His kiss was *the* kiss. The one she'd always wanted, yet never knew she wanted. When she looked up at him, the look in her eyes was new, an open revelation. But before she could fully embrace the joy of the moment, the fear of losing her friend, her partner, gripped her chest. Her body stiffened. He moved back as she looked at his hands on her arms until he let go, then she turned slowly toward the van. The door handle was a blur, and she blinked hard as she fumbled with it till it finally gave. He closed the door with a defeated thud.

He stood in that spot for a minute, watching the side of her face through the window, waiting, but her jaw was set, her gaze focused straight ahead. His legs shook as he rounded the van and patted himself down for the keys. Then he climbed into the driver's seat and started the car.

"I'm sorry," he said.

"I'm sorry," she said.

Her resolve slacked, slipped from her face and crashed in her chest. She looked at her lap, the door handle, anything—anywhere but at him. Looking out the passenger window, the tense lines in her face cracked, and a smile escaped. He had kissed her. It was wonderful. She wanted more than anything for him to do it again. But they had probably just ruined everything they'd built together. What now?

They rode away from Betty's house in the kind of quiet that only comes from having too much to say.

MELODY

2019

"Just a quick midweek update, Sweepers! We're coming to you off our normal schedule with a note from the road! Since the last episode went live, we've uncovered some very exciting information that we've hit the road to track down. We can't say yet what it is or where we are headed, but if we're right, we'll have a very exciting episode for you next week. Until then, keep sweeping!"

The clip Melody had recorded on the way out to Amelia Island ended on a dissonant note. She clicked it off. The sound of her own voice irritated her, the voice she had this morning but couldn't imagine using now. Teasing big news like a network talking head. She went back to the beginning of the clip and clicked 'play' anyway. At least it drowned out the intolerable silence.

"Just a quick midweek update, Sweepers! We're coming to you off our normal schedule with a note from the road..." She looked at Dorian. He stared straight ahead and she could only see one tense eye and one flushed cheek. "...a very exciting episode next week. Until then, keep sweeping!"

Dorian kept his eyes straight ahead as long as he could, holding steady until the intensity of Melody's gaze pulled his own off the road and he looked at her. Without a word, they agreed. She held a finger over the tiny trash can icon and pressed. A message popped up.

"This action is irreversible."

"Confirm delete?'

She showed him the screen and he nodded. She pressed the button: "confirm."

They both looked straight ahead, out the van's wide windshield. The freeway narrowed to highway. Behind them were the wild, reaching shores of north Florida, its marshland greeting the ocean. The scrubland hugged the marsh, the marsh gave way to the forest, and red Georgia clay surrendered to sandy Florida soil, spreading from the forest to the highway's edge. Beneath them, the road unfurled the miles, winding away in the rear view, like ribbon unspooling from a precious old mixtape.

BETTY,
18 YEARS OLD

NOVEMBER 15, 1970

Dear Diary,

I don't know how this happened. Of course I know 'how' it happened. It was the best afternoon of my life.

It was the day after their big show in Macon. The band was packing up the bus, and I was throwing my things in my bag, crying and crying and dreading what I had to tell him. He knocked on the door to my room, and when I opened it and saw him standing there outlined by the high noon sun, I almost changed my mind. Mama could find someone else to take care of her. I couldn't leave him. But I knew even then, I had no choice.

I'll never forget his face when I said those words: I have to go back home. His wonderful, hopeful smile dissolved away as the reality of it sank in, as he realized what that meant for us. I thought for a moment he might turn and leave me there. The disappointment on his face...it was terrible. And it was all my fault. I was backing out of our plan at the last minute, his bus would leave after dinner to drive through the night, and I wouldn't be there beside him. If he got angry and said he never wanted to see me again, I would have deserved it.

But he looked straight into my eyes, stepped through the door, and took me in his arms. He placed his strong hands on my waist, and he drew me close, pressed my hips against his. The heat from outside was still on his clothes and it wrapped all around me, hummed straight through me. He kissed me as if he wanted to consume me, like if he kissed me deeply enough, we might become one person. My body tingled, weak with wanting him, and I melted into him, helpless.

I lowered the blinds. When I drew the curtains, magic dust shimmered through the slivers of sunlight that refused to be shut out, spreading a fan of light across my unmade bed. Dominicus sat down there, at the foot of the bed, and I came to him, stood above him, watching as he undid the buttons all the way down the front of my dress. An irresistible thrill danced over every part of me he touched.

His dark hands on my pale skin were like music notes on sheet music, playing slow and smooth, deep and low, then growing more intense as his breaths came faster, more shallow as we both gave in to the rhythm of our song. The world outside that room didn't exist. The only reality was him, and me, the two of us holding on, giving all of ourselves while we had the chance, sharing one soaring moment of exquisite, aching pleasure. He filled every empty corner of me with every beat, every note, every word he whispered.

"I love you, Princess."

His perfect head sharing my pillow was the happiest moment of my life.

We cried together, and he wiped my tears. He promised we would make it back to each other again, soon. That none of it mattered without me by his side.

What am I going to do? That desperate feeling in my stomach I wrote about last week wasn't just desperation. Not at all. It was Dominicus's child making his presence known.

I want it to be true. I've got the test results in my other hand while I write this, and I keep reading the word over and over. Yes, it still says 'positive,' every time I look. I want it to be true, but I'm also scared to death. I think I'm going crazy. It can't be true.

Only yes, it can.

What will he look like? Maybe it's a 'she.' How will this world treat her? How could I be so selfish and stupid? I'm barely nineteen years old. I have nothing to offer this child. Less than nothing, since my life isn't even my own.

What in the world can I do? I can't keep Dominicus's baby. Not here, not in this town. It would be different if I were with him. But not here.

I wish he would write to me. Or call. Anything.

No way I can hide it. If I'm anything like Mama, I'll get huge. In the pictures from when she was expecting me, she looks like a big old mama bear. It's actually really funny to see, tiny as she is now.

This isn't a joking matter. I am in a lot of trouble here.

So why do I keep smiling?

TABS AND BLANKS
PODCAST

Transcript
Season 2, Episode 17: Final Thoughts?

What a ride this has been! Right, Sweepers? Thank you for joining us this season as we looked into the mystery of what happened to Betty Van Disson. I wish we could have brought you the answer, but we can't say we didn't try. We followed every lead down every rabbit hole in hopes of finding a trace of Betty Van Disson we could share with you, our awesome listeners.

And who could have predicted the treasure hunt this season kicked off? Dorian and I sincerely hope no historic hearths were harmed in the making of this podcast! But I've gotta say: If you tore up your chimney, that's on you...

The thing about devoting yourself to investigating a person is that you find yourself coming out the other side feeling as if you know them. They were, or are, real people after all. They are more than the fascinating story of their disappearance or murder or whatever aspect of their story it might be that fascinates you enough to draw you into their sphere. You inevitably develop a strange kind of loyalty to them. They become like family. You've spent a lot of time and mental energy on them, after all. You spend so much time looking at photos, listening to stories, leaving no thread un-pulled in the hopes of finally finding that person at the other end of one of them. You think about them so much, and so deeply, that their face appears when you close your eyes. You conjure them in lucid dreams, hoping your subconscious will take all the little details, perform some magical calculation, and spit out a solution—a length of elucidating ticker tape—that gives you the definitive answer to the ultimate questions: What should I do? At what point should we let go? How do we convince ourselves to release that person to the fate which has already swept them far away?

After we visited Mrs. Beakman's Avondale home and heard her account, I admit I let myself imagine that Betty found the treasure there that day. There was something satisfying about envisioning her cashing it in for the reward under conditions of discretion and anonymity and slipping off to sip mai tais in Puerto Vallarta for her golden years. I have an overactive imagination. But even I could never have imagined the places this story would actually take us.

There is something important I want to make sure to include before we sign off for this season: after talking to Randell that day in the hospital, I can say that I believe him. Just like the similar case of Nellie Olfort, suspicion came to rest on the husband who turned out to be innocent, at least when it came to their wives' disappearances. I personally believe that Randell had nothing to do with Betty's disappearance and that he didn't know what happened to her. I believe it enough to put my opinion out there like this, before I have hard evidence to support it. On his deathbed, he told us he had taken Betty's diaries and just where to find them. I truly believe he considered taking those diaries his worst offense against his wife and that he may have felt he deserved to lose her for that act.

"Gone from me." That was how he put it. Unfortunately, when we found the box of diaries, where he said they'd be, they were hopelessly disintegrated. The quietly relentless, majestic yet foreboding environs of rural north Florida had claimed them for her in her absence.

Her words were not meant for our eyes.

This story isn't over. There are calls and leads still coming in every day. Who knows? Maybe we'll be back next season with more on the story of Betty Van Disson. That would be great. Betty has a story— her own truth—and it can only come to light if and when she wants it to. Like Nellie's car rising from the St. Mary's River, refusing to let her life be a mystery, Betty too may reach out from wherever she is, and let her story be told.

I'm Melody Hinterson, and this has been The Chimney Sweep. On behalf of myself, and of course the amazing Dorian, a huge thank you to our Open Mouth Productions team, to everyone who has spoken with us this season, and to all you loyal Sweepers listening out there. I believe I speak for all of us when I say:

Betty, I hope with all my heart that wherever you are, you are safe, you are loved, and above all, I hope you are happy.

MELODY

2019

The final episode of The Chimney Sweep was scheduled to go up in a few days. Melody and Dorian had driven into Riverside for some promo shots for the website. She kept her focus out the window, nervously tapping her toes on the floor board as they rode in relative silence.

"Could we stop up here at Willowbranch Park real quick?" Melody said. "I just want to get some shots of the park." Melody said.

Dorian turned on the blinker and pulled the van into a spot, and Melody immediately opened her door, got out, and started walking away. She threw an encouraging glance at him over her shoulder and took off into the park.

"Whoa! Hold on, Mel!" Dorian shifted the news-mobile into park and turned off the engine, hopped out, and slammed the door, hastily clicking the fob over his shoulder as he tried to catch up. Melody was already halfway across the field and heading toward the clearing.

Dorian kept an eye on her retreating figure, losing and then finding her again as she passed behind oak trees and wove through azalea bushes. "Wait up!" he called after her. He caught sight of another figure moving away from the clearing, too far to make out at first, but then—*was that Kina?* The figure jogged away and he looked again for Melody. He saw her wave at the jogger and slow down in the middle of the open field. She looked down, then she turned back and waved him over. "Come on, come on," she said.

She spun around once, arms outstretched, and took it all in before he caught up to her. The oaks and the pines reached up with her, grasping for more, for all the heavens had to give. Life was way too short to live small. This was 'before.' Everything else would be 'after.'

He slowed his pace and she watched him approach. She swung her arm, grandly presenting the surprise that lay at her feet. In the grass was a blanket, brightly colored with a tie-dyed print. Little lights twinkled in the grass around the blanket, and a picnic basket sat to one side. He tried to make sense of it and looked at her, confusion gathering around his eyes. "What's all this?"

Melody sat on the blanket and patted the space beside her. He sat, and she leaned back and lay down on the blanket. "What's going on, Mel?" he said. "What are you doing?"

"It's called a 'grand gesture,' Dor," she said. "You know, like in the movies?"

She clicked the screen of her phone and music started playing. The Allman Brothers' "Blue Sky." His head tilted back and he closed his eyes, and smiled.

Melody watched the back of his head, the short black hair at the nape of his neck, saw him shake his head and swallow hard. She knew his thoughts by the way his muscles moved. She turned up the volume. Finally, he lay down beside her. An emerald oak canopy swayed like gypsy skirts, dappled the sunlight over them, swishing and swaying with the memory of leather fringe ruffled by the timeless breeze. She lifted her hand, holding a silhouette in the sunlight—the missing puzzle piece. He reached for it, took her hand in his. They could almost catch traces of sweet incense and patchouli lingering on the air. They sang along.

"You're my blue sky, you're my sunny day
Lord, you know it makes me high when you turn your love my way
Turn your love my way..."

The End

For James,
the missing puzzle piece

ACKNOWLEDGEMENTS

Endless thanks to my wonderful editor and publisher Arielle Haughee, for your guidance, your knowledge, and your friendship. Teaming up with you was one of the best decisions I've ever made.

Song of the Chimney Sweep street team and beta readers, thank you, thank you, thank you for your support and enthusiasm. I still cannot believe how generous you all are.

Thank you to those who gave of their valuable time and their vast knowledge: author and music historian Michael Ray FitzGerald; Dr. Jerry Urso, Grand Historian Most Worshipful Union Grand Lodge of Florida PHA; Rev. Cn Allison DeFoor and the Jacksonville Historical Society; Ritz Theatre and Museum; journalist Wade Tantangelo.

I'm so grateful for a big, wonderful family. Love you, Dad.

Danny, thank you for your incredible tech skills and web expertise, but also for your support. Dave, thank you for always talking to me about the music.

To my amazing kids Sophia, Isabelle, and Joseph and kids-in-law Billy and Madison: everything important in life revolves around you.

432

Acknowledgements

James, thank you for being the other half of my brain and the holder of my heart.

Interested in learning more about North Florida's musical history?

Buffalo Smith, Michael. *From Macon to Jacksonville: More Conversations in Southern Rock.* Mercer University Press: September 4, 2018.

FitzGerald, Michael Ray. *Jacksonville and the Roots of Southern Rock.* University Press of Florida: October 6, 2020.

FitzGerald, Michael Ray. *Swamp Music.* Hidden Owl Press: December 13, 2018.

Weldon Johnson, James. *Lift Ev'ry Voice and Sing.*

Wynne, Ben. *Something in the Water, A History of Music in Macon, Georgia.* Mercer University Press: October 1, 2021.

AUTHOR BIO

T amatha Cain is a former musician and bandleader. She graduated with honors from the University of North Florida with a concentration in Writing for the Entertainment Industry, and her work has appeared in national and international publications. Winner of the 2020 Royal Palm Literary Award for unpublished fiction and first place in The Experience Poetry Competition, she also writes reviews for Southern Literary Review. She is a member of WFWA and FWA. She is a wife and mother of three and lives in a hundred-year-old bungalow in North Florida, in close proximity to the historic locations found in *Song of the Chimney Sweep*.

BOOK CLUB QUESTIONS

1. Did you or someone you know grow up in the '60s? '70s? '80s? Beyond? What changes have you seen in our culture (race relations, music, politics)?

2. Were you surprised by any of the musical facts in this book? (The first reported performance of The Blues, for instance). Does it affect your opinion of the music?

3. Has music played as big a part in your life as it did in Betty's? What is a song that can take you right back to another time and place?

4. Betty's whole life took a different path than she hoped for herself. What are some ways that family and responsibilities have affected the path of your life?

5. Though Melody was hopelessly in love with Dorian, when he expresses his feeling for her, she initially rejects them. How do you feel about her agency in this situation?

6. And are you glad she 'saw the light' and made her own grand gesture toward him, by showing him how well she knew him?

7. Randell, basically on his death bed, explained to Melody that he was asexual. What other relational factors may have driven him to pursue and marry Betty?

8. Melody and Dorian each did so in different ways, but when Dorian begins to have trouble hiding his feelings, their careful balance is tilted and strained. Do you understand Melody and Dorian's attempt to protect their work and their friendship by denying their feelings for each other?

9. How do you think Belinda's life might have been different had her mother been allowed to keep her baby?

10. How might Melody's life have been different?

11. Do you think 'everything happens for a reason'? Or is it only a tragedy when circumstances change the course of a life?

12. Belinda's adoptive parents were her parents. She was loved and nurtured by the Hintersons. How do you think she will relate to her birth parents now that she's met them?

13. How did you react when the DNA test showed a connection between Melody and Loreen?

14. Has anyone ever taken something very personal to you, like a diary? How did you react? Do you relate to how Betty reacted?

15. Compare Melody's journey with Dorian to Betty's with Dominicus. How do the times and circumstances affect their individual experiences on the path to 'true love'?

OTHER TITLES BY ORANGE BLOSSOM PUBLISHING

B ound by a devastating secret, childhood friends
David, Josh, and Kate take on home renovation
as a means of healing from a dark, shared past.

Their only promise? Friendship first—no hookups.

Only several months after moving into their Baltimore
fixer, the aptly nicknamed Canton Catastrophe, walls
are crumbling, sparks are flying, and promises are getting ignored.

Josh, a paramedic, is plagued with panic attacks, haunted by the past, and sharing a room with David, who he is definitely not attracted to. And then there's Kate. She's having a job crisis, popping pills, and pretending she doesn't notice how distant the boys have grown. And David? The eternally calm, blue-eyed beauty's health is deteriorating and he's mysteriously blacking out.

But when they learn someone may have discovered their darkest secret and is now stalking them--and blackmailing Josh's father, a conservative media personality with secrets of his own, renovation and relationship woes take a back seat. Suddenly, their past is unraveling, and the shocking truths unearthed will have them questioning everything from family ties and friendships to love, loss, and the lengths they're willing to go for each other.

DID YOU ENJOY THIS BOOK?

Please consider leaving a review on <u>Amazon</u> or <u>GoodReads</u>. It helps our small press sell more books!